THE ORPHAN GUNNER

ALSO BY SARA KNOX

MURDER: A TALE OF MODERN AMERICAN LIFE

SARA KNOX

The Orphan Gunner

GIRAMONDO

FIRST PUBLISHED 2007
FOR THE WRITING & SOCIETY RESEARCH GROUP
AT THE UNIVERSITY OF WESTERN SYDNEY
BY THE GIRAMONDO PUBLISHING COMPANY
PO BOX 752 ARTARMON NSW 1570 AUSTRALIA
WWW.GIRAMONDOPUBLISHING.COM

DESIGNED BY HARRY WILLIAMSON
TYPESET BY ANDREW DAVIES
IN 10/17 PT BASKERVILLE
PRINTED AND BOUND BY SOUTHWOOD PRESS
DISTRIBUTED IN AUSTRALIA BY TOWER BOOKS

NATIONAL LIBRARY OF AUSTRALIA
CATALOGUING-IN-PUBLICATION DATA:

KNOX, SARA, 1962– .
THE ORPHAN GUNNER.

ISBN 978-1-920882-28-0.

I. TITLE.

A823.4

9 8 7 6 5 4 3 2 1

TO MY MOTHER, HEATHER, AND TO CRISTYN

Searching of thy wound, I have
by hard adventure found mine own.

Shakespeare, *As You Like It*

Chapter One

Bomber county

It was to be Scotland by way of the Humberside.

Norm was on a pilgrimage to the Old Course of the Royal and Ancient club at St Andrews because he reckoned he'd qualified as ancient, and ought to have a go at it. Olive's interests lay south of her husband's, in Lincolnshire – 'Bomber county', as he bluffly called it.

When they arrived, the Thrifty booth attendant at Humberside airport hadn't upgraded them from a compact to an intermediate car, a subject Norm did not let go until they were a good few miles down the Immingham road. He had the irritability of the arteriosclerotic, and was more than usually convinced that life had it in for him. Now he grasped the steering wheel so tightly that the bones in his hairy wrists showed white where they protruded from the cuffs of his parka. Olive kept an eye on his colour and the quake in his hands, and it was only when he'd left off his tirade about the ineptitude of the English that she roused herself to look about. There were new brick bungalows on Harbrough Road, and beyond these power pylons threaded the north-western horizon with wire – as effective a barrier as barrage balloons. Norm kept slowing the car below the forty-mile-per-hour village limit to cast anxious looks at the horizon, as if – like her – he was wondering how aircraft were meant to get in over all that mess.

She would have found Harbrough unrecognisable if not for the service station in the middle of the village, one section of its iron roofing flexing skyward in the northerly wind. In 1944, the Austin belonging to a fellow WAAF had sat outside that tin shed, waiting on a machine part that was always in the offing but never there.

A few kilometres on from the roundabout they came to shabby little South Killingholme, a fishing village with no sea, its row of houses facing brown waves of soil in fields so newly ploughed the chaff still danced on the road. North Killingholme was less dismal, the grey spire of St Denys Church rising serenely from a stand of oak and hazel. At the crossroads a traffic sign said 'Village Traffic Only' and Olive took this to be a rebuke to the articulated trucks roaring past on their way to Volvo or Grimsby Marine; the Tesco tankers off to the refinery.

Norm wanted to visit the aerodrome right away, as if he, not she, was the one returning. Despite his eagerness, they drove around for some time, puzzled by the new roads and the roadmap, until Olive was tempted to get out and find her way on foot. After all, she'd done it many times before, when she was young, and drunk, and when there'd been a blackout on, and clouds had dowsed the moon.

They had to drive up the road and back again before Norm decided that the turn-off to the industrial estate was the only way onto the old airfield, and still there were the chain-link fences of the tyre outlet, the self-storage barn and the freight depot to skirt before they found somewhere they could nip in. Then, nudged by the distant barking of dogs, they walked what remained of the north-western runway. Years of trucks braking and turning had scoured the bitumen, exposing the pink and white stones of the macadam across which much heavier machines once had run.

They were not the only people there. A man with a Doberman was some way off, and when Olive saw him turn towards them she gave a wave embarrassingly like a salute – her arm and hand more ready than the rest of her to remember the Station. She led Norm around the aerodrome buildings with purposeful dispatch, the decrepitude of the place so great that she could think of nothing to say. Not about the air-raid shelter sunk in hawthorn, nor about the brick exteriors to buildings the roofs of which had long since subsided. At the outer edge of the technical area Norm stopped under the humming high tension wires to photograph the only building still standing. She watched him fiddling with the digital camera, and was grateful for his attempt to salvage something from the place. But everything had already gone from North Killingholme aerodrome – demolished, subsided, rotted, or borne away by vandals. Even the green paint had flaked from the wall against which she would daily lean her bicycle before going on watch in the Flying Control Office. That bike had been pinched so often she'd stopped reporting its absence, since she'd always find it (or one very like it) leaning up against the wall of the NAAFI hut days later. The missing bike seemed to prove that a replacement was nearly as good as original issue, until March of 1944 – when the replacements on which she so relied ran out. After that, gone was gone.

Having taken his photographs, Norm walked on, fumbling with the toggles on his anorak, not watching his feet. She saw that he was tired; had had enough. At the car, she found chocolate to keep his blood sugar up for the short drive back to North Killingholme.

The sight of the village was restorative. There was the close she'd careened along on her bike, taking the short cut to the field from the local pub, and there was the lichgate at the western end of the graveyard through which aircrew and WAAFs had walked to church, eschewing the grander gate at the front. On Church Lane they drove past a line of square-edged bungalows sitting snugly on their sections, cheek by jowl. A bicycle lay on its side in one red brick drive, and a dog lay in the middle of another – the midland meek inheriting the earth. The houses that once had sat on those sections had had their plaster shaken from walls and ceiling nightly throughout the war, and she didn't wonder that they'd gone. The last house on the street was the only one of that earlier vintage, despite the newness of its render and red-framed mullioned windows.

'Here we are,' she heard Norm say.

She was out of the car and through the gate, forcing him to follow – his car keys jingling as he hurried along behind her. Just as she was about to push the door open, Norm took her arm. She turned, but did not snap at him – he'd coloured so much that his moustache had lost the last of its ochre hue.

'Manners,' he mouthed, jabbing a finger at the backlit doorbell.

A woman with eyebrows marked only by thickly pencilled lines let them into the hallway. Although two people could not stand comfortably abreast in the hallway, Olive held her ground at the base of the stairs. She was a small woman who nevertheless occupied a great deal of space, and all her life people had taken her as older or of greater rank than she actually was. Her face was lined from years of having got about clouded in the smoke of Benson and Hedges cigarettes, and her customarily shrewd expression accounted now for errors as likely to be her own as anyone's. This sharp look she now turned on the proprietor of the Bed and Breakfast, much to the other's discomfort.

'I'm Mrs Ainslie,' the proprietor said, putting out her hand to Olive. Norm, whom she could not reach, had to do with a smile.

'Let me show you the amenities.' She pushed open the door to the front room, inside which a grandfather clock was ponderously ticking. 'You'll find breakfast here – ' Olive noted the places set for the next day's breakfast, the napkins in hand-painted wooden rings, and the mahogany wood of the table visible only at its feet, the rest being shrouded in Irish linen.

The proprietor gestured at a closed door at the corridor's end.

'That's my room. You can ring any time before ten at night, after if there's an emergency.'

'We wouldn't disturb you,' Olive said, and followed her reluctantly up the stairs. She wanted to know what the room behind the door marked 'Private' looked like, but had to be content with praising the polished wooden floorboards that had cost the house its Tourist Board rating.

They were left standing in the bedroom that once had been Olive's.

She walked to the place where the bottom of the stairs intruded, and the ceiling zigzagged down into the room. Putting the flat of one hand on the new plaster, she said, 'This was where I used to hang my washing.' Then, in a marvelling tone, 'How did you know about this place?'

Norm was testing the springs in the mattress, and looked up in bafflement. 'Know what?' he asked, and stopped bouncing.

'I used to live here – ' she waved a hand at the window, towards the garden, ' – off Station.'

'Good God! You mean this was your billet?'

'Mine, with Catherine Derrick and Violet Evans. Betty Giles too, until she worked her ticket.'

It was not only here at North Killingholme that Olive had lived off Station – earlier in her war, at Waltham, after the Luftwaffe demolished their Waafery, she'd found herself with three other girls in a two-up, two-down bungalow close to a pub called the Tilted Barrel. Being just off the Peterborough Road, they'd had women from other services to billet. Everyone was on the move during the Blitz and North Lincolnshire had become a vast dosshouse for evacuees, draftees, volunteers and lost souls. At Kingsgate Road they'd put up lorry drivers en route to York or Lincoln or London; they'd found beds for nursing orderlies; and once had let the lumpy couch to a girl in civvies with a beautiful voice. That one was Special Ops, and was later shot by the Nazis running to the Wellington that was to airlift her out of France.

And it was to Kingsgate Road that her best friend Evelyn first had come.

Evelyn had ferried aircraft for the Air Transport Auxiliary, balancing the need to keep the planes moving with the vagaries of English weather. A delivery run might begin fair and then – at some field on the way to, or at, the destination – the fog would lower its white eminence onto the deck, or the rain thicken to a wall, and the pilot would be 'stuck out'. Weather had downed Evelyn at Waltham aerodrome that late autumn day. She'd arrived when the crews were off at their briefing, so there was no one about to be shocked by the sight of a wide-shouldered, long-legged girl jumping down from the wing of the Hurricane she'd been on-ferrying. She'd hung around the field just long enough to cadge a bike from one of the girls helping to bomb up. Evelyn never had to ask for directions, having by then learned from the air every copse, wood, road, lane, church spire, railway line and trestle distinguishing one field from another in all that flat Lincolnshire land. It had only taken her a moment to orient herself and then she'd set off, her feet – still in flying boots – pumping the pedals, her leather flying jacket open, its zips banging against her belt.

Evelyn cut a figure in her uniform, and Olive was one of

the lucky few to see her. That flamboyance was nothing new to her – she'd been watching her friend for years with the kind of wary attention mariners give to weather. But Evelyn's vivacity – her *dash* – surprised even Olive that day. She had arrived at Kingsgate Road fagged out – fit only for tea and toast, a hand of cards and a wash – but her pleasure at finding Olive free, indoors, and alone, had made both of them blush. The delight of that first moment – Evelyn's cheery call from the open back door – had lifted the day right out of Olive's war, where it had remained since in some light limbo of perfection. They had spent the evening sitting cross-legged on the bed, talking. In the small hours of the morning they'd pushed the bedclothes to the floor and, like a pair of housemaids, had shaken the sheet between them and settled the blankets back over cotton tacky in patches with jam from their tea. Then Evelyn had gone off to the spare room. She was known to snore, and even asleep could shout things in such a demanding tone that anyone nearby would wake with a start. At home no member of the household, human or animal, would share a room with her. But that night in Kingsgate Road no noise at all issued from Evelyn's room, and there came no light knock on Olive's door, despite her having started once or twice awake to an imagined one. Evelyn left after the other girls the next morning, and there was someone else dossing in the spare bed a week later, and the week after that.

The inevitability of her thinking of Evelyn, of *seeing* Evelyn with the Irvin jacket draped about her shoulders in the cold little room at Kingsgate Road, now struck Olive. Wasn't that what all of it was about – Bomber county, the rented Opel Astra, Scotland by way of the Humberside? She was edging her way back to where she'd left her friend.

For it was in *this* room that they'd spent so much time together – not the one at Kingsgate Road. It was here that Olive had slept during those mad four months between the Leipzig and Nuremberg raids. Certainly the view towards the mouth of the Humber had changed (the chimneys of the refinery loomed on the horizon, closer than the barrage balloons lit red at sunset, silver in the morning) and a different bed stood – to more or less the inch – where her own once had. But it was her room nonetheless.

Olive heard the sound of footsteps on the stair. Mrs Ainslie had come to tell them there was a tea out if they'd like to help themselves.

Over tea, Olive found it hard to follow Norm's attempts at conversation; his organising of their day – where they first would go; how long it might take to get there. What could it matter? Her thoughts would not lean towards the future – they were not interested in *this afternoon*, or *tomorrow morning*. Olive wondered what might have happened if Evelyn, on that Waltham visit, had stood drinks at the pub and talked cheerily to off-duty crew about aircraft types and the difficulty of flying without instruments; if she'd posed for photographs in the Irvin jacket and trousers that were such a flamboyant variation of regulation ATA gear. What if she'd become unmistakable, then, to the crews on Station – *that plucky girl who flies Spitfires?* If the veterans of the flight later pushed off Waltham to seed North Killingholme's squadrons had known that girl, she'd never have managed to fool them into seeing her as someone else.

Olive noticed Norm chasing a biscuit about his saucer with thumb and forefinger. There was a stubborn patch of eczema on his cheek and his eyebrows needed trimming. Something stirred then beneath her solicitude, and she looked from her husband to the window, as if her feeling was forming out there, beyond the glass.

She remembered snow against the glass, and a coal fire in the grate, and Evelyn reluctant to leave.

If Evelyn had never come to North Killingholme, then everything might have been different – and disaster averted.

'But if things had been different,' thought Olive – moving a hand restlessly over the denim of her trousers, plucking at a stubborn crease – 'I'd never have had her to myself.'

In the late afternoon, they went out for a walk. Olive accommodated Norm's pace, his sudden acceleration to breaks in hedge or wall that afforded a view into neighbouring gardens. To get any effective walking done, she had to tow him along the footpath – down Church Lane and onto Clarke's Road, then into St Crispin's Close with its cottages so like her own one-time billet. In wartime, there'd been couples housed there: brave souls working around the rule that forbade anyone in 'intimate relations' residential duty at the same station. She'd once helped a WAAF and her flight sergeant dig in their back garden for old hooks and curtain rings, so the WAAF could hang the drapes her father had bought, on the black market, for the peacetime price of a motorcycle. The couple had wanted to hide the blackout curtains – '*just to forget for a minute*'. Months later, she'd passed the same house and found another WAAF marking out a vegetable patch, a little pile of seed potatoes by one knee. The girl had acted so proprietary she'd not dared to ask after the last tenants.

'God woman, I'm not a punt,' Norm said, pulling his hand out of his wife's so he could stop and peer through the gate into a garden where two boys were squabbling over a football. Feeling themselves watched the boys came to the gateway and stood in the gap, as solid and ruddy as wood.

'Pass it here, lads.' Norm put up a hand, waved it gently behind his head, while the boys looked on, stupefied with surprise at being addressed.

The smaller boy tucked his chin down to his chest and said, 'Handling foul.'

'What do you mean? *You're* holding it.'

'Holding's nivvir the same as chucking.'

The boys sidled past them and went on down the lane, Norm staring after their bobbing red heads until they'd rounded the corner. His thin neck showed its sinews more when he was angry, and she saw these now come up as clear as the vanes on a waterwheel.

'They've no sense of humour. What did he think I was going to do with his precious ball? It's a wonder the cack-handed toffs at Rugby ever thought to pick the thing up.'

Olive pointed out a trellis-climbing Alfred Carriere to distract him.

He snorted. 'Who'd put a rose that size there? It could knock your bloody head off.'

In the churchyard they poked around the sundial and Norm admired the stonework of the church. She caught him up as he was pulling open the heavy wooden doors, and passed through the gap before him. The pews stood empty, the benches polished from long use, hymnals tucked into their green baize pockets.

'There's your memorial,' Norm said, pointing.

The stained-glass window featured three glass panels in the centre of which the squadron badges floated above a patchwork of fields, below a sky still indigo with night. The names of men who'd died flying from the squadrons of North Killingholme Station were carved on a plaque beneath the window. She knew that Evelyn's brother, the rear gunner of Lancaster LQ-Love, would not be named there. Only through the Commonwealth War Graves Commission could one find the plot at Rauceby with Duncan Macintyre's service number on it.

Then, as she stood in the light from the stained-glass window, Olive remembered Love's mid-gunner, Lawrence 'Lofty' Hilliers, going on about the saint the church had been named for – a Gallic hero who'd picked up his own severed head, terrifying the soldiers of Emperor Decius, his executioners. 'Patron saint of maximum effort,' Lofty had said, knuckles whitening on the hymnal. She thought he'd made that crack at someone's funeral, but it couldn't have been Duncan's. Only six people had been in Rauceby chapel then: the priest, two sniffling nurses, an American pilot by the name of Curtis Crowe, and Olive with her friend from the billet, Catherine Derrick. Lofty was by then in the custody of the Air Force police – he'd never had a chance to visit the person who'd so vexed the authorities; the person who'd lain dying for three long days in that stinking private room, the sheets tented over a frame to keep the cotton from sticking to pinkly glazed skin. In the chapel, hymns were sung, and the priest had fumbled his Book of Common Prayer while he read the service. He'd said 'we consign this body' – no names were mentioned. Then the coffin went to the council-run crematorium so that its furnaces might finish the job begun by melted perspex and aeroplane fuel at the end of the south-easterly approach to the aerodrome at North Killingholme.

Norm handed her the tissue she'd tucked into his pocket before they left the cottage. Feeling that she was under scrutiny, Olive drew into herself: she closed her eyes and pulled her mouth into a scarlet line. She would say nothing about the death at Rauceby, or about the fate of the gunners. Immediate and longstanding circumstance forbade it. In any case, Norm was failing – he lacked the strength to listen to a story that spoke so poorly of its teller. And there were all those years; years like snow banked before a door.

Olive blew into the tissue.

'Right then,' Norm said, rocking on his heels. 'I wonder what the ploughman's lunch is like at the Ashbourne.'

That night she took the single bed by the window and, once her husband had started to snore, pulled open the curtains. Rain was chugging quietly down the corner drainpipe, and on the horizon the pale amber lights of the flare stacks burned. The eeriness of the view contributed to her sense that everything was coming apart, dismantled by the demolition gang of the years: Humberside changed, and Norm depleted, irritable, done-in.

In the past year he'd become snappish, inclined to long silences broken by tirade: immigrant drivers, bank fees, the price of spectacle frames, or the Animal Registration Act – whatever irritation he could seize, and hold forth upon. As Olive stood at the window she abandoned the hope she'd been nursing since he'd suggested they visit Bomber County: that she could tell him about what she'd been involved in at the end of her war. Neither of them was up to it – not him to hear, nor her to tell.

They left the house on Church Lane the next day, and set off northward through Yorkshire, Olive drawing out her husband's service stories while telling none of her own.

It was not until a year after that trip, and a month or so after Norm's death – when she'd received a letter from Lofty's wife telling her that he too had died – that Olive allowed herself to think about the gunners of LQ-Love; that she again called back into memory Evelyn and those long nights spent at watch in the Flying Control Office of her final Station.

They had kept in touch, Love's last gunner and the woman who'd once cut his cap in half with kitchen shears. Every year

Olive would send a cheery card from Sydney to Lofty Hilliers and his wife in New Zealand, even as time refined her Christmas card list to the children of those friends with whom she'd once dutifully swapped season's greetings.

Lofty had died of respiratory complications after a bout of simple flu, an illness free from fuss. When his widow wrote to say that the funeral was 'a bang-up do' she could hear Lofty in the turn of phrase – the NAAFI patter they'd used throughout the war, habits of speech never shaken. Guilty that she'd missed the funeral, she'd promised to send some photographs of Lofty in his prime.

Olive kept her war in the schoolbag she'd once tied to the saddle of the bull-necked farm horse which she would ride, always a length or two behind Evelyn, to school in Orange. It was not often, now, that she looked into that bag. On top of the pile of photos inside it was a picture of Lofty and Duncan posing by the door of the car they'd assembled from spare parts only to have it sit idle in the corner of one of the Lancaster hangars at Elsham Wolds; and beneath that a picture of Duncan in RAAF grey-blue, an open-faced boy sitting on a straw mattress at the camp in Bradfield Park. And so on, and so on, back into their shared childhood: Duncan with his head under the bonnet of his father's Ford; Duncan leading a horse over the back paddock of their farm in the Canobolas Valley. The last in the pile showed a willowy girl sitting rigid in the saddle – everything about Evelyn, even the drape of the looped reins, signalling impatience.

Duncan had sent photographs from Lichfield of his newly formed crew, six young men looking pleased with themselves

– among them Duncan, with his neatly combed corrugations of hair and tailored uniform. She'd thought that the pinched waist of RAAF blues made the men's figures girlish – only the soft-bellied older men at Flight Command could carry it off. But Duncan liked the look and thought it 'aristocratic'. She'd had to agree that one man in the crew had a regal air – Crowe, the American pilot. He had an immaculately trimmed moustache and curling top lip that – even if one missed the silver wings – marked him as a pilot. In the first photo Duncan sent from Lichfield, Crowe was waving at the belly of the Wimpy above their heads, his hand a pale blur of movement. Duncan and Lofty stood flanking him, Lofty with his shoulders hunched, and arms folded high on his chest; Duncan wearing his cap so far back on his head that the collar rim seemed to be the only thing holding it up. Now she paid little attention to Solomon, the bomb aimer, and Derek, the navigator, although she remembered being amused, on first seeing the picture, by the gimlet-eyed glare the latter was giving the photographer. The wireless operator was missing from the shot – he'd flown that day, 'spare bod' for another crew.

A week after hearing that Lofty had died, Olive packaged up the photographs and Duncan's gunnery log, and sent them to Lofty's widow. She kept no copies for herself, and placed the emptied schoolbag behind the recycle bin in the garage, meaning to throw it out. But a few days later a package arrived from New Zealand, the stamps curling at their corners.

Inside was a collection of photographs she'd never seen, and a tissue-wrapped dark blue notebook of the sort shopkeepers once used to keep track of items bought on tick. The handwriting on the pages was tiny, and did not seem to be Lofty's. Keeping a diary was against King's Regulations. She settled herself with a cup of tea in the sunroom to find out who'd had the pluck to keep this one.

The diarist had flown Spitfires from RAF Digby, and he detailed chess games won and books read while waiting for the Tannoy to sound. By the third page Olive knew him, although she could not recognise his catalogue of men dead – or 'as good as': a pilot named Somerville whose Blenheim went down in flames over Cherbourg, another called 'Socks' who'd baled out over the Channel from a cockpit awash with flame; who was saved by air-sea rescue for a long convalescence but could not return to his job as a teacher for fear that he'd terrify the children. And a Pilot Officer named Bentley burned so badly when his Spitfire crashed that his corpse was indistinguishable from the leather and metal of the pilot's seat. It must have been from this business of his friends being burned that Curtis Crowe fled in 1941 – requesting the transfer from Fighter to Bomber Command that would eventually make him skipper of Duncan's and Lofty's first Lancaster, T for Tommy.

About a third of the way through the diary Olive found the entries dealing with Crowe's arrival at the Operational Training Unit:

Crewed up today. Picked the tallest mid-, and the softest-spoken rear gunner, a wireless operator whose first language is French, and a bomb aimer who looks too young to have enlisted. Derek thinks I'm crazy, but if I'm to tempt fate I want it tempted wholesale.

There's another damned dance tonight. Not that I don't like a dance but there's too much expectation about cutting up and – naturally – girls. I wounded myself shaving so I could get out of it on the sly. Better bourbon in the sergeants mess than no beer, a Lincoln blackout, and all those roving fingers.

Have logged as many night hours as day now. The boys call me Dracula. I like the name and when we get a kite of our own I plan to have it painted on the nose. Metamorphosing into smoke at will is surely a better prospect than being turned into kindling like the crew of the Halibag that went down with our wireless operator in it. The bomb aimer got out – he said that as soon as things went grim J. lost his facility for English altogether. The last heard from him was apparently a prayer in Basque. He wouldn't have cut it and might have put us all in danger so maybe it's better the poor guy's gone. Derek's on the prowl now for a new W/Op.

This is our first day of leave since the conversion course started. Caught a (cold, and very slow) train to Lincoln, meant to change there but ended up crammed in a waiting room with about 80 unwashed locals and 3 sheep. The sheep were on their best behavior. Asked when the train was likely to arrive and the brawny female porter said I'd better 'bleeding well not ask' or I'd jinx it. Gave up my seat to a munitions worker the colour of flames in a 'Back them up' poster after it's been tacked up a month. She told me it took her four hours to get home and the children had to do for themselves. Train came, of course too full to take even one of the sheep but a little bit of pushing cleared enough of the platform that I could stretch out for a nap until the arrival of the following train.

We have our W/Op. He's a South African called Van den Graaf and for some reason his hair smells of freshly baled straw. That such a creature comes to be in my crew I take to be an expression of the Lord's kindness to a lonely Yank airman. The only quarrel I have with the man is that he talks in the funny way the Boers have, the vowels squeezed to a point in each word. But so long as the tower can understand him, I don't care.

Reading this, Olive wondered what had become of Crowe. She'd never bothered to find out. Her lack of interest was shameful, and she had no good reason for it. Certainly she'd disliked Crowe, even resented him, during the war. He'd had a habit of getting into everything. Even the fact that he'd served on fighters before bombers seemed an irritating sign of omnipresence. But people she loved had cared about Crowe, and there'd been nothing about him that one could point to and say – *that's what's missing in the man*. He wasn't flash with money, and his best blue uniform – although beautifully tailored – wore at the same rate as his crew's.

She remembered how Duncan had praised the skipper's way with a camera. While he'd turned his lens onto a little ginger cat that had walked out of the fields bordering the aerodrome to adopt him, Crowe had kept his box brownie busy taking pictures of their fellow aircrew. Now that she had these before her,

Olive couldn't agree with Duncan on their quality. There were group shots in which men had been coaxed into the picture by a comradely arm only to be halved, or edged off the emulsion altogether. But Duncan and Lofty and the South African wireless operator always made it front and centre into the shot: it was never *their* arms or legs cropped, their heads lopped off.

It was dark by the time Olive put the tissue back around the diary, and stacked the photographs. She stood at the back door listening to a frog singing and then took the path round the front of the house to the garage. The pavestones were wet – the automatic sprinkler system had begun its cycle.

Slipping the package into her old schoolbag, she put the bag behind the bin again.

Near the diary's end, she had found a sentence she could not face: *Their hands were very alike. I know this because I was still holding one of hers when the nurse came to lay the body out.*

Chapter Two

1938

Olive had had no idea what to pack.

It would be cold in England – colder than the winters in Orange and not nearly so dry. She turned the trunks in the shed out to see what might serve for the trip; there was a pair of overshoes, a woollen skirt and a scarf that might do to replace the one she'd once caught on the branch of a blue gum on the ride to school.

Evelyn's parents had booked a cabin for her on the upper decks of the *Largs Bay*, hull-side – she would be among a class of passengers more than suitable for the daughter of a man who had run a bullock team. Olive was afraid she'd have to stay in her cabin.

By the time her father came in from feeding the dogs, she was packed, the trunks sitting by the front door. After she'd cleared the breakfast plates she stood behind her father's chair and trimmed the hair in his ears with a pair of dressmaker's scissors while he rolled smoke rings round his tongue and out the open front door. Arthur Jamieson thought it was a good thing his daughter was going to see the world before someone took the lion's share and put the workers out.

'You get your bit. Go where they listen to what's said.'

He'd been in Europe during the war: Etaples, Beaumont Hamel, then a convalescent home in Devon where someone finally made sense of what he'd been whispering – night and day – since the stretcher-bearers found him. *A half of bitter*. For a long time after Arthur Jamieson's discharge he'd sworn that English doctors were the best, even if bourgeois sods.

'Just remember,' he said as he wrapped salt into a twist of paper and packed it with the hard-boiled eggs she was to eat on the train. 'You're going there to save Evelyn, not the other way around.' Rolling the thermos in a towel, he packed it on top of the rest of the satchel's contents.

'*Fetching* Evelyn, more like.'

Her father frowned and said, 'They'd have sent Duncan if he didn't have college.' He approved of Duncan's education in the practical, and humanitarian, field of veterinary science. It was better that his daughter should go – all she'd miss was tapping away at the keys of an old Imperial at secretarial school, and she could do that just as easily when she got back. Opportunities for travel routinely came the Macintyres' way – if someone else was to get the chance, then good on them.

With father at one end of the trunk and daughter at the other, they shuffled the thing out onto the verandah and stood waiting for the Macintyres' Ford. When the truck came rolling up the track out of clouds of dust the old farmer planted a kiss on the parting of his daughter's hair and went back inside the house.

Duncan had been playing cricket all summer and had a stockman's tan on his forearms, but the skin above the rolled cuffs was pale. He did not have trouble meeting the eyes of girls of his own age, and he now looked keenly into Olive's, his face aglow with an amiable envy. She'd had her hair cut short for the journey, and now put her palms up to primp reddish brown handfuls of curls. Had these not been tamed by a blue hat with small white flowers on it the effect might have been more marked, but Olive was nevertheless pleased to see she'd made an impression. Duncan had not often seen her wear lipstick, and seemed to find arresting this extra level of emphasis on an already emphatically characterful face – one eyebrow of which was set perpetually higher than the other. He leaned out from the truck door, feet on the running board, and stared admiringly at his sister's best friend.

'You look brighter than a burnished penny.'

Olive blushed. She was not good at taking compliments, even though she suspected the capacity to do so was advantageous. In answer, she held out her valise, and Duncan took it from her. Together they wrestled the trunk into the back of the truck, which sat shaking on its springs.

With Duncan steering around potholes and over corrugations of dried mud, they followed the road by Meadow Creek. Along that same road, years before, two old Irishmen had pushed wheelbarrows crammed with bitten cabbages, dwarf potatoes and dirty carrots to sell in Orange, until the thin soil of their plot so annoyed them that they sold their garden, and the land on which they'd built their shack, to Duncan's grandfather. It was all Macintyre land until her father chivvied out 500 acres east of the valley that became Lake Canobolas during the Depression.

After a few miles Duncan broke the silence to ask whether she was sorry she was going.

'Of course I'm not.' Olive stole a look his way – it was hot in the car, and little stipples of sweat were standing out on his forehead. Duncan's skin had finally cleared; the light mottling of acne scars not nearly so noticeable. If anything, they made him look older, someone to take account of.

Olive was kneading the handkerchief in her lap. She admitted to being a little nervous about travelling.

'Just follow along with what other people want to do. Accommodate,' he suggested, the skin around his eyes crinkling with pleasure at the idea of a cooperative Olive. 'Join in with things. Cribbage, draughts. It doesn't matter what you do so long as you're doing it with other people. You'd be surprised how much it helps to be a part of things.'

'I'm not to play solitaire then.'

'No solitaire, and reading in public to be done in deckchairs only. Never at a table.' She put a knowing expression on her face and, seeing this, Duncan took his hand from the wheel to make the scout's honor sign. 'On my word. Mum told me this when I went off for my first term boarding. She said give it a month and if it didn't work they'd talk about my coming home. It worked. I can get on in most situations now, even when I've no one familiar about.'

'I don't think I'm much of a joiner-in,' Olive said, and looked back out the window. Brindle cows were gathering in the shade of the scraggly brush in the paddocks by the side of the road. As the car passed, a heifer lifted its tail to let fly a stream of faeces.

The drift of Duncan's advice worried her. Joining in was easy for people who dressed and spoke properly and knew just what to say to their deckchair mates, and the smart set forming a four for bridge. While there might be some small hope for her (she'd been a fourth hand at bridge with Evelyn and her parents since she'd matured to the game at the age of thirteen), Olive suspected that mastery of the rules of the greater game remained beyond her.

Halfway to Bathurst, watched by a hungry kurrawong and encircled by ants, they stopped to eat the lunch his mother had packed. Duncan stretched out for a rest, his head on a rolled tea towel, and hat over his face, one leg bent. His was the sort of grace that meant he could drape himself anywhere, and he now lay with such stillness that he belonged as well to the ground as the rocks or fallen branches of gum. Olive was so loath to disturb him that she spent a quarter of an hour trying to divert a particularly resolute stream of ants from roaming up the bridge of his ankle into his trouser leg. Then, she read until he sat up, disoriented. 'I don't know how we're going to get that train,' he said, and looked at Olive in such a way that it was clear anything going wrong, after that, would be her fault.

'You didn't need to drive me all the way,' she said, piqued at his reproach. 'There was a bus.'

'I wanted to.' The way Duncan looked when he said this almost persuaded her that the viola awaiting collection from the storeroom of the sheet-music shop in Bathurst had nothing to do with him taking her to the station there.

He rubbed the dust off his palms and, to Olive's surprise, took her right hand in his. She was not used to people touching her and tried to pull out of his grasp.

'Olive,' Duncan said, in a tone all the more rueful at her so hurriedly having detached herself, 'I can at least see you off.'

And he did, after supervising the porter's loading of the trunk and putting her valise up onto the luggage rail. Then they sat opposite each other for the few minutes before the train was due to depart.

'Any messages for Evelyn?'

Duncan was struggling with the window, trying to shut out the cindery wind. It took him a moment to answer. 'If you tell her not to come back, she will. She's a contrary cuss.' He made a quick perusal of his blunt nails. 'And tell her I'm going to learn to fly. That might get her interest.'

Olive's mouth settled into a disapproving line. 'You can't put your parents through that. Evelyn's been quite enough of a worry.'

'No.' He sighed. 'I suppose I can't. But what I do is different from what you tell her I'm doing, isn't it?'

Duncan regretted this flippancy when Olive sighed and looked away from him. 'Don't be dim, Duncan, it doesn't suit you.'

He sat a moment, the muscles in his jaw working. He seemed

young to her then, sitting there clutching his hat on his lap like a man in a doctor's office.

Olive moved to sit beside him and said, 'Sorry, that was shrewish.' Hesitatingly, she laid a hand on his knee – this would have been perfectly alright, and a natural gesture, had not the young woman in the seat across the aisle looked over to assess them, a cool sweep of the eyes that seemed to say that neither of them knew the faintest thing about the way goodbyes should be made between young men and women on trains.

Duncan slid out from under Olive's hand to stand by the seat. 'All set then. Got your tickets for the voyage?'

She nodded.

'And something to eat on the train?'

She nodded again.

'Right. I'm off. Mum will write you at Aunt Ida's to find out how you're getting on.' He searched the ceiling panels of the train for the right parting remark and found, 'Make sure you keep warm and…look out for chilblains.'

Olive promised she would and leaned out of the train window to watch Duncan's unhurried retreat along the platform, his deft deflections to right or left to let pass porters with carts, or travellers in their last-minute rush for the carriages. As he rounded the corner to the exit, the wind caught him – his white shirt briefly billowing and his golden hair lifted.

At the docks the little man at the fruit stall was reluctant to sell Olive an orange, and kept proffering apples, saying they were better for the stomach at sea. But she eventually left him with thruppence and the fruit she'd wanted, despite his warning she'd be sorry once they found the swell beyond the Gap.

The *Largs Bay* rose like a wall before her, the brass fixings around its windows rimmed with verdigris. Passing up the gangway she was excruciatingly aware of that heaving green space between the ship and the wharf into which people fell, and were sometimes crushed.

A ship's steward showed her to a cabin on 'B' deck, assuring her it was freeboard. Her first impression of the cabin was of how dark it was, and how small. She was to live in a room more confining than her kitchen at home. After she'd unpacked, she reassessed it from the vantage point of a seat on top of her empty luggage. If she lay on the floor, and rolled twice she would come up against something no matter what angle she'd started at.

If this was a stateroom, it was the Luxembourg of staterooms.

She retreated to the upper decks.

The sea was calm in the harbour, and as they left their mooring Olive went astern in the wake of other parties of passengers already formed. There they goggled at the bridge, and at the governor's residence, and a young man with a newspaper folded under one arm pointed at the naval docks and said, more loudly than Olive thought was necessary, 'They seem busy enough. At least someone in this country is taking the threat of war seriously.'

The girl standing next to him – a thick-waisted, pretty thing with a merry expression – was watching the flock of grey gulls following the ship out. 'There won't be a war,' she said. 'Nobody could let it happen, not after the last.'

'But if there is, it'll be decided at sea,' the young man said, reaching up to finger his shadow of a moustache, as if to see it was still there. 'That's our lookout. Sea to every side of us and all we've got is a fish-and-chip navy. *That's* why I'm glad there's a little preparation.'

They were startled when Olive spoke up from behind them.

'It won't be decided at sea,' she said, putting her hands on the rail beside them. 'It's what goes on in the air that counts.'

When the two young people turned to look at her she saw that they were siblings. They had the same brown eyes, and the same something about the mouth: whether it was nose or chin she couldn't be sure. The young man smiled, his lips parting to show uneven teeth.

'Well, that's a comforting prospect,' he said. 'Australia's got even more air around it than sea, so I can't see us being bothered.'

At that the girl looked again at the gulls following the ship out, and Olive thought that she, at least, had grasped her point. The confiding smile she gave Olive seemed to confirm this impression.

'I'm Anne Battersby, and this is my brother, William.'

Olive introduced herself, and said she'd come from Orange, as if her origin was more important than her destination. Now that she had licence to do so, she looked more closely at them. They had the ease of people who'd never born a snub – peers to the

Macintyres in class. William Battersby wore a startlingly pressed suit and even Olive could see it was cut from cloth imported from England, and now on its way back there. Anne Battersby had a silk parasol tucked under one arm, and her white gloves were held closed at the wrist by amber buttons.

In her grey woollen skirt and matching worsted jacket Olive felt dowdy by comparison.

William Battersby announced that he and his sister were off to Plymouth after Southampton. Neither Perth, Colombo nor Aden seemed to be part of *their* itinerary.

'Pleased to meet you, Olive Jamieson. I hope we shall be good messmates.' William took her hand lightly, and shook it, then put his elbows on the rail. The edges of the newspaper he was holding riffled noisily. He glanced at it and with a cavalier flick of the wrist cast the thing into the wind – the pages blistered the water briefly in the declivity of a wave until the wake caught and drowned them.

All three watched the thing go down, as if it was the past disappearing. Then they looked at one another.

'What say we explore the ship?' William asked and, in case the invitation wasn't clear, he added, 'Do come with us, Miss Jamieson.'

Olive realised that she had just joined in, and everything would be all right.

Then there was a week of south-easterly swells. She was too ill for dinner the first day out, or for breakfast, lunch or dinner on the days following. The ship's doctor visited regularly. So familiar did he get with her, and her cabin, that he arrived one morning to a 4 a.m. call barefoot, in a robe, with his eyeglasses askew. The doctor was concerned about dehydration and made her drink a glass of tonic so vile-smelling she had to pinch her nose to get it into her mouth, only releasing the clamp to swallow. Then he'd swaddled her in her own sweaty clot of blankets and led her on deck.

'Look at that sea. Mild as a milk-pond,' the doctor told her. She shrunk out of his grip in embarrassment. The decks about them were empty, the sky full of stars and the smoke from the stacks trailed aft in a crisp-edged line.

The cords of the doctor's robe had come loose and were dangling like bell pulls. He tugged them together and, with great impatience, told Olive to sit on one of the bench seats on C deck, overlooking the stern. Olive could smell new paint on the staves of the seat beneath her.

'The trick,' the doctor was saying, 'is to keep an eye on the flag.'

She looked where he'd pointed – saw the ensign pull this way and that, then buckle into life to press its tongue hard into the wind raised by the ship's progress. Around the ensign the horizon – a grey line on the black sea – swung gently to the ship's roll.

'Now I want you to stay here, looking at the flag, until you stop feeling sick.' She peered into the physician's face – he was unshaven, his eyes puffy from lost sleep. He did not look like a man to be second-guessed.

'Doctor's orders,' he barked, turning to the gangway.

She stayed on deck for more than an hour. Soon dawn reddened the horizon around the rim of the rising sun, it became a magenta line, then a yellow road running the ridge of horizon, and finally a silver blaze of light that swallowed the flag entirely.

She struggled out of her nest of blankets then and went to the rail. A few passengers came strolling aft, and were kind enough to ignore the young woman's irregular dress and makeshift bed, nodding and saying 'good morning' as if they'd met in town, or upon a country road. It was only in appreciating this delicacy that Olive realised her nausea had receded. All that was going on between the sting of chill in her feet and her dry throat was a slow grinding in the gut – not seasickness but the clenching of a stomach shrunken to a fist.

Gathering up her bedding, she went back to her cabin. She had a thorough wash and put on the clothes that Duncan had left – wrapped clumsily in brown paper – on the seat he'd briefly occupied in the train. There was a blue bolero jacket with a hip-hugging skirt, and a hat made from matching material. The shirt had been in the package too, and it was red, with small white polka dots on it, and she was glad the jacket covered nearly all of it. She set the hat aslant – right to left – like a forage cap. It was unfortunate that her pumps were the wrong colour, but the mirror was too squat to show them and she was forced to take the impression of herself from knee to forehead. Since the young woman looking out at Olive seemed much too satisfied with herself, she gave her the orange to hold – the fruit looked ludicrous in the curve of a white gloved hand, and was all but impossible to eat.

Olive found William Battersby on deck, where he was examining the davits from which the ship's boats would be hoist in an emergency. She waited until he'd satisfied himself as to their condition, and caught him up as he passed the entrance to the lounge.

'Brought breakfast, did you?' William said, nodding at her orange.

'My first meal in a week.'

'Allow me.' Unencumbered by gloves, he deftly stripped the fruit of its skin and the two of them shared it standing by the ship's rail, William spitting his orange pips downwind while she watched, envious of the licence given him by his sex.

'We asked to see you, but the doctor thought you weren't fit enough for visitors,' William said. 'I hope you didn't think we'd deserted you.'

'Thinking wasn't my strong suit,' said Olive, tipping her handful of pips over the rail and examining her gloves for stains.

'It's a pity your stomach's not stronger. Anne and I are both good sailors. We can stand a blow.' As he said this, William put a foot up on the lower rail and Olive saw the outline of a muscled thigh beneath the linen of his suit trousers. A strong stomach was not all that he had, apparently. Now she could understand his preoccupation with the maritime threat – the Battersbys were sailing people, born and bred.

In the following days, Olive tried to borrow her new friends' ease. After Perth, as the ship steamed towards the equator, they exhausted each other with hand after hand of suicide gin or swapped novels to laze in adjacent deckchairs, reading. Indeed, they'd sunk so happily into the role of shipboard wastrels that the ship's arrival in Colombo came as something of a shock. The passengers were allowed a day to themselves ashore, but Olive and the Battersbys found their attempt to construct their own itinerary quickly thwarted. Their cab driver delivered them to the only 'decent' club in the Fort district despite their prompting him to drive them about for a bit. In a dining room with potted palms at each point of the compass they lunched with other Europeans – a company dressed for the tropics but eating as if in preparation for an Arctic stint. At half past the noon hour a towering dessert trolley did its clattering rounds. Olive had just eaten her second Boston bun when a young man in cricket whites, foreswearing his *Ceylon Observer*, came over to say they were sitting at Donald Bradman's favourite table – the cricketer had dined there every day after play at the Galle Face Green.

'Really?' The dab of butter William had been about to spread on a scone sat on his knife, forgotten.

Anne and Olive left the two men to their cricket talk and went for a walk, meandering south towards Cinnamon Gardens, not saying much, happy to follow a route that didn't end at a gangway or rail. Every so often, Anne would lean on Olive's arm to adjust the strap on her shoe, her big hands splayed on the cloth of Olive's sleeve and her dark ringlets falling aside to expose the nape of a strong neck covered by a velvety down of hair, sun lighting the whole of that covering as if it were a second, glimmering, skin. They spent the afternoon thus, walking, with Olive letting the younger woman rest against her.

She regretted her walk the next day when her seasickness returned, forcing her to retake her seat at the stern and fix her gaze once more upon the flag until the worst of the nausea had passed. While the other passengers went ashore at Aden she stayed on board, not wanting to risk offending her inner ear. Her stomach remained unsettled until they made the Suez Canal. There, the whole cohort of passengers turned out to marvel at English engineering. But for Olive it was the desert cloven by the canal that deserved the attention, and she spent the through-passage staring at sand dunes from behind which came the occasional grinding roar of a truck engaging its gears, crossing the dun-brown water to her.

After they had passed Gibraltar on the last leg of the voyage, Anne and William raised the topic of her visiting them at Plymouth. The three were lying in their deckchairs in the shaded, starboard side of the ship. Despite the cover, it was hot, and most of the passengers were below. The deck was theirs. Anne put her book down with a sigh and – as if this had been a signal – William set about convincing Olive she'd be better off out of a London she hadn't been in yet.

First it was, 'The air's better.'

Then it was, 'Cheaper rents. And nicer flats.'

Finally he got to, 'We could go sailing. Wouldn't that be nice?'

Olive threw her own book down in exasperation. 'Because I do so love the sea,' she snapped, 'I will take myself to Plymouth to live comfortably on an allowance I haven't got.' Dismissing them, she rolled onto her side. She heard Anne's skirts rustle but by the time she'd turned back it was William who'd gone. Anne was staring into the sky, her book upside down on her chest – the red penguin on the cover walking back towards her chin.

'You're our friend and of course we'd like you to visit. But it's more than that for William.' In the shape of the final syllable she could see Anne's tongue press pinkly against the darker roof of her mouth.

Olive said nothing to that, hoping the subject would be dropped. It was not that she didn't want to visit Plymouth, but that she had no resources to do so. William being driven away by her rebuff had excited her – not so much because he'd shown his feelings but that the interchange had put his sister in a confiding mood. Anne moved her deckchair nearer Olive's.

'William's not usually so easy with girls. He's in a better mood all round, and I know that's because of you.' Olive was about to protest that the voyage might have something to do with it – their untesting leisurely lives – but she foreswore breaking her silence. There was something fetching about Anne's mouth – and she was content for her to talk so long as the confidences didn't get too startling. But Anne had no more to say. Olive set her book before her face and went back to reading.

Now that she had been told that William was fond of her she could not ignore it. She revised her accounts of their time together and took new meaning from the way he might have offered her the salt at dinner, or opened doors for her, and given her his hand whenever they were about to mount the stairways between decks. She saw now how carefully he'd been slicking his hair, and why he'd bought that paper flower for his buttonhole from the purser. She knew, too, that William was just the sort of fellow she *should* go for – lively, intelligent, easy in the world. But her overwhelming feeling was one of agitation, as if his affection – or any like it – was a threat. Perhaps her discomfort was a result of the imminence of their arrival in Southampton. There was no time now for romance, and whether William should woo her or not was pressing less on her thoughts than the rendezvous ahead – Evelyn come to fetch her to London.

It was all so confounding that she had to go to her cabin to think, and the thinking terminated readily in a nap, by which time it was dinner. William and Anne turned up at her door acting as if nothing had happened. In the dining room their conversation ran freely and the evening card game was strained only because all three made poor losers.

Before turning in, Olive went on deck again. To port lay the dark ridge of coast they'd been skirting for some hours. She was tempted to ask the crewman smoking at the rail where the ship sat on its course, but couldn't bring herself to talk to him. He had brawny arms covered with soot, and a blackened face in which only his eyes showed; these ringed by skin glowing palely in the moonlight. Passenger and stoker stood watching the shore slip by in silence. He took one long last drag on his cigarette and threw the butt away; it spun out from the ship in an arc until the wind pulled it through a knot of sparks into darkness. Olive risked a glance then, and saw him staring at her with a frank, assessing gaze, the sort of look her father gave horses at auction. There wasn't enough to nerve him because he nodded and went below, muttering a goodbye that sounded oddly like 'Near Miss'.

Chapter Three

Bank holiday

At disembarkation gangways sprouted from the smooth line of the hull as trunks, and bags, and items of crated furniture were transferred to the dock. There were more gramophones than anyone had imagined, and at least four caged birds – one of these a white cockatoo, the feathers at its crown fanned into rigid spikes.

'Poor thing,' Anne said, leaning out over the rail until Olive felt the vertigo her friend obviously did not.

'It's probably had a more exciting voyage than we have. Everyone trying to get it to speak, and now all it can say is, "Polly gone. Polly gone".' William craned his neck to scan the crowd. 'Fancy teaching a bird geometry.'

Olive recognised the joke with a tight little laugh and looked back over the rail at the packed dock. Down in that crowd was Evelyn, years older than when she'd last seen her. Evelyn – the writer of infrequent, if loving, letters; letters to which she had or had not replied, but had in any case kept in a jarrah box by her bedside – the kind of box a person could lay hold of quickly if the house caught on fire. Olive stood on the tips of her toes to stare at the crowd, but told herself she was not looking for Evelyn – so great was her dread at not finding her.

She became conscious of Anne pulling at her elbow. It was time to go.

Together they braved the crowd at the bottom of the gang-plank, and she walked closely behind William. He was clearing a path. She didn't see Evelyn, at first – not with William in the way – and then she was suddenly *there*, beside her, and it hardly mattered that he was still ploughing on ahead. They stood in a circle of sweetened air – Evelyn's unfamiliar perfume – and Olive looked at the friend with whom she'd been so angry. She was taller than she'd been when she left Orange, as much as seven inches taller than Olive. Evelyn had a habit of squinting when she talked to people, as if they were some distance from her or stand-ing in hard light. This was not because she had any infirmity of sight – her grey eyes worked with remarkable efficiency, and were at that moment energetically taking Olive's measure.

'Look at you, bustier than ever,' Evelyn said, luckily at moder-ate volume. When Evelyn leaned forward to kiss Olive the red silk scarf she'd looped about her long neck slid loose, exposing her décolletage; the lines of bone rising and falling under skin marbled with cold.

'Your fingers are freezing,' she said and, laughing, began chafing her friend's hands between her own.

Olive stood self-consciously canted towards Evelyn and waited for the Battersbys to finish their hugging and handshaking.

It was a minute, then, until quiet was secured.

She felt a palm press against the small of her back. William's. She saw Evelyn look from the hand to his face, and take a small step back from them.

'This is Miss Jamieson, Father.' Anne was introducing her.

'Pleased to meet you,' Olive found herself saying. In order to concentrate, she appraised Battersby Senior. He suited his name; looked like the sort of man who'd appreciate a fry-up. He was small and round and his suit fitted snugly at his waist, and at the tops of his beefy arms and shoulders. She could meet him eye to eye. 'This is my friend Evelyn Macintyre,' she said. 'Evelyn flies aeroplanes.'

'Does she now?'

Evelyn stood more than a head taller than Mr Battersby, and he beamed up at her. To the old gentleman's credit, he shook her hand without registering the oddness of the gesture from a woman half his age.

'No point in my offering a lift, I'd say.'

In reply Evelyn jangled the keys she'd been holding, silver against skin ruddy with cold. Olive could see that her knuckles were chapped.

'We have a car, but thanks for thinking of it.'

Wanting now to be getting on, Olive kissed Anne on the cheek and touched William's arm. He put his hand over hers and she could feel the ridges of callous on his palm. Afraid she'd turn out to be lying, she said, 'I'll see you again. Soon, I'm sure.'

Both the younger Battersbys waved at Olive when she and

Evelyn turned at the end of the quay. Olive was surprised how easily she could pick them out of the crowd, and she felt oddly lost as she raised her hand to wave a last goodbye.

Evelyn stood watching her, clutching the car keys against her bony chest. Since she'd dressed that morning for her friend, Olive found this attention awkward, and all the more so because she had no idea what Evelyn thought of her now. So she stood looking along the quay longer than was needed – Anne and William and their father being long since out of sight. When finally she turned, it was to see Evelyn flex her shoulders and lift her head, then set her feet apart as far as her narrow skirt would allow. She put herself into this pose with the faintest affectation, like an artist's model new to her trade.

She saw that Evelyn's dress sense had not changed. The direction of her tastes was due less to her mother's attention to style ('Don't put blue and black together dear, you'll look like a bruise') than to her accusation that Evelyn was 'gawky'. While the adolescent Duncan was free to lunge about, and break things by mistake, and walk slope-shouldered through the house, Evelyn's deportment was a source of reproach. Something sterner than reproach was needed when Mrs Macintyre found out that Evelyn had worn her brother's cricket whites to a game between rival Protestant parishes in Bathurst. Bowling for the Presbyterians she'd economically dismissed two of the Methodist batsmen before being recognised, and sent off. Olive had been the only person to see Evelyn play, and she alone appreciated the gameness of that grace; the mercurial energy that got Evelyn onto the pitch and kept her there through two innings. After the cricket incident, Evelyn was not let out of the house for a fortnight, and by the time Olive saw her, she'd changed. She'd been reined in. Thereafter she walked more on the toes and less on the balls of her feet, and did not appear in public without a smudge of rouge or lipstick. Evelyn had assumed a proper style, but a perpetual air of dissatisfaction was its price.

Olive put down the hand she'd been waving and caught up with Evelyn.

'Now it's just us,' she said, glancing shyly up into her friend's handsome face – the broad jaw, and wide brow, and the deep crease of a dimple above the left side of her long mouth.

Evelyn replied, eyes sparkling, 'You can hold onto my jacket if you like. Don't want you getting lost on your first day. What would I say to mother and father? And imagine the signs: *Lost, on or about November 4th, well-dressed colonial girl. Reward offered.*'

'How much?'

'How much what?'

'The reward. How much would you pay?' Saying this, Olive threaded her arm through her friend's. Evelyn's warm arm in hers made her reply that much more teasing.

'Oodles. An absolute fortune. Say five pound?'

'Penny-pinching Scot.'

Evelyn took the valise from her and gave it to a boy sitting on the bumper of a racy looking two-door saloon car. The boy, whose trousers were belted by rope, accepted the bag with a stony face that lightened only when Evelyn passed him sixpence.

'See that goes in the boot. And there's another two bob for you if you go find the porters for Miss Jamieson's luggage.'

Evelyn opened the car door for Olive. The windscreen was spotless, and the upholstery smelled like one of Mrs Macintyre's best handbags. 'Penny-pinching Scot I may be, but I do a fair turn at spending *other* people's money.' Evelyn patted the steering wheel. 'Aunt Ida needed help choosing a new car. I said it was cheaper to buy one that had fewer doors.'

'And she was taken in by that!'

'Anthony Eden having one was a bit of a clincher.'

The boy was on his way back, leaning into his task like a bullock in harness. He had the trolley in tow, but no porter.

Evelyn turned over tags, and tugged at locks, then sent the boy away with his coins. Olive could see her in the rear-view mirror, her back rigid, and one foot tapping. Apparently there was more luggage than space for it in the trunk.

Evelyn leaned in the open car window to announce they'd have it sent on and before she could object had gone to find the porter.

They trailed a slow-moving lorry away from the docks, its canvas loudly flapping. Since they were creeping along and Evelyn didn't have to keep her eyes on the road she turned to give Olive one of her winning looks.

'Be a dear and don't tell me off. I came for you, not for your luggage.'

Olive was about to object to being managed when the wing

beat of the canvas sounded more loudly. They could see the lorry driver's face as they overtook him, and he didn't look happy. Evelyn pulled the Morris in tightly in front of him, and smiled into the mirror when they heard his horn.

Olive wavered between admiration and embarrassment at Evelyn's driving, but she did love the way she sung the names of the villages they passed – trilling *Waterlooville* and *Woodmancote* and *West Ashling* at the top of her voice. She also took the bends in the road with one hand on the wheel, and the other tap-tapping the top of the bench seat behind Olive's head.

'Brighton Sands for afternoon tea,' Evelyn said, patting the picnic basket on the bench seat between them. 'Lunch even.'

The tide was out at Brighton, although that made little difference to the English daytrippers with their deckchairs turned to face the teashops and hotels on the promenade. They lay with the crowns of their heads pointing out to sea, many with handkerchiefs over their faces, for the autumnal sun was unseasonably warm, and there was no wind. Evelyn and Olive ate looking seaward. Beyond the edge of the pale sand, the sea was a glittering line – a presence perfectly proportioned to the land, and quite far enough away for Olive's liking. Had she known it would be years until they'd see again such an uninterrupted stretch of sand, such a benevolent sea, she might better have appreciated it – but the mined dunes strung off by wire and the anti-invasion barriers like foundations of buildings swept out to sea were still to come. That sunny day the appeasers were busy – not at all put out by the urgent scenes she'd seen on William's Churchman

Cigarette cards: bombs swept from vegetable gardens by housewives with scoop and hoe; gas-suited figures on a raid party.

After lunch, they carried their shoes and stockings to stroll along the jellied sand until a young man – barefoot but in his bank holiday best – told them the tide was coming in and they'd better watch it.

Olive's father knew about English tides, although the waters he'd seen at Scarborough were placid enough. He'd told her how some tides might come in four times a day, or gallop faster than a Derby winner to drown clam-gatherers, and sweep cars from isthmus roads. But the tide they watched that day came in so slowly a man could roll a barrel of molasses up the beach without getting his heels wet.

Olive was disappointed.

'Bother this,' said Evelyn, but not – it turned out – about the slowcoach tide. She stopped walking and took her friend's hand, her thumb absently stroking Olive's. Olive scanned her face. Reading Evelyn was largely a matter of guesswork – she kept most of her feelings close-hauled, even if her physical dispensations were generous.

'I'm not ready to take you to Aunt Ida's,' Evelyn said. 'Let's see whether there's a room free at the Ocean Hotel.'

Olive had no idea where the Ocean Hotel was. And the prospect of being taken there by Evelyn was as daunting as it was exciting. She could be alone with her friend, but she had no nightwear or change of clothes – the baggage having been sent on. And she'd never stayed at a hotel. Her father's advice on the subject was to *follow the girl with the towels, if anything needed doing*. And Mrs Macintyre had once said that it was perfectly all right for English ladies to drink in public houses and hotels, so long as they kept their hats and gloves on.

So she followed the hatless, gloveless Evelyn off the sand. As they threaded their way through the crowds on the promenade her friend explained that the Ocean Hotel was popular, and new. There were salt baths out the front, and a ballroom inside with an American style bar backed by a mirrored wall. Evelyn knew this, but not the niceties: the rooms cost two guineas, which was more than they could afford.

'Shall we stay for the tea dance?' Evelyn asked as they trailed back through the lounge of the hotel.

Olive felt herself blushing. 'I'm not dressed for it,' she said, and was appalled to hear the shadow of a plea in her voice. She wanted something to put between herself and Evelyn, something on which she could concentrate that was nothing to do with her. Looking about the lounge, she told Evelyn to wait for a moment and went to ask a man with both editions of the *Times* whether he might let her have one. He rolled the thing into a parcel for her gladly, and his wife added to it the copy of *Homes and Gardens* she'd just finished.

She had only been a few moments, but Evelyn was already sick of waiting. 'I take it this means you don't fancy a dance.'

'Not today. I'd like to settle in somewhere.'

They walked to the car in silence, no longer arm in arm, and Evelyn drove too fast towards London, and Hampstead, where they were long since expected, where tea was ready, a bed had been made for Olive, and water warmed for their baths.

Evelyn's Aunt Ida was the smallest person in her family, so small her footwear was custom ordered from a shoemaker in Mayfair in a child's size but to the season's fashion for ladies. As they had tea, Olive began to see why Evelyn had talked her aunt into purchasing the little coupé – a larger car would have dwarfed Ida Douglas. When she was seated her feet barely touched the carpet, despite the generous heel on her brogues.

'Evelyn tells me you're wanting to find yourself employment. A secretarial job, is it?' Miss Douglas asked, the reediness of her voice made up for by her perfect diction – the punch of consonants, the glide of vowels. She was taking a second section of cream cake onto her plate, so didn't see Olive jump, nor hear the teacup she was holding ring against its saucer. 'Don't feel you must rush from us,' she said. 'My sister is very fond of you, as is Evelyn, so you're welcome for as long as you care to stay.'

One of the Jack Russells – Eeny, or possibly Mo – stirred from its place by the fire, stretching its legs, and rolled onto its back. Olive patted the coarse, curling fur at the ridge where its ribs met. It jerked a leg in the air.

'Thank you, you're very kind.'

After tea, they went to Olive's room. Evelyn stood by the end of the bed, and kicked the trunk lid open with one strong swing of her leg.

'I'm wondering how much dresser space you'll need. There's

no wardrobe here so your clothes will have to hang in my room.' She lay back on the bed, plumping the pillows to make herself comfortable. Behind her the line between the bottom of the blind and the windowsill gave onto a sooty sky.

From the trunk Olive took the dresses she'd packed and laid them over the end of the bed by her friend's feet, putting one down after another in the hope she would have no time to see how dated the styles were, how worn the fabric.

Evelyn watched the pile grow. 'I don't know how my mother could have let you come away like this,' she said, lifting to her face the green dress Olive had worn for an interview to the Secretarial College at Bathurst. The gold catch of its white belt clinked. 'What do you intend to do with this?'

'Wear it.'

Then she pointed at the sleeve of the oilskin jutting out of its greaseproof paper wrapping. 'To the Orkneys, or Sheerness in a gale?'

'It always rains in London.' Throwing down the skirt she'd been holding, Olive said, 'I've not come to have dinners at the Savoy. I'm here to see you home. My clothes ought to do for that, or am I to be found wanting for a few strips of fur and a crease-free macintosh?'

Evelyn seemed to find the pressed tin of the ceiling interesting. After a minute she said, 'You're welcome to something of mine. I have two decent overcoats.' She was not looking at Olive, but at the pile of clothes.

'I'm round where you're flat, in case you haven't noticed. And the hem would be too low on my calves. Surely you're more observant than this in the cockpit.'

At that, Evelyn's face closed. Her good humour was like a barrage balloon in heavy weather: likely to drag anchor, and potentially incendiary. 'I think you're mistaking me for your young man at the docks. It's not *my* business to notice how your dresses hang and how you fill your pleats.'

At that Evelyn pushed herself off the bed and left the room. After a moment Olive heard the kettle whistle downstairs, and she nerved herself to move.

It took some effort not to cry. She had to watch her face in the vanity mirror until she was sure it would behave, and then she got out her cold cream and wiped off the make-up she'd so carefully applied a few hours before. Evelyn came in a half-hour later looking conciliatory, and carrying a towel. Olive followed her friend to the bathroom wordlessly and was relieved that she did not ask to stay.

She found that it was hard work not thinking when immersed to the chin in warm water. Her thoughts did wander. To keep them in check she read the *House and Garden* she'd been given in Brighton, the pages picking up a hem of suds. There were pictures of Hitler's mountain home: the 'handsome Bavarian chalet' with its jade-green colour scheme and Hartz mountain canaries trilling from cages in every room.

The fact that she thought there was soon to be a war on made her feel better. The awful situation in Europe and the friend she'd never been able to manage merged in her mind: both invited things to happen that were exceptional to the rule; both were bound to be a source of compunction where she was concerned.

Thus relieving herself of responsibility for anything she might in future do, Olive dropped the magazine she'd been reading by the side of the bath, and dozed, as a crocodile might, water lidding her nostrils.

Olive saw Evelyn in the evenings. More often than not she'd arrive with Civil Air Guard cadets in tow, girls who'd sit in the parlour discussing stalling speeds, trim and navigation, while a baffled Aunt Ida fed them teacake or macaroons.

Olive would sometimes sit in on these gaggles, if only because she'd inherit Evelyn once the last of the girls had put up her umbrella, or donned her macintosh, to brave the drizzle on the way to the Hampstead underground. Prised from her party of admirers Evelyn would contract to a manageable size, could be asked to stack plates, gather teacups and even set the table for dinner. She was lining up the dessertspoons with the knives the evening Olive broached the subject of their going home, to Orange, and the farm. Throughout the idle, enjoyable days she'd spent walking on the Heath, or reading on a bench next to Whitestones Pond, Olive had been dimly aware that it wasn't just Evelyn avoiding the issue.

'I'm meant to take you home.' Olive put the last water glass down in its place, facing the engraved lily to the edge of the table.

'I'm not going.' Evelyn stuck the tip of her finger between

knife and fish-knife to space them evenly. 'I told Mother that in not one but two letters. One of those – ' she said, pointing a spoon at Olive, ' – sent in May, in good time to stop you coming.'

'It probably gave her the idea to send me.'

'I'm used to my parent's gestures, not their plans,' she said, smiling crookedly. 'That's why I'm over here in the first place. I know what I'm after, and have a much better idea how to get it than they ever could for giving it to me.'

Having set down the last of the cutlery Evelyn stood away from the table to admire her handiwork. 'Napkins?' she asked.

'They're in the sideboard.'

The sideboard was one of the many pieces of furniture lining the walls of the dining room, all of mahogany fearsomely polished. These bulky pieces did at least put a stop to the arabesques and curlicues of the wallpaper that – when looked at sideways – seemed to crawl and spiral. The sight of Evelyn fussing over a simple chore was only slightly less exhausting than the pattern on the wallpaper. Olive sat in the chair Ida had put by the door to allow an elderly maid to sit while waiting on her dinner guests – she'd drawn Olive's attention to it as 'Timmin's chair', and it felt just that little bit less peculiar to sit in it than to be introduced to it.

'You shouldn't refuse to go until we've talked about it properly. I feel like an idiot coming all this way for a simple no.'

'For God's sake stop taking it so seriously,' Evelyn said, peering into one after another of the sideboard cupboards. 'I'll pay back your fare and you can stop feeling guilty.'

When Olive didn't answer she pulled the entire napkin drawer from its recess and brought it over to her, presenting the neatly ironed squares of napkins for her perusal. 'What do you think, red or white?' she asked.

Disgusted, Olive pushed the drawer back at her and went to fetch the serving dishes, and by the time she got back to the dining room Evelyn had laid one red place-setting between two white. Olive put her plate on the red.

There was just the three of them for dinner, and Evelyn rattled on about flying, and how many more girls there were than places for them in the Corps. Her aunt couldn't seem to get over what they wore in the cockpits of their Magisters or Tiger Moths.

'It must get awfully windy, and cold.' Ida paused over the cutting of her poached pear. 'Not everything can be covered by a scarf. And those girls have such beautiful complexions.'

'The Gladiator has an enclosed cockpit,' Evelyn said.

'Yes, but that can't be said of all such contraptions. I've heard the girls talking. One of them said she'd thought about using *grease* against the cold, like the Eskimos.'

'That was a joke.'

'It may well have been, but the poor girl had a point all the same.'

Evelyn set down the fork she'd been using to skewer her pear while she shaved it down to the core. 'We're perfectly comfortable up there – '

' – and safe?'

'Safe as houses.'

'I'm accountable to your mother, Evelyn,' Ida said. 'Don't be flippant.'

Evelyn changed the subject. 'I think I've got a job for Olive,' she said.

Her aunt looked sharply at her. 'Not at Stapleford?'

Evelyn raised an eyebrow, surprised. Olive doubted she could see beyond her own attachment to the aerodrome. 'Of course it's at Stapleford – in the annex to the control tower. Nothing very technical – a bit of filing, and record keeping, minding the telephone, running messages. That sort of thing.'

'It doesn't sound very interesting.' Ida had her spoon poised above her pear, and it wavered as she looked at Olive. 'I should think you could do better.'

'She could,' Evelyn agreed. 'But I can run her out, and back, and she won't have to be cooped up in some office through a city winter.'

'Even so – '

' – I'll be cooped up in an annex through an Essex winter.' Olive moved her chair back from the table and apologised for interrupting Ida. 'I'm not meant to be here for winter. Perhaps that's not clear. I thought Mrs Macintyre had written to say I was coming to fetch Evelyn home.'

Ida's expression showed bewilderment. 'There was nothing of the kind mentioned in the letters *I* received. And Evelyn's parents sent her to me. Why on earth would they be asking for her back?' She peered at her niece as she might at a tradesperson come to the front entrance of the house – a look of disapproval tempered by need. After a moment she put her napkin by her plate and said, 'Oh. I see.'

Evelyn leaned over the table towards her aunt, and covered the hand now lying loosely by the place setting. 'I don't want to go. If there's a war I can make good use of myself here.' Glancing at her friend, she added, 'As can Olive.'

'But Olive wasn't sent to make a use of herself generally, she was sent to bring you home. You could at least notice the effort your friend's made to fulfill your parents' wishes, even if you have no intention of obeying them. And if I were you,' she said crisply, moving her hand out from under her niece's, 'I'd think hard about what I say next.'

Evelyn looked from her aunt to Olive and then down at the tablecloth. Olive felt uncomfortable and would have left the table but since it was her fault they were having the conversation at all, she was bound to stay. She tried to catch Evelyn's eye but her friend would not look up. Outside, the night had closed in, and rain blew against the window so that it rattled in its frame. The rattling, and the ticking of the clock on the mantelpiece, was the only noise in the room.

Evelyn finally spoke. 'Flying is what I do best and I'd like to keep doing it. If that's selfish then so be it.'

'It's this inability to repent at being selfish that gives me pause.' With back straight and small head lifted, Ida stared at her niece until Evelyn began to blanch, and stutter.

'I'm...sorry to disappoint,' Evelyn stood so quickly her napkin dropped to the floor. She stacked the plates. (No one else would come to clear – there'd been no servants in the house since Timmins – of 'Timmins' chair' – had died.) After rolling the cores of the fruit into a single dish she took the lot out to the kitchen.

When she'd gone, Ida said, 'How odd that I hear of this only now.' Her voice had dropped, and she leaned nearer Olive, glancing towards the door as she did so. 'You don't think that a letter meant for me ended up in someone else's pocket?' Then she patted at her neatly set curls, as if they were out of place. 'You know Evelyn better than I do – is she that kind of person?'

'Not at all.'

'That's some comfort.'

'Yes it is.'

'And I wonder if she mightn't be right – about her being better use here.'

This startled Olive. 'Might she?'

'Might I?' Evelyn said from the doorway, where she stood with cleaning cloth in hand.

Ida glanced her way, and shook her head. 'Perhaps, but you're the last person who needs to hear it.'

'So,' Evelyn said, batting at the crumbs on the table with her cloth, chasing as many to the floor as those she caught in its damp folds, 'I'm not allowed to *enjoy* being right.'

'And I am not allowed to enjoy a quiet evening,' said the Ida who loved a good conversation. 'Sit down Evelyn. And stop trying to clean.'

Evelyn sat.

Ida went to get the sherry decanter from the sideboard. She poured each of them a glass.

'I'm responsible for you, Evelyn. Your mother is worried about mustard and chlorine and phosgene gas, or bombs levelling the house – and those are sensible fears. I've been stupid not to think of sending you back.' She added thoughtfully, 'If you'd let yourself be sent.'

Olive saw Evelyn glance at her, perhaps hoping for her support, but she merely got up to draw the curtains against the increasingly loud sound of rain.

'I'm sorry my parents are worried,' Evelyn said. 'But it wasn't necessary to send Olive to escort me back to Sydney, as if I'm sick or a child. I know what I'm doing here. And I'm doing something that's useful, if getting this country ready to deal with the war that's coming could be called useful.' As she spoke she laid one long-fingered hand over her breastbone, as if she'd set upon a recitation and was dramatising some element of it for the audience.

Ida sighed at that. 'Perhaps my lecturing you is unfair,' she said, fiddling with the stem of her sherry glass. 'But it's very difficult distinguishing your sense of duty from your self-interest.'

Evelyn was frowning, her thick, dark eyebrows drawn into a line, and Olive – afraid Evelyn would say something they'd all regret – put in, 'It couldn't hurt to stay.' Then she turned back to her task of twisting the curtain sash cords off their brass fixers.

'I do hope you never have cause to remember saying that,

Olive,' Ida replied and the legs of her chair scraped the floorboards as she stood to leave the room.

'What did that look like to you?' Evelyn asked, going to fetch herself another glass of sherry. 'Capitulation?'

'More like resignation.'

'Lord! I do make things difficult, and they're not meant to be.'

Olive didn't say anything to that. Evelyn's belief that things were meant to be easy was a measure of the distance between their worlds. In any case, Evelyn seemed to enjoy making things difficult, because it was in difficulty that the strong feelings of others might be encouraged.

'That job you were talking about – ' Olive started to say, but Ida popped her head round the door to tell the girls she'd arranged for a fourth hand at bridge Friday night. Would they be free?

'As birds,' Evelyn said, leaning in to hide the decanter from her aunt's view. Ida went back to the telephone to pass on the happy news.

'The job's real enough,' Evelyn said, 'if that's what you're wondering. But do you want to stay for it?'

Olive noticed that Evelyn did not look at her as she asked this, but peered at the arabesques of the dark wallpaper at the corner where their flowing converged, in a knot, beneath the ceiling. She was used to Evelyn being direct, and took this as a sign that the answer to the question was important to her. Smiling, she hooked one errant curl behind her ear, and replied, 'Why not?'

Chapter Four

Jetty

Five out of seven mornings in the following weeks they got up early for the drive through the still dark Islington and Hackney streets and out into the country to Romford. At Stapleford, Olive would see Evelyn on and off throughout the day – she liked to have her cup of tea in the annex, where there was a chance of getting warm in one go, rather than that uneven roasting and freezing that seemed to go on in the training cockpit of the Magister.

As Ida had feared, she found the work at the aerodrome dull. But having a measure of independence made up for the drudgery of the work. More importantly, she now had a reason for being in England that wasn't about Evelyn.

She'd not long been at Stapleford when the Control Tower was fitted for wireless. The first she heard of this was when Evelyn came rushing in from the field with one of her favourite Civil Air Guard cadets, a creamy-skinned girl named Marjorie whose double-barrelled last name she was always forgetting. Marjorie spoke a form of public school English Olive had never heard before. A simple yes came out 'yah', and what Marjorie would do with a word like 'opera' or 'bangalore' could only be guessed at. Marjorie was the most popular girl in her group, and hers was the name most often on Evelyn's lips.

'Some berk doesn't want to be diverted,' Evelyn said as she passed through the annex for the internal stairs to the tower.

They could hear the plane approaching the aerodrome, the sound of its engines bouncing around in the low ceiling of cloud. The ground crew had come out from the hangars to see what was going on and Olive stood in the annex door for a moment but the wind was favouring their shelter, not her own, so she went in search of an alternate vantage point.

Normally, the air control tower was off-limits, but the aerodrome administrator nodded agreeably to her.

'Watch,' he said, winking. 'Way of the future, this is. All they have to do is follow the beam in, and bob's your uncle.'

She hadn't a clue what beam he was talking about, and there was nothing to watch.

He saw her bafflement. 'Range signals set up between four beacons.' With his palms perpendicular, he put one hand over the other in a cross. 'The A and N beams converge but each has a different sound. If a pilot comes in at the right bearing and with a straight and level attitude they can hear they're on a true course. So long as they don't go banging into anything, they can follow those beams in nicely.'

Apparently this pilot did not think so, for a man's voice came over the loudspeaker. 'Canopy's too tight, shan't make it today. Sorry for the bother.'

The controller leaned into the microphone and replied as politely, 'Cloud cover is 800 feet at North Weald.' Then the sound of the visitor's engines eased, and disappeared.

The aerodrome administrator was keen to clear the tower. Thinking the whole thing a fizzer anyway, Olive made to leave but paused when Evelyn and Marjorie didn't follow. They were bent over the wireless unit, examining its workings, and she saw Evelyn settle her hand on the younger woman's back, and idly stroke it. Olive caught the words *signal strength*, and *frequency*, and then they were laughing at nothing in particular. She turned and went quickly to the door.

The short winter days lengthened, and when spring came visiting pilots joined the mechanics in impromptu shooting parties, coming back to the aerodrome from the adjoining fields with burlap bags full of the coiled corpses of hares to distribute to the staff. Even then, the landowner neighbours were tolerant of the foibles of 'their' flyers, and, as possibility turned to probability then certainty of war, other sights became more familiar at the field: housewives with bottled preserves or invitations to passing civilian pilots to 'overnight', and girls with brightly coloured headscarves come to welcome pilots to land.

Olive's stint at Stapleford came to an end serendipitously. She had the offer of work at the West Hampstead library, and took it. She'd begun to feel isolated at the aerodrome, particularly since Evelyn had starting spending her lunchtimes with Marjorie.

On being told of the new job, Evelyn was annoyed for a few days, sorry that she'd have to commute to the aerodrome alone. But Ida was immensely pleased – librarianship was the right occupation for a bright girl like Olive, and when her niece's friend ended a week of accessioning, cataloguing and shelving convinced that there was little difference between one type of drudgery and another, Ida would hear nothing of it.

'Librarianship,' Ida announced, pushing her eyeglasses above the horn of bone at the bridge of her nose, 'is an improving profession. Stick to it.'

Olive's great boon was the books. Nobody at the library seemed to mind if she was gone for an hour at a time, browsing instead of shelving, and she could borrow what she liked. Soon Evelyn's room had to accommodate stacks of Olive's books as well as her clothes, but her domination of the space merely pointed up the fact that Evelyn herself was never in it: certainly not that summer, when she began stopping out with Marjorie's family, or Marjorie's friend, or Marjorie's cousin just down from Oxford. These absences always had something to do with Marjorie and the little universe of the rich into which she'd been inducted.

One Sunday, Ida rose early and went to fetch the girls only to find her niece's room empty. They were to have walked to church together, enjoying the morning, and now – Ida told Olive as she leaned against her doorjamb like a slowly leaking sandbag – how were they to do that? A telephone call was the least one could expect. But there hadn't been a call, had there?

Olive stood, clutching her robe and not knowing what to say.

Her room was still in its state of nether-worldly darkness – the drapes drawn. The unlined yellowy-gold of the curtain material glowed, lighting the room as if for the first act of a comic opera.

Ida looked set to stay in her doorway, and unless she were shifted Olive couldn't go to the bathroom. So she went to draw the blinds and said, with more conviction than she felt, 'Perhaps the road was fogged in. Or she was on a training flight and had to divert to another aerodrome.'

'Even so, I'd expect to hear from her. You don't think something's happened?'

Olive couldn't imagine anything bad happening to Evelyn. She wasn't the kind of person to whom bad things happened and was the most competent woman she knew. If Evelyn wasn't home it was because she'd meant not to be, but she could hardly say that to her aunt.

The idea of Evelyn delayed by fog finally got Ida out of the doorway, and Olive chivvied her down to the kitchen for a cup of tea. By the time she joined her Ida was peeling the apples for the pie to follow the Sunday roast and had reconciled herself to her niece's absence.

But Evelyn didn't stay gone. She came bustling in with an armload of freshly cut flowers, and with her hair out. She was in fierce health. Although the circumstances of her morning didn't seem to have been conducive to the application of make-up, Evelyn's lips were as red as Olive had ever seen them.

Evelyn lightly kissed her and said, to Ida, 'Do say there's time for breakfast – I'm famished.'

Ida put more elbow than was necessary into dicing the apples into eighths. Evelyn raised an eyebrow at Olive, who frowned at her so deeply that her jaw hurt.

Evelyn said, 'Well, if you're ready to go – '

Ida slapped the hand reaching for the single whole apple still on the draining board. 'Where have you been?'

'Marjorie's parents put me up. We flew to Sussex, and dined with them. I meant to call but couldn't find a moment.' Evelyn had lost some of the rosiness in her cheeks and Olive thought for a second how unlikely it was that she was still living with her aunt in a place like Hampstead. She always had to explain herself; to make appearances. It wasn't a situation she'd fallen naturally into, as Olive herself had. Evelyn was more comfortable the further she was from a domestic situation. She belonged in transit, and was happiest in the company of taxi-drivers, station masters, bus conductors, building contractors, pilots (of course), or telegraph and telephone operators – anybody whose business it was to administer the movement of things or persons from one place to the next, or whose career it was to orchestrate a change from one state of being to another. This principle extended to doctors, but stopped short at clerics. Evelyn hated talking to vicars, and Olive wondered that morning whether she'd chosen to stay out Saturday in the hope she'd miss Sunday service.

'Next time make more of an effort. I was worried about you. I won't say more about it because – ' Ida turned to arch her suggestion of an eyebrow at Evelyn, ' – we have already discussed the matter of your selfishness.'

At that, she gave Evelyn the apple, took off her apron, and went to the hall mirror to set her hat properly. Evelyn stood behind her making helpful suggestions, her long face looming in the glass above her aunt's. They made a comical pair, one so short and wide, and the other tall and lean, one dressed in a sober blue woollen suit and the other in culottes the colour of cherry blossom; a neat oriental silk jacket hanging open over her plain white shirt. The embroidered edges of the jacket bumped gently up against the hall sideboard as Evelyn leaned in to the mirror, lipstick in hand.

'Go on,' she said to her aunt. 'Let's see how this suits you.' Holding the older woman's chin – bristled with the occasional sprouting hair that Ida had missed – Evelyn put her own colour to her aunt's lips.

Olive watched them for a moment. She was happy at their reconciliation, but felt oddly excluded. Neither Evelyn nor Ida looked away from their reflections when she passed them on her way to search between the piles of books in her room for her one good handbag.

Throughout that summer Olive saw little of Evelyn. She'd spend her weekends at the London flat or country house of one or another of the friends to whom Olive had never been introduced. Home was what Evelyn came back to when she'd had a row with – or about – Marjorie, and then she would be too bright, or moody, or spend all her time stretched out on the couch in the lounge, cushions plumped around her head, reading a book. On other occasions Evelyn would throw herself into some cleaning project. Once she polished all the metal in the house, including the brass trim on the fold-out bridge table. When she was in one of these moods, Olive left her to herself, but would sometimes stand at a doorway for minutes at a time, unobserved, watching her read, or polishing silver, or – sometimes – sleeping with one sinewy arm laid over her face.

Some nights when Evelyn was home she'd lie on Olive's bed and tell her one story after another – her polished anecdotes, the sort she saved for dinner parties, or long train journeys with friends. At odd occasions Evelyn would tell the same story twice, and though Olive might get up off the bed and go to stand, frowning, by the window, she'd seldom protest the repetition. She was glad to have her there.

When their conversations turned to more serious matters they tended to suffocate. By not going back to Australia the pair had disappointed Evelyn's parents. So when talk veered towards home, and Olive's plans in staying, they would hit an impasse, and Evelyn would fiddle with the edge of the bedspread or stare into her empty cup of cocoa, perplexed.

It was during one of these silences that Evelyn suggested a trip to Plymouth. She'd drive, and Olive could visit the Battersbys. Evelyn made the suggestion carelessly, and when Olive agreed to it, she looked sorry she'd come up with the idea in the first place.

Chapter Five

A Turn at the Tivoli

Evelyn drove the Morris coupé with her characteristic dash, and had to be convinced to stop at Athelhampton, near where Thomas Hardy was born. She could not see the point of their staying at a bed and breakfast there, rather than another twenty miles farther on, but eventually Olive prevailed. Showing she was not completely without a sense for the importance of literature, Evelyn went to sleep with a copy of *Tess of the D'Urbervilles* under her waterglass, while Olive sat up reading. Every so often she'd have to tell Evelyn to turn onto her side – whenever the first whiffling breath announced the intention of a snore.

When at her breakfast the next morning she suggested they take in Hardy's house, Evelyn was dismissive.

'What's so important about a pile of old stones once lived in by a genius? The stones won't be any different for it, will they?'

But when Olive slumped in the passenger seat, signalling a sulk, she got her way. They diverted to Cerne Abbas to see the Giant scoured into the chalk there – Evelyn chattering away as she followed her up the hillside. She was saying that it was alright, really, that they'd come, since a good many of the cairns and mounds and stones of antiquity were quite unknown until some aviator made something of them from the air.

That was too much. 'Oh for pity's sake – ' Olive exclaimed, 'let's just have a bit of quiet scenery!' Evelyn did pipe down then, and she was able to get some sense of the giant, its pebbly contours. One leg stretched out to their left, and another to their right. When Olive realised where they were standing, she let out a laugh.

'We're on its privates.'

But this only prompted Evelyn to a new, and much more dangerous, topic of conversation.

They had started clumsily down beside the right leg of the Giant, Evelyn taking smaller than usual steps beside her. Their progress slowed, and then Evelyn stopped altogether and asked, 'Have you taken any lovers?'

She tightened her lips, and didn't answer. Evelyn added, 'But I am perhaps the one person you *wouldn't* tell if you had.'

Olive slipped then. Evelyn reached an arm out to steady her and she looked along it, up to the face Evelyn had opened, and set, for her. Evelyn's dimple had deepened, and her grey eyes were very bright.

'I don't ask about your affairs,' she said, and despite having spoken shortly, she took Evelyn's hand and linked her fingers with her friend's. When Evelyn looked down at the hand holding hers Olive saw the pale lunette of ear upon which the edge of her hat rested; the delicacy of the ridge of skin.

'No you don't, more is the pity.'

The rest of their descent was made in silence, the ground being uneven and the incline steep.

Back at the car they sat at either extreme of the platform seat – Olive with one leg out the open car door – and shared tea from Evelyn's thermos. It was a relief when Evelyn started the car and they set out for Plymouth. There was a thing or two still to be seen on the chalk hills of Dorset, and she kept her face turned to the window. After a while, Evelyn broke the silence to announce they'd make Plymouth for tea. Being used to flying distances, she tended to optimism about ground ETAs, and it was no surprise to Olive that they arrived at the Battersbys in the dark, when all chance of sharing dinner with their hosts had passed.

Anne was standing on the steps of her father's stone terrace as they pulled up. She was in a heavy coat, scarf and hat, and only her big, pretty face was showing. Then William came out, and bounded down the steps in one go, dodging his sister, to open Evelyn's door for her. With Evelyn's bag under one arm, and Olive's under the other, he stood on the pavement looking awkward, the collar of his generously starched shirt cutting into his neck just beneath his Adam's apple. Olive thought that the only perfectly relaxed person among them was Evelyn – she stood examining the early Victorian ironwork of exterior lamps and fence rails, her hair lifting in the cold wind from the sea.

Evelyn raised an eyebrow at her, as if to say, *I'm along for the ride, you do the honours*. With breathless dispatch, Olive reminded them how they'd met at the dock months before and, the reintroduction over, they trooped inside.

Battersby Senior was away in London for the weekend, chasing contracts. He'd gone into the manufacture of nautical instruments and the drawing room shelves were filled with brass and steel mechanisms. Evelyn perused these, her cooling cup of tea forgotten, while the others sat in their unforgiving Regency chairs, talking.

Olive was delighted to hear that Anne was training as a nurse – delighted, that is, until she started going into details.

'Blood I can stand, and wounds, but I've fainted twice since starting ward work: once when I assisted in a minor surgical procedure for varicose veins. Did you know that when they pull them out they're black and they *writhe*, just like snakes do?'

Olive pictured this, and was sorry she'd done so.

'And I passed out when I had to change the dressing on the foot of an elderly man with septicemia. The smell was awful,' she said, wrinkling her nose. 'Before you know it, I was out cold on the floor, with the old gent yelling for help. I came to facing the matron's shoes. I was mortified, and had to make out it wouldn't happen again.'

'You should try the smell below decks at the end of a watch rotation during a gale if you think that's bad.' William had joined the merchant service, and was on leave. When Olive asked why he'd not joined the navy Anne glanced at her brother and then into her teacup.

'There's a dance on at the Tivoli tonight, if you're up to it,' she said.

Evelyn put down the compass she'd been handling. 'Let's,' she said, looking more or less in Olive's direction. 'We've been sitting in a car all day and could do with a dance.'

William, who had that day made more effort dressing than anyone else in the room, looked down at his serge, touched his shirt-front nervously, and mumbled, 'I'd best go change.'

'He wanted to join the navy,' Anne said, when he was out of the room. 'But our father was against it. When war comes the Government will make the merchant service a reserved occupation and William will be stuck. There'll be rows then, I bet.' She started gathering up the tea things. 'Not that I'll have to witness them. I'll be in a nice quiet hall of residence.' Seeing Olive's commiserating look she laughed and said, 'It's not too bad – only four to a room.'

Evelyn had finished examining the brassware around the shelves and now put in her bob's worth. 'Olive never went to a boarding school. She's not had to learn to put up with people the way we have.'

Hearing this 'we' Olive felt a savage satisfaction at the fate of the Romanovs in their basement, and the red hats at Etaples. 'Oh, go put a dress on,' she snapped.

Evelyn looked down at her trouser suit. 'I can't go like this, then?' For Anne's benefit, she added, 'Olive would be ashamed to be seen with me.'

Olive did not contradict her friend, although she was not

ashamed to be seen with her, and liked the way she looked. Evelyn wore everything with confidence and grace, and she had an infallible sense for how to stand, or sit, in such a way that people got pleasure from looking at her. But right at that moment she didn't want to look at Evelyn, and most certainly didn't want to enjoy doing so. It was infinitely more satisfying to send her away – even if 'away' was just upstairs for a few minutes.

Before she left the room Evelyn looked back at her, one hand on the doorframe, and smiled that rueful, winning smile of hers.

'Your friend's a bit of a character,' said Anne, carefully.

'She'd like you to think so, anyway.'

Anne was kind enough to say nothing to this.

The dance hall was packed with couples of all ages, and the stage was barely large enough to accommodate all the members of the band. There were tables ringing the room, and William claimed one of these by putting four bottles of stout down, one in front of each empty chair. But the four of them barely had time to drink, and no breath to waste on talk, between dances. Olive did the foxtrot with William, then he asked Evelyn to dance and those two did a circuit before Olive was able to reclaim him, at which point both Anne and Evelyn disappeared into the crowd.

By the time they'd gathered again as a party, Anne had made herself a friend – a young man with ears pink from the exertions of dancing, while Evelyn brought to the table a man at least twenty years her senior. He had gold cufflinks on, and a fob watch – the chain of which must have been a hindrance when dancing. Before seating himself, he carefully fitted his camel-hair coat over the back of the chair he'd pulled into their circle.

'This is Bob,' Evelyn said. 'Bob's in trade.'

Bob nodded coolly, and lit the cigarette he'd just that minute offered Evelyn.

'Trading what?' Olive yelled.

'Whatever makes a bob.'

'Thus the name,' Evelyn added. 'Bob's a handy man to know.'

'In times like these,' said the man himself, nodding.

'How's that?'

'I've got an eye on the docks. Millbay. Sutton. Southampton. Interesting places, those, in times like this.'

William put his mouth close to Olive's ear, so close that she felt his moustache brush against her cheekbone, and said, 'In times like these, my foot. I hope someone does him for receiving.' He downed his drink and stood, waiting for her to do the same. 'If you'll excuse us, that's our shot at the Lindy hop.'

Olive hoped he was joking, and was relieved when they buried themselves amid the other dancers to do a more gentle turn: cant, rather than swing. She didn't have to concentrate on her feet, and William had a good sense for where they were going, threading the space between other couples. Soon they had danced their way through the crowd to its edge, and come hard up against a potted palm. If ever there was a time, and a place, for a man to kiss his dance partner, it seemed to Olive that was it, but they stood there like lumps.

After a minute William asked his partner if she'd like some

punch and although Olive knew that the to-do of fetching the drink would help the moment pass, she shook her head.

'Sit down then?'

The benches around the wall were full, as were the chairs at the tables. Another gaggle of young people had taken their table, and a new circle of glasses sat about their own. Olive could just see the top of Evelyn's head as she was swept through the crowd of dancers by that crook Bob. Anne and her beau were nowhere to be seen.

'I think I'd like some air.'

The couple stood at the entrance, the light rain blowing in every so often to dust their shoes with water. A few latecomers passed them on the way in, but otherwise they had the space to themselves, the marquee lights humming soothingly overhead.

Olive felt muddled – with alcohol, and something else. Perhaps the stress of her first attempts to dance the modern style – all that pushing and pulling and flinging to and fro – had made her light-headed, unsure of her balance. She leaned against William.

'Would you like me to kiss you?' he asked, so quickly Olive almost missed the critical word. She thought of the stoker smoking his cigarette on the voyage out – the way he'd looked at her – and nodded her assent.

They kissed, hurriedly at first, then – seeming to satisfy themselves that it could be done – in earnest. Olive was self-conscious, wondering whether she should open her eyes slightly, or not at all; whether she might open her mouth to let his tongue in rather than have it keep bumping at her teeth. When she looked out through her eyelashes and saw that William's eyes were firmly closed, she let him have a proper go at kissing her. The hair at the nape of his neck was prickly under her palm. When her fingertips grazed his earlobe his whole body seemed to quake.

That put a stop to things.

William stepped back from Olive, and wiped a hand over his face. But she was not to be put off – feeling close to something that could set her to rights. So she followed William and put her face up to his, catching the scent of his aftershave, and of Evelyn's perfume – she'd dabbed this at neck and wrist before leaving for the dance. This time she kissed him, and did not confine her hands to his neck, but stroked the bunched muscles in his shoulder blades, following the line of his body down to where his shirt tucked into his trousers. Her palms came to rest on the edge of his leather belt.

William took her hands and held them firmly together in his own, at the same time pushing her away from him. He was very red in the face.

'I'm sorry, I didn't mean – '

'It's not you,' he said, letting go of Olive. 'We must get a grip on ourselves.' He took out a cigarette and lit it, smiling roguishly around the butt – very sailor-like. 'Don't misunderstand me, it's because I like you that I don't want to be that way.' Smoke curled from his nostrils, and he blinked at it, his irises expanding so that the distinction between brown and black momentarily disappeared. 'It cheapens things.'

'Oh,' said Olive, feeling cheapened only as he said it.

The couple stood for a while looking out into the rain, and then Olive suggested they move back inside. As she went to go, he took her hand and held it, and then kissed her on the top of the head.

'Please don't think badly of me,' he said, as if his were the only appetites that needed explanation.

It was much hotter inside than it had been when they'd left, and the floor was packed. There was no chance of a seat, so they stood at the edge of the dance floor. Olive waved at Anne as she and her partner passed, doing a foxtrot, and in reply Anne flapped the hand she'd been drumming on his back.

William motioned at the floor, 'Do you fancy it?' and when Olive shook her head he went back to watching the dancers rather too intently. The next time Anne appeared, William excused himself and went to cut in on his sister. Her partner linked up with another girl, and off they whirled.

The dance floor was spilling out towards the tables, and Olive had backed up as far as she could go, but still the dancers brushed by her, the men giving her their assessing looks. Then it was Evelyn and Bob swinging their way through the crowd. Seeing Olive, Evelyn stopped. She said something to Bob and he went off towards the bar.

'No room here.' Evelyn had to put her face close to her friend's to be heard. 'Let's dance,' she said, and pulled Olive onto the floor. They passed a few other girls in pairs, some too young for boyfriends, others chary of a male partner's intentions. Evelyn settled into the lead without a misstep – one hand linked with

Olive's, pushing down on her wrist to guide her, and the other holding her lightly at the small of her back.

'You're good at this,' Olive said, more breathless now.

Evelyn looked down at her and quickly away. 'Dancing's dancing,' she said. Then, laying her cheek against Olive's so that the lobes of their ears touched, Evelyn added, 'If that's what you were referring to.'

Evelyn swept her partner past a young couple doing a vigorous swing step, then she pulled her close again, until Olive could smell the Pears soap and chamomile with which Evelyn had washed her hair.

'You've kept yourself scarce the last hour.'

'I was getting some air. With William.'

Evelyn looked at her friend from her crooked arm's length, a frank assessment that said she had no need to ask what they'd been doing.

'I suppose it's about time,' she said, steering her partner back to the dancing's edge. They broke to face the floor, and hadn't been there long enough for Olive to form a rejoinder when Bob sniffed them out. He had fresh drinks for two in his fat pink fists and a fine sheen of sweat stood on his skin – the hair at his forehead had stuck to it.

Olive heard him say to Evelyn, 'Thought you'd flown, my duck.' After giving her one of the drinks he put the freed arm about her waist.

'I'm off to find William,' Olive said too loudly, and pushed her way back into the crowd.

The rest of the night Olive spent dancing with William, and they left the Tivoli as the band packed up its instruments. Evelyn did not disappear, as Olive had expected her to, but came out of the milling crowd after the last dance, rosy-cheeked and alone. The four of them walked back through the rain, jostling for umbrella space on the narrow footpath.

The next few days Evelyn made herself scarce – she had discovered that Bob had a yacht, and spent much of her time on the water. Perhaps, like Anne, she wanted to leave William and Olive to it. The four of them did picnic together on the Sunday, Olive lying in the sun with her head on Evelyn's lap to watch Anne decisively beat her brother at chess. But Evelyn seemed – that day, and for many days thereafter – remote.

When the two friends left Plymouth, William stowed their luggage in the car, and checked under the bonnet, not willing to trust them to chance. Then he wiped his fingers clean of oil before taking a tissue wrapped package from his breast pocket. This he shyly handed to Olive.

She looked up at him – at his warm brown eyes, and too narrow lips beneath the neatly trimmed moustache. Inside the tissue paper was a silver locket on a chain, and inside the locket were the tiny, dried flowers of the Sweet William plant. Pleased, but nevertheless troubled, she let William drape the chain about her neck, and cinch it.

Some miles down the road, while Evelyn was looking steadfastly through the rain-dappled windscreen, Olive folded the collar of her shirt over the chain and nub of the locket.

Chapter Six

First casualties

Olive was not to have such a generous amount of time with William for another two years, although she regularly sent him letters. Her clearest feeling about their relationship was a concern about how to behave when next they'd meet.

When war was declared there was a moment when Evelyn decided it might be best to go back to Australia after all. She'd come home after being gone for days; encouraged Ida into some household project to pass the time until Olive finished work, and then dropped everything to follow her friend upstairs, draping herself diagonally over Olive's bed.

'If we were to board by the end of the week, we could be home in time to help put down the fertilizer.'

Olive saw that her eyes were puffy, the mascara fat on her lashes. She got Evelyn to make enough room on the bed for her to sit.

'Are you homesick?'

'Lord no,' Evelyn said, squinting up at Olive. 'I don't need a case of the flim-flams to see the sense in getting out – ' she waved a hand at the window, ' – of all this.'

'Of course we should get out, but that's not the point. What's brought this on?'

Evelyn sat up, pulling her knees to her chin and hugging them. 'It's just so bloody unfair given the hours I've put in. Along comes this fellow from the Civil Aviation Authority and says that's the end of inessential flying, and inessential flyers. Just like that. Of course inessential flyer means any woman who happens to be doing it.' She pulled her scarf off and twisted it between her fists as if it was the throat of the man from Civil Aviation. 'Marjorie's already given it the shove. She's gone back to her daddy's estate in Sussex to think about how she might make herself *useful*. She'll probably do her bit for the war effort by joining secretarial pool. Christ!'

Olive kept her mouth shut, but put a hand on Evelyn's knee, and patted it gently.

'What about it, Olive. Shall we go home?'

Olive was shocked when a tear slid down Evelyn's face and banked just above her dimple. Evelyn quickly rubbed it away.

'But I can't ask you to. You've got William.'

'Don't cry,' Olive said, and put her arms around her. 'You'll be alright.'

'I won't – ' Evelyn said, her lips moving against Olive's shoulder, ' – not if I'm by myself.'

'You aren't by yourself. You've never been.' She held Evelyn's face and kissed her forehead, resting her lips on a dark eyebrow. She could feel the muscles in Evelyn's scalp working as her jaw clenched, and relaxed. Although she was moved by Evelyn's misery, a small, mean voice now spoke up within her. *Now* – it said – *you know what it feels like to be abandoned.*

Evelyn never cried for long, and in a minute she was dabbing at her eyes with the handkerchief Olive had proffered.

'I'm not going to tell Ida that I've finished with training the Air Cadets. And I'd thank you not to mention it either,' she said.

'I won't. Anyway, there's nothing to tell. If we stay you'll find a way back up into the air. If we go, you'll just knock around the farm feeling useless and we'll never hear the end of it,' Olive said, pretending that was what the fuss had been about.

'Thanks,' her friend said, smiling. 'You're a brick.'

Olive thought that Evelyn without Marjorie could only be an improvement. Perhaps she'd stop talking like a Chalet School girl. More importantly, she'd see more of her – the star of Evelyn's former attentions having finally set.

Oddly enough, she enjoyed those otherwise awful first months of the war. Civil preparations had reached a confusing pitch with the evacuations – the buses and trains were a shambles, and children were everywhere. They were nightly plunged into the darkness of blackout, and a man down the road knocked himself unconscious by walking into a lamppost. It was a very strange time, but people seemed to know what was expected of them, and if they did not there was always someone to correct their ignorance or error – personally, or by announcement. It was a world of new measures.

At home, the radio was constantly on, and Ida began collecting a 'War Economy' file: a repository for official pamphlets, council booklets and notes she'd written on the responsible running of the household. At the library, too, things changed. The cataloguer at West Hampstead brought a radio in and it sat, its dial glowing, on the bench above the volumes of the *Encyclopaedia Britannica*, the spines of which Olive had been reinforcing. She was up to GEL-HOM when Morris, the middle-aged ex-accountant who'd recently taken the job as head librarian, announced he was off to join the RAF. Olive kissed his cheek and congratulated him in the first – for her – of many such scenes.

Evelyn's urge to return home waned after a quiet week in, a few evenings of which she met Olive after work for a stroll over the Heath. But like all such periods of quiet for Evelyn, this one quickly passed. Before long she was towing targets for the Army Air Corps.

Evelyn's war started in that businesslike way.

Olive's did not. It did not start with Chamberlain's sombre broadcast of September 3rd, nor with their being plunged into sudden darkness. She was oddly ignorant about politics, and listened to the radio news with a thin idea of context and almost no sense of proportion. Consequently, she let herself be led by other listeners. If Evelyn kept her eyes closed during an item Olive would ignore it, but if her eyes popped open, or Ida shushed them when they weren't making any noise, she would put down her book and listen.

All September, she got about in a daze. Some things were out of kilter (like the blackout) while other things went on as they'd always done, or more noisily than before. The restaurants and dance halls and cinemas were packed, the shelves of the shops still full. War wasn't made by declaration – not if the shops of Oxford, Bond and Regent streets were anything to go by.

Olive's war started one day in October when the library was closed. She might have stayed home to read but Ida was making an inventory. Ida's war preparedness campaign called for everything to be taken out of the kitchen cupboards and pantry and off the cellar shelves, then put back in its proper place – a place made proper by being recorded in a notebook. Olive did not want to get mixed up in that, so she took the northern line to Camden Town and walked to the Zoo.

She'd planned to buy a bag of peanuts for the monkeys, but on a whim bought aniseed balls for herself. Just one of these small, hard sweets could be sucked for a half-hour, and it struck Olive as the perfect choice for the abstemious wartime palate. She got a bob's worth, which was more than a person could eat in a week, considering a day's worth would make her tongue cat-rough; too sore to allow her to enjoy dinner. So she doled out sweets to the animals as she strolled past the enclosures. The wild dogs pushed at the balls with their tan muzzles, sniffing loudly and looking at Olive with wide, startled eyes. The lioness rolled on the aniseed, swishing her tail like a house cat excited by the wind. The monkeys followed the flight of the sweet with jaundiced eyes, and would not bestir themselves. And then there was the beaver. Olive thought it would take no notice, but it rooted around in the spot where the aniseed ball had landed and lifted its head. Then came a terrific cracking sound from between its busy jaws. Olive hurried away from the beaver's enclosure, shamefaced, but the sound of crunching followed her all the way to the bears. She went on without seeing A. A. Milne's inspiration and walked as briskly as she could to the first covered enclosure she could find.

It was dark in the reptile house but the thick, green glass of the terrariums glowed dully. She pressed her face to the cold glass of the first case and scrutinised the mass of leaves and branches and papier-mâché rocks. A spider was visible, but nothing else. The next space was as cluttered, and as empty. After reading the signs describing terrapins as terracotta-hued and hard to see she looked as carefully as she could for the snake in question, without result. Then it was a quicker look into the next glass window, and the one after that, all onto emptiness, or at the home of animals so exquisitely camouflaged there could be no point in having them on display.

At the other end of the reptile house Olive stood blinking in the sunlight to get her bearings.

'Awful shock isn't it?'

The young man who'd spoken was sitting on a bench nearby. He was pasty-faced and had red-rimmed eyes – was, all in all, the negative image of Olive's stoker. Like her, he was blinking. Olive thought he'd been referring to the sunlight but when he put his head down into his hands and his shoulders hitched she saw that wasn't what he'd meant at all.

'Where did they go?' she asked, thinking of the trains full of evacuated children.

He kicked the rubbish bin by his feet and it rang dully. Then, before Olive had a chance to stop him he had the lid of the bin off, and had tipped the round mouth of it towards her. He did not need to look himself – having laid them in there, coil after sticky coil, he knew which lay on top of which.

'Gassed them, we did, while they was dozing' the keeper said. 'I'd be laughing if it weren't so horrible.'

Olive had a thought then that made her want to run out of the zoo. She had an urge to find the first open space she could and lie down with her face in the dirt.

They had started with the low animals (the ones – in Renaissance paintings of the Last Judgement – harrying the souls of the damned) but they would carry on with their quiet gassing until every hutch and aviary and cage was empty.

It was with this apprehension that Olive's war started.

Chapter Seven

What Evelyn was like

The library stayed open through a winter so bad that any warm public space was seen as a boon to public morale. Olive accession-stamped, issued borrower cards, shelved books and catalogued 5x3 index cards on quiet afternoons with the radiator hissing beside her.

Her memories of the war's start would be almost obliterated by the much heavier stamp of the years immediately following – routines that cast all other routines into relief. Those first few months were like time at the dock before a long sea voyage: the ship is still berthed and one can sense the thing's size; its capability; but there's no rolling, or yawing, and the deck doesn't vibrate under one's feet. Just like that, they were waiting to be getting on: the biddies in the West Hampstead Branch Library, the farmers, the clerks and shopgirls, the women – like Ida – at home, the poor bloody infantry milling to war, the aircrew in their Whitleys tossing uncut piles of leaflets out over Germany in the hope they'd hit some Boche on the head. The lot of them, baled up by the bore war.

It was a relief, then, when mail arrived from Orange – from the war at home, so different from their own. Evelyn's brother, Duncan, was still hard at work at the Veterinary College of Sydney University, but was obsessed with the prospect of war, and his place in it:

Nobody can seriously expect me to sit tight here while there's a war on. How is my encyclopedic knowledge of the reproductive disorders of pigs of any use right now? I can't pretend that my place in the university regiment is anything to be going on with either. We drill like drongos, and the uniform would embarrass a bullet. Between the regiment and study I'm stranded. No cavalry, no horses, no point for a training in veterinary science in wartime, even dad gives me that much when we talk about it. Of course, he doesn't want me to go, and neither does mum. But if we don't choose, someone will choose for us so I'm going to sign up for the Empire Air Training Scheme. 'Hurry up' says the poster and I'm taking it at its word. I shall be a pilot before you know it.

From there he moved to domestic matters, including a detailed account of how each of the farm dogs was doing, and a description of the house cat's abscessed tail.

But the next letters saw Duncan still at university, and his parents wrote of their relief: so many men had volunteered inductions would take a year. The youngest Macintyre had been given a satchel full of reading and a lapel badge to show that he was aircrew reserve. He'd been told that a course in mathematics might do him a world of good. Other than that, he was to cool his heels until his intake course number came up. At no time did anyone mention the fact he might not make pilot. Everyone then thought (Duncan included) that a boy from a good family, who could sit a horse as well he could, would be a dead certainty for pilot training. It was just a matter of time, and Duncan spent this at his study, and – during the break – helping around the farm.

So Evelyn and Olive were able to get on with their war without the worrying sense that he was in it.

What made Olive volunteer for the Women's Auxiliary Air Force was not the sense that she was missing out, nor the need to keep up, but the effect of her watching Evelyn evolve into a creature of duty. Even before the Nazis squeezed the British Expeditionary Force out of Northern France, Evelyn was gearing up for her own maximum effort.

While the air-time Evelyn put in for the Army Air Corps was modest, she had to fly in all weather – and heavy rain or fog made those doses of air-time hard to take, even at ten pound pay. And the chance that a trainee gunner would shoot wide made Ida witless with worry. It was a relief for all when Evelyn came home with her bags and the news that she'd found another way to fly, one that meant not getting shot at – not routinely, at any rate.

The three of them sat in the front room, Evelyn hugging one of Ida's over-stuffed cushions in lieu of the dog. Olive sat beside her with her feet folded up underneath, one bare sole just touching Evelyn's leg. Ida faced the two younger women on the couch, her game of gin rummy forgotten. Her hand had drooped so that Olive could see every card in it.

Evelyn explained that she'd been asked to join the women's section of the Air Transport Auxiliary, delivering training aircraft. The increase in air-time was considerable, and she'd be bound to get more variety than the old Puss Moth day in and day out. What pleased her particularly was that she'd been asked, invited, *recognised*, by female flyers she'd never met. The confraternity she was entering was more elite and less girlish than her entourage at Stapleford – the women a minority among a larger group of pilots.

'Americans too,' she said, as if these were a class mutually exclusive from men. 'I'll be based at Hatfield aerodrome, in Hertfordshire – so I won't be far away. Just up the London road. There are Nissen huts for us near the field, and we have our ration books to give over, if a hotel billet is in the offing. I'll not have to pay anything on fitting myself out – Nancy Goodhope's given me her Irvin jacket, trousers and leather flying boots. The lined ones,' she said, looking at Olive as if she'd understand the difference, and the attraction. For her aunt's sake she added, 'They're much more flattering than the skirt and jacket. And practical, given the cold. A good flying jacket is much better than three jumpers. And trousers are far more dignified than a woollen skirt that's prone to ride up, or blow about.'

'You'd have thought they'd make some provision for females, to distinguish them properly,' Ida said. She herself swore by a woollen skirt, and now smoothed its edge over her own square and dimpled knees.

'There is the Sidcot suit,' Evelyn said, staring into the empty centre of the rug as if she could see one planted there on legs kept erect by the solidity of its padding. 'No one wants to wear the thing. The poor girls who do have to go through doors sideways.'

The other girls weren't girls at all. Most of the volunteers were older women, well established on the ground and in the air. Most were independently wealthy. But it was the lower-middle-class Amy Johnson whom the war had brought to reign as Queen of the Air, after years skulking in the counties under the pseudonym Audrey James. That Evelyn had been asked to join the ATA only a month after Amy Johnson ratified her as an aviatrix – she'd been confirmed, borne up, and that night in the front room there was no denting her pride, no matter what niggling detail of uniform, housing or pay Ida brought to her attention.

This happened in June of 1940. The street signs had disappeared, France was falling and invasion fever had set in. A story appeared in the papers of a vicar in Wapping who went out into his garden to find his four-year-old daughter holding a bucket and staring up at the sky. The bucket, she'd told him, was for catching parachutists. Olive presumed they were to emulate this level of preparedness, in spirit if not in fact, but her preparations consisted of sandbagging the windows in the library and taking the books off the top four shelves of every stack to improve their stability in a blast. This only made the library staff's work harder and irritated what borrowers they had left. If a reader came in wanting the *Lives of the Saints* there it was, at the bottom of the first bay by the door – but Darwin, Homo Erectus and the whole of anthropology had vanished, 301s that had been on the top of the neighbouring stack.

It was late June when Ida suggested Olive take herself off to Hatfield too. Ida felt she had the sense that her niece lacked, and could be relied on to make an impartial report. Olive was given two days off from the library – enough time to get there and back, allowing for the state of the wartime train timetables.

She arrived at the Stonehouse Hotel just after eleven and, it being fully billeted, had to make do with the offer of a cot in Evelyn's room. While she sat in a comfy chair enjoying a pot of tea, the girl went to set up the room. Returning for Olive's tea things, she stood with the tray balanced on one forearm and a pile of folded sheets draped over the other. When Olive asked for the key the girl told her to wait until Miss Macintyre returned. Even her bags had been taken hostage in case she was faking an association with Evelyn.

Olive was puzzling over this when the girl said, 'I think they're smashing. Perfect ladies, they are, when they go out every morning. Then we hear the planes go over and I think it's *them* up there.' She hitched at the sheets and used one black shoe to scratch the instep of the other. 'You're sure you're not with the newspapers?' she asked, eyes narrowing.

It didn't seem to matter that Olive had said she was Evelyn's friend. Evelyn didn't sound like an Australian. Olive did. The housemaid couldn't find the social code to read her by.

'I'm not, honestly.' Olive said it as nicely as she could – it wasn't the housemaid's fault they had nowhere to put her.

'Right then.' The housemaid smiled, and all the thinness went out of her voice. 'Why don't you have a poke about the village. It's dead boring here until the guests come in. There's a nice place for a bun down the road – much better doings than here,' she said, leaning towards Olive conspiratorially. 'To tell you the truth I'm off out of here next week to join the WAAFs – they'll be the first trained to fly when they ease up on the rules, and volunteers will get first dibs. That's what Miss Macintyre says.'

The girl went about her business then and, returning her attention to the window, Olive saw a kestrel hovering above the field at the other side of the road. She watched it until it plunged out of sight behind a hedgerow.

Volunteering.

Olive's father had opinions about volunteering. First dibs in the last war meant an early death and a name too high on the honor roll to read. But things could be different now. Service would get her out of the library; out from under the weight of Ida's generosity, and away from all the reasons she'd come to England. It would be a way through the war; a kind of remedy for her rootlessness.

Outside, the kestrel had reappeared. It flew off at a diagonal until swallowed by the fringes of grey cloud that – some miles off – had resolved into a thicker train.

Rain.

If she was to get any walking done she'd better do it now.

There was no wind, which was why the rain hung in torn curtains on the horizon. Contrarily, Olive walked away from the old town, knowing that she'd have nowhere to run when the weather arrived – she'd been cooped up on a bus for several hours and fancied a proper walk. She didn't consciously aim for the aerodrome. She had no idea whether it was east or west of the village, since no aircraft had flown overhead in the time she'd been at the hotel.

Olive followed the track furrowed by bicycle tread, and veered naturally through what once had been the stile to a walker's right-of-way, and had since been cleared for bicyclists. She followed the hedgerows, and the fences, and passed the gate to a manor house obviously requisitioned: a young man in khakis sat astride a motorcycle on the other side of the gate and he waved at her, and she at him, before she went on down the path.

She knew she'd come to the aerodrome before either runway or hangars were visible – the smell of aviation fuel hung in the air, a smell familiar to her from Stapleford. Then it was just a matter of skirting the scraggly hedgerow with its breaks filled by barbed wire, and signs threatening trespassers with death. She found the sentry box at the gate and the guard on duty frowned at her, knitting his brows so that his cap brim sat low upon the corrugated bridge of his nose.

'This is a secure site, lass. Can't let thee in just on a say-so,' he said, although Olive had a difficult time of it catching the guard's meaning, so distracted was she by his accent and the dark star of the birthmark on one cheek. 'Every Tom, Dick and Harry would have his popsy here for lunch and then where would we be? Folk on this field have business being here.'

'I'm after Evelyn Macintyre,' Olive said. 'The *female* pilot.'

'Why'd tha not say so in the first place?' He stomped into his booth to ring the Station house.

A few minutes later (spent under the sentry's regard, and in silence) Olive saw Evelyn appear, walking across the grass field from a low set of buildings beside the control tower. She was wearing a neat blue uniform: skirt and jacket and a white shirt buttoned up to the neck, the collar rims pinning the knot of a tie the same blue as the rest of the uniform. She was dressed for the outdoors, but without – for once – one of her drooping scarves.

Ida would have been pleased to see her niece so respectably turned out, but it was not the respectability of the get-up that made an impression on Olive, it was the neatness of it; it's implication of an asceticism ordinarily foreign to its wearer. Olive was so taken aback by the uniformed Evelyn that she did not move to kiss her, and it was Evelyn who folded her arm through her friend's and walked her through the gate.

'I'll have her back in an hour, promise,' Evelyn told the sentry.

'You're lucky you caught me,' she said, squeezing Olive's arm and waving her free hand at the sky. 'No flying today.' Evelyn looked critically up at the leaden skies and her eyes lightened; pupils retracting as the reflection of the clouds covered her irises. 'Not that I mind. I get a day with you.'

She took her guest along the track beside the ring road. Bicyclists bumped along past them, but otherwise the perimeter was their own. Except, that is, for the rabbits. Each time she saw one of these, Evelyn would mime the taking of a pot shot.

'Take that you little bugger,' she'd say.

The week before a young RAF type had made a neat landing only to have the weight of his wheels cave in the pitted core of the field. The Gladiator had flipped and killed him.

'Done in by rabbits,' Evelyn said, shaking her head. 'Not what I'd like to have the wing commander write to my family.'

They skirted the hangars on their way to the canteen. Evelyn had promised Olive the bun she'd missed, and a cup of tea. She was the only person in the hall without a uniform although there were so many variations of these that she didn't stick out too badly in the dark blue dress, and solid coat, she'd that morning picked to wear. After getting their well-steeped tea from the urn, and sticky buns from a Leading Aircraftwoman they sat at the only empty table.

'You've got an admirer at the hotel,' Olive said. 'The girl who does the rooms.'

'You mean Helen Sewell of Sandridge. Don't be mean about her.'

It had not occurred to Olive to be mean, not until Evelyn mentioned the possibility.

'You've been telling her stories and now she's all shine and fervour for the WAAFs. She'd more likely end up doing that – ' Olive nodded in the direction of the girl picking up cups, ' – than she would flying planes.'

'I never said anything about flying. Once they pass the manpower bills, there'll be so many people to deal with they'll just slot them in wherever. It's better to do it now, while you've got some say about where you might like to go, and while there's someone with time to listen.' She flicked a look at Olive. 'Not bad advice, if I say so myself.'

'Duncan tried. It didn't get him anywhere.'

'Aircrew is something else again. It takes years of training to produce an airman. That pilot – ' here she dropped her voice, and leaned in close to her friend, ' – who went in last week was in training for over a year. He'd had two flights in an Operational Training Unit, and then someone offered him a nice safe hop to dispersal, and the *rabbits* got him. You can't begin to imagine the cost of that little exercise. And that's not counting the damage to the plane.' She took a bite of her bun, and talked around it. 'Which is why we don't fly when the weather packs in. The planes are worth their weight in gold, and so are the people who fly them.'

Olive thought if that were true it would be a slow air-war. She'd never seen so much rain in her life – not to mention fog, drizzle, and that mist the English hadn't dignified with a name. How she longed for the dry air and looming thunderheads of home.

Evelyn had finished her bun and was eyeing the uneaten portion of her friend's. Olive dealt quickly with that by eating it.

'They'll eventually need more people for non-operational flying and will have nowhere to get them. All the men will be in the services, or reserved employment. And then what?' Evelyn asked.

'The temptation of Helen of Sandridge and a thousand other poor girls. You're the devil down the back garden in the Anderson shelter. Join up, you say, and throw off the burdens of your sex.'

Evelyn laughed. 'I don't think many round here are seeing their sex as a burden. Look at this little lot and you'll see where a uniform gets you.'

Olive could see that the hut was full of couples or potential couples, although there were too many men. They sat about in lounging groups, most as near to the windows, or the counter, as they could get, for in the light from one of these the white smocks of the girls reached a tempting translucency, and at the counter the girls were at the beck and call of the men. At one end of the hut a NAAFI girl – forgettable face alive with a blush – was being chatted up by a young man who looked like he might have done better. Olive saw this but thought it proved nothing – after all, what interested her about the service was its ability to *foreclose* the question of romance. She – like Evelyn – could put herself out of trouble.

She was mulling this over while Evelyn – imagining joining-up was the farthest thing from her friend's mind – put long minutes in trying to convince her to do what she'd already decided on.

This irritated Olive. So did the way Evelyn kept harping on about the 'drab' life of Helen Sewell, the poor girl picking up the dried crusts of sandwiches from the dining room floor, and toting the guests' dirty sheets and wet towels – how much better she'd be out of domestic service, and in a uniform; the nasty business of social class forgotten.

'Oh give it a rest,' Olive snapped. 'You don't give two hoots about Helen Sewell. She's just some little cinder cast skyward by your war. A figure. An example.'

Evelyn put down her cup in surprise at her friend's outburst.

'Poor girl,' Olive added. 'To think she's got a crush on you.'

Evelyn stirred the teaspoon in her nevertheless empty cup. She glanced at the shelf above Olive's left shoulder – its orderly rows of white jugs and gravy boats; its stacks of serving dishes – and then looked back at the disorderly mix of emotions on her friend's face. There was reproach there, and envy, and something else – something that looked almost like an invitation.

'Don't be absurd,' said Evelyn, enunciating carefully. 'She's a *housemaid*.'

'Unlike the lovely Mar– ' Olive nearly said the name, but clamped her mouth shut on it at the last second. Mentioning Marjorie meant addressing questions she did not want to face.

The question of what Evelyn was like, for instance. And – harder still – what Evelyn might want.

Being flippant seemed the safer course. So Olive said, 'Since when do housemaids put anyone off? England's built on the long-suffering compliance of the lower orders, whether it's skirts or bayonets lifted.'

Evelyn smiled at that and – true to her class, and to Olive's friendship – would not be further drawn.

Olive carefully skirted the question of Marjorie, but there was more that needed avoiding than that. There was the subject of Evelyn's parents footing the bill for Olive's fruitless mission to get her to come home; of Evelyn using Ida's home as a flop when the whim took her; not to mention the way in which she'd taken on the attitudes and demeanor of an English debutante to cover something more than a stubborn streak of boyishness. Olive was constrained in what she could say, and not just because of the difficult question of what Evelyn was like. More constraining still – and uppermost on both their minds – was the question of what Olive was like; what Olive needed.

They surrendered their cups to the LACW (pronounced, by Evelyn, 'laquer', which seemed to Olive an attractive ranking) and went back out into the drizzle without pushing the conversation further. Evelyn walked her to the gate with the brolly every so often banging on the top of her forage cap: Olive, as Evelyn put it, was a bothersome short arse, and never more so than when an umbrella was needed. Evelyn then surprised her by giving over the umbrella altogether. She backed up under the eaves of the sentry box, crowding the poor man, and grinning at her friend.

'I do take care of you, you see.'

'Loik me own dear modderrr,' Olive acknowledged.

'Get Helen to pour you a bath!' Evelyn yelled at the departing Olive. Then she stood to watch her pick her way between the puddles, jumping from one dryish spot to another, muddy water splashing onto her stockings and hem. She waited until she could no longer see her friend then turned back towards the pilots' lounge.

Helen did draw Olive a bath, and gave her a scented soap to use, so that she felt ashamed of how she'd used the girl – just as Evelyn had – to voice some stupid idea about the war.

The pilots returned to the hotel from the field at afternoon tea time, four women and seven men. Evelyn came into the lounge with her friend Audrey and a one-armed Yank she introduced as Mike.

They sat down in the corrugated cushioning of the easy chairs Olive had tried, in turn, and rejected. Dexterously, Mike rolled a box of matches up his palm, pushed the insert out, and up-ended a matchstick as one might a stick in pick-up-sticks. He saw her watching, and grinned around the smoke from his cigarette.

'You should see me juggle. Four balls, kid, and none out.'

'Mike's a regular octopus,' Audrey said, glancing warmly his way. 'Don't bother feeling sorry for him.'

'What's with the "no feeling sorry" story? I deserve a sympathetic thought.' He picked his glass of beer from the tray and proposed a toast. 'Here's to long hours and lousy pay. And to fools like me.'

'That's the spirit,' Evelyn said, patting Mike's knee.

Olive took a sip of the beer, steeling herself for disappointment.

Mike winked at her. 'The English are great at a lot of things, but right now this isn't one of them.'

She found herself capped in a cone of din with Mike at one side of her and Audrey at the other, and it was the American's stories that kept them going until someone, foolishly, asked her what life in the outback was like.

'The only outback I know is the dunny. The lavatory,' she yelled, just as there was a lull in the general hubbub. She sat straighter in her chair to brazen out the gaffe. After a wave of song from the group around the piano had subsided, she let them in on a few things about Australia.

Kangaroos did not hop down Sydney's streets, or down the streets of Orange; drovers did not ride camels, and people owned – and drove – cars. What's more, she said – waving her empty glass for emphasis – the Australian Army and Air Force both had their own perfectly adequate commanders, and weren't just bodies for Britain to dispose of as she wished – like they did in the last war, when (and this she would later remember saying, word for unfortunate word) the corpses of Dominion soldiers made filler for the holed walls of dugouts at Gallipoli and the Somme.

That phrase would stick with her, as would the look on Audrey's face. In sorting Evelyn's friends, Audrey would consequently allocate Olive a position well beneath decency's horizon.

Olive sat holding her sweating glass and cursed Duncan, what with his *just join in and you'll be fine*. Had he been there that night she'd have throttled him. It was a relief when she could finally retreat to her cot. She'd underestimated the strength of the beer, and overestimated her manners.

Evelyn had been talking to other people all night, and as soon as the lights were out she expected Olive's attention. Olive had just turned her cheek to the pillow and taken hold of its corner to slow the room down a bit when Evelyn said something about the car, of all things. *Why hadn't she brought it down?* Olive mumbled that it wasn't hers to take and then Evelyn said something that – while hardly sobering her – put sleep out of reach.

'I had a letter from Marjorie. She wants me to come up for a weekend. I was wondering whether I should.'

Olive considered how long it had been since Marjorie had packed in flying to head home to the manor. Four months, at least – long enough for Evelyn to have got on with things, to get over it. But it seemed she had not.

Olive turned onto her back and tried to see the ceiling. Her temples throbbed.

'You could say you're too busy. That you can't get leave.' Olive did not know whether she was required to give a firm 'don't'. *Don't* would say more than she wanted, and she could hardly say 'yes'. Her best hope was that Evelyn would go to sleep and forget the question had been put. But the stillness on the other side of the room was such that Olive knew she hadn't.

Finally she said, 'Why ask me?'

Evelyn sighed. 'Because you know what it feels like – being left, when a thing's unfinished.'

This was too much for Olive. She sat up and was appalled to find herself shouting: 'That's precisely why – if you had any decency at all – you'd spare me the question. How dare you! If you want to see Marjorie, then see her, don't get up a committee about it.'

She heard the thud of heavy army blankets hitting the floor, and then Evelyn was beside her – the dark warmed, solidifying.

'I'm not asking for your permission. But this constant disapproval and evasion I cannot stand.' Olive felt a light touch in the hair at her right temple where her curlers pulled most tightly; the place from out of which the worst of her headaches came.

Olive lay back down, away from the hand and from Evelyn. She lay as though frozen.

Evelyn sighed. Olive felt her breath, and turned her face aside.

'Thank you,' Evelyn said and the springs sent up a cry as she got back into her bed.

Olive lay, feigning sleep; sunk in the darkness of her own blackout.

Chapter Eight

Cranwell

After an exhausting train journey from the WAAF recruiting station at Kingsway, Olive was billeted for induction at the Grand Hotel, in Harrogate. The Yorkshire sky seemed larger and brighter than its London equivalent. And the Grand Hotel *was* grand, low as it had fallen. There were staircases wide enough that, walking abreast, two girls carrying kitbags and with gas masks swinging under their arms could make it from the foyer to the fourth floor without the straps of their masks getting caught on anything. While some of the girls had to make do with a dormitory arrangement in what once had been a ballroom, Olive and three other girls shared a room that looked down on the gardens and onto the caps of people streaming in and out of the hotel.

The indignities of those first days were tamed by the comfort of their accommodation. It was a matter of exercising patience most of the time, and organisation the rest: there were Free From Infection inspections (queues and questions), kitting out (more queues and questions), and then they were all to have an interview with a WAAF officer that Olive was warned would steer the unwary girl into whatever trade was most in need of bodies.

So she sat before Assistant Section Officer Coombes on a seat the leather of which had been warmed by one girl after another – a warming accumulative, not from long indenture. The assistant section officer was young and not particularly good-looking, but she was flawlessly turned out in her uniform. Olive imagined that this mix was conducive to an advance in rank.

'You're Australian?' The section officer asked as if she doubted it.

Olive nodded, waiting.

'Farming?'

'My father's a farm manager.'

The section officer sat back, the file before her drooping towards the desk. 'I see.'

Olive saw that she did, and added, 'But he owns land now.'

'Good for him.' The section officer let the file drop completely, and folded her hands over it. 'I think you've done a very decent thing volunteering. You might otherwise have fallen through the cracks and become one of those rare people not to have their business minded by others, but here you are. And what are we to do with you – ' she glanced back at the file, 'Aircraftwoman Jamieson?'

'I don't much mind where I'm stationed, so long as it's not *too* cold.'

'Not dead keen on Scotland then.' The section officer's smile said she had no influence in such things. 'Any idea what trade you'd like to muster in?'

Olive had had her bit of clerical work at Stapleford, and felt she was up for something more. She explained that she'd worked at an aerodrome, and been involved in the use of the newly installed radio-telephone sets. She made much, too, of having replaced fused valves on the crystal set at the West Hampstead library.

She had been dismissed, and was walking from the office when she realised there was something she'd much rather have done than work the wireless. She'd have *liked* to be a truck driver. But by then the section officer's door was shut and girls lined up waiting for it to open were all staring at her, so she went off to a first-aid lecture and while other people thrust arms up to ask ridiculous questions (like the appropriateness of a tourniquet to the throat in the case of a head wound) she pondered the prospect of a war spent at a switchboard.

The morning after the lists went up Olive and the other girls were woken at three a.m. They had their breakfast fairly chucked at them, and by four the sleepy young women were staggering out into the dark, bowed under the weight of the gas capes rolled on their backs; the respirators and groundsheets tied to their shoulders. Each of them dragged a suitcase. The cohort was formed into columns of three and marched to a train where they were crammed – as many as could fit – in each compartment; girls draping every which way in an attempt to get comfortable.

Throughout the train ride (south, once more) Olive's imagination had stuck on the 'telephone' part of the trade description, but the first days of training at No 1 Signal School, RAF Cranwell, were much more interesting than she'd expected. She mastered Ohm's law – voltage and wattage – and struggled with morse while the Luftwaffe bombed London. In the evenings she'd call Ida to see whether she and the house were still standing, and in the days would sit at the end of a trestle table – with other WAAFs and with RAF wireless operators bound for the bombers – in a room darkened for them to learn to read the letters flashed by the Aldis lantern. After a few weeks of that Olive was pulled from the group – marched out, as if she was a stirrer being sent to the headmaster's office. The instructor told her that she had no chance of making the required eighteen words in morse per minute, and that her efforts, and his, might be better spent elsewhere. Had he bothered to ask why she was lagging she'd have told him it was the fault of the passages they'd been given to transcribe – columns from the *Daily Telegraph* and the *Times* that Olive thought it her duty to think about, as well as read.

So she moved from morse – those spirits tapping at the tables of imperfect mediums – to the spirit world of radio. Olive learned that resistance and coupling were neither political nor moral topics, and that inductance had nothing to do with compulsory military service. In theoretical lectures she was taught the behavior of radio waves and how to differentiate waveforms, while on the practical side she learned to take apart her set, then reassemble it, and to work repairs on its body and aerial – all of which involved the mastery of minor electrical and mechanical skills, and a particular familiarity with the soldering iron. The radio-telephone operators carried their soldering irons about in little holsters, as if the application of a bit of melted flux might be required at any time to hold the world together.

It was during training for R/T that she again met Marjorie. Evelyn's favourite must have tired of life at the manor, and had joined the WAAFs. Now she was a demonstrator, teaching correct pronunciation of the alphabet to a bunch of bluebird radio-telephonists. This made it hard for Olive to avoid her – even if she stood at the back of the circle, worrying her last pristine cuticle and hoping no one would call on her to squawk. (The other WAAFs laughed at her accent, and she was worried that the squadron officer would transfer her out of signals.)

'Get in closer,' the WAAF non-com standing behind Olive said. 'You can't see anything from here.' So Olive elbowed her way into the inside of the circle, nearer to Marjorie and the Marconi.

'Helleau, Monkey Fo-wer Fife, Monkey Fo-wer Fife, this is Jetty answering. Receiving strength thuh-ree. Can you repeat?' Marjorie turned to show the trainee WAAFs how she was shaping the words. Her mouth was unnaturally set and her accent more marked than ever – as if she was sending herself up. She got a recognition signal quickly, but when one of the younger WAAFs was called upon, all she got from the depths of air was a puzzled challenge: *Hello Nemo, repeat?*

During her first few weeks of training Olive's calls never went as surely out into the dark as Marjorie's had, no matter how hard she studied the Ohm's law chart on the wall of the classroom where they learned the principles of signals strengths, phonetics procedure ('speaking in character'), and set maintenance. She stared at that chart as much as she did at the cardboard cut-outs of aircraft that hung from the ceiling, spinning slowly nose to port every time someone opened the door. Although the chart's corners were curling, and the paper was yellow, someone had thought it useful enough to keep its pride of place just behind, and above, the instructor's head. 'Englishmen,' it told them, 'Invariably Support High Authority Unless Vindictive.' How comforting, too, was it to learn that, 'The Managing Owners Never Destroy Bills'. And the last line on the chart sounded to Olive like one of the slogans popular with the poster-wallahs of wartime ministries: *Remarks When Loose Play Jangling*.

One evening Marjorie came to sit at her table in the mess, and although Olive saw the younger woman notice her, she let the moment pass, unacknowledged. It seemed easier to behave as if they'd never met, had never been introduced, and knew no one in common. Nevertheless, this meeting prompted in Olive a disorienting loneliness. There was no shortage of company in the married quarters where she'd been billeted, nor at the Marconi. Why had she managed only a nodding acquaintance with the other operators?

Olive studied the women of RAF Cranwell, calculating, as she did, her difference from them. There were parades to fall-out into, and fatigues to do, and jankers for about a thousand possible disciplinary infringements – one of which was to forget, as Olive did, to take to mealtimes the knife, and fork, and spoon issued to her upon arrival. She learned that a mess was not a cafeteria, and if a girl got the WAAF cook's back up she might find her plate one day covered in peas, the next by gravy with nothing beneath it. Olive took to beaming at anyone with a ladle just in case.

On any day, along with classroom demonstrations on use of the sets and principles of radio-telegraphy, they would be lectured on gas, hygiene, discipline, first aid, standing orders, air-raid precautions, aircraft recognition and the proper way to care for their kits. The frequency of the hygiene advice was unsuccessful in compelling the English girls to wash. Many of them had come from homes without baths; with detached or shared privies – and they seemed to be allergic to water: they paddled, but did not swim, and they washed whatever they could decently reach with a flannel, but did not bathe. Olive never saw her roommates naked, not even in the billet, since they struggled in and out of their clothes like good Catholic girls, shedding one skin under another. Some simply went to sleep in their underclothes without changing. When Olive first discovered this, she took to showering ostentatiously and – with her hair wrapped in a towel – would walk the married quarters corridor to her room. There she'd sit on the end of her bed with a greatcoat around her shoulders and tend to her feet.

Olive imagined that she was leading by example, that her converts would dash to the showers, and come born again out of that baptismal font, hygiene nuts to the last. None of which happened. She found instead that no one would join her table at breakfast, and that it was always her set on the blink when she came back to the classroom from lunch. This went on for a week, and then a girl with the newest style of 'do' – her tight curls cut to arc back from her neck just above the collar – poked her head round the door of her room just before lights out.

'They think you're stuck up,' she whispered in a voice that might have been pitched to calm a testy horse. 'And you make them feel like they're rubbish.'

The girl had a lovely voice, and was too well spoken to have no commission.

'Oh,' said Olive, ineffectually. 'I didn't mean to.'

'Well, that's alright then. We need to get on with one another to make a go of this.' The girl looked hard at Olive until she nodded, and left after saying she'd see her at breakfast.

This was her introduction to Aircraftwoman 1st class Catherine Derrick. After Cranwell, they would meet again – in Lincolnshire still, at North Killingholme. Olive could never catch her in rank, even though Catherine Derrick reached the plateau of her ambition before the war's end, and passed up a commission. Her enthusiasm was radio; she didn't want to advance beyond the technical; didn't want to be – as she put it – just a hand to stir the people pot. She pursued her own voice on the airwaves right into a cushy job with the BBC, and that voice would be familiar to thousands of children during the 1950s when she read storybooks for an after-school broadcast.

While they were at Cranwell, Cathy kept herself out of the general run of assignations and flirtations. She went to dances, and was as sociable as the next girl, but didn't get involved. The other girls thought this was due to cautiousness and a commitment to the higher duty of war work, but Olive saw it as something else. Cathy was choosey. And when, late in the war, she made her choice, she was to do so with fierce deliberation, single-mindedly, as if those years abstaining – surrounded by people being caught up, or let down, by love – had left her starved.

The first morning Cathy joined her at the table for breakfast she let Olive have her bacon, although it was the rare morning they were given it. Usually they were faced with a grey lump of porridge congealing at the centre of the plate.

'Vegetarian,' she'd whispered. 'Don't tell anyone.'

'You must be mad,' Olive said. 'English food's bad enough without cutting the decent half out.'

The other woman shrugged, and set to her plate of oats, and bread with marmalade so thickly spread on it she had to hold the slices with both hands. There was nothing anaemic about Cathy: she had eyes the blue of pressed cornflowers, and regularly managed to get away with pencilling the mole on her cheek into a beauty spot. For some time it was rumoured in the Married Quarters that before the war Cathy had been an actress – a story that accounted for the voice, and for the affectation of the spot.

Having discovered a friend, Olive set about testing her. There were a great many men at Cranwell, and although their billets were at the other side of the camp, servicewomen could meet them in the canteens, at the Station cinema, and at dances. No matter what charmer she put in her way, Cathy showed nothing more than a genial disinterest, and the most attention Olive saw her give any man was to the chaplain. He led services in a church jury-rigged in a hangar for the duration of the war – the blades of a Hampden's propellers welded to form the cross. But it turned out that all that there was between Cathy and the chaplain was her singing voice and his abilities with the piano.

It was from Cathy that she learned standing orders, and the finer points of King's Regulations. It was also from her that Olive learned not to be flattered by attention.

'The fact that they like you means nothing,' Cathy told her one night as they walked from the NAAFI back to quarters, hand in hand because of the blackout's perils. 'It's what *you* feel about it that matters.'

If Catherine Derrick was master of herself, so was she of others. She could deftly avoid being disciplined but demonstrated great skill at dishing out punishment to non-commissioned officers of lesser rank. Not long before their training ended, she confided to Olive that her aim was to be 'well in' with the squadron officer, so that a request that they be attached to the same station might get some consideration.

But when Olive made Aircraftwoman 1st class and was able to draw her thirty shillings, the promotion came with the postings. Olive was to go to Waltham while Cathy had been kept at Cranwell – she'd made herself indispensable to the wrong people and was to be put on instructing.

When the time came, Olive hugged Cathy over the lump of her kitbag while the driver of the lorry looked on sympathetically.

'Write me if you have something to say,' Cathy said, characteristically unable to put a thing the way one might expect it. Olive put her face into her friend's shoulder for a moment, and then Cathy was pressing a packet wrapped in newspaper into her hand. She looked down at it. The paper was darkened at its corners and tacky to the touch.

'Lamb chops. Your aunt will know what to do with them,' Cathy explained. Olive had a 72, and was to go to Ida's before reporting to Waltham. 'My father's a butcher in Louth.'

Olive realised it was now too late to ask how a butcher's daughter ended up with such nicely rounded vowels and rolled r's. (She would later learn Cathy had taught herself the Queen's English the way banjo players in the Appalachia learned bluegrass – one ear pressed to the radio.)

'Lamb chops,' Olive echoed, and hefted the package. 'But I've got nothing for you,' she added guiltily.

'Well, that leaves you in my debt, and I shall enjoy the thought of you exercising your thoughts in search of reciprocity.' With that, she saluted Olive, and added, 'Now off with you.'

As she was driven towards the gate Olive looked back: Cathy was a blue flag with a tip of white – her waving hand. Then all she could see from the Leyland was a wall of hawthorn as they followed the curve of the lane towards the main thoroughfare.

Chapter Nine

Extraction

After a month of watches in the Flying Control Office at Waltham, Olive was an old hand, filling her pad with a scrawled log of aircraft arrivals and departures. She wrote swiftly and corrected her log before she went off shift, walking out onto a field sometimes full, and sometimes bare, of aircraft. The grass was flattened and streaked, scarred by multiple landings, by run-up and take-off, and if a flight went out on a daylight sortie grass seed rose from the fields so that off-duty ground crew and WAAFs would come into the NAAFI with eyes red from sneezing, and sit plucking the serrated heads of grass from trousers, or from the facings of skirts.

In the early autumn, if time and weather allowed, she'd lie in the long grass beyond the chance lights to read her mail. There were letters from Duncan (Barrack E, Zone 2, Bradfield Park); letters from Ida with cinnamon and sugar poured between the folds of the paper; letters from Olive's father – one squared page of writing that was invariably news of the farm. And then there were

Evelyn's letters, sent from Hatfield, blue ink on blue stationery.

Evelyn suggested they meet to share a leave. While it would have been a reasonable suggestion that they meet somewhere within striking distance to them both (Northampton perhaps), Evelyn's cavalier 'let's drive down to see Aunt Ida in her new cottage at Collingbourne Kingson' set Olive slashing at the grass with her foot. A 48 was scarce, and petrol even more so, but such elementary matters as these had not occurred to Evelyn. Duncan's letters demonstrated a better grip on reality, but when he wrote triumphantly that he'd frustrated the attempts of the selection board to categorise him as a navigator, Olive saw – in Duncan – his sister's too easy sense of the world. Of course he'd be a pilot. Of course she'd motor over to Wiltshire.

These ungenerous thoughts about her friends did not go unpunished.

Her teeth had been bothering her. She couldn't say which tooth, and neither could the friend from the clerical pool who braved a look into her mouth.

'It's the medical officer for you,' the friend said, popping the wad of cardboard Olive used as a mouthguard into the waste-paper basket.

But Olive neglected to go. Her face swelled, the jawbone seeming to droop. She kept to herself – wrapped, as she was, in a fug of pain. But there was no avoiding Marjorie. She, too, had been posted to Waltham from Cranwell, and now got about with a gang of admiring younger WAAFs. It was Marjorie and a group of her friends who saw Olive coming out of the

Station flicks, and it was Marjorie who said, the words carrying distinctly in the cold still air: 'I didn't know they were conscripting Mongoloids.'

Olive would have slapped her if she could. But the force of her feet hitting the concrete jarred her head so badly she could only plod on towards the Waafery, like some great Neanderthal on the way back to its cave.

The following morning at breakfast she held Evelyn's letter in front of her face. Marjorie would not be able to mistake it – the paper was from her own private stock. She'd kept Evelyn in good supply.

She fanned two sheets, this being what was needed to cover the expanding width of her jaw.

The letter had been sent from Hatfield. 'Darling,' it began. Evelyn then quickly disposed of the news that Olive was missed, and that a letter would be welcome. The real business of the letter was her description of a Lysander flight in which she'd managed to get 'tangled in the soup':

I got myself into some cloud – from my last visual reckoning of landmarks – 8 or 9 miles from my destination field. I descended and couldn't find clean air and then unwisely (and against standing orders) decided to go back up and see whether I could go over the top of the muck to find out where I was. Out I come and – since I've lost some sense of my bearings – I don't have the foggiest notion what I'm looking at on the ground. I can't descend safely any lower than I am, and if I go back up I might become hopelessly lost, and could even blunder into the cables of the barrage balloons anchored to shield the Liverpool docklands. So I stooge about for a bit not knowing what to do. My mind is blank, I haven't got a clue, and it occurs to me that this might be how it happens. Not mechanical failure, but all systems operative and with nowhere to land. Then I saw a railway trestle and crossing, got a fix on my position and was back in the daily task of delivering an aircraft – saved just as banally as I'd been lost.

The last sentences took up the arch tone of the letter's start: 'I hear from Marjorie that you look well, and will take that as a broader indication of your welfare.' Over the final entreaty, 'Do write', were three deeply scored 'x' marks.

It was true that she hadn't written. Olive had meant to punish her friend, and her silence did seem to have exercised Evelyn's imagination, or conscience – why else would she suggest they meet?

Looking around the edge of the paper she saw Marjorie, in among her gaggle of friends, sitting with such erect carriage she might have been on horseback. No doubt Marjorie had written Evelyn to give an update on her condition – in her letters Olive would hardly look well.

Olive's swollen jaw prompted the squadron officer to pull her out of the line filing from mess. 'Be in the medical officer's hut in five minutes,' she said, having taken the WAAF's miserable measure.

The Station MO had his gramophone playing, the needle surfing the wave of the warped disc at every turn. It was a Sousa march, chosen to discourage malingerers. Luckily he could at once see that Olive wasn't one of these.

'Open,' he said, without preliminaries. Then he peered down his nose into her mouth and she saw him blink and grimace. 'Wider!'

The swelling of her jaw forbade it. The MO harrumphed and, without asking Olive to sit, went back to his own chair.

'What you've got I can't fix. You'll have to see a dental surgeon.' At her look he added, 'Abscess in the recess of the jaw.' He bent to scrawl on his notepad and, ripping off the greying sheet, passed it to her. 'There's a dental hospital in St Albans. You'd best get yourself there.' With that she was dismissed.

Olive reported for duty in the Watch Office, and went to bed after a dismal supper of tea-dampened toast.

She thought it was proof of her willpower when the pain in her jaw began to ease. The dark cast to the skin of her right cheek was gone by the next afternoon, so that when the station officer came to check on Olive she could honestly report a return to health.

This reprieve held until winter, when the Waafery was bombed. Olive was briefly billeted at Kingsgate Road. It was then that Evelyn – stranded by fog, and anxious that she'd not yet had a letter from her friend – bicycled from Waltham aerodrome, where she'd just set down a Hurricane.

She had seemed so bluff and beautiful that day, banging the bicycle handlebars up against the outside wall of the kitchen and yelling for Olive to put the tea on, like a husband home from work for his dinner.

They'd sat at the kitchen table and Evelyn read her letters from home, letters she carried in an ever more creased package stuck inside the front of her Irvin jacket. Struck by the fact that there were none of her own letters there, and by Evelyn sitting across the table from her – cheerful, not offering a single reproach – Olive had gone upstairs to get her own letters from Orange to reciprocate and Evelyn had patiently put up with paragraphs of Arthur Jamieson raging at the tyranny of wartime committees. Then, when it was getting dark, Olive put the marg and jam onto the breadboard, and sliced six pieces of bread so they could carry on with their tea in bed. The two women sat cross-legged at opposite ends of the mattress and talked about Duncan. Evelyn spoke quietly and with such measure that Olive could tell she was angry with her brother. She told Olive that Duncan was not faring well in his Elementary Flight Training School at Deniliquin – every time he went up in an aircraft he'd get airsick, too sick to have the coordination and concentration that flying demanded. He was hiding the sickness, hoping to brazen out the training until he'd get over it. But the thing was that people never did. Airsickness was an affliction that wouldn't shift, like palsy, or a harelip. Evelyn was about to render judgement on this when Olive's teeth let out a clattering round of chatter, so Evelyn took off her leather jacket to drape it around her friend's shoulders, then – since she was herself now at the mercy of the night air – pulled the bedding right up over her shoulders and head. All Olive could see of her was one pale hand. This she'd sent out foraging for the last of the crumbs of bread and jam, index finger dab-dabbing across the board. Only after they were both sufficiently warm had Evelyn taken up her line of thought. The whole business of Duncan cracking hardy was a fool's strategy. He was afraid that he'd be scrubbed as a pilot – that they'd designate him ground crew and keep him in Australia and out of the fun. And for that conceit he was risking his own life and that of his flying instructor.

Evelyn poked her face out of her clot of blankets then and glared at Olive as if she was the offending Duncan. One blonde curl had formed itself into an upside-down question mark on her forehead.

'I don't approve,' she'd said, and then, showing great likeness to her aunt, 'I cannot help but worry.'

A second passed and then Evelyn heard herself and rocked forward, laughing. Their foreheads touched and they swayed back to their respective ends of the mattress, its springs creaking beneath them mirthfully.

Olive later imagined that the thing that put a stop to their conversation was a sudden preoccupation of the air outside: rain so heavy they could not hear each other speak, rain that would turn the grass by the runways into a bog, and would spread glistening slicks of oil over the macadam. The rain had made Olive think of the night outside, and of the morning's watch. She did not know what the rain made Evelyn think about. Perhaps it signalled the end of the fog, and the need for her to finish her delivery. Perhaps it was simply that it gave her the pip: rain again! All Olive knew was that there seemed to be no point in talking anymore.

After that visit, Evelyn's letters got warmer, more intimate, than they'd been for months. She still went on about aircraft types, but would now broach the subject of other enthusiasms – including Marjorie, about whom they had *generally* agreed not to speak. Evelyn's Marjorie was unrecognisable to Olive: that gamine who could hold polite conversation in two languages was nothing like the corporal with the immaculately crimped hair who'd let every girl in the Waafery but Olive use her pink nail lacquer. In general, their letters drifted to safer subjects: to Duncan, and to rationing (Evelyn had spotted cold cream in a department store in Lincoln). In this way the tone of their correspondence cooled again, and no matter how sorry Olive was that it had done so, she could not prick it back to life.

At the year's end there came heavy snowfalls; the bombers returning with ice on their wings. The newspapers' contribution to Christmas cheer was the announcement that the butter ration was to be reduced again. Olive passed her spartan Christmas on Station and – after a misadventure eating the single toffee laid by her plate at New Year's Eve dinner – her toothache came back; the ball of pus reforming in her jaw.

For several days she got about so muffled in scarves that no one had a chance to see the swelling, but a surprise Free From Infection inspection put an end to that. The other girls were dismissed, and Olive was left standing at attention in nothing but her winter-weight blackouts with the MO and the station officer bawling her out.

She did try a home remedy for toothache, and lay on her

bunk reading while waiting for it to take effect. She had three letters from Duncan that had come together. In one of these he lied about his reasons for being washed out of Elementary Flying School: that he was not tall enough, or that his legs were too short. Duncan was 5 foot 8, and thought Olive was stupid enough to believe he'd been washed out because his feet couldn't reach the pedals for the rudder of his Harvard trainer. But Olive had seen Duncan re-buckle the stirrups on a saddle after his father – a compact Scot – had sat the horse. She knew he had long enough reach in the leg to suit any cockpit layout. All that rang true in that letter was the rueful way in which he'd been dismissed, the instructor taking him aside to say, 'You've had it cobber.' That, and the note of rising enthusiasm as he embraced his bad fortune, as many young men would do – gleeful that they'd still get to see their war.

Duncan had chosen air gunnery because it was the quickest way in to active service. He'd been designated 'Leading Aircraftman' and sent off ahead of his Initial Training School draft to complete his training. Overseas. First to Auckland from where his second letter was posted on Christmas Eve. The troopship had berthed to take on its complement of RNZAF trainees:

We've had two days in port, lovely sunny days that light the red roofs of the houses here. But the first night was a bit of a shock as Kiwis have an idiosyncratic way of doing a blackout: no house or interior lights but the odd neon sign still glowing for reasons I cannot fathom. Perhaps they like the aesthetic effect? Makes the cinema easy to find anyway.

Saw a piece of marvellous rubbish with Bob Hope in it called 'Ghost Breakers', and laughed so much at one point that the Jaffa I'd just popped in my mouth popped right back out again and hit the back of the head of the chap in front. He wasn't pleased but once he saw my uniform he was as nice as could be and even ended up apologising to me (what for, I don't know).

From Auckland, they'd sailed to Suva, where the purser's boat took the mail to shore. The complement of trainee airmen stood at sullen rest at the ship's rails, having been denied leave. They'd been crammed eight to a cabin, and it was too noisy for Duncan to read his untranslated volume of Hugo's *Les Misérables*. Thrown out of the solace of his Hugo, he'd had to follow his own advice and 'join in', befriending a Kiwi gunner nicknamed Lofty who in peacetime had been a mining engineer in the west coast coal pits. Lofty had broken the hearts of the recruiters for the Army Engineering Corps by choosing air and .303 shell over dirt, dynamite and well-placed pontoons.

By the time Olive read the last of Duncan's letters she'd forgotten he'd lied to her. She dozed with their pages spread on her chest, the bar of the heater ticking down into a chilly and ashen silence. Somewhere after midnight fever gripped her and in the morning she carried it with her to her watch. On seeing the state of the WAAF reporting to duty, the Flying Control Officer sent her straight to the MO, but the MO took one look at her and withdrew to his office, leaving her with the clerk he'd ordered to type the medical pass.

Olive was to go to London, to the dental unit at Hill End Hospital, St Albans. There she sat on a bench in the bare garden for an hour watching white civilian and khaki military ambulances creep up the icy gravel of the drive. It was only when it started to snow that she followed them in.

There were cots set up at the side of the entrance hall and all along the inner corridor but since it was near noon, and the Luftwaffe had not been over for a daylight raid all week, these stood empty, the exposed canvas lined and stretched. From the desk she was sent to the back of the building and then up a stairway edged with pigeon droppings.

When the nurse put the rubber tube for the nitrous oxide over Olive's nose she said, 'You must breathe regularly,' and stroked the back of her fingers. 'If there's pain, don't hold your breath.' The nurse gave her hand a little squeeze and walked out of sight.

Olive's head was braced to the headrest so all she could do was listen to the hiss of steam escaping from the steriliser, and the bright sound of the tongs hitting the wall of the tank as the nurse chased the instruments about. The dentist had not arrived and so the nurse was cheerily whistling the refrain from 'A Little on the Lonely Side', breaking off every now and again to direct a comment at Olive, as an animal lover might converse with an unfamiliar dog or cat. She'd given the patient up as gone, and rightly so, for when she came to tap her on the hand Olive felt the touch as a rapping at a distant door.

She was breathing regularly, saliva pooling under her tongue, when the dentist finally came to inject the anaesthesia; and she was breathing deeply by the time she felt her teeth being stirred about in her jaw. The pliers made a sound like church bells and Olive had opened her eyes and was trying to free her busy mouth to tell the dentist how beautiful it was to hear them ring again when she saw Evelyn, her gloved hands holding the bunched ends of the scarf draped about her neck. Olive held her breath and Evelyn's face rushed at her. The ironical tilt to the head and the cast of her eyebrows said 'Happy now?'

Still Olive didn't breathe. Only when the grumble of the drill replaced the sound of ringing did she take another whiff of nitrous.

Evelyn had come after all.

Olive had telegraphed, not thinking how the short message might sound: 'St Albans, Hill End Hospital. Emergency surgery 11 a.m. Thursday. Can you come?' And she had.

The halter of laughing gas was taken off Olive some time later and the dental surgeon stood before her dandling the hose.

'You have three less teeth than you had this morning. One of your wisdoms was impacted and two others had roots like boar's tusks. Not an easy set of extractions, I can tell you.' At that, he hung the face mask back on the gas canister and put his finger in her still open mouth to tamp down the last dressing. The curly hair on his wrist tickled her cheek. He said to someone behind her, 'She's going to have a difficult time of it with bleeding and that sort of thing. Salt mouthwashes every two hours, but not until tonight.' He tilted the wrist he had in front of her nose so that they could both see the time. 'You're a plucky little WAAF – putting up with all that without a general anaesthetic – so you'll be fine.'

'What can she have for the pain?' Olive heard Evelyn ask.

'All we can offer is aspirin.' The antiseptic-scented hand stopped fussing inside her mouth as the dentist leaned back. 'Distraction does a better job,' he added. 'Find your friend something to think about.'

Evelyn took Olive out into the early winter dusk and held her shoulders while she spat blood into the snow bedding the bare garden. They stood, hip to hip, looking at the rosy stains.

Evelyn rearranged Olive's scarf so that its ends were well tucked away from the blood. 'There,' she said, rather too emphatically, and glanced into the darkening sky. 'Let's get you out of here before we're at the mercy of the glimmer lights.' She sat Olive in the car, its windows lightly crusted with snow, and put something into her hand. It was the two wisdom teeth that had lasted the distance of the extraction, two perfectly healthy teeth. The only harm in them had been their tenacity, their desire to stay put, to hold fast with their complex skirts of root twisted in the jaw.

Olive felt sorry for them, and for herself. 'What happened to the other one?' she said thickly.

'It cracked up.' Evelyn looked surprised that she'd asked. 'They took it out in pieces.' Then she pulled in her lower lip, held it with an eyetooth thoughtfully. 'The dentist thinks there's nothing left, but it was hard to tell under all that blood.'

'Oh,' said Olive, and opening the car door spat red into the gutter again.

Chapter Ten

Confidences

Evelyn drove Olive to Hatfield, and to the Stonehouse Hotel. Helen Sewell of Sandridge had long since gone and the only person at reception was a thin-faced woman with spectacles that looked like they'd been issued by His Majesty's Prison Service. The stairs seemed to flex away from her feet as she walked up to Evelyn's room. No sooner was she through its door than Evelyn made her step out of her shoes and get into bed.

While Evelyn was away having her dinner, Olive lay propped up against two plumped pillows, a bowl balanced on her chest into which she'd spit bloody saliva every few minutes. Her face felt no less swollen than it had before the extraction – no less painful. She was a cartoon chipmunk, ineloquent and lumpy-cheeked.

The candle had burned down half an inch when Evelyn came back, and she'd no sooner put the sheets on her cot than the air-raid siren went.

'Here we go.' She sat on the bed and put an arm around

Olive's shoulder. 'The *distracting* dear old Luftwaffe. Can't have that.' And, flicking back a lacquered plume of hair, she pulled her cot up so that there was no space between it and the side of the bed she'd given over to Olive. She drew close the candle and, stretching out beside the invalid, began to read aloud the letter she'd just received from Duncan in Canada. Evelyn fell into the familiar gentle rhythms of her brother's voice but had to bawl out some sections emphatically as a vaudeville comedian to make herself heard above the planes.

Duncan and Lofty and the other men of their draft had docked at Vancouver and were sent by bus to New Westminster, where a long line of Pullman cars sat waiting for them – the sort of cars train robbers, or Indians, were always chasing in the movies Duncan saw back home. Their train steamed its way up through the Rocky Mountains by the Fraser River, Lofty enthusing about the engineering of tracks and tunnels and bridges. But Duncan was too busy staring out into the woods to pay any attention – the word had come back, by Chinese whispers, that someone in the carriage ahead had spotted a bear.

Lofty only wanted to know whether it was draught or lager.

The troop train passed through Calgary, through Medicine Hat and Moose Jaw. At Portage, while the train took on coal, a girl passed outside the carriage windows handing out packaged lunches. When she appeared at their window Duncan told her she ought to be careful: all that running around would get her 'knocked up'. The girl gave him a look of horror and spilled coffee all down the window sash. Lofty pointed out that *that* particular expression had a different meaning to Canadians; that the girl had gone off in fear of her virtue.

It was at Portage that Lofty struck up a conversation with a young civilian in a crisp white shirt who'd come to ask if they needed any 'candy'. He was a Mormon, from Utah; and told Lofty – with a twinkle of his prospector's eye – that he'd come in the company of an elder to find converts. Lofty informed the young man they'd been amply provided for in the food and beverage department. But might he not see to their spiritual needs by providing a Book of Mormon? When the young proselytiser told Lofty he'd have to go to a meeting first, and Lofty remonstrated that they were a bit indisposed in the meeting department, the Mormon had smiled, showing his not inconsiderable teeth, and moved on to a more promising window.

At the mention of teeth Olive waved at Evelyn to stop. 'Aspirin,' she lisped, and sunk into the bedding so that it bunched to hide her mouth.

Evelyn sighed. 'You've had enough for one night.'

But the Luftwaffe weren't in agreement. One of their bombardiers put a string of bombs near enough the hotel that the ceiling puckered and plaster dust drifted down on them.

'Aspirin!' Olive yelled, because it was the only anodyne on offer, and the only thing she'd been thinking about that could rise out of the noise intact.

Evelyn got out of her cot and went to the dresser where she'd put the bottle of pills. Olive watched her walk, her slim feet neat inside their service issue brogues. Evelyn had been lying on her cot fully dressed, with her shoes on.

'Why aren't we in the air-raid shelter?' Olive asked, forgetting the aspirin even as her friend rolled them into her palm.

'Because they're not bombing *us*. If we were in North London we'd be in a shelter.'

Olive put the sheet over her head then and sucked on the chalky pills. Evelyn tugged at the edge of the blankets until Olive shifted to let her in beside her.

'It's not the Anderson shelter, but it's cosy,' Evelyn said. It was a single bed, and there wasn't much room, so she cupped her hands beneath her chin, pulled her elbows to her chest and lay, her nose not more than four inches from Olive's. After a moment she said, 'There's a couple of Crosse and Blackwell crackers at the bottom of the tin, if you want to share them.'

'I do not,' said Olive, through lips still swollen. Evelyn leaned over the side of the bed to get a handkerchief, and this she balled to gently dab some blood from Olive's mouth.

'It would be my luck to get you here, and you too ill to enjoy.'

'How – ' said Olive, pausing for the next word, ' – would you propose I be enjoyed?'

Evelyn's reply was to shift her face closer to her friend's so that they were, of a sudden, breathing the same air. Both could smell camphor, and linen. There was plaster dust in Evelyn's hair.

Olive shut her eyes. With her legs bent she could feel the wool of Evelyn's uniform skirt against her knees, and beneath it, the warmth of her skin.

'I feel awful,' she said. For all that she felt awful, that feeling was not her preponderant one.

They lapsed into silence, still lying face to face, and when the walls of the room shook at some explosion much nearer than the northern suburbs of London, Evelyn grabbed Olive's hand and squeezed it. But when Olive opened her eyes she saw that her friend had relaxed, and had turned her head so that she was squinting up at the ceiling. Light from the flickering candle made threads of shadow on her cheek and forehead, her hair having come loose from its lacquer.

'Duncan says his friend Lofty is theologically-minded,' Evelyn said, as if in continuation of a thought. 'That's why he wanted the Book of Mormon. Apparently he's got the Talmud, the Apocrypha, even the works of Confucius. Something about his needing to be able to converse with as many Gods as possible where they're going.'

Olive leaned up on her elbow. 'I wouldn't think there'd be more than one God in Winnipeg.'

Evelyn laughed. 'I think he means bomber command. Not so much an inhospitable place as a perilous position. The scripture is insurance. Duncan calls it Lofty's "backup plan in case of emergency". Clearly there are higher authorities than wing commanders and air vice marshals to be remonstrated with should the need arise.'

Olive's teeth wanted to chatter but something had happened at the dental surgery that made it impossible for them to do so.

'I don't know,' she said. Then, surprising even herself, added, 'I don't really care.'

Evelyn frowned. 'I do. I can understand putting one's trust in a book. I feel much the same way about my Hutchinson's. Or my handling notes.'

Olive was about to say that those were very different things when Evelyn threw the blankets back and lay there blinking at a newly formed crack in the ceiling – a dark line wavering in the light of the dying candle. She sat up and struggled with her shoes, then – obviously too tired to care – toed each shoe off by the heel, ignoring the knotted clump of laces.

'So, do you want to hear the rest of the letter?' she asked, fetching the pages from the floor.

Though sleepy, Olive was not ready to relinquish her time with Evelyn, so she listened drowsily to her friend read about the arrival of the draft in Winnipeg, their detraining in the yard to the sound of hundreds of men's boots crunching through the frozen snow that bedded the rails. The cohort had been bussed south-east of Winnepeg to a stretch of land just desolate enough for a gunnery and bombing school. There the trainees turned out to hot food and tea. They'd formed lines in the dark outside the shower block where they were to wash three days of soot from their bodies. Everyone was glad of this but Lofty, for whom a patina of coal dust was natural.

Lofty and Duncan had joined the end of the line for the showers, and when the men before them had finally shuffled through to a thorough wetting, it was their turn. By then, the makeshift stalls were empty. The gunners stood back to back in separate stalls beneath the sputtering taps and Duncan turned once to see Lofty cradling the blackened nub of soap against his chest. His friend was weeping.

As she read this, Evelyn glanced up at her and Olive saw that it was for *this* the reading had been engineered. Her friend's voice took on an alarming jollity as she read the last paragraph, underpinning Duncan's false note with her own:

We're bunking in the same old biscuits of straw we get the world over. Lofty lies a yard or so off, and he's snoring. I am fagged out and finish this letter by sending my love.

Evelyn folded the letter to put it back into its envelope. 'He signs it "Hope you're in the pink".' Nodding at the bowl of bloody spit Olive was pulling towards to her mouth, she added, 'I shouldn't think he meant it literally.'

Olive put her hand over Evelyn's. 'They're just homesick,' she said, authoritative as a doctor diagnosing an illness he's never had.

The hotel was quiet; the drone of the bombers' engines receding. Evelyn let her hand lie under Olive's, and Olive felt the fingers beneath hers arch and settle, arch and settle.

'All I know – ' Evelyn said after a moment, catching her lip with her teeth. 'All I know is that I'd have been happier if Duncan hadn't committed to writing that he'd seen his friend weep. And I'd have been happier if his friend wasn't inclined to weeping.'

Then she shaped her body to Olive's on the narrow bed, tucked her fists under her chin and – as the all-clear sounded – went to sleep.

Chapter Eleven

A happy accident

Olive's first letter from Lofty arrived the day she was to start a 48. She was to spend it in Collingbourne Kingston, with Ida and Evelyn, having got heartily sick of the Lincolnshire weather – whole weeks at a stretch overcast, frosts lasting a fortnight. The only ground clear of snow that February had been burned black by the heat of a full load of fuel exploding when a Wellington bomber crashed, killing all four members of the RCAF on board. She had cleared them for take-off two minutes before. Such things happened, but the WAAFs did not talk much about it. Olive did not talk about it at all.

So, she was off to Ida's, sitting in a seat by the window with her rumpled canvas bag on her lap, looking at Lofty's letter instead of the landscape. She saw with dismay how fat the letter was, and hoped there was no expectation the reply would be as weighty. But on opening it she found a single Comfort Funds sheet wrapped around a sheaf of newspaper clippings of the sort that occupy the outer columns of pages eight through to ten of the less respectable papers, the kind of stories that appeal to people who ignore vital news of the military situation to read about a goat found suckling a baby.

In the pile of clippings was the story of the 'Young Miner's Singular Mishap' – a colliery worker who blew his nose so hard that his eye popped out; the shooting of the 'Isle of Wight Monster' with its slow and deliberate movements; the American man with two hearts (the land of plenty!); and physicians baffled by a five-year-old Peruvian child who'd reached maturity and was sliding into old age after having been bitten by an unidentifiable species of spider.

The last item in the pile was from the *Daily Mirror* and must have appeared when Olive was busy transcribing into morse articles from that paper's more prestigious rivals. As she absent-mindedly handed the conductor her ticket she converted the headline:

..-. --- .-. --. . - ..-. ..- .-.. - .-. .- ...- . .-.. .-.. . .-. ...

The article noted that 244,000 items had been left in London transport vehicles and terminals. This treasure trove included 47,000 umbrellas, 26,000 pairs of gloves, 30,500 handbags and 48,000 tin hats, gas masks and rifles.

Olive thought that Londoners could not have reconciled themselves to war if they were leaving such things on the bus to Bethnall Green. Still marvelling, she turned to the letter itself. Half the page was taken up by a pencil drawing, a good likeness of Duncan lying belly-down on a cot, chin in hand, reading. The sketch bore the caption *Page 5, Les Misérables* and below this the letter began, 'Hello Olive, You sound so broad-minded in your letters to Duncan – ' She shook the page, and cursed. What was Duncan thinking, reading him her letters? ' – that I'm guessing you'll not think too badly of me for writing.'

The only correspondent I have is an old Jesuit in Christchurch, and he's half blind. I run out of paper before I've written a paragraph because I have to make the words big enough for him to read. And since you can read like an ordinary person, I thought this a more efficient use of paper. Anyway, Duncan thought you'd like this picture, and instructed me to send it. If your life is anything like ours you could use the entertainment. Not for nothing do they march us to the flicks for our daily dose of Nelson Eddy or the scintillations of 'Alf's Button Afloat'. And then there's the popular music. Jolly old nonsense it is too. *If I only had wings I'd fly fly fly like a birdy in the sky! Nighty-night, sleep-tight toodle-oo*. I like a singsong as much as the next man but I do not think the world works along the lines of *Wishing, make it so*.

What's all this, you're thinking. Look out! you say, I've been latched onto by a madman.

I'm not mad, just a tad worried about what we've got into. I like to put what I think on the page and hope you don't find me too rude. Duncan says you're the kind of girl a person can say practically anything to, and he's not one to listen to me when I'm melancholy, *he's a rainy days don't bother me* kind of a boy and I'm like that poor beast on the Isle of Wight, terrifying people all the time with my slow and deliberate movements. And we know what happened to *it*, don't we?

What I'm actually writing to say is that I'm looking out for Duncan. I've always thought it would be nice for someone (I don't know who) to get a letter saying that *I* was being looked out for, EVEN if it was a letter like this one.

Hope this finds you well.

Regards,

Lawrence Hilliers.

What a strange egg, thought Olive as she folded the letter around the clippings. But his handwriting didn't look barmy. It was a bit too elegant, the letters sloped but not falling forward and the seraphs on the ends of each stroke nicely proportioned – not like her own shocking handwriting with its letters marching along upright as toy soldiers. Back at school she'd been strapped on her writing hand so often her letters should have begun to run obediently at a crouch, but they showed no sign of doing so.

A group of aircrew in their best blues boarded at Ludborough. A few bluebirds followed, smiling at her as they passed through to the following carriage in the dim hope of a seat. The men were from RAF Binbrook, and Kelstern. They sat four to a seat, laughing as the one on the end bounced regularly off the bench and into the WAAF on the seat nearest theirs. After the third jostling the WAAF put down her magazine and, in a tone of feigned anger, told him he might as well sit in her lap since he seemed to have formed such an attachment to it. They were still at it when she got off to change trains at Helpston.

It took some time to get through Wiltshire to Collingbourne Kingston, and she was grateful to be off the train crowded with soldiers on their way to Tidworth Camp. Stepping down onto the tiny halt beside the rails she gathered the edges of her coat, put her bag between her vital organs and the worst of the wind, and walked the mile to Ida's cottage, where that same cold wind was sucking the coal smoke out of the chimney.

Ida was in the kitchen, darning in the light from the front windows while taking the heat from an Aga indistinguishable in colour from the green tweed of her Women's Voluntary Service uniform. She'd joined at Hampstead and transferred the vocation to Marlborough after one of the Jack Russells was killed by shell fragments falling from the West Ham AA barrage. Now a discouraged Ida was adapting to the provinces. Poorly, Olive thought. Village life was an enigma to her, and she wanted moral support in her attempts to enter into its mystery – Evelyn and Olive would surely come stay? Ida said her house was always open to them, although Olive knew she bolted both front and back doors before retiring to bed with her book.

The surviving dog, Mo, had not taken well to the loss of its sibling. It put its sharp nose in the air and barked at Olive. Ida told it off and it tucked tail and disappeared under the table.

'How were your connections?'

'One bus that didn't run, two late trains and a service police corporal who didn't like the look of my leave pass. Not a bad run really.'

'You should have come through from the north. It's always faster to avoid the London conurbations.'

'Perturbations.'

'Precisely,' Ida said, putting down her fabric shears and standing to give Olive a kiss on the cheek. 'You're just in time to help me do the pairing.' She waved at the pile of socks on the table, their various shades of khaki. 'Pairing' was Ida's own tidy-minded invention – she liked to send out socks in pairs aesthetically forged by identical densities of dye, or wefts of the wool.

So Olive took her bag to her room upstairs, washed at the basin and went to help Ida. Even if it was a waste of time, pairing was restful – like shelling peas or shining silver, and she was perfectly happy to rummage in the pile for the darker or lighter khaki or air-force blue sock to complete its partner.

Late in the afternoon she took Mo for a walk up the hill on the permissive path through the Manor pastureland. At the top she stood looking down at the cottages and lanes of Aughton while the Jack Russell nosed off through the bare blackberry vines in search of rabbits. Ida had stayed in for the man with the lorry who was coming to fetch her socks, and when Olive left she was filling blown eggshells with mustard to put down for the rats. Ida did not approve of trapping, or poisoning, and would have liked a barn cat, but the dog wouldn't stand for it. Mustard eggs were the kindest way she could find to keep mice and rats from her larder. 'Scarcity be damned', she'd said about the eggs – the only time during the war Olive heard her make such a proclamation.

When she got back to the cottage Evelyn was there. She still had coat and bag on, and her gas mask was dangling under her arm. She'd hitched a lift from Maidenhead, and come the last way in the lorry delivering the darning, and was now standing by a sock-strewn kitchen table remonstrating with Ida.

'You should be down at the old school hall with the other ladies in the communal darn-up.' Seeing her friend, she smiled, 'Olive thinks so too, don't you?'

'Of course.' Olive hung the leash on the nail by the door, and the dog ran to Ida, its claws clicking on the stone tiles. Evelyn's cheek was cold when she kissed it, and her ears were positively frozen. She pushed her nearer the Aga.

'Do put the kettle on since you're there,' Ida said to Evelyn; then to Olive, 'Gloves off in the house, dear.'

Olive pretended not to hear. 'It *would* be nicer doing all this – ' she waved at the table, 'with a bit of company.'

'I'd rather be in my kitchen, working at my own pace, in my own way.'

'Supplying your piece-work project puts an unnecessary dent in someone's petrol ration,' Evelyn said, in her best scold's voice.

'Nonsense. It's a quarter mile to the school hall from here, and he has to pass right by.'

Evelyn shrugged, and put a fingertip on the jug's surface to test it. Her hands were red, and raw, with cold. All that time spent in the freezing air had irreversibly altered a constitution meant for warmer climes. She stood there, now coatless, her leather gloves sitting on the table, pink fingers hovering near the enamel of the jug. Her only concession to the weather was a scarf she'd left too loosely looped to be of any use in keeping out the cold.

'So, what's up this weekend?' she asked. 'What's the plan?'

'I wouldn't have thought you needed a plan,' Ida said, putting her darning aside. 'Spontaneity is more your thing, isn't it?'

'I love a Wiltshire village as much as the next girl, but in my experience they're not much chop in the spontaneity department. We need a plan.'

Olive said that she planned to walk, and read. 'And to write to William, Duncan,' remembering the letter in her bag, she added ' – and to his friend, Lofty.'

Ida and Evelyn both looked at her oddly, and she felt obliged to explain.

'Duncan's far too trusting,' said Ida. 'Heaven only knows what poor soul he's let latch on. I don't think you should write back to this fellow. It will only give him licence.'

Evelyn rolled her eyes and asked to see the offending document. She skimmed it while they sat having tea, Ida shooting disapproving glances up from the sock she was working on.

'Interesting.' Evelyn did not read the clippings. They sat in their little pile on the table where Ida eyed them, probably thinking of the salvage drive. 'He certainly can draw a picture.'

Olive wondered whether she meant that literally.

After dinner, Evelyn suggested they walk to the pub for a drink, and Olive agreed despite her reluctance to go back out into the cold. Evelyn made a joke of it, winding Olive's scarf too many times around her friend's neck and chaffing her gloved hands as they walked down the lane. She was in a good mood but just a bit too bright, and the way she lavished physical attention on Olive made her wonder what was up.

Far off they could hear the uneven throb throb throb of a bomber's engine – the enemy's, not their own – and stood listening until it faded. A dog barked, and a voice from a blacked-out house nearby told the animal to pipe down.

Olive and Evelyn walked on, looking for the glimmer lights that marked the front door to the public house.

'It's bloody dark,' Evelyn observed, as thousands before her must have, and Olive was just thinking how dark it was when her foot connected with someone's porch step. She pitched forward and fell – clumsy with the burden of gas mask and winter coat – the heel of her left hand scraping over the uneven stone of a cottage wall and her right arm taking the weight of her momentum. She howled, and a door opened just by her head, the blackout-curtain flipping aside for a second.

'I think she might have broken it,' Evelyn told the person who'd come out into the street.

Olive heard a man's voice say, 'Let's help her down the road a bit.' She thought, *he wants to get rid of me, the unchristian sod*, but then he went on to say, 'The doctor's always in the pub evenings.'

Olive's arm was hot, and not answering to her. Evelyn propped her up as they walked the last stretch, her arm around Olive's shoulders.

'Bloody hell,' said Olive, 'it's bloody dark.' But then they came into the light and noise and warmth of the pub, at which point she began to feel better. The man who'd come out of the house that tripped her had his ARP helmet on, and the look of a man meant to be somewhere else. He put his face too near hers and asked, 'You alright love?' then patted the unhurt arm. 'I'll be back in a mo' to see how you are.'

After propping her on a stool, Evelyn leaned over the counter to ask the publican which of the drinkers was the doctor, and he nodded at a tall man at the inside corner of a booth otherwise filled with farming folk. The room was spectacularly empty of khaki and blue and Olive's uniform drew so many looks that Evelyn had caught the doctor's eye even before she'd got to his table.

'You've made a job of this,' he said, massaging Olive's arm just below the elbow.

'Shouldn't you have a bag?' she asked, raising her perpetually arched right eyebrow higher than usual.

'I don't need a bag to see you've gone and broken your arm walking about in a blackout.'

'But we had to walk about to get here.'

'Should have been more careful then.'

The doctor wanted to pass her off with a splint but was convinced (by a fiver from Evelyn) to take them to his practice, where he mixed the plaster of Paris and properly set the bone. All the while he went on about 'his pint' as if they couldn't have done with one.

Back at the pub Evelyn put a double whisky into Olive's hand. 'That's you off for a while,' she said.

Olive thought that might be the case. She would have to ring the squadron officer to get her advice. While there were lighter duties, too many routines on a bomber station required personnel to be able-bodied. Gas drill with one arm would be laughable, if not impossible, and it might be difficult to dress let alone kit out complete with tin-hat and gas mask. No, thought Olive, feeling the full effect of the whisky, she had a good stretch of leave coming – longer than she'd see under ordinary circumstances.

It was arranged for Olive to report to the nearest RAF station, Upavon, where the opposite number of her squadron officer would authorise her leave. From there she could hop a lift back along Devizes Road to Collingbourne. In the end Evelyn drove her both ways, eking out the petrol she'd need to get back to the White Waltham Ferry Pool, from whence she planned to cadge a delivery flight back to Hamble.

Olive had her signed and counter-signed leave papers safely stowed in her jacket pocket and was wondering – as she looked out the rain-spotted car windows at the view – what on earth she'd do at Ida's for a month, when Evelyn said, 'You could stay with me. Aud's room will be free, and I'm sure we can find you a seat in the Anson for the trip down.'

When she'd got no response from her friend she added, 'Ida won't mind, and you'd be bound rigid if you stayed here.'

Olive couldn't argue with the fact that she'd be bored, but she thought Ida *would* mind – lonely and out of sorts with the war as she was. Still, she didn't contradict Evelyn, who was frowning out at the road.

'Where will Audrey be?' Olive asked.

'With her husband in London. Now that he's got a War Office job she's packing it in.'

Olive imagined it would be a struggle living off two ration books, in a place totally unfamiliar to her, and with her arm in a cast. She'd have to housekeep, as she would be the one home all day while Evelyn was off delivering aircraft hither and yon. *A silly idea all round*, Olive thought as she looked out at the bare branches of the trees bordering the lane.

She spread her fingers on the empty stretch of seat between herself and Evelyn, and stuck out her lower lip in a pout. 'You explain to Ida then.'

Evelyn turned to glance at her and, laying her arm along the top of the bench seat, said, 'Don't you worry about a thing.'

Chapter Twelve

Chop girl

By the time Olive arrived at Hamble, Spring was overdue and although she didn't yet know it, Duncan and Lofty had finished gunnery school, embarked at Halifax, crossed the Atlantic, and disembarked in the south-west of Scotland.

And William – in a ship not forty miles off the Southampton docks – was applying for leave, Olive's telegram in hand. Hamble was handy to Southampton, and the war had finally brought them together.

His reply read: *Coming. STOP. Will call about arrival. STOP. Can't wait.*

Evelyn arranged a room for William at the Royal Southern Yacht Club, where he would be within walking distance of their cottage on the hill above the village. She made clear that this was just one option – he was welcome to stay in the cottage if that suited better. Leaving Olive little to do, she cleaned, queued with the ration book at the butcher shop and, when the wait came to nothing there, made whispered phone calls to a friend who knew the black market. The weather had been bad for several days since Olive's arrival, and there'd been no flying. Evelyn was at a loose end but one that she warned would soon be tied, and for some duration. Mucky weather created a backlog of planes that would need immediate shifting, and since nothing happened immediately, the shifting might take some time. She'd be away from home for several days and Olive – she said, waving around her at the sitting room she'd just cleaned – would have the house to herself. There was butter, and bread and jam just bought. There was a cigar (still in its wrapper) and two fingers worth of brandy in the decanter, should William want it. To cap this, Evelyn promised someone would be round with a roast of beef, and Olive was not to wait for her to return to cook it.

So comprehensive was Evelyn's generosity and so definite her desire to make herself scarce that Olive felt a growing dread at the prospect of William's arrival, and Evelyn's departure. All she could think was that *she* wasn't prepared, no matter what the state of the house and larder. And God only knew what she was going to talk to William about, and what they'd end up doing with all that space and privacy.

So, the evening before William was due to arrive, Olive sat glumly in her chair by the fire and watched Evelyn going over her handling notes. She kept them carefully stacked in the satchel she took on flights, along with the parachute, logs and chits, so there was never room in the cockpit for more than one small bag of clothes in which she had packed bloomers and slacks, a single shirt and woollen jumper. Her scarf and gloves sat on the chesterfield next to her, and her coat was thrown over the back of it.

She looked ready to leave at a moment's notice, although they had the whole night. William would not arrive before noon, at the earliest.

Olive came over to sit beside her on the couch. The notes she had open before her were on the Walrus, an amphibious craft. She'd never flown one, and any new aircraft had foibles in the air or on the ground that the notes would try – and only very occasionally fail – to convey.

'Are you nervous?' Olive asked, because Evelyn seemed to be – was pulling agitatedly at the one curl she tended not to lacquer.

'Of course not,' she said. She put the booklet down and tapped its spine with her forefinger. 'Not so long as I have these. But aren't you nervous about William?' When Olive blushed, Evelyn looked away, twisting the lock of hair more tightly about her forefinger. 'You must be excited.'

'Certainly.' Even to Olive's ears that sounded non-committal, so she added, 'It's a relief to have him safe from the sea.'

'You should make the most of the time you have.'

Olive looked hard at the side of Evelyn's face; saw the pulse at her throat working its slow magic under the skin. 'As should we.'

'We've got bags of time yet. I promise we'll do something nice next weekend – get ourselves to Southampton to look at the bomb damage.' As she spoke she gathered up her books, stacking them so that the edges were even, the Walrus notes on top. 'Off to bed for me then,' she said, closing the lid of the satchel and putting it next to the little bag with her clothes and toothbrush in it. 'I have an early start.'

'But it's just past eight!' Olive protested.

'I fancy a read in bed. It's always warmer under the covers than it is down here. Warmer still for two.' At the word 'two' her eyes swept up to Olive's.

A blush rose on the younger woman's cheeks and – this time – did not retreat. 'I don't know what you're talking about,' Olive said. Evelyn blinked at the evasion, and – masking a yawn – stretched so that the hem of her blouse was pulled out of the waistband of her trousers. It hung askew beneath her cardigan.

She told Olive not to be obtuse. 'Mind you,' she added, 'we've got by for years not saying what's on our minds.' She stood clutching the wing-rest of the armchair, anchored by it. One finger tapped the fabric. 'How am I to be persuaded to stay up for another hour? What entertainment do you have in mind?'

'We could play Ludo,' Olive suggested weakly after a moment.

Laughing, Evelyn let go the chair and came towards her, bending so swiftly that Olive pushed back against the cushions of the settee in alarm.

'I'm just kissing you goodbye,' she said, and slipping a cool palm over the nape of Olive's neck, and nestling the ball of her thumb just beneath her ear – she lifted Olive's face to her own. Olive caught the scent of her lipstick: beeswax and pencil lead. Then she turned aside.

'The fire,' Olive said, and jumped up to stir the coal in the grate, rolling the lumps until red showed through the skin of ash. When she looked back Evelyn had gone. She heard the bedroom door close with a solid thump.

William called from the Southampton docks to say he was going to try to hitch a lift, but he might have to walk some of the way. Olive gave him the best directions she could. He sounded younger on the phone than she remembered.

The wait was excruciating, and there was nothing for her to do to fill it. The housework had been done and she'd prepared the tea things, banked the fire and put a warming iron in the bed of the guest bedroom in case (she told herself) William needed a kip when he got in. So she sat down and wrote letters in an ugly left-handed scrawl: one to Duncan, with a note to Lofty appended, and a page to her father telling of her broken arm. She was just starting a letter to Ida when the doorbell rang.

Olive took a quick look in the hall mirror before going to answer the door and saw a pale face with dark smudges under its eyes. And the auburn had vanished from her curls. Whether this was from age, a wartime diet or English weather she couldn't tell. Her hair was brown and nondescript – just as she was.

'I'll just have to do,' she thought, neatening her lipstick. After smoothing her dress and checking that the seams of her stockings were straight (black-market, a gift from Evelyn) she opened the door.

William had his kitbag over his shoulder and was smiling at

her in a way she'd quite forgotten she liked. Still his hair stood in those unruly dark waves, and he was no more able to grow a beard to go with his moustache than he'd been a year before.

He stood kneading his cap until she moved aside for him to enter. At the bottom of the stair they bumped into one another, and there was a farce of 'You first' and 'After you' until finally she led him to his room and showed him where to put his bag. Then there was the embarrassment of the bed to contend with: its covers neatly – enticingly – laid back. They were out of there quickly. Leading William towards the parlour Olive faltered and went on to the kitchen – a place as neutral as Switzerland.

She put an egg on for him, and had poured the water into the teapot before either of them said anything.

Then he asked, *Flying is she?* and she said *When there's weather like this they're always on the go.*

Better than yesterday, he said.

She agreed and tapped the top of his egg with a knife before setting it down in front of him. 'It's soft you like, isn't it?'

'Anything other than powdered, and I count myself lucky.' He fell to eating and they were spared having to talk. After demolishing the egg and three pieces of toast with jam he pushed his plate away, but before she'd had a chance to reach for it, he'd carried it to the sink, rinsed, and set it on the draining board.

'I haven't been able to do that for a while. I like being back in a kitchen.'

He leaned comfortably against the bench with his ankles crossed.

'There's a fire in the sitting room,' Olive said.

'Righto then.'

By then, William had seen the whole of the house, missing only the WC. Olive now waved at this as they passed. In the overly warm sitting room William sat next to Olive on the settee; making his presence all the more definite by picking up the fingers of the hand protruding from its cast and holding them on his calloused palm.

'Does it hurt much?' he asked.

'It itches like mad. I've been using Audrey's knitting needles to scratch, so *now* it hurts.'

He laughed. 'Sounds like someone should keep an eye on you – stop you playing with sharp objects.'

'I can crack nuts with it.' Olive hefted the cast to show him how. 'It makes a mess of walnuts though.'

He was laughing heartily, just as he used to do when she'd dance her victory jig after a win at suicide gin. Olive was so pleased she'd amused him that she leaned over and kissed him on the cheek, which only stopped his laughing.

'There's a room for you at the Royal Yacht Club but you might as well stay.' This came out in a rush, after which Olive looked down at her lap. 'There won't be talk since no one knows I'm here.'

'Olive – '

'It's what I *want*.' As she said this she saw it was true – truer now than it had been when they kissed on the steps of the Tivoli. Of course she wanted William to make love to her: why wouldn't she? If they had allowed themselves to get properly involved she might have been spared her subsequent doubts. Olive was suddenly annoyed at him for being so gentlemanly.

Upstairs in the room they'd fled a few minutes before the two disrobed in nervous silence. Olive got under the covers and pushed the lukewarm heating iron to the bottom of the bed with her foot. William sat on the side of the bed, his back to her, struggling to put on one of the rubbers he'd had the foresight to bring. She concentrated on the delicate hollows at either side of his spine above each muscled buttock; comforted by his lack of expertise in what she imagined had, for many, become a reflex task.

Her broken arm felt lumpish and unromantic, so she tidied the sheet over it, wishing it were a prosthesis she could detach for the duration. Then William got under the covers and she had to forget about her arm.

It was a narrow bed, and although there was no room for reserve, he seemed to be holding himself as far away from her as he could. Still she could feel the weight and heat of his thing pushing against her thigh. It fascinated her more than any other part of him – even his face, the prominent sinews in his neck, and his slightly shaking shoulders could not compete. It bumped towards her hand like something with an independent purpose. He groaned, and as he bared his teeth his narrow top lip hitched on his single long eyetooth, and dimpled. Everything she did with her hand she saw immediately expressed in his not-quite-handsome face, and she wished they could do without the prophylactic.

He leaned over her on shaking arms, and his face was hidden from her as he looked down the length of his body to check that the rubber was still secure. When he'd satisfied himself that it was, he let the weight of his lower body down on her, arching his back so that his erection pressed into her stomach. She reached down to re-position him, but when she touched his penis he groaned suddenly and pushed against her, his whole torso quivering. Something had clearly happened.

His forehead, leaning just below her right breast, was damp and heavy.

'I wanted to be careful.' He said this to her ribs as she stroked the back of his head.

'Yes,' Olive replied, her lips gluey. They lay for a while like that, William stroking her good arm. They must both have dozed, because when Olive next spoke the candle had burned down two inches.

She asked whether William had another rubber. He started and looked up at her.

'I want you to try again,' she said.

He blinked. His hair had come out of its waves into sweaty curls, and he shook these in puzzlement.

'That's what prophylactics are for – ' Olive went on, ' – to make it safe to go *inside*.'

William got out of bed to rummage in his kit for the rubber. This one he put on as shyly, if more quickly, than the last.

The second time they made love Olive held him and again watched his face fill and change, but it seemed to her that he was keeping part of himself aloof, watching her, and when she'd guided his penis, and wriggled her hips experimentally to find the best position to take it, he'd looked amazed – as if she was about to burst into flame, or evaporate into thin air.

When it hurt her William would stop, or shift his weight, always muttering 'sorry' as he did so. They were both sweating, and when finally they detached from one another Olive saw that the surface of her cast had gained a white stippling of something that looked like mould.

'Oh no, I got the plaster wet,' she cried, and set about drying it with a sheet. Then she noticed that William had white smudges all over his left side and upper arm, and she swiped at those too. 'I hope I haven't done any damage,' Olive said, and his eyebrows shot up. 'To the cast,' she added, waving the white wedge, and he looked relieved.

After enduring a long few moments of William peering at her, Olive closed her eyes and felt him relax in turn. Soon he was dozing lightly against her shoulder. She knew he needed the rest but she was sorry to be left alone with her thoughts. As soon as it was dark she slipped out of bed, put on her dressing-gown and went downstairs to the kitchen to wash – as she and Evelyn customarily did – at the sink.

The fires had gone out – the whole downstairs was damp with cold and smelled of coaldust and, inexplicably, cabbage. After staring at the sitting room grate in consternation, she cleared the ash away and picked through the wood piled beside the fireplace – much of this was damp and refused to burn and since she knew they had to be frugal with coal she didn't know what to do to get it going. It was Evelyn who'd set the fire each morning. Not since Ida's had Olive had to start fires, cook dinners, or clean, and she was at that moment too tired to learn over what once had been second nature. She sat crying, in the dark, making herself colder by the minute.

Olive knew she'd have to get the fire lit, or go back to bed with William. And even if she could not warm the living room, the kitchen stove would need heating. They had to eat sometime – three bits of toast and an egg would already have taken William as far as it could.

After a few more earnest attempts she managed to get the stove going, and heated herself some milk hoping it would help her sleep. She heard the lavatory door shut, then, a minute later, the roaring complaint of its flush. William came to stand in the doorway in his pyjamas and robe.

'Is there anything up for tea?'

She was sitting at an empty table; an empty stovetop behind her. An explanation seemed required. 'I didn't want to wake you.'

'I woke up because I was ravenous.' Two red buds of a blush rose on his cheeks for a second. 'Aren't you?'

Olive didn't know *what* she was but did gladly make herself busy with dinner. It was too late to put in the roast, she explained, but that meant they'd have something to look forward to tomorrow. Clumsy with self-consciousness, she let the onion she'd pinioned with her cast roll off the chopping board. William chased it to the skirting board then made a show of bowling it overarm into the sink. They smiled at each other then and for a while everything was easier: eating, conversation, the hand of cards she made him play and even his leading her back to bed just as the clock chimed eleven – nine o'clock; double summer time at the fag end of winter.

That night the Luftwaffe bombed the Southampton docks and Olive stood with her face pressed to the frigid glass of the window, the blackout curtain folded around her like a second robe, watching the searchlights from the AA batteries to the east and west of the city meet where the German bombers were. At times she could see the serrated stone top of the tower of St Andrews lit by the glow of the burning docks or the swing of a searchlight and once or twice she could even pick out the dark lines of the masts of the yachts at the Royal Yacht Club against a much lighter sky.

She was dispirited, but not by the bombardment. Her stomach felt light, and somehow wrong, and it was not the air-raid siren that had woken her – she'd been shocked out of sleep by the wayward conviction that she might be – must surely be – pregnant. Behind her in the bed William slept on. He was used to worse dins than these. Sometimes, on quiet nights at shore, he had told her, he would wake up panicked, thinking the ship's engines had stopped.

She stood by the window, after the all-clear's sounding, until there was nothing but dark at the glass. Even in two pairs of woollen socks her feet were freezing, and the water in the jug by the basin was already forming a thin skin of ice. She knew it would be cold tomorrow and she'd need to be more efficient with the fires. With that thought she finally went back to bed.

They had three days together. Despite the cold, they walked, and when they were not walking, read, or listened to the radio. Conscription had been extended to women, and even voluntary services like the Home Guard and Civil Defence had been made compulsory. The radio gave them notice of this or that new duty, or scarcity, and they were exhorted – even by the evening's bill of popular songs – to save better and work harder.

The Americans were not about to rescue England and her Dominions despite their having joined the war. As he told her over their last glass of brandy, it didn't matter how much the United States War Production Board rolled out of America's factories or farms if ships kept going down in the Atlantic. William knew all about ships going down in the Atlantic and when he walked off down the hill, kitbag on his shoulder, Olive watched him go and wondered if that knowledge might get him through. Perhaps if he saw enough, it wouldn't happen to him.

But of course it did.

Chapter Thirteen

Gossip

Evelyn had been home a week when Olive found out, by chance, that she'd not been off the aerodrome ferrying Spitfires from one tiny grass field to another during William's visit. At the end of each day's flying she'd be lounging in the well-warmed sitting room of the aerodrome mess and, later, walking to the house of a fellow pilot. Olive discovered this when she overheard two of the other female ferry pilots talking as they wheeled their bicycles over the cobbled lane that fronted the grocer shop, the thinly stocked shelves of which she'd come to search for a tin of salmon.

They were wondering – and not quietly – what was up with Evelyn Macintyre, and why she'd not gone home the weekend before.

'Well, she did break up with that girlfriend of hers,' said one.

The other girl, a brunette with tight curls around a too-wide face, stood on the pedal to bump over the stones for a yard or two, then turned back to her friend.

'If she's fancy-free she could have made a pass at home.

Perhaps it didn't work and she was asked to sleep out. Those types can be trouble. I couldn't live with one.'

The other girl shrugged at this and they walked on up the road, palms flat and fingers splayed on the seats of their bicycles.

Olive stood under the grocer's faded marquee, her back to the forming queue, clutching her shopping bag too tightly. It was not until an older woman touched her elbow and told her she'd miss out that she roused herself to join the queue.

'You're very quiet,' said Evelyn that night when she switched off the wireless.

'I was listening.' Olive nodded at the light fading on the dial, then picked up her book and passed Evelyn the newspaper. Evelyn made no move to read it.

'You're worried about William.'

'Yes,' Olive said. Worry was everyone's *fait accompli*, and she felt able to discuss it. 'And about Duncan,' she added.

They'd neither of them had a letter from Duncan, and Olive imagined him somewhere out on the Atlantic, perhaps at the exposed edge of a convoy. Duncan and William both at sea. Olive called their faces into mind, but no sooner had she done so than her imagination veered off to conjure spots of flame on the Southampton docks and two women pushing their bikes up the hill, gossiping. A pulse began to beat behind her right eye and this made reading so uncomfortable that she sat with the book in her lap as if the words might launch themselves off the page of their own volition.

She had told Evelyn that William had stayed at the cottage. Her friend had merely nodded at this; had neither fussed nor pried. And now she knew what lengths Evelyn had gone to – she had put herself out to give them time alone together. Olive couldn't decide whether this was from selflessness or something more awkward – the sort of thing she'd read about in novels of sensation, books in which the stepmother connives with the seducer in the daughter's deflowering. Perhaps Evelyn thought a sexual assignation was what Olive needed – after all, she'd intimated as much before.

Evelyn flicked through the pages of the newspaper.

'They've added rolled oats to the points ration,' she said, moistening her finger to turn the page. 'And they're threatening to do something drastic to conserve the wheat supplies.' She looked up at Olive as if she was peering over bifocals. 'What kind of drastic do they mean, I wonder. Stockpiling? Or blending the flour with sawdust?'

When her friend didn't answer she went back to scanning the columns.

Furious at Evelyn, and in an attempt to make sense of the feeling, Olive said, 'You didn't need to slope off and stay with someone else on the weekend. That makes me feel like I've had a dirty little affair.'

Evelyn put the paper gently down and folded her stockinged feet up under herself. Her expression was mild, even a fraction remote. 'I was trying to let you get on with things, and if I'd said I was going to stay with someone else it might have made you even more self-conscious. You'd practically jittered apart at the prospect as it was.' Then, in the voice she'd used as an instructor, she added, 'It's easier to make consequential decisions when they're not surrounded by clutter. Too many people in the house or the need to consider other people's motives – that's clutter.'

Under the press of her emotion, Olive's hazel eyes had deepened to the green they'd been when the two of them were young; when – for a year or so – they had seemed accountable only to each other. 'If circumstances had been different I mightn't have had to make a decision,' Olive said. 'You might have made it easier for me by being here.'

'Oh to believe you mean something by that,' Evelyn replied, and looked out the window. 'Whatever the case, my being here wouldn't have made it easier for William.' With that she tilted her paper back to the firelight and appeared to read.

It was a minute or two before Evelyn looked up again. Olive was crying, noiselessly, head down. The pale cotton bib of her dress was already spotted with tears. Evelyn came to kneel by her chair, picking up her good hand and squeezing it – which only made Olive all the more woeful.

'Olive – ' whispered Evelyn. 'If I did the wrong thing, I'm sorry.'

But Olive shook her head. That wasn't it.

'Do you feel bad about what's happened? About the weekend, I mean?'

She shook her head at that too, thinking it unfair to William that she should feel bad.

'Then why are you crying?'

Olive didn't really know why she was crying, but said, 'Because I wasn't very much fun for him and – ' she steadied her voice, ' – he deserved better.' Only after she'd said it did she wonder whether it was true. Who but the undiscriminating sat in a cold kitchen, weeping, when they could have been in a warm bed? Even her misery now was proof of her unfitness as a lover.

'I'm sure that whatever you feel happened is quite different from what he thinks. I'd be very surprised if you'd done anything less than delight him. And if you didn't it was because the leave was so shockingly short. A 72 is hardly conducive to a person throwing themselves into a situation body and soul.' Sighing, Evelyn joggled the hand she was holding. 'These aren't things you can worry about. You'd be better off predicting the drastic measures around grain conservation. Really.'

Olive fished out a handkerchief and blew noisily into it.

'There you go,' Evelyn said, and pushed the damp hair back from her friend's face. 'William is lucky to have you,' she added, but Olive was blowing her nose and did not hear her.

While Olive composed herself Evelyn rooted about in the cupboards of the sideboard. She came back carrying the Ludo board.

'Pity we don't have a third,' she said, looking into the box at the brightly coloured counters.

'And a fourth.'

At that, Evelyn's mouth tightened at the edges.

When Olive received a letter from Anne Battersby describing the bother of being stationed in Bournemouth, and the constant lectures about hygiene aimed to keep the nursing staff away from the thousands of men passing through the town, she did not picture Duncan and Lofty among them. But the trainee gunners were already there by the time a letter from Duncan arrived – the first he'd sent from shore, written as he sat at a trestle-table in one of the warehouses at the Glasgow docks, served tea and scones by Red Cross ladies whose accents he could not understand.

He wrote nothing about the voyage, except that they'd been anxious. Instead it was, *I'm halfway through Hugo now, lucky me!* And, *we're off to Bournemouth.* The letter ended with the complaint that everybody was to get disembarkation leave but the gunners, who were *desperately needed.*

Olive got her letter before Evelyn, who didn't seem too bothered. Perhaps she didn't want to have to deal with any more revelations of the type slipped into the letter from Winnipeg. Bournemouth, Duncan wrote, was an unending round of church parades and lectures. The urgency of the needs of the RAF didn't seem to be in evidence.

A letter from Lofty quickly followed. Duncan's friend described Free from Infection inspections by the Committee for *Pubic* Safety. The gunners avoided these by going out walking to the barricaded beach with its tank entrapments. There were mines in the sand and – he'd heard – a courting couple had been blown to bits the week before. Not to mention the drain on wandering dogs that nobody but Duncan seemed to worry about.

The letter's tone was morose. Lofty had heard that the production of bombers had got so out of control, the workers so hard pressed, that when the bomb aimer on a newly delivered Stirling opened the bomb-bay doors over Bremen a sleeping factory worker fell out with the incendiaries. *Gives a new meaning to the term 'shiftwork'*, he wrote.

Olive wondered what people thought of Lawrence Hilliers. The censors didn't seem to mind him – his letters had curiously few marks of the blue pencil, and the only excisions were the writer's work: blots and scours of second-thoughts that made a mystery of every page. There seemed to be something Lofty wasn't saying, but since *he'd* chosen to write to *her*, Olive thought he ought to get on with it, and write what he meant.

In her last week at Hamble, she found that the number of letters she was getting from Lofty exceeded those from Duncan. But she was none the wiser for it.

Evelyn was the first down in the mornings, and she'd fetch the post, and Olive's cup of tea, and then go back upstairs to plump Olive's pillows so that her friend could sit, nestled in their warmth, while she pulled both sets of drapes aside.

Then, looking at the window, Evelyn would pronounce on the weather. Clear, she'd say, or, clear enough, and if there was cloud there'd be a number, 'It might break at 900' or, 'The ceiling's down to 200'. Her days were ruled by such numbers and she liked to test them on her tongue. Meanwhile Olive would be testing the tea. This was as sweet and white as the girls taken prisoners by pirates in the books she'd been reading, daily, since coming to Hamble – row upon row of Victorian adventure tales had been left on the shelves by the owners of the house when they were put out by wartime requisitioning. She read the heroic adventures of boys from Eton who'd found themselves in the Sudan, or whichever hot and difficult place bred bravery in the better sort like mould on week-old bread.

One of those books would be sitting on her night-table, next to her waterglass, each morning Evelyn measured the clear air, and if the assaying was lower than 800 (ferry pilots could not fly if the cloud were lower than that) Olive would take up her book. If higher, she would get up, because Evelyn would be gone all day, and not home until late, and breakfast would be the only meal they'd share.

One morning, in her last week at Hamble, Olive saw Evelyn slip a letter into the pocket of her dressing-gown: an envelope of the sort then becoming scarce as razor blades, or rouge. Marjorie's stock of blue paper. Needless to say, she did not break open the blue envelope at the breakfast table, but read instead from a long letter sent by her mother.

One of the house cats had been found poisoned, and Mrs Macintyre was wondering whether she should tell Duncan.

'Of course she should tell him,' Evelyn said. 'If he can't deal with the death of a house cat he shouldn't be where he is now.'

'That's a bit rough. They're altogether different things.'

'What rot. You forget he's training to be a vet: they don't just motor about doing acts of charity and kindness to animals. He has to be hard-headed about things.'

Olive bit each corner off her slice of toast and thought about that. There was a difference, even if Evelyn couldn't see it. Hard-headedness was a prerequisite for action – but a good many things happen over which people have no control, and take no part. Once, during a flash flood at the farm one of the Macintyres' working dogs had been swept to a sandbar in the middle of the creek. The children watching could see that the islet wouldn't last long, particularly as the agitated dog kept scrabbling at the soft edges. Duncan had run back to fetch a stout rope, and then he'd gone in, the water foaming around his shoulders and back, and over the black nose of the pup as he'd carried her safely back through the swollen creek. Later that same day Mr Macintyre rode out to check the flood damage on the property. His horse had floundered, and fallen badly, and he had had to shoot it.

'Duncan doesn't need to know,' Olive said. 'You might think it's a fuss over nothing but I'd like to spare him what I can – even if it's only little things.'

Evelyn sighed and went back to the letter, this time reading silently.

When she'd folded it back into its envelope Olive said, 'So I see I'm not meant to read it.'

'What's got you in a spin?' But she asked this so remotely Olive could see her mood wasn't about the letter from home, but the one she'd slipped into her pocket on coming in from the hall.

Evelyn left the house not long after that, her boots crunching through the spring frost that had settled overnight on grass already burned brown from cold. Olive had the house to herself.

Although she knew that wartime had elevated snooping from a venal to a cardinal sin, she went upstairs to Evelyn's room. But the letter wasn't in the pocket of the robe Evelyn had thrown over the headboard of the bed, nor was it on the floor beneath it.

It was in the obvious place, as it turned out: in the drawer of the desk beneath the window, on top of a pile of envelopes, not all of which were of Marjorie's private stock. Some were the usual creamy-yellow pulp issued in stores, and canteens, at every station across the country. Olive was pleased to see that Marjorie had had to make do like everyone else. Then, she almost shut the drawer to go downstairs – but she wanted to know what Evelyn's relationship with Marjorie was like: whether they used pet names; had anniversaries, and aspired to the domestic routines of peacetime. She wanted to know how closely the relationship of a normal man and woman might be mimicked.

So she sat on Evelyn's bed and read all of Marjorie's letters, the last first, and then the earliest, skipping through the family news, the descriptions of who'd worn what to the hunting meet, and the bureaucratic saga of Marjorie's attempts to get approval to stable her roan mare near Waltham. She was clearly worried that the horse would not be safe during the months of the blitz when bombs did fall in, but also around, Waltham.

But in the main Marjorie's letters expressed only two kinds of anxiety: frustration and embarrassment. If deeper feelings existed, the writer had not confided them to the page. Most of the letters' contents were indistinguishable from the chat exchanged by ordinary friends. If there was anything odd, or freighted, it was to be found in Marjorie fending off her correspondent's moods, enthusiasms and passions.

The letter that had been in Evelyn's dressing-gown pocket was less placatory than the rest:

March 21st, Waltham.

E –

You must understand that while I shall always be fond of you, a friendship will require a restraint on your part that I am not confident you possess. It's this doubt that has forced me to omit you from the guest list. I'm also painfully conscious of the fact that you've pleaded with at least half of our old friends to 'talk to me' – as if I was a morally wayward child to be schooled in some wiser course of action.

The fact is that the sort of affair we've had could not go on. Even you must know this. I wouldn't say that Matthew is my way of making sure that we both move on – that would be a dreadful watering down of how I feel, and a simplification. But he does make things easier. What you call *performing to expectations* is actually something much more basic than that – I want to be secure and comfortable. In times like this that's nearly impossible, and being with you – in times like this – entirely so.

It would be better for you if you understood this.

Take care,

M

After putting the letters away Olive went below stairs and sat on the couch, trying to banish the fact of her snooping to an immediate but nevertheless inaccessible past. It didn't help that she kept wondering about Evelyn's side of the correspondence, the side she'd not seen.

She knew she'd done a terrible thing. Intruding was bad enough, but spying was worse. Too agitated to read, she put on her coat and a pair of too large Wellingtons and sloshed out of the house and down the lane for a walk to the Yacht Club over fields sodden with spring thaw. Each day there were fewer yachts and more naval and coastal command craft. Olive watched the activity around the boats until she became conscious that she was visible from the lounge of the Club – the lounge frequented by ferry pilots. So she walked on to where the coastal track became too difficult to be negotiated in wellingtons, and stopped below seed buckthorn bushes still stubbornly in winter fruit. Gulls and great, grey-breasted fulmars wheeled threateningly about in the air above her head.

Olive wondered what might make the intrusion excusable, a lesser evil. Speaking aloud, she told the gulls, 'I was worried about Evelyn.' The wind pushed the words back at her. No, that wouldn't do. The truth was that she wanted evidence of her friend's suffering, and its cause; she wanted to know that the life Evelyn had chosen was wrong – a mistake.

Guilt made Olive insensible to the cold – indecisive – despite the fact that her one good hand had mottled red and white and, like the rest of her, needed to be taken back to the warm indoors. The wind from the sea made her eyes sting, and then begin to run, but she stood for as long as she could bear it, even longer, as penance.

Chapter Fourteen

Battle tactics

415732, Leading Aircraftman Macintyre, D

'A' Flight, 27 OTU, Lichfield

26 April, 1942.

Dear Olive,

We'll be here for a couple of months, and I'm hoping for some time off for a shufty around Birmingham – not much chop after London, but it's amazing what fun one can find in air-raid shelters. The good news is that we'll be crewing up here, and the CO has assured Lofty and me that we'll be crewed together as gunners. If only they'd told us that in Macdonald rather than leaving a note on our service records – someone can't have looked too hard at the files after Bournemouth because they separated us. For refresher training, no less, which was a bit on the nose. Either they thought we had brains the size of mice or that we'd been on the Atlantic so long we'd forgotten the business end of a Browning! Mess and sleeping quarters were arranged by nationality so Lofty went his way, and I mine. There was one hut for Canadians, one for South Africans, one for Kiwis etc. You can imagine what sort of atmosphere this created: if there'd not been an assortment of aircraft cluttering up the field we'd have had a rugby tournament. But they're not so hard-headed about things here. The major division seems to be by crew assignment, although I've noticed that the navigators and pilots get about together anyway. Gunners are pretty low on the pecking order but everyone is frightfully decent to everyone else as no one knows yet who they'll be relying on up there. We're none of us self-sufficient.

Anyway, it's off to bed for this gunner. There can't be many nights of ease left to me – we're bound to get our first night-flying in sometime in the near future. Oh, and did I tell you we're in Wellingtons? They're a bit long in the tooth now but perfectly serviceable. When I look at them I can see where the slang word 'kite' came from: Wimpys are a bit of doped cloth over a frame. They look like they'd float if you could find a bathtub big enough to put them in. Comforting thought that.

Did you get the ball I sent you? I bought it from a GI in Bournemouth. They're actually for making he-men out of pint-sized nothings but if you spend two hours a day squeezing it, your weak arm will be as good as new.

Hope you're well.

Your friend, Duncan.

Olive had a steady stream of letters that month from Lichfield – Duncan writing about training and life on Station, and Lofty airing whichever complaint was uppermost in his mind. In one letter he wrote to say that Maisie and Ethel were getting on nicely. She assumed this was a pair of friendly WAAFs until the following page made it clear that the two characters had been invented by a whimsical Lofty – Maisie had endured an attack from the gunnery leader on her buttons, and Ethel had failed to master the skill of 'knotting the compass'. In a scribbled postscript Lofty said she'd certainly hear more of Maisie and Ethel; and that it was only right she should – something had to exorcise the Boy's Own Adventures she'd read, and rattled on about, the month her arm was broken.

The number of letters dwindled once the crew started night-flying but Lofty did write to say he'd been scared witless on his first night flight as the mid-upper gunner in their Wellington. The darkness was so immense he found it hard to believe he'd ever be able to see anything unless they shot first and he saw the tracer. And if that was the way it was going to be, what point was there to anything? Lofty's next letter had no news in it at all, just an account of a dancing class in which Maisie and Ethel learned the 'Butterfly Corkscrew'. Lofty had drawn a little sketch with the caption 'ompapa-ompapa-ompapa' beneath it:

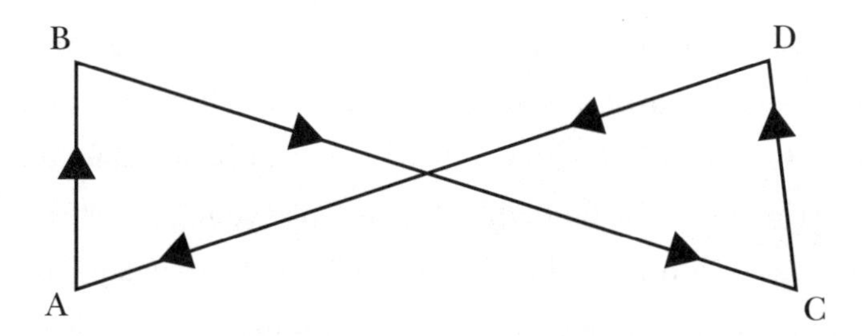

The thing that irked Maisie and Ethel about the Butterfly Corkscrew was that A-B-C-D-A was meant to put them back more or less where they'd started, except they kept finding other dancers in their place once they'd got there. So whenever they danced the Butterfly Corkscrew someone would end up having to leave the dance floor, even as the music went jauntily on.

Olive didn't have the foggiest what Lofty was on about until she got a letter from Duncan on the topic of battle tactics. If something iffy turned up the gunners were to tell the pilot to corkscrew to port, or to starboard. Jig the wrong way and you might collide with another plane in the bomber stream, or move into the sights of a fighter. The ultimate object was to jig about so much that the trailing fighter would lose patience and go find someone else to harass.

Such was the dance of the Butterfly Corkscrew, first step to last.

Olive liked Lofty's version better. She found it hard to imagine Maisie and Ethel at peril in the air.

When the time came, Lofty's grand plans about crewing-up unravelled. The best of the best found each other over breakfast at the mess or over a watery beer, and on that crucial morning in the hangar the elite stood chatting in companionable huddles while the rest of the flight drifted about like young people at their first dance, Duncan and Lofty among them. Olive imagined them leaning diffidently against some wall, waiting on all-comers, easy and self-contained. Something must have made the American pilot, with his navigator in tow, stride purposefully out of the milling crowd to ask the antipodean gunners to join his crew.

Duncan wrote: 'up came this Yank called Crowe, very smooth looking, and old, to ask us to crew *for* him. I could feel Lofty bridling beside me at the way it had been put and I thought, Bother this! I'm not going to have him blow it just because he's bolshie, so I said "Why not?" and shook the pilot's hand.'

With that buttoned-up, the four of them trawled for bomb aimer and wireless operator. It took them half an hour, but they found two men who were bright of eye and steady of hand; who had enough fat on their bones that they wouldn't be 'nervy', as Crowe put it. Duncan and Lofty had their crew.

Olive had to wait some time to hear more about the new crew, and when she did get a letter it was two days before she could open it, the paper being too wet to get the thing out of the envelope whole. A package of mail had slipped out of the waistband of her skirt as she rode from the Direction Finding Station back to the Waltham aerodrome, and the Waafery. She'd felt it go, so brought the bike to a skidding halt and fumbled around on the dark path, brushing through grass and mud and heaven knows what to find the wad of papers swelling in a none too fragrant puddle.

She collected the post for the four girls in her room, and they would kill her if they didn't get it. And there was a letter from Evelyn in the pile – she hadn't heard from her in a month, not since she'd left Hamble to get her cast off. Stowing the sodden mail in the face of her gas mask, Olive rode on down the dark lane while the bombers on the battle order for that night roared overhead, one after the other, to join the stream. She pedalled quickly on, sliding through the turns in the lane as if it was lit and the ground beneath her dry.

For the next few days the letters lay on a strip of carpet where the sun might catch them, and if it was cloudy, the bar heater was turned on and the envelopes turned and tended by whichever girl was off-shift. So Olive eventually came back to quarters to find her three letters – the paper crimped, and the ink on one badly bled – laid out on the foot of her bed.

Evelyn was on notice that she might be at Hamble only a few more months. Spitfire production was levelling out and the transport of bombers was a more pressing concern. By winter she hoped to be at no. 1 Ferry Pool at White Waltham. She'd already had the promise of a cottage to share at Waltham St Lawrence, and wrote that she'd not be sorry to see the back of the Hamble ferry pool, nicknamed the 'Bloomsbury Group' of the service. Olive thought of the two women with bicycles outside the Hamble grocer and wasn't surprised.

Beneath Evelyn's stories of aerodromes left and arrived at, barrage balloon placements suddenly shifted, and the tribulations of weather, Olive sensed tiredness and frustration. But when she unpicked page from crimped page of the final letter to find one whole section blotted and unreadable, Evelyn's misery had to be intuited from the one line legible. This was not the usual polite 'And how are *you*?' but 'Have you seen anything of Marjorie?'

Olive had not seen Marjorie. No one had. She'd been granted leave for her wedding, and for a brief honeymoon. So in her reply she glossed the question completely, running on about films and dances and gossip from the station, and spending one long paragraph retelling Ida's news: the Spitfire that bounced on the thatching of a neighbour's roof, ruining it, and the less dramatic matter of the Collingbourne Kingston Bakery having finally closed. 'Poor Ida – ' she wrote, 'no more crossing the road in the hope of a scone.'

By the time Olive did see Marjorie her broken arm had filled out; was no longer fish-white and puny, and she had given up being ginger with it. It was early morning – they were expecting the bombers back and Olive's set had gone on the blink. She was sorting through the resistors for what she suspected was a dead cell, solder and coil of flex at the ready beside her, when she heard Marjorie's nanny-bred drawl. As Olive turned to have a look her world wavered. She could smell burning hair, and her arm ached all the way up to the shoulder.

The Flying Control Officer caught her by the elbow, saying 'What dog? You're mad woman!' and bellowed for someone to bring a cup of tea, then he steered her out of the office to prop her at the rail, overlooking dispersal. It was dawn, and the flare path was changing colour, losing its green hue.

'You've had a shock,' the Flying Control Officer said. When she just stared at him he harrumphed and went back into the tower, passing her on to the WAAF nearest to hand. It was Marjorie, then, who came to press a steaming mug of tea into her hand.

'That could have been nasty,' Marjorie said diffidently. Olive thought of the hundred or so times she'd been told to make sure that there was no current running into the R/T unit before unscrewing any of its facings, or examining its parts. She had muffed the simplest, most commonsensical rule of her work, and would have felt awful about it had the idea that the dog needed feeding not kept getting in the way. She waved a hand around looking for a bowl until Marjorie, amused, reached out to stop her.

'I should sit down for a minute if I was you.' Then, knowing very well they had to keep the area at the doors clear, and that chairs could not be left out, Marjorie added, 'The steps will do for now.' She patted the wood to check whether it was too cold, or wet. Olive thought how good it was having her there: she blocked the wind, which was – at that time of morning – still fresh.

'You got married.' Olive's voiced sounded dull to her own ears, as if her skull had thickened.

'If that's congratulations, thanks.'

'You're welcome. Oh bother,' Olive said, feeling stupid. 'That's not what I meant.' She took a sip of tea. It was very sweet, and hot. 'I mean it was unexpected. That you got married.'

'Delightfully so.' Marjorie laughed, and when she shook her head Olive caught the sharp smell of the chemicals they'd used on her permanent wave. 'Would you like to see a picture?'

Olive should have guessed that Marjorie's husband was aircrew – and since she knew the face in the photograph, was on squadron nearby. He wasn't exactly handsome, and must have been a good ten years Marjorie's senior.

'Matthew's hoping to get his wings,' his wife said, tapping the brevet in the photo. 'It was flight engineer or ground duty.'

'I hope you'll be very happy.' Olive handed the photo back and Marjorie slipped it into the pocket of her jacket where it would be within easy reach.

'Do you have one?'

Still muddled, she for a minute thought Marjorie meant cigarette, but then she took out her identity card and opened it at the fold to show the passport-sized photograph of William she carried.

Looking from the photograph to her face Marjorie said, 'I wasn't at all sure you had a boyfriend. From what Evelyn said.'

'What did Evelyn say?' She was shocked that Evelyn had talked about her at all.

Marjorie couldn't reply immediately as the first of the returning aircraft came in for landing then, on one engine, lit by the luminescence of the flare it had dropped while circling the field. The two women watched the fire tender race along the ring road and out of sight. As there was no explosion the Wimpy must have come down safely, and others followed it in moments later. The air was throat-catching: fuel and sulfur from the flare blending with the smell of burning hair that Olive fancied was her own phantom addition to the stink.

It was too noisy for conversation so they leaned in the doorway of the Flying Control Office to watch the letters of the planes returning go up on the board. One flight from the squadron had sent five, the other six, and of that initial return, eight letters went up. In a couple of hours there might be a call from another aerodrome. Crews turned up in all kinds of places: Olive had even known one to make an 'emergency' landing at a field in the south-east of England so the navigator could visit his mother in the neighboring village.

They leaned in the doorway and no one bothered them. Olive began to feel invisible. She had fouled-up her duty for the morning and would have to explain herself to the squadron officer, but right at that moment there was nothing to be done about it.

'I'll walk you back to the Waafery,' Marjorie said, taking her elbow in as proprietary a manner as the Flying Control Officer had done. She inexpertly lit a cigarette, squinting at the smoke, and when she passed it over to Olive there was lipstick on the butt. Olive drew on it, and saw her hands were shaking.

'Can you manage your bike?'

'Not to ride, no.'

So they wheeled them along the track.

'What did you mean when you said Evelyn hadn't let on I had a boyfriend?'

'Evelyn wanted me to feel that she had options, and that mine was not the upper hand. She was not very subtle in that regard.'

Olive hoped that Marjorie wouldn't look at her but of course the other woman did glance up then, taking her in quickly, before looking back at the ground just before the bike's leading wheel. Olive was shocked by the indifference of that look, even if – a second before – indifference had seemed no challenge to her, and something for which she might be grateful in the circumstances.

'I don't know what you think – ' Olive said, because she'd begun to suspect she did.

'Evelyn told me about it. Your adolescent fling.' Marjorie sounded the sibilant in the last phrase derisively. 'Evelyn gave the impression that all you needed was a bit of prompting. To take up where you'd left off.' Her tone seemed to suggest that impressions were all Evelyn had to give.

Olive stopped walking, the bike cumbersome on the end of her aching arm. She swallowed a mouthful of bile.

Marjorie turned and, seeing her, laughed. 'I didn't credit it. A crush isn't indicative of anything.'

Olive understood that this was how Marjorie saw herself. She was putting distance between her girlhood and the concerns of the moment: war-work, a service marriage, daughterly duty, and the responsibilities of her class.

They walked the rest of the way back to the huts of the Waafery in silence, and Marjorie, blonde braids bouncing on her narrow back, went to show off her wedding photos to some more interested WAAF. There would be questions about the honeymoon, and the ceremony – normal questions that Olive hadn't thought to ask.

For a while she stood picking blackberries off the tangle of vines poking through the hawthorn hedgerows, the sun warm on the nape of her neck. She was not thinking of anything at all: there seemed to be a great deal of unoccupied space inside her, whole continents of it – her own little untouched world – and she felt if she could just keep standing there it would all spin onward forever. It was only when she was full of fruit, and had sucked what purple smudging she could from her fingers, that she went to her room. The bed was as she'd left it, the blanket pulled tight, and folded into hospital corners. On the deep half-oval of the windowsill above her bed sat a ceramic cat Duncan had sent from Canada, and a round grey stone she'd picked out of a creek bed in the Canobolas Valley and had carried 10,000 miles to Lincolnshire. She closed her fists around these sun-warmed shapes and lay on her bed listening to the hubbub of girls coming off-shift, and when someone poked their head around the door to ask whether they could borrow her curlers she pretended to be asleep, and – not long thereafter – actually was.

The next day Olive had to explain her laxity in servicing her set to a WAAF non-commissioned officer. Luckily the warrant officer was a mumsy sort who could be counted on to be merciful. She was lectured on the perils of inefficiency and then the warrant officer sat back in her chair to ask how Aircraftwoman Jamieson had been getting on generally.

She surprised herself by saying she'd like to transfer stations, and the WO nodded, knowingly, and told the young WAAF that while that sort of thing wasn't for the asking she'd see what she could do.

'This isn't – ' the WO asked, just as she had saluted and turned to go, ' – due to a man? Because that sort of trouble can be had at any station, and a change of scene might do less good than a change of attitude.'

'No ma'am,' Olive had replied, 'I have a fiancé in the merchant services.'

She was dismissed and went to fetch her bike for the ride to the control tower. At the bike rack, her dormitory room-mates, Joan and Maggie, stood waiting for her, a sprinkling of cigarette butts at their feet. They had clearly been there some time. Olive was still a few yards off when she saw the paper in Joan's hand – a single, greying, sheet.

Olive had seen scenes like that before: the waiting huddle of friends, the bad news gently broken. She had watched such exchanges as one might an avalanche on a distant mountain face – thankful not to be the one in its path. Now she was the one about to be swept up, and buried. It was her head the sky was falling on.

She was so sure it was Duncan, or Evelyn who'd died, that when Joan passed the telegram into her hand and she read that William Battersby was missing, presumed killed, the first thing that she felt was relief. Then her stomach lurched as she realised she'd just two or three minutes before used him as an excuse – the word fiancé tripping off her tongue, a lie so pat she'd not even noticed it.

She dropped the telegram, and the wind caught it. Maggie pinned it under her shoe, and then slipped it into her friend's pocket – as if it was a legal warrant, duly served.

'Let's go have a cup of tea,' Joan suggested, and they each took one of Olive's elbows and frog-marched her to the NAAFI to sit her at a table in the sun. Joan leaned across the counter to whisper to the girl from the Women's Voluntary Service, who nodded and looked over at Olive, just for a second, but long enough that she could guess what had been said.

She's had her telegram. (As if there was one for everyone).

Olive was holding her white utility teacup so hard that Maggie had to pry it out of her grip. After a bit she said she was ready to go on duty, and they walked her to her bike.

'Are you sure you're alright?' Joan asked, for form's sake as much as anything.

It was not until she came off watch that Olive was able to write to Anne Battersby. A short letter was all she could manage. She wrote that she hoped to see Anne soon, and that she'd be keen to hear any information she might get about the sinking of William's ship.

Sealing the sheet – its one paragraph of upright writing, the blue-black ink blotched where the nib of the pen had caught on rougher patches on the paper – Olive decided to walk to the postbox on Louth Road, near the neighbouring village of Holton Le Clay. She'd often strolled along the right-of-way that joined farm to farm, and village to village, following the narrow – sometimes nearly invisible – permissive paths that skirted woodland and pasture, and passing fields in which the wheat had grown tall. Some of the fields had now been ploughed under and flies rose off the turned soil to follow her. The blackberry at the side of the lane down which she walked lay in thickly banked, dusty ridges, giving off a rich molasses smell. But that afternoon she did not stop to pick any, nor did the pheasant lumbering into flight from the thick grass startle her. She walked on beyond the postbox, letter still in hand, to climb the stile that would take her north of the field towards Waltham village, and the windmill.

Servicemen and women at Waltham aerodrome had formed an attachment to the windmill, but none more so than the aircrews in their returning planes. Once they saw its slowly turning sails they felt they were safe, and home. For those approaching from the ground, rather than the air, it was likewise reassuring. Olive had never seen a windmill until she came to Lincolnshire – and to her it was an edifying piece of pastoral scenery. She'd walked to it practically every week since being stationed at Waltham. Now she could see the tops of the vanes as they rose over the copse of hazel trees and, as she got nearer, could hear its creaking. At the mill race she stopped to sit on the wall in the late sun. Back at the field, some cautious pilot on a pre-flight check was running up a Wimpy's engines – one of these fuel-starved from the sound of its coughing. There might still be time to see to the problem, and if there wasn't the aircraft would be grounded as unserviceable and the crew assigned to fly an alternate. Some pilot might now be cursing his thoroughness: had the problem come to light once they were airborne they'd have to turn back, and would be spared an operation. But that, too, had its drawbacks: early return meant a trip not counted, and a crew no nearer their magic number of thirty operations.

The crops in the field were blazing in the last of the sun, and she looked away to the dark brown water of the race. There'd been no magic number for William – not forty convoy escorts, twenty-five crossings of the Atlantic, fifty sightings of the barrage balloons of the Southampton docks on return to port. His crew had simply gone on until their ship was sunk, and the survivors assigned to other vessels. Those, too, might sink. And so it would go on.

When he'd visited at Hamble, William had told Olive about a nurse who'd survived the sinking of the *Titanic* only to die on the *Lusitania*. She could still hear him say, 'Who'd have that rotten luck?'

47,000 umbrellas,
26,000 pairs of gloves,
30,500 handbags,
48,000 tin hats,
73,741 allied aircrew,
25,000 merchant seamen.

Visit the Lost and Found. If you can correctly describe the item, it's yours.

Chapter Fifteen

Crew

The warrant officer was good to her word. Olive was granted a change of scene for her grieving, and was sent across the Humber, into East Yorkshire, to spend seven lonely months at Holme Upòn Spalding Moor. The Flying Control Office there was a particularly depressing one, done out desk to floor in a brown linoleum constantly polished by a crash tender crew left idle, as were the R/T operators, when no planes were nearby in the air. Sometimes after the crew had done their mopping and buffing Olive would take out the shove ha'penny board and they'd have a game to pass the time.

While at Holme, she saw none of her friends. She would have had to cross half of the country to get to Evelyn. And the hundred miles to Wiltshire, where Ida fretted, or to Lichfield, where the gunners were completing their final training, were distances she couldn't manage. What free time she had was spent walking the moors, or in the warmth of the hall at Market Weighton where picture shows were screened, and dances held for allied servicemen and women. Of that time Olive was to remember very little, detached as she was – an escaper's compass spinning at the end of duty's thread.

She did get letters, although the gunners' productivity declined after they were sent to 103 Squadron at Elsham Wolds, one of the many aerodromes just south of the Humber. Evelyn was more reliable. Mail from her came weekly, although the tone of her letters was pinched throughout winter as she lost patience waiting for the move to White Waltham and her conversion to 'heavies' – four-engine bombers, like the Stirling and Lancaster, with which scattered squadrons in 5 Group had already been equipped. Olive thought it only right that Evelyn should wait longer for a conversion course than her brother had – by then Duncan and Lofty had survived most of a first tour of operations flying Wellingtons, those commodious, stable airframes that could go no higher than 12,000 feet fully loaded. There was nothing so obliging to the enemy's flak batteries as a Wimpy, and over the target they risked sailing into the tonnage that rained from the bomb bays of the Lancasters and Stirlings above.

Duncan never complained. To him, the Wimpy was a dear old plane, and its low ceiling of operations a blessing. Most of the drama went on above, and a Wellington's crew got a much better view of the target than most. Duncan made the Wellington's flaws sound like virtues. Lofty, on the other hand, was even-handedly disparaging about every aspect of operations. Olive couldn't trust either of them to be honest about how they were getting on, because aircrew never were – not to each other, not to the intelligence officers at interrogation, nor to anyone on station – with the odd exception of confidences imparted to a trusted medical officer, or squadron leader – and *they* weren't telling.

She had a letter from Anne Battersby only once, when Anne wrote to say she'd heard that William's ship had been the first of two in the convoy torpedoed that night by a U-boat, and it had sunk with the loss of all hands. There was not much to be seen – just the flash of the fuel tanks reported by men on the dogwatch throughout the convoy. The fire had been snuffed out when the ship broke in two, and sank, in less than five minutes.

Olive read Anne's letter in the crowded NAAFI, under the weird white glow of the snow still packing the windows. Every spare hand had been diverted to clearing the field so that the bombers might take advantage of the break in the weather to join the battle order. Olive was on a break from this, her hands mottled pink and white even after a half-hour indoors.

In the last page of the letter Anne told Olive she was getting married; that she wanted to put the loss of William behind her. She had wedged into the envelope a photograph of her brother with two other sailors busy on deck on a make-and-mend day. Olive might have been grateful had the photo not set her in mind of what she'd said the day she got the telegram – her smug reference to a 'fiancé out in the convoys'. The shame this roused in her was greater, even, than her grief. He'd deserved better than that.

Olive was transferred off Holme in February of 1943 and posted to East Kirkby, at the very edge of the Lincolnshire Wolds, near the tiny villages of East and West Keal. The sea was not so accessible as at Waltham, and there was no breaded cod and chips to be had – just that strange combination of fish balls and chips (the fish balls made of potato, so one ate a double serving of starch). The distance to the grubby promenade at Cleethorpes was greater, too. But the hardstandings were familiar; as were the crews and their airframes, and Olive was glad to be back in Lincolnshire, near to Duncan, and nearer to Evelyn.

By then it was late winter. There was still snow in the fields, and winds that tore through the hedgerows and made the trees talk. The rabbits were thin, and wary with being shot at by underfed, ever-hopeful land-girls. In the mornings when her watch ended Olive would cycle back to the Waafery, scattering rabbits before her as she went.

She had hopes of seeing Duncan and Lofty, but before she was due her first leave, the crew of T for Tommy completed their 30th operation, and the gunners took themselves off to Cornwall for a month, living out of rucksacks as they bicycled between villages. By the time Olive was able to remonstrate with Duncan about not having visited, he and Lofty were back in Lincolnshire, instructing air-gunnery at Manby.

She finally met the gunners, by accident, one market day at Louth. She was wheeling her bicycle along Eastgate, idly looking for Derrick's butcher shop – she meant to ask Cathy's father how her friend was getting on, and where she'd been stationed. From the square came the insistent bleating of the sheep brought in for sale. She'd had to pick her way through them on the way into town, and their black faces turned towards her were pinched in complaint, tiny in comparison to their winter growth of wool. Although there was little point in heading into the market square, the noise drew her. While the farmers stood about talking, their land-girls leaned on the backs of wagons or sat with dungareed legs dangling over downed gates. Olive had never known what to say to these women. She'd seen them at service dances, and was on nodding acquaintance. Out of uniform Olive felt exposed and garish, and somehow frail – but she wondered how much worse it was for these girls – their skin ruddy from sun, their hands calloused, and their arms thick with muscle.

Down the end of the road where the sheep were penned the animals were stirring. A little knot of ewes went leaping over the backs of those in front of them as three men came running through the pen. From a distance Olive could recognise the pale blue uniforms of the RAAF and of South Africa. So fixed was she on identifying shoulder flashes that she didn't think to look at the faces of the men.

They came towards her, trailing their fingers over the animals' humped, woolly backs and laughing uproariously at the commotion they'd caused. It was Lofty that Olive recognised first – not that he looked much like his photographs. The hair she'd thought dark blond was actually a coppery red, and he was much better looking than she'd imagined. The odd thing about him was the way his facial features seemed to crowd together: his eyes were close set beneath the straight, and solid, line of his eyebrows and there was but a narrow gap between the top lip of his cherubic mouth and the end of his nose. He was, for this reason, not particularly photogenic. But animated, his face was an altogether different thing. Olive saw Lofty, and *then* she saw Duncan, his cap set back so far back on his head it looked about ready to drop off.

One of the farmers shouted, 'Get ya great clod-hopping feet away from them sheep!'

'Unhand me, grey-beard loon.' Lofty proclaimed this to the farmer standing a good five yards from him. The man huffed, and turned his back in disgust. 'There,' Lofty said to the airman beside him, a tall half-ringer with South African flashes at his shoulder, 'I told you I was a gorgon. He'll be stone by midnight.'

They were not looking in Olive's direction. Duncan had fetched out a hipflask and all three seemed intent on drinking from it. Duncan crooked his elbow sharply as he up-ended the flask, sucking out the last of the spirit. The skin of the wrist jutting from the sleeve of his best blue uniform was paler than it had been, but no less delicate. The back of the hand she could see was still hairless, and she couldn't help but reach out to touch it.

Olive's hand must have seemed to Duncan – attention fixed, pie-eyed – a phantom floating in from nowhere. But then he located the shoulder to which the arm belonged, and then the head, and face: the pointed chin and snub nose, the eyebrows at different heights, the cat's eyes. And suddenly Olive was swept off the ground, up onto the gunners' shoulders.

At this, the sheep – that had started to settle – turned their blunt heads at the noisy group, and recommenced their worried bleating.

'Winkette! Winkette! Winkette!' Duncan and Lofty chanted the local term for a pretty girl with all the conviction of Lincolnshiremen. 'Winkette Waafy!' they cried as they marched Olive around in a little circle. After a turn or two, and much to her relief, she was set down.

'Bugger me!' Lofty said and then, nudging Duncan, 'Bugger us!'

The South African opened his mouth to say something but – drunk though he was – seemed to think better of it.

'Olive,' Duncan asked, wonderingly, 'what are you doing here?'

'I've been sent to fetch you.'

'By *God* – ' Lofty said, nodding solemnly at the South African. 'She's been sent by God. To put us on the path of righteousness.'

'To fetch us?' Duncan echoed.

'That's right. To put you on the path of the next pub so I can catch up, you sots.'

'Oh. Right then. Wizard.' Duncan waved at the taller of his two friends. 'Olive, this is Martin Van den Graaf, but we call him – ' and she thought he'd said Ray until he repeated the nickname. 'Faye's our wire op. We're just having a wing-ding while he's down from Cranwell. Get us all out of the bind.'

Duncan was looking nervous, as if expecting her to disapprove of their drunkenness. In fact, she rather admired it: it took real application to get blotto in a Lincolnshire pub, many of which had jury-rigged signs propped by the front door to say the beer had run out.

'Lead on, then,' she said, giving Duncan a gentle shove. The four of them made their way to Upgate, giving the farmers a wide berth.

There was only a desultory drinker or two in the pub, in civvies, and an American pilot chatting up the only other girl in the lounge. They took a table under the front window and while the wireless operator went to fetch the pints, Lofty and Duncan sat looking at Olive with such satisfaction she'd have thought there was a finder's fee.

The South African set down the drinks and folded himself into his chair.

'That Faye thing – ' he said, nodding at Lofty, ' – is just their joke.' He leaned forward confidingly. 'But they're not *always* joking. Our boy carries your photograph as his good luck charm, you know,' he said, and looked with disappointment at the headless, barely effervescent, pint in his hand. 'Every operation, next to his heart.'

Duncan was blushing, the red creeping up from his collar to his cheeks, where it stayed as two solid points of colour on his otherwise pale skin.

Lofty sprung to the other gunner's defence. 'Faye's shooting a line.' He nodded at the South African disparagingly.

'I do have that photograph of you riding Putter,' Duncan said, and even though the look on his face was anything but funny,

Olive laughed, because she thought it was probably the horse, and not the rider, that prompted him to carry the picture. There could be nothing less romantic that a pudgy thirteen-year-old on a Welsh pony.

'Well, I could elaborate but I won't,' the South African said with the gravity of the truly inebriated.

'And what's your good luck charm?' Olive asked.

'A baby's booty,' he said, and then, after what must have been some profanity in Afrikaans, he added, 'Not mine.'

'Here it comes – the Peter Pan thesis,' Lofty said, but the South African had laid hold of his pint with real vocation and had nothing more to say.

'And,' Lofty rapped the table to get Olive's attention, 'since you ask, I take a lump of coal from a *very* unlucky mine – on the principle that lightning won't strike in the same place twice.' He took a pull on his own beer, and grimaced.

'I saw lightning strike in the same place once,' Duncan told Lofty loftily.

'So which was it, once or twice?'

'Twice, I told you.'

'He's telling the truth,' Olive put in. 'There was a big gum hit by lightning on the Macintyres' property, and the scorch marks showed two distinct strikes.'

'And *I* saw it.'

'He did,' she confirmed, nodding, thinking it best not to overexcite Lofty with the story of the young couple struck by lightning the same day at a church picnic outside Bathurst.

But Lofty was already overexcited. New Zealand, he said, did not get much in the way of lightning strikes. 'Our God is decent that way. He lays sheet lightning over the sea sometimes – it lures the snapper and warehou to the surface. Makes the fishermen happy.' Lofty would have gone on if Olive hadn't weighed in. As she spoke she tried very hard to imagine the man called Lawrence Hilliers with whom Duncan had shared a cabin on the troopship bound for Fiji – the taciturn man who was down on gambling. What had happened to him?

She changed the subject by asking the wireless operator, 'What about your home?'

He blinked. 'South Africa.'

She let the question settle for a moment. If there was one thing a WAAF learned quickly, it was how to talk to a man on a jag.

'J'burg,' he mumbled, and Duncan filled out the name for his friend, clipping the vowels to imitate his accent: *Jo-henness-burg*.

'Since you're so chatty,' Lofty said to the South African, who was blinking rapidly at him, 'why don't you fetch us another round?'

Once the wireless operator had gone back to the bar, Lofty leaned over the scarred top of the table and said, 'His brother was killed in the Western desert. Fighting Rommel's lot. They gave him two weeks leave but the poor bugger didn't know what to do with it – he got himself board with an old lady in town here and turned up in our mess, because that's all he knows.'

'Ask Faye to take you to the flicks.' Duncan had to whisper as the South African was on his way back to the table. Both gunners lifted their knees so he could slip past to his perch, where he sat, oblivious to the freighted looks his friends were giving Olive.

She thought the gunners had very little sense for the importance of the proper moment – there was something touchingly boyish about their inability to see it. But it wasn't for her to point out the clumsiness of their meddling.

The solicitousness of Duncan and Lofty for their W/Op was in no way surprising, but throughout the next few hours the four of them spent in the pub, or bicycling around the lanes of Louth, they were oddly shy about the other members of the crew. Lofty did mention the flight engineer a few times, calling him 'Dear Old Auntie' as if the man was memorable for his eccentricity, not his proximity.

It wasn't until Olive made the point of asking after Pilot Officer Crowe that she noticed this reticence. She was curious as to why Crowe, who was an American, had stayed with 103 Squadron when the 8th USAAF were in need of experienced pilots. She'd phrased her question carefully, stressing the pull of duty – the thing risen to; not the thing abandoned.

There was a long silence, during which a cloud of rooks lifted from an oak in the meadow, whirled noisily, and resettled. Duncan, looking through them at the thinning cloud, muttered, *they'll be flying tonight, poor sods.*

For a second Olive took this as an answer to her question, until she remembered Crowe had been packed away for a stint as instructor. He might very well be flying that night, but it wouldn't be on operations.

'So how *is* the skipper?'

There was another silence. Even the rooks had put a sock in it. Lofty and Duncan and Faye were walking ahead of Olive, and as she waited for one of them to answer, Duncan swapped hands so that he was wheeling his bicycle with his left hand, rather than his right, putting it between himself and the other two men even though the bike's front wheel kept wanting to turn right, and was bumping against his shin.

Lofty, glancing nervously at Duncan, said, 'The skip's flat out as a lizard drinking.' The phrase came out with such vaudeville timing that all three men laughed.

By and by they made their circuitous way to the crossroads at which Olive hoped to find a lift to East Kirkby. The boys were apologetic about not being able to take her to the Station gates, as if all three of them had been reading the same book on etiquette the night before. In any case, they elected to wait with her until someone stopped, and they did all stand there, three airmen and a WAAF clutching her bike handle with one hand and holding the front of her coat closed with the other. It was getting cold and none of the passing traffic had stopped at Lofty's wave.

Eventually Olive said with heavy emphasis, 'Why doesn't just one of you stay?' and Duncan and Lofty had scrambled for their bikes before their friend had time to react. The gunners kissed Olive on the cheek and rode off, yelling a final goodbye over their shoulders. They'd not said a word, nor given any sign, to their W/Op since running for their bikes.

Olive looked at the head of the lane – the opening between the hedgerows was losing its distinctness as the last light drained from the sky. Soon passing drivers wouldn't be able to pick them out from the dark mass of the hedge behind, and it would take more than a flash of leg to show up in hooded headlights. Van den Graaf moved closer to Olive and, putting a gentlemanly hand on her elbow, edged her back from the rutted side of the road.

'Would you like to take in a picture while you're here?' she asked, nerved up to it by his hand on hers.

'I'd like that.' But he sounded remote, and she wondered whether he'd remember.

To make sure, Olive asked for the telephone number of the place he was staying and although she had just the exchange name and three digits to remember, she had to keep saying it over to keep it in her head, and this took some part of her attention. It was then that he started talking. He told her that she didn't have to go out with him as a kindness, that he was quite alright, and would get on with things. There was nothing to worry about, nothing at all, and that was the point really. The worst had passed – they'd made it through thirty operations. He confided that it was the sudden *lack* of tension that was wearing. At Manby, where Duncan and Lofty were, the gunnery instructors had taken apart their mess and stacked all its furniture in a pile just so they could have something to do.

'Will you re-form the crew?' Olive asked carefully. 'When everyone's been off in different places instructing?'

'It would look strange if we didn't. Some men do an extra tour just to keep a crew together.' The South African lit a cigarette then, turning away from her to blow the first draw of smoke, face hidden. 'The devil you know, and all that.'

The flare of his match must have caught the eye of a lorry driver, for a Leyland with mud streaked up the sides of the cabin pulled in. The WAAF driving leaned over the bench seat to open the door.

'Alright there love? Or is this smooth job making a nuisance.'

'Oh no, he's a friend,' Olive replied. 'I could do with a lift to West Keal. Or East Kirkby, if you're going that way.'

Van den Graaf helped her stow her bike in the back of the lorry, then mounted his bicycle, one hand for balance on the still sign-less post that marked the crossroads. Olive kissed him quickly on the cheek, and told him she'd call.

As the lorry lurched into gear the driver – forward as any London cabbie – said, 'There's no point crying about it. Half the time they don't want you because they're scared you'll be the one left dangling. Better not to start, I say.' And she patted her passenger's knee.

But Olive was crying because it was William's roughening cheek she'd kissed.

Chapter Sixteen

Flat spin

She could not often find a time and a place to be with the people in her life that mattered. They were at distant postings, or leave could not be found when it was needed. Someone would be on duty when she was off. And then there were the dead and the missing, those undarnable holes in the weft of her wartime world. But in the summer of 1943 she and her friends had three days together at a cottage on the Yorkshire coast, in Robin Hoods Bay.

Evelyn had suggested the destination, and secured their accommodation. She'd wanted something far from the war. There was an army base at Mappleton, and barrage balloons tethered to the coast there, but despite the intrusion of the odd bobbing mine the pressing concerns of seafaring Yorkshiremen were still fouled nets, uncharted wrecks and gales. The starkest change the war had made to Robin Hoods Bay was the evacuees settled in local households, children whip-thin and dark-skinned; their elbows and knees flecked with the pale scimitars of scars they'd got scrambling from cove to cove, over limpid-covered rocks, in search of smuggler's caves. Robin Hoods Bay was a summer place, and holiday-makers still came to walk barefoot on the grass, down to the seawall, or down the cobbled lanes to the slipway, pale in their togs, with the thin scrap of a towel thrown over their shoulders.

Olive arrived by way of a train from Pickering, through Grosmont, to Whitby, and came by bus over the rutted lane above the ruins of the abbey, where sheep stood grazing among its stones. From there the bus turned south-east to the crossroads for High Hawsker, Flyingthorpe and Robin Hoods Bay.

How happy she was! The sun was out, and she'd been given a freshly baked scone by a girl off to WAAF induction at Scarborough. Her connections had been good, and she'd not once had to go without a seat, or (as was often the case) without a train. Her pass for the 72 was folded safely inside her identity card. Not since York had she seen any military police, although civil guard, ARP and fire wardens were much in evidence, marked by their armbands or the letters stencilled on the tin hats they carried. Nobody had asked her business until she'd arrived at Whitby, and then it was just to see whether she might need help with her bag.

The bus laboured up the road towards the brown cap of heather on the moors, its passengers willing it on, and the relief was general when they began the descent towards the fishing boats and cottages of the bay. She was set down by a dusty hedgerow next to a row of tall houses that once had been owned by sea captains, and now were the possession of businessmen from

Manchester and Hull. The windows of these were curtained or shuttered; the flowerboxes on the sills empty. Olive might have thought the place evacuated had she not been walking towards the sound of a fretting engine, and the gull-like cries of children rising from behind the seawall. At the brow of the final slope upon which the village stood she stopped to watch a man leading a horse in harness up the steeply cobbled street. The horse was skittish, unsettled by the blue sparks shooting up from its shoes where they struck stone. The cobblestones were slick, and dark – as if those streets were the sluiceway down which water had been poured to make the sea.

Luckily, Olive did not have to go down the way the horse had come. Evelyn's letter said: 'at the top of the hill veer right. When you see the path to the seawall, head for the narrowest alleyway you can see'. 'The Openings' was a tiny curved way cut between stone cottages leaning in towards each other at the eaves; the cobblestones of the street uneven as teeth in a too-crowded jaw. Ammonite Cottage was not difficult to find since someone had stamped the render with the crenellated claws of fossils.

As she put up a hand to knock on the door, the white mesh of a curtain twitched in the window beside it. Duncan's face appeared, framed by the heavy tresses of the blackout curtain. Then the door was open and he was standing in it.

'We haven't finished clearing up.'

She followed him into the house, blinking in the gloom of the tiny kitchen. There were dirty dishes lining two sides of the table, rows tidily arranged by some drunk.

'Never mind about that,' Duncan said, catching at the canvas of her kitbag, 'the lounge is sparkling. You won't have any complaints – '

Lofty came in then, the grey strands of a mop head arranged in a fringe over his forehead and the mop's handle stuck down the back of his trousers. 'I bid you welcome,' he squawked. 'Maisie Curmudgeon at your service. And this – ' he waved at Duncan, ' – is Ethel Light.' He swept back out.

After a pause Duncan said, 'Your room's very nice. Perhaps you'd like to see it? There's not much going on down here. Faye's so teased out he's in bed,' he said, leading her into the sitting room. She saw how changed Duncan was from the last time she'd seen him: the skin under his eyes pouched and dark; his complexion generally sallow.

She promptly told him so.

'I'm fit as a fiddle as far as the medical officer is concerned. You're just not used to seeing my English pallor.'

Olive looked doubtful but said, 'It's probably just that you look odd in civvies.'

Duncan's green corduroy trousers were held up by suspenders, and tucked into them was a clean grey shirt.

'When I first got into this clobber I felt like I'd gone on an op without a parachute.' He ground his teeth and then smiled at her. 'But that was yesterday.' Holding open the door to the lounge, he said, 'Quick, before Lofty decides to do another circuit.'

From the sounds upstairs Lofty had gone to wake Van den Graaf. They could hear cries of 'wakey-wakey' and a banging that sounded like a broom-handle on a wooden floor or the surface of a door. This clamour was followed by a wounded silence.

Lofty came down the stairs, muttering, 'It's not much chop when a person can't wave a mop around without being assaulted.' He palpated a spot on his abdomen. 'Aimed for the soft parts too, like he'd been doing bayonet drill.'

'I'd say he took a dim view of your trying to shift him.'

'That one could sleep until the end of days – Christ doing his final judgement tap dance; bells ringing; trumpets blowing; golden ramparts falling while Flight Sergeant Van den Graaf, *sancti*, takes a nice zizz.'

Olive put her bag down and Lofty stepped neatly over it to plant a kiss on her cheek. He smelled faintly of beer, and soap.

Furniture had been shifted to clear a space at the sitting room's centre. The pile of the carpet was spiked in some sections and flattened in others as if someone had been wrestling on it, or dancing, but now the sun lay pooled there, shining in through two windows giving onto a view of the sea, the cliffs to the north of the bay and a blue sky empty of cloud. A high-backed chair had been placed before each window – the seats facing the bottom of the frame as if deep in conversation, wood to wood.

'That's our widow's lookout,' Lofty said, seeing where she was looking. 'We're very big on widows looking out,' he added, 'what with the war on and women scarce.'

'Someone ought to put a cloth over his cage,' Olive said to Duncan, then – pushing her bag towards Lofty with one foot – 'Why don't you make yourself useful by taking this upstairs.'

'Bossy bloody Australians,' Lofty genially observed, picking up the kit. 'Excuse me while I see to the lady's bags.'

When he'd gone Olive flopped down on the couch and kicked off her shoes. The breeze from the open window felt delicious on her insteps.

Duncan lowered his voice and glanced at the stairway. 'Lofty's alright really,' he said, offsetting the disloyalty of making sure he'd gone. 'Just a bit rough around the edges. He's the direct opposite of Faye – he *doesn't* sleep. Hasn't since we came off ops. When they scrub an op, everyone cuts up in the mess and then they turn in. Not Lofty – he reads, or takes long walks in the night, but his horizontal pursuits are severely limited.'

Olive raised the eyebrow most ready for ascent. 'Horizontal pursuits?'

'You know what I mean,' said Duncan.

Sitting up, she looked out the window at sea the colour of dying bracken, a frill of mauve at the shore. The coastal water from the Humber estuary up to the Tyne was coloured by the soil of the cliffs upon which it fed – Yorkshire worn down at its seaward edge.

Taking up her thought again Olive asked Duncan whether he was sleeping well. The lines about his mouth and eyes might have been from fatigue but could just have easily been sculpted by smiling – that smile she'd seen him freely bestow on cats, dogs and horses.

'Oh, I take a crack at it now and then.' When she frowned at him he added, 'The MO will tear strips off a man if he doesn't sleep between sorties. Believe me, I'm in fine fettle.'

But not as fine as Van den Graaf, whose snores were making the plates in the sideboard jitter.

There was time before lunch for Olive to have a wash and put her feet up so she stretched out on the bed in the room she was to share with Evelyn – once she'd deigned to make an appearance. Evelyn had reserved punctuality and predictability for that part of her life given to war work. The rest of her world was left to guess and to God, as it always had been.

Olive had not seen her since Hamble. When she heard the warm timbre of a woman's voice in the rooms below, she surprised herself by pulling the sheet over her face. The idea that they were all under one roof had suddenly paralysed her.

Evelyn had taken her shoes off before mounting the stairs, and so came silently in. When Olive heard a floorboard by the bed creak she hoped it was the nettlesome Lofty, or Van den Graaf, awake and finally come to greet her. But she could not resist throwing back the sheet to check, and there was Evelyn plucking the ATA cap from its perch on her permanent wave and tossing it onto the chair over which Olive had draped her jacket. Grabbing the board at the foot of the bed, she rocked it.

'Where's my hello, lazybones? I'm standing there five minutes thinking you're still on your way before Duncan puts me right. This is no time for relaxing. I want attention.'

'Can't I give you attention from a prone position?' Olive

propped herself on the pillows and made a half-hearted attempt at bringing the knot on her tie nearer to her neck.

'If you make room.'

'Your colour is high, and you're sweating. You look like you've just run a 500-yard race. I'm not having that on my bed.' But she nevertheless inched over to let her friend sit.

'You look as fresh as ever,' Evelyn said, but Olive thought it empty phrasing, and untrue. All of them had aged, if Evelyn the least. Her war seemed to have kept her young, while her juniors had caught, and passed, her.

'Flatterer,' Olive said, and taking one of Evelyn's calloused hands in her own, turned it palm up. 'Look at that life line – it's longer than the Nile.'

'A good thing, if I'm only to see you once a year.' Evelyn detached herself and shrugged out of her uniform jacket. She let it drop onto the bed, then pulled the bottom of her shirt from the waistband of her skirt, flapped it, and left it open to the breeze.

'*Years*, they get shorter all the time. Don't you know they've put them on the ration?' Olive yawned and sank back into the prone position she'd formerly occupied. 'I feel absolutely knackered.'

'What you're experiencing is relief; the short-circuiting of all those busy little WAAF circuits.' Evelyn flicked her shirt tail to draw the breeze, and smiled down at her friend. 'No amount of flux will fix it, so you might as well let yourself go unserviceable until you sign back in with the duty officer at the station.'

'Unserviceable, am I? And there's me thinking I'd caught something on the train.'

Evelyn was still fidgeting with the free end of her shirt, so Olive said, 'Don't stand on ceremony with me. If you're that hot, take the bloody thing off.' And she pinched one of the buttons out of its hole for her.

Evelyn lifted the twisted coiff of her hair, exposing the line of her throat and the soft skin on the inside of her forearms. Olive picked another button open with fingers keen from the delicate work of feeling bunched wires, to find the one frayed, or burnt. As she undid the buttons Evelyn lowered her arms obligingly to shrug off the shirt.

Olive was shocked to see that her friend wore the same unglamourous underwear she did – the straps of her brassiere frayed and stretched, and the cotton weave of her 'twilight' bloomers thinning, transparent in places, where it was visible above the waist of her skirt. 'My God – ' said Olive, surprised by the ordinariness of Evelyn, ' – what a sorry sight we make!'

Then they were both whooping and rolling about on the bed; Evelyn pulling herself upright every so often to mime a kind of Mata Hari shimmy.

'Go on then, let's see you,' she said, plucking at Olive's shirt front, and she obliged by doing her best imitation of a tart's twirl out of the scratchy WAAF shirt. The breeze from the window prickled her skin, and she felt the day's sweat drying as the delicate hairs on her arms rose and stood to attention.

'I've got you half-naked already, and I've been here less than half an hour. That must be some kind of progress,' Evelyn said, her heavy lids settling until her eyes became a shining line – like the edge of sea they'd seen at Brighton Sands. She spoke so lightly that Olive imagined they were sitting there half-naked in protest against three years of service life, and in homage to childhood summers spent in places too hot, and too sparsely populated, to instill a proper English terror of exposure. She couldn't let any other interpretation of the scene stand, and was relieved when Evelyn left off that train of thought and fell to examining her shoulders, and the skin of her upper arms. She seemed to find both unsatisfactory. 'There's never enough vanishing cream to spare for my arms. I'll be scaly as a crocodile by the time the war ends.' She picked up Olive's wrist to give her arm a critical once over. 'But look at you – bloody perfect. Not even a freckle.'

Olive looked too, and smiled. Perhaps those staggered watches – many during night-time hours – had their benefit.

Like her brother, Evelyn had lost weight. Meals must have been a haphazard affair, and a busy day's ferrying meant lunches or dinners missed. Her arms did not have that soft cushion of fat considered stylish pre-war, but were all sinew, and her breasts – never large to start with – had shrunk proportional to the growth of muscle. The wrestle with rudder and throttle, the winding up and down of landing gear, had taken its toll.

'We should get you some lunch,' Olive said, picking up her shirt. It was only when Evelyn stood before the mirror smoothing her clothes into shape, then her hair, that she felt a vague sense of regret that she'd suggested they join the others. But Evelyn was already retouching her lipstick in quick economical strokes, making herself presentable for the boys.

Olive's toilette was a more peremptory affair, and she followed Evelyn downstairs with a face bare of make-up, and with her shirt untucked, but since Van den Graaf was sitting on the couch in his pyjamas she felt she'd cut the right dash. Duncan did the introductions, and the South African patted down his unruly coxcomb of hair before taking Evelyn's hand to shake it. Then Lofty came in from the kitchen waving an ordnance survey map to call them to lunch and before too long the five of them had crowded around the kitchen table, jostling elbows as knives and forks were distributed; margarine and jam spread on bread, and quarters of apple balanced at the edge of plates. The overall chaos at table was increased by Lofty's insistence that he spread the map.

'The target for tonight is Ugglebarnby,' he said, tapping a spot on the moors that looked, to Olive, too far inland to be an attractive destination.

'Ugglebarnby?' Evelyn asked, knife poised over the slice of bread she'd been buttering.

'Ugglebarnby. Bugger all defences you see. Open wide, it is. Just begging for it.'

'Begging for what?'

'Colonial invasion. The lot of us against the lot of them: best drinkers win. Come in with perfect visibility and go out blind.'

'But we have no way of getting there.'

'Nonsense. We have a car.' Lofty tapped the map again, and then smiled. 'Actually, I do think we should take a dekko, if only because I like the name of the place.'

'Why waste the petrol?' Van den Graaf asked. 'There's pubs here we can walk to.'

'But all of them are down the hill and that means coming back up,' Lofty said, glaring at his W/Op. 'I'm allergic to an order of things that puts the descent before the ascent: it's not bloody natural.'

Duncan reached for the jar of strawberry jam and put it down on the map so that it covered most of the eastern edge of the North Yorkshire Moors. 'I agree with Faye. Why drive somewhere to get drunk when we can do it perfectly well here?'

'So getting drunk is the aim of the evening? You have decided this, despite the fact that ladies – ' and here Evelyn nodded at Olive, ' – do not get drunk, merely tipsy?'

The men flinched, and Van den Graaf's chin sunk an inch or two closer to his chest. Duncan blushed. But before he could pull a reply out of the stutter forming, Olive said, 'I fancy getting stinking,' and leaned down to rub the place on her shin where Evelyn had kicked her.

'Maybe a couple of quiet pints down by the slipway. After a good long walk. Just enough to get whistling,' Evelyn said, trying not to look at her brother. 'After all, we can't really let our hair down, not on a 72, not with duty looming. It's different for you lot.'

Duncan stared.

'Then again,' she said, her expression blank as the Mona Lisa's, 'I could be pulling your leg.'

'Oh thank God,' Lofty said, 'I was beginning to feel parched.'

'I *was* serious about the walk, if anyone fancies it.'

The South African said he intended to go back to bed and read, so it was just Lofty and Duncan and Olive who followed Evelyn down the cobbled street to the slipway. The fishing boats were in. The four of them stood for a while watching the hubbub, and Lofty spoke to a man who, among all his peers in rubber and brine-aged leather boots, wore flying boots, the sheepskin on the inside rims greasy and matted.

They moved on up beyond the harbourmaster's cottage to the break in the seawall where the track to the cliffs began.

There was a Labrador. It appeared from the beach, its coal-black coat damp and flecked with sand, and fell into step at Duncan's heels as if he'd trained it from a pup.

'Oh hello,' he said to it.

The dog trailed them as they walked towards the edge of the farmland, and the flowering heather. The heather was miles from them yet, and stayed that way, but they walked towards it as if it were the only possible destination. The path pointed them at the far tops of the moors but took them down towards coves cut deeply into the shore. At Boggle Hole they rested, and Evelyn doled out the scones she'd carried wrapped in a tea towel tied neatly at its four corners. The grass was scraggly and hard by the brook in the place where it had carved the cove and widened into the sea. Olive folded her jacket under her bare legs and sat on that, while Duncan and his sister braved the ground.

'There are meant to be smuggler's caves here,' Duncan said, looking around at the unpromisingly piled dirt where the cliff had subsided and, further up the hill, at the thickly clustered coronation trees with their shiny scarlet berries.

'Supposed to be all along this coast, but we can't find them,' Lofty added. 'I thought if I nabbed a child it might be bribed to lead us to the caves, but a bob to them is a bob not put to a pint, so...' He turned his hands up in a gesture of surrender. 'In any case, they show no sign of speaking English and I've no money to spare for an interpreter.'

'Don't you speak child?' Olive asked, and Lofty did something fetching she'd seen few men do: he wrinkled his nose.

'I don't speak cockney.'

'Balls!' Duncan said, passing a crust to the dog. 'You were surrounded by eight-year-olds yesterday, and you seemed to be talking about *something*.'

'I was busy bargaining for my life. Sign-language. Didn't you see?'

'I saw plenty of hand gestures. Particularly when you handed out those toffees.'

'You need your dark glasses, old man. The glare was playing tricks on you.'

'Which reminds me,' Evelyn said. 'I have a new pair for you back at the cottage, Duncan. They're American. Lovely dark lenses.'

'The sort they wore until 1941 so they couldn't see the war,' Lofty said, and lay back with his arm over his eyes.

Olive spread the lapels of her jacket and lay down too, leaving Duncan and Evelyn to catch up. They had not seen each other for years, and she wanted them to feel easy. For a while, her mind hung onto their conversation (night-sight, and how to preserve it) and then she let go of her friends, and of the afternoon.

Their stop at Boggle Hole was not so brief after all, and the sun was appreciably lower in the sky when the four started north again. She and Lofty took the lead so as to leave the Macintyres to themselves. Surprisingly, Lofty had little conversation to make unless it was to ask the names of a tree, or flower: many of which, to Olive's shame, she could not identify.

Nevertheless, she explained the drill passed on to her by Catherine Derrick in their strolls around Cranwell. Birches have triangular leaves, while laurel has long thickly clustered leaves, and hazel, oval leaves with hairy undersides.

'I know a few men like that,' Lofty put in, and she frowned at him.

'Elms on the other hand,' Olive went on in the singsong tones of instruction, 'have rounded leaves with serrated edges that look rather like the leaves of the beech, but paler and more gently serrated.'

'Beech smeech,' Lofty said. 'They've got nothing on the ones we have on the west coast in New Zealand. Our beech has black bark with little hairs on it, and on the end of each hair is a drop of dew as sweet as maple. Now there's a tree!' They'd walked under an oak, and the ground of the path was strewn with fallen acorns – making a precarious surface to walk on. Lofty reached out an arm to steady her.

'I hear you don't sleep much,' Olive said, bored with botanical talk.

'Me?' Lofty looked surprised. 'Someone's been talking a load of guff. I sleep like the dead. It's just that I take my time getting there. Anyway, look at Faye, he sleeps too bloody much.'

'And Duncan?'

'It's not Duncan's sleeping habits that worry me.'

He caught the sharp look Olive gave him and shrugged. 'Weight-loss. We had some chairborne types come and weigh us, and they were busy with their tape measures too. The MO says it's a sign of fatigue. Flying stress. But I think it's just that we'd not had our operational meals for a while: duff weather's hard on the stomach.' He glanced back down the path at Duncan, who'd stopped to throw a stick for the dog.

'What does he do about the airsickness?' Olive asked, watching Lofty carefully for a reaction. While she presumed he knew she knew, she could not be certain.

The mid-gunner's face closed. 'He takes a pillowcase on every trip, and dumps the sodding sodden thing over the channel on the way back. That makes a cramped trip even nastier but there's not much else he can do short of fess up. Which – ' Lofty crossed his arms, ' – Duncan's not about to do. Airsickness is listed as a symptom of flying stress, and he's not having anyone put *him* down as LMF. So it's the bag for our boy.' He kicked at an acorn, and it shot away into the shade beneath the trees. 'Duncan is going to have to start keeping himself in better shape if he wants me to come in with him after the war. I'm not tying my interests to a scarecrow.' At this, Lofty tried to look nonchalant, haughty – as if he could pick and choose what to care about, and who to care for.

But when Olive asked, 'Got plans, have you?' he looked hopeful – happy to have shared prospects. He told her that they might set themselves up farming hops in Nelson, or perhaps he'd give orcharding a go. Duncan had already written to his father to ask whether any work could be found for Lofty on the farm at Orange.

'You know...for after,' he added shyly.

Olive said she thought the Macintyres would be lucky to have him. His training as a mining engineer was bound to come in use.

Lofty could see the sense in that. 'Farmers do love a bit of dynamite,' he said. 'When they can get it.'

They walked in silence – Olive watching skylarks dogfight in the air above a copse of birches – until Lofty asked, 'Will you be about then? I mean – ' He lapsed into a stutter, and looked away from her. 'I mean, obviously, you'll be off home after all this.'

'Oh, I don't know.' The end of the war was such a dim prospect that she couldn't see the point of planning for it.

'I thought you would, though,' Lofty added, his cherubim's mouth making a question of the statement.

Olive just smiled at him, saying, 'Let's turn around now.'

And they did, catching the Macintyre siblings in their slip-stream. Olive had Evelyn to herself while Duncan and Lofty marched on ahead, home towards their beer. Evelyn seemed pleased with her brother's news, and if there'd been anything to worry about in his health, she'd not seen it. From what Olive could gather much of their talk had been about people and animals at home, or about life in the air, 'upstairs'. Technical things Olive wouldn't be the least interested in, or so Evelyn said before lapsing into a silence, and a mood, that Olive didn't think she deserved.

It was not until they were in the pub that Evelyn revealed what was bothering her. She'd been going on about what a thrill the shift to White Waltham was, and the conversion course to 'heavies', a course she'd done with a full complement of male pilots who couldn't help but stare. Those weren't the first odd looks Evelyn had had: when she'd delivered Spits and Hurricanes she'd been gawped at by pilots on operational fighter stations. But things had changed since then, and the appearance of a woman in the pulpit of a Lancaster should have been perfectly predictable.

But that predictability was the very thing that bothered Evelyn. She'd flown so many types that she was running out of surprises. What she wanted was a change, and she'd been talking to pilots of the Atlantic Ferrying service – those men who flew Liberators on the long haul from the coast of Canada to England, aircraft crowded with newly trained aircrew and materiel safer in the air than on the sea, or empty but for the odd important personage. But no women flew that route.

'I'm tatered. It's time to re-muster,' she said, and drained her pint. 'And what will I be? A spark-plug tester perhaps, or a cook.'

Then looking at her friend, she said, 'Perhaps I could follow Olive into the signals trade. White Waltham to Waltham should be a step up.'

'East Kirkby,' Olive said, but Evelyn didn't hear, had closed her eyes.

'I'm fighting the same war as you, but with the blood squeezed out of it.'

'Left you the sweat and tears then,' Lofty said, taking the empty pint glass from her hand.

Van den Graaf had drooped towards the table but this did not stop him from pronouncing, in the ringing voice of prophecy, 'You don't want blood. Blood is ugly stuff.'

'Frightful,' Duncan put in sharply. 'But let's not talk about it.'

Van den Graaf took the reproach amiably, turning his attention to Lofty at the bar, as if he expected him to come back one pint short.

The little group drank more and talked about dances they'd been to, and about films. Nobody talked about the war itself – how well, or badly, things were going. There was only the odd CineReel to go by for news as no self-respecting mess or canteen had newspapers in it, and if it did, the pages were open at the funny papers. Likewise, the radio – if any of them had time to listen to it – would be tuned to music broadcasts or to radio comedies, to the Big Bands belting out Glenn Miller or to ITMA, Ali Oop promising 'I go, I come back', a phrase that every pilot in England seemed addicted to, and that more than one had used on Olive after she'd told him to pancake his aircraft at 2000 or

3000 feet, stacking the queue for landing. The most contentious topic broached that night was rationing – Lofty expounding upon the evils of the black market and those wicked people who drew double points by using fake identification papers.

'Watch out, your moral high-ground is showing,' Olive said, pleased finally to meet the man who'd thrown a deck of cards out the porthole of the cabin on their troopship.

'It's not morals, it's practicality.'

'So you won't be wanting any of the chocolate I've brought?' Evelyn asked in her most innocent voice. 'Or the bed in the cottage? Or the RAF petrol in the tank of the car you drove up from Manby?'

'Don't you come the acid with me. We got that fuel fair and square by coupon swap,' Lofty replied, slouching further into his seat. 'And if some rich bastard wangled himself a cottage by the sea I'd prefer it go towards making men in the service happy than to his dirty weekends with some piece of nice from Picadilly Circus.'

Van den Graaf's forehead hit the table with a smack.

'Drinks too much, he does,' Lofty said, looking mournfully at his own pint. 'Do you think he'd mind if we finished our drinks?'

'Mind? Him? He's insensible.' Duncan pinched the South African's earlobe to make his point. Van den Graaf blew out his cheeks in a sigh.

So they finished their pints, and the last of the whisky in the hipflask the publican had been kind enough not to notice, and dragged the wireless operator up the hill.

Back at the cottage, Faye regained his vim about the time Lofty suggested they play spin the bottle. It was Lofty's idea to go one verbal and one physical payment by turns: either the kiss or the answer to a question.

That was complicated in its results, in as much as any of them could remember, the morning after. But several things happened – among the questions and answers, and the kisses bestowed – that would stand out in Olive's memory. Late in the game Duncan spun the bottle, a less than vigorous spin he might have imagined would end pointed at Lofty, who'd asked too many difficult, theological, questions and whom Duncan richly wanted to serve. But the bottle spun to a rest in front of the drooping South African. Van den Graaf perked up at the idea he was going to get to kiss Olive until she told him he had to take a question.

'And you have to answer truthfully – no bumf.' (They had banned bumf after Lofty's 'What is God?')

Olive leaned into the circle of legs, propping herself against Evelyn's knee so as to get closer to Van den Graaf's pale, sweating face. 'Why do they call you Faye?'

Van den Graaf swiped at his forehead, brushed back a hank of unruly hair. 'We've all got girls names,' he said. 'On Tommy. Because of the kite's nickname. Starlet.'

'Answer the *specific* question,' said the stickler, Evelyn.

'I'm sure that Maisie and Ethel have an opinion, but since it's my turn, that's all the answer you'll get.' This came out with gravity. 'Satisfied?'

'That's a bit off course,' Evelyn announced.

'He evaded the question,' Olive added.

'That wasn't evasion. That was my bloody answer. Why can't I just snog someone and be done with it?'

'Spin the bottle, Faye,' Duncan said, and the South African did. It turned a quarter circle to point at the younger, then the older, Macintyre.

'No kissing then,' a crestfallen Van den Graaf said. He was rapidly losing interest in the game.

Duncan picked up the bottle and pointed it at his sister, 'If you could kiss anyone here, I mean *really* kiss them, who would it be?'

'Well, darling, *you* naturally, since you're my brother.' She was smiling, looking cool. 'Your courage, your cheerfulness, your resolution: what could be more attractive?'

'Faye's right. You're not playing this properly.' Duncan stood up, still clutching the bottle. 'If it's just going to be piss and wind I'm off to bed, and bugger you lot.'

'Bugger you too,' Van den Graaf muttered and, crawling onto the couch, turned his back on the room and went to sleep.

Lofty, Evelyn and Olive sat looking drunkenly at one another.

'Religion was a safe topic. You ban religious talk and all you get is sex sex sex. Stands to reason really.' Lofty lay back on the rug, linking his fingers behind his head. 'Then someone gets hurt. A maiden loved, an idle word, and there you have it: a comrade lost.'

'But we weren't talking about sex, were we?' Olive asked, lifting a bottle of beer to the light to see if it still contained any liquid.

She lay down so that her face was very near the gunner's, so close she could see the faint mark of the rash on his cheeks from his oxygen mask. Lofty opened his eyes very wide, his brick-coloured eyelashes trembling.

'There's my girl,' he said, so gently that Olive's throat caught at hearing him.

She put one fingertip into the cleft of his chin. 'Why do you call him Faye?' she asked.

Lofty closed his eyes, and she felt his jaw clench.

'Oh Lord. That. Let's just say he made an almighty fuss when the beast tried to snatch him – the beloved *hero* beast, the crew's one and only. Captain Kong.' His eyelids flickered, but did not open. 'And if the other crews think we're a bunch of *girls*, why not make a joke of it? That's the form. If we make it a good laugh, no one gets hurt. The crew take care of each other, and *do not* air the dirty washing in public.' His eyes opened for a second and he added, 'Not that the washing is dirty. It's the minds of them watching it wave about that are dirty.'

'One more question,' she said as quietly as she could, although she knew that Evelyn was listening. 'Why did you cry in the showers, just after you arrived in Macdonald?'

Lofty's eyes sprung open again. 'That was *Duncan*, not me. The last time I cried was when I couldn't shift three tons of fallen rock off the mouth of a mine on Mount Rochfort.'

'Oh,' said Olive.

'And let's say no more about it. Careless talk, you know. Costs lives.'

'Remarks when loose play jangling,' she added.

'True enough,' Lofty said from the floor, and there was quiet.

Evelyn looked at her. Then, putting a finger to her lips, she picked up her shoes and crept up the stairs. Olive followed.

Once they were in their room, Evelyn said, 'Duncan was testing to see what I'd think of a trainee crying like that. I should have known he was writing about himself.' She looked at Olive, her eyes very bright. 'But he seems alright. Whatever it was, he got over it. Don't you agree?'

'I have no idea.' Olive spoke to Evelyn's reflection while she busied herself before the dresser mirror, slopping water from the bowl as she dipped and wrung the flannel. 'About any of it. They're so cagey. Why should we believe Lofty when he says it was Duncan? He probably thinks everything is better left to the imagination anyway. That way it could be either of them, or neither of them.' She tugged the brush through her hair so vigorously that Evelyn took it out of her hands.

'Most things *are* better left to the imagination. But I'm just thankful there are enough unimaginative people in the world that some things go on beneath anyone's notice. I'd rather not know that Duncan was so scared – or homesick – that he was driven to tears. But I am glad to know he felt safe enough to cry in front of his friend.' Evelyn tapped the tortoiseshell back of the brush against her thigh, and Olive felt the conversation – like the room – turn, and shake her. Evelyn was saying, 'Unlike you, Olive – there's no point sharing things with you. You work things out, and then keep them to yourself. You're marvellous at starving the possible.'

When Olive glanced up at herself in the mirror she could see her face was blazing. 'Some things are impossible, no matter what you think, or do,' she told Evelyn, and her reflection. 'That's only being practical.'

'Oh yes,' Evelyn said, her voice tight. 'I have heard a great deal about the virtues of practicality. You'd do me a favour not to mention the word again.'

She put the brush down lightly, bristle-side down.

Chapter Seventeen

The naming of parts

At the end of their leave Van den Graaf and the gunners drove south through Yorkshire, over the wind-torn Humber Bridge, to North Lincolnshire and the aerodrome at Elsham encircled by dark-soiled fields planted entirely with cabbage. Duncan's letters to Olive complained about the view, and the bike ride down to the village – easy coasting down Vicarage lane but a long haul back with bellies full of beer. Lofty wrote of his campaign against the gates to Lord Yarbrough's Estate – a monumental arch of stone narrowing the Scunthorpe road that had claimed the lives of several night-riding motorists, including an American fighter pilot stationed at Goxhill. The Americans had laid a wreath on the eastward leg of the arch but it was Lofty who'd scrawled *Victims of Feudal England* over Yarbrough's stone.

On odd occasions one of the gunners' letters might come with a scribbled note from Faye on the last page, but these were polite scrawls about picture-shows Olive should look out for, or songs he liked. And there was a period in the middle of October when she had no mail at all; when a slim parcel of letters was held for her somewhere at Group while she moved to the newly forming station at North Killingholme. The land below Skitterbeck was already full of aerodromes, but the Air Office thought one more could be made to fit – Lincolnshire not covered enough for their liking by brick housings, by hardstanding and hangars and Nissen huts and bomb stores, by tractors never used for harvest, by crew-bus and fire-tender.

When Olive stepped off the lorry, kit on shoulder, she had the usual trudge to the WAAF site. It was well away from the aircrew mess – strict separation of personnel being one of the first principles of airfield design. She soon discovered the advantage of the remoteness of the WAAF depot – it sat near Killingholme Road, and squarely between two pubs: the Black Bull at East Halton and Cross Keys at South Killingholme, both of which were popular with Americans from Goxhill whose tailored uniforms, and deep pockets, she'd grudgingly come to appreciate.

But the proximity of the pubs was not nearly so pleasing as the fact that Catherine Derrick had been plucked from the Flying Control Office at Bardney to join the complement of WAAFs at North Killingholme. The upheaval of her own move was eased for Olive by the presence of her friend. Cathy had advanced in rank – she was one of the most senior WAAFs in the Flying Control Office, and was not tethered to the Marconi. She was directly responsible to the flying control officer, and Olive was responsible to her. None of the R/T operators wanted to disappoint the butcher's daughter, for to do so meant forfeiting one's share in the Lincolnshire sausages sent from Louth. These were ferried by a female dispatch rider who'd once arrived with a string of pork sausages swinging about her neck.

At North Killingholme incoming crews shared quarters without rank distinction, sergeants with officers, and one crew mixed with another. Lines of allegiance were drawn by likenesses in position and trade, so it was perfectly natural that a corporal like Olive should share a room with a twenty-year-old from the East End, and a warrant officer.

At the start of the operations at Killingholme only one squadron was flying – 550, very few of whom Olive recognised from her time at Waltham. The squadron had been restocked with men just out of their long training, men whose uniforms still held a crease and whose buttons shone. Many would die before their buttons could lose that burnish. By early November a new squadron, 629, had formed.

Olive had a few weeks to adjust to the new station, and since the routines of duty were the same as they'd been at Holme, East Kirkby and Waltham, she settled quickly. But for Duncan and Lofty, and the crew of T-Tommy at Elsham – just eight miles to the west – the month was not so kind, and routine was little comfort. No matter how many groups of men stood outside the mess at breakfast to second-guess the weather, mugs of tea steaming in their hands, any opinion on the state of operations was pure conjecture. Orders came down, targets were picked; Group, Squadron, and Flight were selected for duty, and finally the crews on the battle order listed – but a Lancaster might be queued for take-off, and all members of the crew nerved up, only to have word come down that the operation had been scrubbed. Uncertainty was an airman's routine: would they be at war, or whooping it up in the mess?

T for Tommy's crew was tired. When the battle order went up for the Hanover raid, Van den Graaf saw one more pin in the map, a target in an endless succession of targets, some far away and some farther still. The middle distance of Germany's industrial north was not such a long way off, but it was a drawn out, jittery journey for a wireless operator who'd taken to swallowing his benzedrine tablet, and the mid-gunner's as well.

On the day of the Hanover raid, Van den Graaf went to crew assembly and then to the wireless operators briefing. Then he walked the gunnery leader's dog around the perimeter track – Lofty saw him from a distance, throwing a thin curl of tyre-rubber for the dog to chase. He seemed cheerful enough, and had no problem demolishing his egg and bacon. The WAAF radio-technician who met Van den Graaf in Tommy for an equipment check thought something wasn't right, he was a little too solicitous about the set – made her take the facing off and then stood staring at the perfectly sound fixings as if it would mis-wire itself before his eyes.

Then, when the crew was suiting up, Van den Graaf took off his Mae West and laid it on the bench. He told them he could not go on – he'd lost his nerve and couldn't risk the rest of the crew by stuffing up. Duncan was putting on his kapok outer suit, bent double to snap the fasteners over his flying boots, breathless from the press of the layers of clothes around his midriff. One of the studs came off in his hand just at the moment Van den Graaf announced he'd had it.

The flight engineer closed the door, and leaned on it. Crowe took off his flying helmet and held it the way a man holds a pair of gloves on entering a theatre.

'I understand,' he said. 'We all do.' Crowe's dark eyes were amiable, and mild. He looked around at the crew, holding each man's gaze, forcing what nods were slow to follow. 'But – ' Crowe added gently, 'understanding doesn't get the job done.' He told Van den Graaf that the day was long in the tooth and they'd be unlikely to find a replacement. Surely he could see his way clear to fly one more operation? It wasn't as if *they* didn't trust him.

'You'll come right, Faye,' Crowe cajoled – adding, for reasons no one could fathom – 'It's only a hop to Hanover.' Then, waving his gloves towards the door, Crowe asked Duncan to take the wireless operator out, to see that he get 'a nice cup of tea' – despite the fact none of them liked to drink before an operation. Duncan put down his parachute and Mae West and went to his friend, careful not to look into the South African's sweating, pale face. After the two had gone, the rest of the crew discussed their options. Lofty's expression was more pinched than usual, his lips compressed into a line. He was for letting Faye go. 'It's what he wants,' was all he could say. The navigator, Derek, thought they should call the MO and ask his advice and the bomb aimer thought the worst that could happen was they'd be unserviceable as a crew and might therefore miss an op.

'Not the worst for Faye,' Lofty said, and that shut them up for a moment. But when Duncan brought Van den Graaf back, he'd pulled himself together; was apologetic.

'I'll be alright.'

'We'll keep an eye on you,' Crowe promised, slapping the South African on the shoulder.

When it came to it, this was difficult to manage. The navigator's position was hard up by the wireless operator's but once the Merlins were roaring, and Derek had closed the curtains that kept in the navigation light, he might as well have been in another Lancaster. He was in any case kept busy throughout the flight – too busy to babysit the South African.

Lofty tried his best to look out for his friend. Several times he'd clambered down from the mid-upper turret to look along the fuselage at Van den Graaf sitting, sallow-skinned, in the green glow of his dials. But checking once or twice was all he could manage and on the flight back when Duncan saw the shadow of a Fokker-Wulf, Lofty had to keep his post, staring out through the frozen perspex, his parachute clenched between his knees.

It wasn't until Lofty noticed that he was more than usually cold that he'd let himself down from the mid-upper turret, jelly-legged with fatigue. Not seeing Van den Graaf at his set, Lofty crept clumsily over the wing spar, past the rest bunk and spare oxygen bottles, and on through the obstacle course of the crowded fuselage.

The wireless operator's position was empty. The pages of Van den Graaf's log were riffling under the flying helmet that had been placed there to hold it. Lofty felt cold on the strip of skin between his goggles and his mask and looked up – he had passed beneath a square of night sky where metal ought to have been. The emergency exit was gone. And there on the fuselage floor a neatly packed parachute lay.

He picked it up. For a second he thought it was his own, dropped in the excitement, but he still had that. He had his hands full of bloody parachutes, and *one* of them clearly hadn't worked. The WAAF safety equipment worker who issued them made the same joke before every operation. She'd say, *Bring it back if it doesn't open*, before thrusting the thing into the waiting hands of the crew. And it hadn't opened, had it?

Lofty shook the packs of silk in his hands and breathed jerkily into his mask. There was a laugh rolling about in his chest and he let the thing go, bashing the parachutes together like cymbals.

Lofty had not plugged in his intercom, and its cord now jerked and swung in front of the waist ties of his Mae West. The crew could not hear him laughing: certainly not Duncan behind the armoured doors of the rear turret; nor the navigator just up the fuselage – at the back of the pulpit, behind his confessional curtains. But something did make Derek pop his head out, red light bleeding around the gap in the blackout cloth he held clutched about his shoulders – so that it looked to Lofty like a severed head floating out at him.

The gunner fumbled for the socket by the dinghy stowage and plugged in his intercom.

'*What on earth's up?*' the navigator asked, his voice tinny in the earphones of Lofty's flying helmet.

The skipper chimed in, 'Mid-gunner, is there a problem?'

'Only if the lack of a wireless operator is a problem,' Lofty said and bit down on another jittery laugh.

Intercraft communication on a sortie was generally a disciplined business. There was never unnecessary chat, and what talk there was was framed by speech so formal it would have fit proceedings at the Old Bailey. Everything about the gunner's response was therefore wrong. Derek was so alarmed that he came fully out of his possie, and reported crisply, 'The exit above the wing spar is open.'

'Thank you navigator,' the pilot said.

Lofty felt like he had on Oxygen Starvation Drill, and wondered mildly at his nitrogen levels. Even allowing for the timbre-changing intercom, his voice sounded in his own ears more tightly than it should. And he couldn't stop laughing. His mind kept giving him an image of Faye taking off his flying helmet and mask to climb out of the hatch. That hatch was just ten feet behind the dome of the mid-upper turret, ten feet behind Lofty's head, and he'd missed it all: Van den Graaf sucked off into the dark – gurgling up the drain of an upside-down world.

It wasn't a bit funny.

'See that the mid's oxygen is working, would you Nav?'

'I'm coming up,' announced a fourth voice.

'Stay in position, rear gunner.'

Derek, meanwhile, had taken hold of Lofty and was fiddling

with his oxygen bottle. He unclipped it from the line, tapping it sharply on the glycol tank, then stretched and massaged the line before reconnecting it. Then he placed the mask over the gunner's face like a doctor administering ether to a patient. After a moment, Lofty fixed his own mask and waved the navigator away.

'I'm coming up,' Duncan said again.

'I'd appreciate it if one gunner stayed put,' the pilot replied.

'No.'

Crowe's voice changed then, and Lofty could hear the wear in it. 'Duncan, please.' He followed this imprecation by asking, 'You didn't see a parachute open, rear gunner?'

Lofty sighed. 'How could he, if the bugger didn't take one?'

At that the intercom fell silent, although each man in the aircraft could hear the tinny echo of the Lancaster's engine through his earphones, a castrato accompaniment to the bass roar the Merlins actually made. Once he'd started breathing normally, Lofty put down Van den Graaf's parachute and clambered back along the Lancaster to his position. There was static in his ears, the sound of a crew with nothing to say. He swivelled the guns, doing a lazy scan of the available air, willing himself not to turn and look at the emergency exit above the wings. He thought he might see the South African clinging to the airframe, glittering strings of ice in his hair.

Chapter Eighteen

Prophecy

For Tommy's crew it was a longer than usual return leg across the North Sea, and there was little talk until the bus set them down at dispersal. In the interrogation hut the crew sat, arms crossed, smoking their cigarettes with a little more vigour than usual. Crowe left it to the mid-gunner and navigator to fill in the WAAF intelligence officer, a non-com seasoned by years of hearing from crews what had gone right, and wrong, on operations. The intelligence officer knew that Tommy's wireless operator was not the first man to jump out of a bomber without a parachute, but he *was* the first that crew had known, so she kept her voice light, and made herself smile at the bomb aimer's crack about the wireless operator having failed to follow the proper procedure for parachute drill. On the margin of one page of the report she penned a short notation, meaning to have a word to the medical officer: 'Rear gunner wept in interrogation.' Men certainly cried after operations, but seldom in front of others. They'd find a quiet corner of the aerodrome – the blast and air raid shelters nearest to the interrogation building were popular places after a particularly hairy raid. But the sight of that young man sitting in his chair, sobbing, a wet-ended cigarette in one hand, was another thing again.

That morning Lofty carried a saucer of milk for Duncan's cat from the mess and both gunners sat on Duncan's bed watching the cat drink, its pink tongue darting in and out of the milk as it watched them, amber eyes wide. Lofty sat with his arm draped over his friend's shoulder. The South African's bunk was nearest the window: they'd tossed a coin for it. Now the bed looked particularly empty with the light lying in it instead of him.

In the evening, Lofty went to the mess alone, sitting away from the other drinkers with a pint warming in his hand. The only person he spoke to was Crowe. The skipper had managed to get his gunners a 72-hour leave; Lofty thought it was probably down to Duncan.

So they filled up the car with RAF petrol and drove down through Lincolnshire, stopping at East Kirkby. There the Duty Officer told them that the WAAF they were enquiring after had been sent to another station. The two unshaven non-coms in their frayed best blues must have made a pathetic sight, because the duty officer told them the name of the posting. But Olive's new station was north, and the gunners were heading south, so they drove on to London to lose themselves in an assortment of servicemen's clubs and hotel dining rooms.

While the gunners were on leave Olive received a letter from

Lofty – one page of Comfort's Fund stationery describing Faye's suicide. For a day she carried the letter about with her; read and re-read it as if some fresh examination of the thing might answer her questions. There was no number at which she could contact them, and she didn't have a pass due for a month. All she could do was wait.

Neither Olive's waiting nor the press of feeling behind it was lost on Cathy. She was of the opinion that war produced far too many stoics and when Olive – exhausted by a duty in which three aircraft had gone missing – sat weeping on the cold floor next to the bath, she held her hand, cooing, 'There now, that's the way, let it out' as if the thing being vented were not tears, but poison.

'You could call your friend Evelyn,' Cathy sensibly pointed out. 'I'll have a quiet word with one of the clerks on the section officer's staff. I'm sure she can find you a line since there's no ops on.'

Olive rallied at that. She was not on watch again until midnight and there was ample time to put a call through to White Waltham. It was Tuesday – domestic evening – and although no WAAF personnel were allowed off Station, the chocolate ration was due. There'd be a mad rush on the canteen, and consequently few competitors for a line out. Just in case, Cathy sent her off to the administration building with a Fry's Chocolate Cream Bar for the telephonist.

'258 Littlewick Green, you're through now,' the telephonist said, as delicately as she could around a mouthful of chocolate, and then stood to let Olive take her seat. Olive was trying the aerodrome office at White Waltham. After the day's deliveries Evelyn would often hang about to await the arrival of the last Anson load of pilots taxied in from their destination fields. Luckily for Olive, she was there.

'I was in the mess making up for a missed lunch,' she said, not prefacing the statement with a hello. Then she added, less brightly, 'You're feeling low.'

'Lofty didn't say much about what happened.'

'There was a raid on Leipzig.' Evelyn said this in a flat voice. 'That's a long way for them to go. And to a new target.'

North Killingholme had contributed aircraft to that raid, and Olive knew how far away it was from the hours they'd had to sit in the Flying Control Office waiting on the returning planes. Leipzig was not as deep within Germany (nor as heavily defended) as Berlin, but the crews considered it a dicey target because it was new.

Olive tapped a nail on the bakelite mouth of the receiver. She was puzzled. Leipzig was the target two nights *after* the operation on which Van den Graaf had died.

'What's Leipzig got to do with it?'

A silence on the line was followed by Evelyn's asking, in an uncharacteristically small voice, 'When did you last hear from Duncan?'

Olive's stomach rolled. 'I got a letter from Lofty. About Faye going missing on the raid to Hanover.'

There was a silence on the other end of the line, and Olive knew that it was a place-holder for bad news.

In a weaker voice, Evelyn told her that T-Tommy had failed to return from the Leipzig raid. The Lanc had been seen struggling against the strong easterly winds not forecast by the meteorological officer and, with the rest of the stream, had bombed the cloud above the city. Then, despite Crowe's habit of flying the Lancaster outside the bomber stream so as to avoid the night-fighters drawn to it, Tommy took its place in the mass for the return leg. Perhaps the navigator had been wounded or they'd had some kind of instrument failure and Crowe did not want to risk drifting off-course – following the other returning planes might have been the best way back in such conditions. When the stream was over Holland a tail-gunner in a Lancaster from Waddington saw Lancaster PM-T with one of its engines on fire. He counted three parachutes clearing the craft before it went in, on fire. The gunner of a 3 Group Stirling flying three thousand feet below the Waddington Lancaster had seen the wing of a neighboring aircraft deflate the canopy of a parachute...

Evelyn paused, and her voice brightened as she spoke to someone at her end.

Under the teacups, she said, which made Olive think of the shell game played on Brighton Pier – the punters asked to pick the right cup. Wistfully, she whispered to herself, 'Tommy is under the teacups.'

'I beg your pardon?' Evelyn asked, and quietly finished her story.

During the Leipzig raid, Duncan and Lofty had been fast asleep in their beds at a hotel in Charing Cross after dancing all night at a Combined Service hop. Now, without knowing it, they'd become orphans.

Duncan had sent her a telegram the next morning – luckily there'd been no flying that day and she'd been able to get permission to go to London to see him.

'I can't talk about it on the telephone,' she now told Olive, 'but Duncan isn't in good shape. When I saw him he looked like someone just out of a coma. Even Lofty's near the end of his tether. There wasn't much I could do in the time I had – I talked about home as much as I could and made sure they both ate properly and then I saw them off at Victoria Station. I haven't heard from either of them since.'

Olive had been listening quietly, polite in her relief. Tommy had gone in, but had done so without the people she cared about on board. 'Duncan and Lofty are alive, that's what counts.'

There was a silence on the line, and then Evelyn said archly, 'Don't be so cold-blooded.'

Olive bit her lip. 'All I meant was that it could have been worse.'

'It may get worse yet. The war gives ample time and opportunity to bad luck.'

Evelyn said this with such bitterness that Olive knew there must be something else. 'What's up?' she asked, and eyed the telephonist. The girl was licking chocolate off the ends of her fingers, like a cat washing.

'I'm worried about Duncan, and won't be about to keep an eye on him. Our father's had a fall and broken his hip. He can't work and it's going to be a long while before he'll be able to. They want me to come home.'

'They've always wanted you to come home.'

'It's different now.'

She could not see how, nor could she see the source of Evelyn's new-found sense of filial sacrifice. She traced her fingertips over the switches on the board and said, 'It would be better if Duncan went.'

'Of course it would. But he's not on his own recognisance, and I am.'

Olive saw that was true. Duncan couldn't choose, and if he refused to fly he'd only spend the remainder of his war sweeping out hangars or sluicing down ablutions blocks; alive but invisible – no wings, no operational pay and as far from home as ever.

Olive said, 'I'm glad you're going.' But what she actually felt was a cold, blank terror – she'd come to England to bring Evelyn home and now Evelyn would go home without her.

Evelyn was silent for a moment, and then she said, around what sounded like a smile, 'Liar! Anyway, nothing's decided just yet.'

The telephonist gestured at her, spinning an invisible ball on her finger. Olive blinked stupidly for a second, but when the telephonist made to pull the plug from the socket she took her meaning.

'I have to go,' she said to Evelyn, and passed over the receiver, beaming at the telephonist. 'I don't suppose I could make another call?'

There was not a smudge, not a shadow, of chocolate on the fingers the woman waved at her. 'You don't suppose right.'

Olive trudged back to her hut and found Cathy and her roommates sitting cross-legged on their beds at make and mend. Betty was knitting new thumbs on a sorry looking pair of gloves, the corner of her tongue poking out as she frowned down at her stitch-work. Cathy was filling in the holes in her winter-weight stockings, and two pairs of blackouts sat next to her waiting their turn. On the inside of the waistband her name was just visible.

'Guess what?' Cathy asked. Her lipstick was crisscrossed with pale stripes from where she'd pressed a row of pins between her lips.

'What?' Olive said tiredly. The cover on her bed was cold when she sat on it, as was the room itself.

'I've got us permission to move into digs.'

Betty gaped. 'You never!'

'RAF willing, and no other hitches.'

'How did you do it?' Olive asked, impressed despite herself.

'You know they're down on us mixing in, and the new Education Officer has ideas about preparing female members of the service for a return to their peacetime roles. There's to be *classes*.' At this idea, Cathy widened her eyes so that she looked like a cinema idol. 'I've seen the schedule – baking, dressmaking, how to iron a damp skirt, that sort of thing. Then there's the Recreational Training. Decorative stitch-craft and – ' she put down her darning and did a little jig in front of her bed, ' – tap-dancing, if you can believe it.'

'Ger'over. You're full of it,' Betty said, forgetting the diction she'd been practising for days.

'This is the pukka gen,' Cathy said, signing a quick left vest pocket – right vest pocket – knot of tie – belt buckle – cross. 'I suggested that domestic duties were better learned in a domestic situation and they actually went for it. We're to have one of the cottages in the village.'

Cathy saw the look on Olive's face and, misinterpreting it, said, 'We'll still get to mess here. And won't it be nice to have a home for the rest of the time, a real place of our own?'

Olive thought about that for a minute and came up with an image of the Macintyres' house in Canabolas, Evelyn sitting on the porch with the dogs.

'Wonderful,' she said, and lay back on her bunk.

Olive showed very little interest in the move, but she did eventually pack her kit and – with the bar heater clutched awkwardly under one arm – walked over the fields, and past the church, to the house at the end of Church Lane. Cathy wanted to celebrate, and she'd wangled a tin of spam from one of the Americans at the Cross Keys for that purpose. The new housemates ate standing around the kitchen table: they did not have any chairs.

Evelyn had tendered her resignation to the ATA, and written Duncan to break the news that she was bound for home. It was, by then, early November, and Olive, like Evelyn, was worrying more and more about Duncan. He was in the infirmary with influenza, and Lofty was left to fly as a spare with crews short of their complement. It was just as well there was not much flying to be done since the autumnal fogs had rolled in from the Humber.

Lofty went to the hospital every day. He would pull a utility chair close to the edge of Duncan's bed and sit, his knees just touching the neatly tucked blanket, and read the fever patient his mail.

Duncan had been in the infirmary for two days when Lofty read him Evelyn's letter, with its news that she was off home. Sounding cheerier than usual, Lofty talked about brightening prospects. He told Duncan that he'd been before the wing commander – they'd had 'a full and frank discussion', after which the Old Man had come around wonderfully. He'd arranged for their posting to a new squadron, where they could crew together. And they were to get leave: they did not have to report to the new station until early November.

'*Everyone* gets a fresh start,' Lofty said. He patted Duncan's knee and, putting the glass of water within reach, waited for a reaction to the news.

'Thank God,' muttered Duncan through cracked lips.

Lofty went back to the crew hut. Since he had the place to himself, he stretched out on his bunk and took up the battered copy of *The Prophet* he'd borrowed from some donnish type long since gone for six. But the lines on the pages moved as if on a gyro, and he couldn't concentrate.

His meeting with the wing commander hadn't proceeded as smoothly as he'd represented it to Duncan – had been no victory.

The wingco had been wondering what was to be done with them.

Gunners were in demand: but not two at a time. *A brace. A pair –* , the wing commander had said, stroking his moustache. – *So hard to place.* Then, as if beginning a verse by Housman, he'd added, *There is a squadron forming –*

As far as the wingco saw it, the gunners had two options: to stay in 103 and take their chances, or to join the new squadron at North Killingholme, and crew together.

Lofty had considered this, frowning. They would have a shorter tour if they stayed, but would fly in different crews. He'd never gambled, and had no head for figures, but reckoned this shortened the odds that one of them would buy it. The prospect of a Lancaster and a crew hut not shared with his friend swayed him. In any case, Duncan might not hold it together, having lost Faye and his skipper in such quick succession.

Then there was the fact that Olive was at North Killingholme.

After Lofty had volunteered their services for the new squadron, he'd thought that would be that. But the wing commander had not dismissed him.

'Now, don't take this wrongly,' the wingco had said, 'but I should like to know: was Pilot Officer Crowe a pansy? Things have been said about –'

Without thinking, Lofty put in, 'Not about me, Sir.'

The wing commander had been moved to wonder about Curtis Crowe. Didn't Hilliers think it odd? Fighter Command, honorable service: and nothing to show for it but the rank of pilot officer in a bomber crew. Then the wingco rumbled on about not minding what the man did in his own time – so long as his inclinations didn't taint the crew.

At the word 'taint' his upper lip had lifted disdainfully.

Now, as the lines of poetry Lofty had been reading dipped and wavered, he heard the wingco's parting comment. *I'm just telling you – the wisdom of discretion, and all that.*

Not a victory, so much as a dismissal.

It was getting late in the afternoon, and the day seemed to balloon and stretch – hours that work couldn't fill; that were unendurable without company. Since he and Duncan had lost their crew and become spares everybody was a potential crew-mate, but each was nevertheless a stranger. The canteen would be noisy, and full, and Lofty didn't want to show his face there while others sat about in a briefing, and were soon off to war. His eyes lit on the cracked delft china of the saucer Duncan kept for the cat, and he got up to go in search of it. He'd not seen the cat since he'd nudged it off the end of his bunk in the small hours of the morning. Duncan would have seen the thing inside hours ago, would have made a nest for it in that pullover he kept spare, the one now matted with ginger fur.

Outside the hardstanding was slick with rain, its surface dotted with puddles black in the early dusk. Lofty called the cat, feeling like a fool, and when it didn't come he fetched its plate and hit that lightly with a knife. If it had been a dog, it would already be at his heels, and Lofty – a confirmed lover of canines – soon got tired of calling. The cat was probably off somewhere making short of the rodent population, or hunting birds, and would bring its prize back to show him when it was ready.

He did not think about it again until the next day, when he woke after a night not spent vying for leg-space. The dish of milk was untouched, the fat on its surface yellowed and congealing. He intended to look for the cat after breakfast, but the battle order was posted and he was down to crew with H for Harry. There was a strange turret to check, guns he'd never fired before, briefings to attend, and a crew to meet.

That night 103 flew a minor operation, leafleting – a few aircraft fluttering down over Germany along with the propaganda. *Wasteful bloody use of resources*, thought Lofty and the crew of H for Harry, once they were back at Elsham.

When they'd appeared at mess for their well-deserved operational breakfast it was to a gerfuffle. Lofty saw at once this was not the usual sort of flap – men to-ing and fro-ing between tables, talking loudly and joking. The atmosphere in the room was like that of a strike-meeting at the mine: the men sullen, talking desultorily in little groups, as if – in their twos and threes – they feared an informer in their midst. H for Harry's crew had come late – the last crew out of interrogation – so the pilot, a young Canadian named Cosgrove, had to ask one of the waiters what was up.

'They've arrested some character, billed him for subversion until they can find a proper charge. The CO went troppo – told the bugger he'd undermined the morale of the station and would be court-martialled and in detention before he could say Mother Brown.' The waiter, a thin-faced man too old to make aircrew, stood worrying the napkin he'd been about to set on the table.

'What did he do?' the navigator asked.

'Fifth columnist,' put in the flight engineer before the man could reply. 'There has to be one or two of them lurking about.'

The waiter waved the napkin at that dismissively. 'No such thing. He'd been poisoning animals. The CO's dog, for one. Bloke's barmy – hates animals like we hate Hitler.'

'Then I jolly well hope they hang him,' the flight engineer said, fastidiously scraping the uncooked white from his egg before settling to the task of eating.

Lofty ate quickly, wiping the remnants of yolk from his plate with a slice of toast collapsed at its centre. Back at the crew hut, the men who'd not been out to war slept on, blankets pulled up to their ears. To Lofty, they looked like kiddies. He crept quietly about, taking the razor and block of soap from his kit and shaving quickly, the bloody nicks made by the over-used blade dripping chilly pink water back into the bowl.

He set himself a search grid, working outward from the crew-hut, taking in all the places a cat might wander: the kitchen, the admin blocks and through the long swathes of uncut grass at the edge of dispersal. It was there he found it, fur matted and dew-wet, its freckled lips bared and frozen in a rictus of pain. Lofty looked down at the little corpse expressionlessly for a minute and then went back to the canteen to get something to wrap it in. It was a fat packet of newspaper, then, that he carried over to the shooting range so he could borrow a shovel. A group of new gunners were banging away at clay pigeons to keep their hands in, and they stopped long enough to tell him where the tools were kept.

'Better sign it out or there'll be trouble,' one of the sergeant gunners yelled after him, but Lofty couldn't be bothered, he just slammed the door of the concrete shed and walked off with the shovel.

He buried the cat in the long grass by the perimeter wire, under a sign that warned of low flying. While he crouched there fussing at the soil, the ground under his heels thrummed as a Lancaster on a daylight sortie thundered up the runway towards its air. Since it was the last thing he'd read, so the first thing to mind, Lofty spoke a few lines from *The Prophet* aloud, feeling less stupid than he had when calling the still-living cat to its dinner.

'All your hours,' he told the little pile of hard earth he'd turned, 'are wings that beat through space from self to self.' After a pause he added, ' – or not,' and headed back towards the warm mess for a cup of tea.

The hardest thing was telling Duncan.

'How are you, old cock?' Lofty said, as he pulled up a chair and tossed two Fry's bars on the bedcover. Their chocolate ration had just come in.

Duncan was propped against his pillows, and had the sleeves of his dressing-gown rolled up his pale forearms. He looked surprisingly bulky and businesslike and Lofty made the mistake of thinking his friend was on the mend.

Duncan had been playing patience and the cards lay all aslant on his blanketed lap. Lofty craned his neck to see the cards in his hand, 'Jack on queen,' he said and tapped the place in the pile his friend had missed.

'Oh, right, didn't see it.' Duncan slid the queen of hearts over the face of the Jack. 'The nurse says I'll be fit for release tomorrow.'

'Good show. That's our holiday started.' Lofty shifted uncomfortably in his chair. 'But I have a bit of bad news I'm afraid.' He should have stopped then, because Duncan said *yes* placidly and went on turning up the cards. 'It's about the cat.'

Duncan put a five of diamonds on a four of clubs, then a king of spades on an ace of hearts.

Lofty reached out to stop him, saying he thought it was a one-way pack in patience, but Duncan evaded the hand and laid down the card he wanted.

'Just tell me about the cat.'

'I'm afraid it's dead, old chap.'

'Is it?'

'One of the erks went barmy. He thought cats and dogs were wicked and set about doing away with them. With poison.' Lofty stumbled in the face of his friend's silence. 'I'm sorry, Duncan.'

The tail gunner brushed the cards from his lap with a sigh and sunk back under the covers. He shut his eyes and his pale, bluish, eyelids flickered. 'Oh,' he said, and a tear hovered above the cheek turned nearest the pillow. 'Oh,' he said again, with the surprise of a man hit by spent flak.

'It was probably quick,' Lofty said, hearing his own lack of conviction beneath the murmuring of the nurse who'd come to give the man in the next bed his bedpan.

'Just leave me for a bit, would you?' Duncan said, so quietly Lofty almost missed it.

Duncan was not released the next morning. The nurse told Lofty he'd taken a turn for the worse and she wanted the MO to have a good look at him. A proper look, she said, her round face dimpling.

'Why?' Lofty asked, suspiciously.

'To see whether he's fit.'

To that, the mid-gunner had nothing to say. If Duncan wasn't fit, if they took him off flying duties, he'd be safe, and his war would be over. So long as the dispensation came without shame Lofty couldn't see a problem with it. He could manage by himself: it was only a matter of going up and coming back and not being blown out of the air and killed. Surely one could get by better than two, odds being what they were. Not that anyone spoke of the odds, and Lofty – whose mind turned from gambling with a distaste learned from the Dominican priests who'd raised him in his Westport orphanage – shied at making bets with himself.

But later that day Duncan turned up in the crew hut, looking more drawn than ever and – if it was possible – thinner. He sat on his bed and smiled wanly at Lofty.

'Ops on then?' he asked, and Lofty nodded.

'Some other blokes up for it tonight, so you can rest, old son.'

Saying this Lofty thought 'old son' an apt description of his friend: a boy grown old unexpectedly, and his dependent. 'Fancy a brew?' he asked, looking about the room to see whether he'd left any trace of the cat to trouble Duncan.

'If you like.'

So they walked over to the NAAFI, Lofty glancing nervously into Duncan's face. He let his friend buy the buns, and – that evening – the beer they drank without their customary enthusiasm.

After their second, Duncan looked over the top of his pint, and asked, 'Why do you think he did it?'

'Faye?' Lofty twisted the glass in his hand thoughtfully. 'Impossible to say.'

'Perhaps he knew something was going to happen.'

'Oh he knew something alright, since he didn't sleepwalk his way through the emergency hatch.'

'No, I mean he knew something would happen to T for Tommy.'

Lofty had nothing to say to that. He'd not made up his mind about the prescient forebodings of aircrew. Certainly he knew cases of men who'd announced they weren't going to make it, and didn't. And if soldiers killed at the front in the last war could appear as spectral visitors to family back home, then why not men foreseeing their fate?

The thing was, Lofty didn't want to know what was going to happen. Ignorance was by far the preferable option.

'Difficult to know really,' he said, carefully. His friend was looking at him with such intensity that he opened his mouth to say more, but Duncan beat him to it.

'Curtis knew. That's why he got us leave. He wanted to make sure I'd be alright.'

On hearing the skipper's name, Lofty stiffened and put down his glass. 'You can't know that, Duncan.'

'It's what I choose to think. That he'd tried to spare me.'

'The skipper was trying to spare you, but not *that*. He was just giving us a rest, which was bloody decent of him and if by any chance he's survived I'll be the first to shake his hand and tell him so.'

Lofty looked around the mess. It was emptying out, and there'd be no waiting time at the counter. He stood and reached for Duncan's glass but something in his friend's face stopped his hand. He let it close, the fingers loosely curled.

Suddenly Lofty knew that it was Duncan who wouldn't make it – he was sitting there like a man already dead.

'Is that pint coming any time in the next century?' the tail gunner asked and Lofty scooped both glasses up to his chest and went to the bar, glad to have his back turned on the apparition.

Chapter Nineteen

Ping-Pong

The call sign for 629 Squadron was Ping-Pong. Some air-ministry wit had tired of signs sounding like Oxfordshire cottages, or the houses in a public school, and for 629 had filched the name of a once fashionable sport. Inclement weather and tiny backyards had made table tennis the perfect choice for a leisured middle class unable to afford snooker. The R/T operators could hardly mistake Ping-Pong for another phrase, and it bounced between aircraft and tower hundreds of times throughout the final months of Olive's war.

The new squadron was ready for battle. Below the tower three of its Lancaster Mk II's sat on the hardstanding – the black and dark green of their camouflage markings as yet unblemished.

Olive was missing Evelyn terribly. A letter from Duncan she'd received that morning told how he and Lofty were about to join Evelyn at Ida's, and Olive felt – not for the first time – envious of the generous amount of leave allotted to aircrew. But the news that they were afterward to join 629 Squadron here at North

Killingholme so cheered her that she had to share it. She found Cathy leaning over the sink in the kitchen, eating toast – she preferred to do this than to use a plate, thinking it kept the crumbs off her uniform.

'That's the practicality of our living here – ' Cathy said, dandling her fingers under a freshet of frigid water from the tap, 'somewhere you can get your courting done in private.'

Olive shook her head at this, and ran back up the narrow stairs to her room. How could she imagine she thought about Duncan that way? Cathy was so upright in her own affairs – why should she assume her friend was any different? But it occurred to her, then, how little she had talked about her feelings. Cathy knew that she worried about Duncan; that he'd long been one of her better correspondents, and that they'd known each other since they were children. It was not such a leap to imagine he might be a potential beau.

Downstairs, she heard the door slam, the sound of the gate opening, and the bicycle sliding in the gravel in the lane. She put Evelyn's letter down and went to put her coat on.

At the end of her watch a call came from the duty officer to say that a flight sergeant from 103 was being escorted over to the tower, where she was to meet him.

The daylight that met her was little different from the dimness of the Flying Control Office itself – Lincolnshire had turned out another dourly grey day. She stood by the wall of the admin building waiting for Lofty, her coat about her shoulders.

'It's three back to the gate then,' she said, when Lofty arrived with the sentry. She pushed the handlebars of her bike into the gunner's hands.

His face fell. 'Will you not see me?'

'I will, but not here.'

'Wonderful. I was going to suggest an outing.'

'Not to the pub,' she scolded. 'We have a cottage in the village. This can be a proper visit – something you'll need to get used to when you're stationed here.'

Lofty took the look she gave him mildly, and said, 'Oh yes, right,' but a little too vaguely for her liking.

The reason for his reticence became clear once they'd left the aerodrome. Ivy's coupé was parked at the side of the lane by the stile leading across the fields to the church, and there was a figure at the wheel. When Olive saw the red-knuckled hand waving out the window of the Morris she realised it was Evelyn.

'Fancy a drive?' Evelyn asked breezily. Olive blinked, and looked again. Evelyn had a diamond earring centred on the neat lobe of each ear, and was in civvies.

'Olive wanted to go to her place.' Lofty jerked his head in the general direction of the church tower. 'In the village.'

'Not on your life,' Evelyn said, and stretched a hand out to examine her nail polish. 'I want to see Thornton Abbey. There's nothing so cheering as a ruin not made by the Luftwaffe.'

Since she had not yet seen the abbey, Olive agreed, and went to prop her bike against the fence-wire bordering the aerodrome.

'We've got a bit of a picnic lunch, if you're hungry,' Evelyn said, looking at her friend's angular profile. 'Nothing on the ration though.'

'Bloody rabbit food,' said Lofty and pulled a face.

The Morris coupé was a single-seater so Olive sat between Lofty and Evelyn, hands on lap and shoulders hunched.

'Is Duncan alright?' she asked.

But Evelyn was peering out over the hedgerows, and was not listening. She pointed east, past the railway signalman's shack and the rail bridge. 'Goxhill is behind that wood,' she said. 'I delivered my only Mustang there.' The forearm protruding from its red sleeve was still muscled, though it was odd not seeing it framed by blue serge.

'When are you going back home?' Olive asked.

'Never mind about that,' Evelyn said, slowing the car. 'Look!'

The carved figures above the gatehouse tower had loomed up over the tops of the trees bordering Abbey Farm – cowled and crowned heads facing the North Sea to greet the returning planes.

'There's a sight you don't see every day,' Evelyn said, just as the trees rose to obscure it.

There were no other cars at the wayside, although the muddy verge was marked by the tyre-tracks of a score of bicycles. A cold wind blew the three visitors through the arch of the gate-tower. Not even Lofty paused to scrutinise the names and dates carved into the stone by eighteenth- and nineteenth-century tourists. The abbey itself was unprepossessing. The only part accessible that still had the shape of a habitation was away from the main ruins, and surrounded by grazing sheep. This building had thick walls and a roof, and there were even raised stones along the sides of the inside wall that made serviceable seats.

'Ye olde air-raid shelter,' said Lofty, and went in, out of the wind. The other two followed.

When they'd sat down Lofty looked at Evelyn, and she back at him.

'What *are* you doing here?' Olive asked.

Lofty clenched his teeth and leaned forward, hands clasped, elbows on his knees, looking for all the world like a union agitator about to propose a strike.

'Right,' he said, 'I'll give it to you straight.' But *straight* did not equate with *immediately*. He sighed, took off his split-arse cap and ran stubby fingers through his hair, and Olive had to prompt him before he said, 'We want to get Duncan out of operations. And out of the war.' Saying this, he shook his head, as if it were resisting the proposition.

Olive stretched out her legs, putting the heel of one shoe on the toe of the other to make a footrest. 'Why stop at him? Why not get the whole of Europe out as well?' She laughed, but they did not join in.

'Duncan's had a basinful. He won't make it in the shape he's in.'

Evelyn settled back against the stone. 'I agree. He barely held himself together after hearing about the Leipzig raid.'

'Then get him to report sick. The MO will see he's not fit for operational duty.'

'Brand him LM-bloody-F, more likely,' Lofty said. 'Our MO is a dim bastard – he thinks flying stress is restricted to pilots and navigators. If a gunner loses his bottle it's seen as malingering, since the job's not that hard to do. Supposedly.'

'And Duncan won't wear an accusation of Lack of Moral Fibre,' Evelyn added. 'Not after what happened to Faye.'

Lofty looked down at the clumps of dirty wool blown into the shelter, and scuffed at one with his boot. 'We're orphan gunners – we've got no crew to speak for us; no one to back us up if we go to the wing commander,' he said. 'Duncan doesn't want to be seen as unfit. The only way to get him to stop cracking hardy is to break him, or get him out.'

'And what if you're wrong? What if he can manage?' Olive frowned. 'In the sense that half of Bomber Command can. By muddling through.'

'The thing is – ' Evelyn said coolly, tucking her chin into the fur collar of her coat, ' – we have an idea. But you have to keep your head when we tell you.' She sat up very straight, then – enunciating each word as if she'd been the one in R/T – laid out the gist of her plan. 'Duncan goes home to the farm and I come to the new squadron with Lofty.' She let out the breath she'd been holding. 'There.'

'We've thrashed it out – ' Lofty began, but Olive's look stopped him cold.

'If you mean what I think you mean, it's – absurd.' She considered her rebuke, and finding it wanting, added, '*You* are absurd, and hardly fit to help Duncan. You're proposing to put on a man's uniform; to live in a crew hut and fly in a Lancaster. To do a job you're not trained to do.'

'Yes. I'm proposing exactly that. And I can do it.' Evelyn said this so firmly, and with such hope, that it was painful to hear. So, thought Olive, *this* is how you sort your doubts about going back.

Evelyn would not be embarrassed out of her idea. She put her chin up, and her grey eyes shone. 'I'm not afraid of this. I can do what my brother can't. The war provides no other options, nor any other means – *honourable* means, that is.' Evelyn shut her eyes for a second, as if to keep the idea – the plan – free from the sullying light of law, logic and practicality. She was, in that moment, more beautiful than Olive had ever seen her.

She added, quietly, 'We have the wherewithal and the will, but what we lack – ' she opened her eyes and looked at her friend, ' – is you.'

'All for one and one for all,' said Lofty, so nervously that his voice went up an octave. 'Practicalities don't count for much. It's what people do with them that makes the difference.' Like Evelyn he did not wish to be drawn on the details: the documents and photographs to be doctored and forged, the bribes and black market contacts.

'*There's* a word for what you're talking about,' she said, looking from Lofty to Evelyn. 'Desertion. Why don't you give it proper due.'

'It's only desertion as far as King's Regulations are concerned,' Evelyn archly replied. 'I'm Duncan's sister, and you're his friend.

What duty do you suppose that obliges? And how can it be dereliction of duty, if someone stands in for the defaulter? If I were to sum this up in a word, it wouldn't be "desertion", nor anything so base as that.'

Olive twisted in her seat to look at her friend, and asked, 'What, then? Duty? Sacrifice? Preparedness?'

Evelyn merely smiled, and looked down at her long-fingered, calloused hands.

'This isn't the cricket pitch at Bathurst,' Olive added, 'and we're not playing a game.'

'Nor am I as unprepared as you think. I had flights as a supernumerary gunner with the Army Air Training Corps. And Lofty can take me out to the firing range every day we're not on ops.'

'Evelyn's a dab hand at the shotgun with clay pigeons – '

'Which are *so* like Me-109s and Fokker-Wulfs.'

Lofty blinked. 'Shooting at things isn't the main business of an air gunner. Keen eyes and a cool nerve is what's needed, and Evelyn's got both.'

'We're talking about a short period of time, too,' Evelyn said, then, as if it was an afterthought. 'Just long enough to get Duncan out.'

'What if that's long enough to get you killed?' She paused to let this sink in. 'And what about the Free from Infection inspections? There's a fright in store for any medical officer wanting to lift your privates with his ruler.'

'Christ, I didn't think of that.' Lofty sank lower in his seat.

'I'm willing to chance my arm. We both are.' Evelyn glanced

at Lofty. 'And I think we can convince Duncan to go along. He trusts us, and he's so tired.'

'All Duncan's decisions have to be made for him at the moment,' Lofty said. 'Why not his friends making them, rather than command?'

'But *this* decision!' Olive exclaimed, so loudly the sheep grazing near the open mouth of the cellar bolted, their hooves pitting the over-grazed ground.

Lofty clenched his jaw. 'If Duncan tries to stick it out, it will kill him. And I'm not having that.'

'All they'll see is a new rear gunner. Just another man in worn RAAF blues.' Evelyn looked hard at Olive. '*You* can choose to look at it that way too. Just think of it. Your childhood sweetheart thrown into service on the same station as you.' Evelyn flicked a loose strand of hair behind one ear and watched her struggle to find a response. When Olive opened her mouth, no sound would come out of it.

Lofty was looking at his boots, and seemed not to be listening. 'I'd like to think of Duncan being safe somewhere,' he said slowly. 'It's not as if I have anybody else to ferret away.'

'You're both putting me in an impossible position, and for what?' Olive asked. All they had was a hunch that Duncan wouldn't make it. And what was a hunch? It had all the substance of piss on the tyre of a bomber.

Evelyn watched Olive, wide-eyed, waiting.

But Olive merely stood up and walked back to the car.

They drove her to where she'd left her bicycle, and very little was said. Evelyn and Lofty seemed to have accepted the fact that she wasn't going along with them, and all that implied. He kept his face pointed at the window, his eyes shielded by aviation glasses. They passed through East Halton, and it was not long before they were opposite the aerodrome. Evelyn pulled the Morris in to the grass verge and Lofty shifted to let Olive out.

Watching them drive off towards the Immingham road and Peterborough, something rose up inside Olive.

She saw herself walking the seawall at Goxhill Haven, under the shadow of the barrage balloons; walking the grassy path with someone in RAAF uniform, a gunner's brevet on their cap – someone who offered a steadying hand as she climbed the stile by the reservoir. It was Evelyn she saw, not Duncan. Evelyn in RAAF blue, holding out a gloved hand.

Chapter Twenty

Four of the Seven Dwarves

Olive was not privy to the conniving, and the plotting, and the forging of documents. It was only later that she learned the lengths to which Evelyn had to go to make the ruse work.

Duncan was to wait at Ida's until he could board his troopship at the Liverpool docks. He'd be bound for the Middle East before Christmas, and home not long after. Before he could do so, several sets of documents would need doctoring, including Duncan's own identification papers and Evelyn's E.2 card (the photograph and middle name changed to allow Evelyn Ames Macintyre of the ATA – a young man whose duty had been served – to board his ship home). Evelyn also paid her forger to produce a letter from a Harley Street physician testifying that the bearer was in private treatment for a 'gentleman's disease'. The Station medical officer gave far more attention to the problems of officers than he did to those of men in the ranks. If the issue of a Free from Infection inspection came up, Evelyn would present the letter, relying on the discretion of a man who thought himself of the better sort. That there might be a commission in the offing for Flight Sergeant Macintyre couldn't hurt. Evelyn would get Duncan's uniforms – uniforms that Ida had altered, at his request, to accommodate his 'weight loss'. In those first days on station, Evelyn was to rely on the tendency of personnel to place a member of aircrew by looking first at the leather name-patch on their tunic. High casualty rates had made people shy of each other's faces.

Olive read Ida's letters carefully for evidence that she knew what they were doing. But she only wrote that it was lovely having Duncan and Evelyn to stay, even if the business of feeding them *was* a trial. Nor did she know what to make of Lofty – what with his odd habit of reading a book while walking into rooms, or up stairs, or out on his constitutional in the fields. The tone of Ida's letters was reproachful. 'Duncan,' – she wrote – 'is not nearly so good as you at pairing the socks.'

At North Killingholme, Olive worked her staggered watches. One evening she and Cathy and Betty and Violet went to see *The Great Dictator* at the Station picture house, but were done out of the end of the film when the air-raid siren sounded, and they had to spend a frozen hour in the shelters while the Luftwaffe bombed the Immingham docks.

Her greatest pleasure disturbed, Cathy sought an alternative line of entertainment – paying one of the WAAF drivers a quid to fetch the gramophone she'd bought in Scunthorpe. This sat untouched for a week next to the radio in the lounge because she'd not got anything to play on it. The day the orphan gunners from Elsham arrived, so did Cathy's gramophone records – a job lot she'd found in a *Times* advertisement. She had no idea what the collection comprised – all the advertisement had said was that it would appeal to 'the open-minded enthusiast'. As the four WAAFs sat on their lounge floor flicking through the heavy stack of 78s, Cathy warned them they had to be as open-minded as she was.

'This is too pretty to play,' said Violet of the blue shellac disc she'd slipped out of its cover. She peered at the label. 'What's a Poldini when it's at home?'

Cathy took it off her. '"Dance of the Dolls", I've heard of that.'

Olive thought she was fibbing, but didn't say so.

Had they stayed up the whole night they could have got through the pile. As it was, Cathy had the late watch and banned her housemates from listening to anything until she was back in the house.

Olive was surprised the next day to find Cathy awake just four hours after the end of her watch. The butcher's daughter walked into the kitchen, still clumsy from sleep, and sat down at the table. She had her hairnet on, a coat thrown over her nightgown, and a cigarette – in full defiance of gravity – clinging to her damp lower lip.

'Toast?' Olive asked.

'I could kill some.' After a yawn, Cathy said, 'Your friends turned up to look for you. The gunners from Elsham. They brought us a cabbage.' She pointed at the pantry.

Olive put too much pressure on the breadknife, and the slice she'd pared from the loaf fell to pieces in her hand. It was such shoddy stuff, that wartime bread.

'Oh,' said she. 'How did Duncan look?'

'Which one was Duncan?'

'The quieter one.'

'He didn't say much, it's true. But he did mention he was keen to see you.'

'Ah.' Olive put a piece of toast on Cathy's plate. Perhaps they had lost nerve and it really was Duncan wanting to see her.

'He gave me this letter for you, from his sister.'

Olive was irritated that Cathy had saved this bit of information for last, and when Cathy pulled the letter from her coat pocket she could not stop herself from snatching it – only to find it unaddressed; the envelope saying nothing of its sender.

Cathy regarded her with bafflement, and blinked as the smoke from her cigarette drifted into her eyes.

'What's eating you?' Olive snapped.

'Too much Poldini. It's bad for the disposition, apparently,' Cathy replied, seeming determined to remain genial.

Olive wedged the envelope under the edge of her plate. As soon as Cathy had gone back to bed, she tore the thing open and read:

Dear Olive,

This will be my last letter, for obvious reasons. I'll be here a month or so until embarkation. I sleep a great deal, and can't rouse myself even to read, or walk. Ida calls me her convalescent. I don't like to think of myself as one of those nervous types who can't hold a bowl of soup without shaking all the liquid out of it – but it's true that I can't do the job anymore, and Evelyn saw through me, and knew that at once. She'll probably do a better job at being me than I ever could.

Be good to Lofty. If it weren't for him I'd never have made it this far.

And try not to worry. This war has been such a stupid bloody lark from the beginning, how can what we're doing now be any worse?

Perhaps there'll be time for a long talk in the future, and if somehow it turns out that there isn't, I want you to know that the war – and T for Tommy – gave me something I'd never had before, and I'm grateful for that, even now.

It wasn't losing Faye that did it, in the end. You do know that, don't you?

Your friend, Duncan.

PS Be a good girl and burn this.

After being a good girl, Olive sat at the table lighting one cigarette after another, adding tobacco ash to what remained of the letter. Duncan's gratefulness had made him too confiding. Olive didn't want to know – in her experience, knowing things got you into trouble.

Olive was not on watch until four, but when Violet arrived home she grilled her about the battle order. Was 629 flying? Five aircraft were, as far as Violet could remember. But when she said it was Apple, Item, Love and two others she'd forgotten, the letters meant nothing to Olive. She had no idea what flight and crew the gunners had gone to.

'Take my coat, it's already good and wet,' Violet said, holding out her dripping cape. Olive looked from it to the glass in the door, already covered by the blackout curtain. It was almost dark, and raining again. How inauspicious.

She rode to the aerodrome, where the aircraft sat quietly at dispersal, their full load of bombs aboard. The Station was wrapped in the boredom of the wait. Olive bicycled past little groups of ground crew sheltering from the rain under the wings of the Lancasters, men debating the finer points of hydraulics or pneumatics, or grousing about the effect on the airframe of hard landings. A few hours later Olive saw the planes up; and then they were back from bombing Cannes well before her watch had ended. She bicycled home at a quarter past midnight and went to bed having not once seen – or heard news of – the gunners from Elsham.

In fact, that night, the two of them had flown in Lancaster LQ-Love, over the tops of English cloud to the clear skies of the South of France. The night was perfect for the Pathfinder force before them, and the red of the target flares was one of the most beautiful things Evelyn had ever seen. She'd watched the flares, and the fire caused by the incendiaries, out of the corner of her eyes, squinting into the dark centre of the sky above the docks at Cannes.

Small stuff, Lofty said when Olive met them in the NAAFI the next day. She'd biked to the Station two hours before her shift was to start and had already been to the sergeants and the officers mess, and had collared a young fellow from 629 running the perimeter road to ask him whether he knew the two new gunners who'd joined the squadron the day before. He was so embarrassed at being seen by a WAAF in his callisthenic clothes that he'd clutched his narrow chest and stared. It was only on Olive's third visit to the NAAFI that she found Love's gunners.

They were sitting at the least popular table. This tended to rock, and often a cup of tea or a bun landed in the lap of the person seated there. The chock under the short leg of the table was forever falling out, and veteran personnel had learned to wait for another seat to come vacant, or to drink their tea standing up. Lofty had one arm clamped down on the table surface to keep it steady, and the other he was waving at Olive.

How blithe Evelyn looked sitting there in Duncan's uniform, cap aslant on a Brylcreamed wave of golden hair! The easeful way she slouched in her chair shocked Olive – Evelyn was too familiar with her role. She must have done this before, and not just at the cricket pitch at Bathurst. But if that wasn't unsettling enough, the sight of Evelyn in her brother's proper place brought Duncan – amiable, affectionate, loyal Duncan – and his last confidence, back to her. It was Curtis Crowe that he'd found on Tommy – Curtis Crowe that he'd found, and lost. The thought of this, on top of the sight of Evelyn, so rattled Olive that she had to veer off to the counter to ask for a cup of tea.

'Are you right with that?' Lofty said, coming up behind her.

'Fine,' Olive replied, balancing her bun on the saucer's rim for the trip back to the table.

Put the tea down, she told herself. *Go on – sit*. She sat down. But looking into her friend's face was more difficult. There were the wide-set bluish grey eyes, the straight nose, the unblemished skin of the cheeks (so different to her brother's face); the dimple in her left cheek beside lips chapped and bare – and all of that framed by the trim authority of the uniform: the jacket lapels smoothed and straightened; the belt tightened lightly so as not to bunch the jacket beneath it; the buttons burnished. Even the brevet looked as if it had been brushed.

'Good morning,' said the rear gunner. The voice was not much lighter than Duncan's, but lacked the astringency of his accent.

Olive thought Evelyn would have to watch that tendency – her brother never had such airs.

Turning to Lofty with relief, she asked him about the op.

'Small stuff,' he said, 'and not easily bitched. I could see the rail-yards clearly, so the bomb aimer could too. Until the smoke from the fires covered them again – and whether it was the marshalling yards burning I couldn't say. That's what I told the intelligence officer during interrogation. How should I know how it went? I just count my rounds, keep my log, and go for the ride.'

'I was so busy trying not to ruin my night-sight that I didn't see much of anything on the ground,' Evelyn said, when finally Olive looked at her again.

'And it was alright? I mean – you were alright?' she asked, and Lofty had to tell her not to whisper.

'Duncan did us proud. And since we've got a sprog crew they should count themselves lucky to have us. I only hope *they're* up to snuff.'

Olive thought that was hardly fair of Lofty. 'Who are they?'

'Sleepy, Happy, Bashful and – ' Lofty looked to Evelyn, ' – who have I forgotten?'

'Doc.' Evelyn was practising rolling a shilling over her knuckles; she stopped long enough to look at the ceiling to find the last name. 'And the wireless operator. Blue.'

'Is Doc the skipper?'

'Sergeant Pilot Arthur Pendleton, optometrist. He has 20/20 vision and is very proud to own the same number of shoes as Winston Churchill.' Lofty shrugged. 'Doc's got a good head as a pilot. He did exactly what the bomb aimer told him to do over the target, and there's some that don't.' He folded one finger down on the hand he'd raised. 'Happy is the navigator, and one could hardly find a more obliging chap. The bomb aimer is called Sleepy because he's never been caught napping, and once made some poor pilot do five dummy runs on a target.' Lofty was by then doing Churchill's victory sign. This he pointed, like a pair of horns, at Evelyn.

' – and Bashful is the Flight Magician. Apparently he's still a virgin,' she said, shrugging, and smiled faintly at Olive.

'And Blue must be the wireless operator, because – '

Lofty raised an eyebrow at Olive and said, 'Why do you think?'

'Because he's an Australian?' she ventured. 'With ginger hair?'

'That old chestnut. Luckily I came pre-equipped with a nick-name.'

Olive looked back at Evelyn, at the face stripped of make-up and the neatly knotted tie hiding a long, pale neck with no jutting Adam's Apple.

'And what do they call *you*?'

'They call me Duncan.'

Chapter Twenty-One

Tussor Yokel

The Station was quiet for the first week the gunners spent with their new squadron. There were daylight training flights, weather permitting, and the crew of Love went up five days out of seven, one of these on a fighter affiliation exercise and the rest of the time on cross-country hops, the gunners sighting on dry stone fences and air. The squadron leader wanted to be sure Love was functioning properly as a crew, so he kept them busy.

Olive was relieved they were not on operational flights, although she worried about them – off watch and on – as if they were. The long winter nights were on their way, and with them would come the opportunity for long-distance raids. Love's happy little hops over Lincolnshire, Nottinghamshire and the Peak District could not last.

In the middle of November the raids on Berlin began. The gunners' old squadron had been moved to Ludford Magna, near Louth, and were stood down while a refit was done of their Lancasters, and they consequently missed the fireworks extravaganza over Berlin that the rest of the Group was treated to. As 550 Squadron was still in the process of sorting itself out, the operational business of North Killingholme reverted to the new, relatively untried, 629 Squadron. If Lofty regretted his decision to move squadrons, he didn't let on.

Love flew twice to Berlin that November, on the first and last operation staged to the Big City that month. Once would have been enough for the gunners but Bomber Command never sent its bombers anywhere once.

Olive was off rotation the night of the 18th, but Cathy was hardly surprised when her friend turned up in the Watch Office just before midnight and asked to stay. The Flying Control Officer frowned at the young WAAF but said he'd oblige on the condition that she fetch everyone tea, and stand relief, as necessary.

Sitting on a stool at the end of the ranked wireless sets, Olive waited. Worried that the trip might be too much for Evelyn, it had been impossible for her to stay away from the Tower, to which word from the returning planes first came. But she had not expected the first call to Tussor Yokel to be from LQ-Love.

'12.45. Bang on. They win the cigar,' the Flying Control Officer said as he watched the number go up. In the next hour, Love was followed home by every Lancaster sent out, a full complement safely returned.

Cathy had ignored Olive most of the night but now she came up and squeezed her elbow. 'Berlin isn't so bad after all,' she said and pointed Olive towards the doors. 'Go home and get some sleep.'

She woke to the sound of someone hammering on the door. When she peered around the blackout curtain she saw Love's rear gunner, in her bulky greatcoat; boots planted wide on the stunted grass.

She'd been expecting Evelyn but was nevertheless taken aback, and her hesitance expressed itself in her not knowing how to dress. Since the household had to save on coal, and the sitting room fire would not be lit, she decided to dress for the cold, rather than her friend. Putting her coat over her dressing-gown, and winding her scarf around her neck, she went to let Evelyn in.

'Are we alone?' Love's gunner asked, peeling off her gloves and using them to wave at the top of the narrow stairs.

Glancing through the open kitchen door Olive saw there were no dishes on the board. Nor were there any muddy pairs of shoes at the front door. But she answered with a lie – saying she thought Cathy was asleep, upstairs. 'So we can't talk for long. And we'll have to be quiet.' And with a finger to her lips, she led Evelyn into the sitting room. They sat facing one another in easy chairs tufted with age and weeping kapok. Olive's coat was bulky at her waist, and she folded her arms to settle it.

'I feel as though we've done this before,' she said, and thought – *when William came to stay in Hamble*. Then, to get herself as far from that impression as she could, she added, 'You're finished. It's over.'

'Thank god. It was hell.' Evelyn shook her head. 'And if it's hell when we all make it back, I can't imagine how I'm going to cope when it gets hairy.'

Evelyn had thought Olive was referring to the operation, but she'd been driving at something larger.

'I meant you must be ready to give up – to end *this*.' She tapped the badge on Evelyn's cap, where it sat upon the side table.

Evelyn squinted over a frown. 'Not at all. Although I'd be happier if I didn't have to go back to Berlin.' She scratched a rough patch of skin on her jaw, one of a number concentrated around her mouth. 'I think I'm allergic to the mask. It's given me eczema. As if I don't have enough trouble with my skin already.'

Olive smiled, relieved by the familiarity of Evelyn's pre-occupation with her complexion. 'You'd better not talk like that back in the crew hut.'

'Why do you think I came here?' Evelyn put her head up, listening to the sounds of the house about them, the windows rattling in their frames. There came no telltale creak of the boards in the stair, so she added, 'I'll tell you about it, if you like.'

She explained that the worst of it had been the cold. The heated flying suit she'd been issued worked well, but anywhere skin was exposed she'd quickly lost all sensation. Except for her eyes. When she and Duncan were at Ida's, he had run through the things she'd need to know in the rear turret – one trick he'd told her was to learn to do without goggles whenever the Lancaster was at its most vulnerable. That meant nothing to keep the cold out of your eyes for the whole time the aircraft was over Europe. Evelyn found it hard to concentrate, to think of anything other than the agony of blinking; each slide of the lid over the congealing surface of eye. This battle between the urge to stare wide-eyed into the dark and the need to blink became all the more excruciating when her wakey-wakey tablet took effect somewhere in the darkness over Kassel. Then Evelyn had started at Love's shadow on the cloud below them, and had hosed the empty air with .303.

Mercifully, there'd been little flak getting to the target, or over it, because the bomber stream was hidden from the batteries below by a low ceiling of solid cloud. What a long way to go with a light meal of bombs in the belly, what a long way to go – freezing and jittery and scared – to a target no one could see.

'There was too much time to think,' Evelyn said, absently stroking the patch of the dried skin by her mouth. 'Too much time by myself. With the doors of the turret closed it's like I'm not in the aircraft at all – it's as though I'm being dragged along in the darkness outside.' For a second she looked embarrassed, and Olive smiled to encourage her. 'I'm used to being in control, and to little bouts of solitude in the air. Ferrying, I was never in the air for more than two hours on a single hop, and that was in daylight. Imagine how I felt about six hours at 21,000 feet, with the perspex icing-up and my eyelids sticking to my eyes. I wanted someone to say something on the intercom, but chatter is forbidden and the whole operation went on in this ghastly silence – unless it was the navigator piping up to say we were crossing the enemy coast or over the target or near the flak defences or whatever. I'd have killed for a rousing chorus of *I've Got a Sixpence*.'

They both smiled at that, remembering Lofty's story about

Curtis Crowe: Tommy's pilot sang during every bombing run – a breathy and not particularly tuneful rendition of *Whistling in the Dark*. He'd had no idea he was doing it.

'Perhaps you can provide a song next time.'

Evelyn shrugged. 'But you know one thing? I don't regret it. Awful as it was, it was immensely interesting – and I couldn't get around the oddness of the fact that I was there at all.'

Odd wasn't the word the police would use, but Olive knew it was too late to say anything of that sort to Evelyn now – she'd become one of those people requiring careful handling, someone who needed listening to, but of whom one did not ask questions – not unless you were an intelligence officer. Where aircrew was concerned the talking – or the silences – had to be left to their discretion. And whatever else she'd been, Evelyn now was aircrew.

'I'll make us a cup of tea,' Olive said and went back to the kitchen, not expecting Evelyn to follow, but she did, looking through the cupboards for the cups, and passing her the tea-cosy.

'You have to stop helping – men never do,' Olive whispered, jamming the thing down on the pot.

For the next week Love reverted to its non-operational flying, to blessedly short hops cross-country. Before each flight Evelyn would go out to the Lancaster to check the ammunition belts were running smoothly through the guns. If she found everything in order, she'd report to the crew chief at dispersal before going to a late breakfast. In this way she avoided the mass of men, and while that meant missing the best on offer at the mess, the cooks and waiters always managed to find something for the late-rising, underfed gunner.

During this respite from operations Lofty once again lost his facility for sleep, and increased his intake of alcohol. He went alone to the pub, or to drink in the mess, as they had decided Evelyn shouldn't drink with the crew, or the Flight. Lofty did the relaxing for both of them, in the process losing a week's pay when he was pinched by a policeman at East Halton for dubbing a WAAF on the handlebars of his bike. Lofty's excuse that he was capitalising on manpower had not gone over well. *Capitalise on this*, the policeman had said, handing Lofty a copy of the complaint he'd written in his little black notebook.

All of which Lofty saw as an excuse for another beer; and grounds to lie awake, brooding, through the long hours until the aircraft came back to the field. This should have been seen as worrying behaviour, but the only person worrying about Lofty then was Lofty.

For her part, Olive was busy fending off Catherine Derrick's questions. With whom was she going to the picture show? Was she to have company for the dance? Where was her sweetheart brooch; her photo; her special song on the gramophone? To shut her friend up, Olive played Vera Lynn's 'Harbour Lights' on the gramophone, again and again, and for a while Cathy crept about her carefully, and did not mention romance.

Olive's sister WAAFs were, in any case, all business when on duty at the Flying Control Office. When Olive came on watch at 4 p.m. on the 26th of November, just as Cathy was coming off, the latter was characteristically matter-of-fact about Love being on the battle order for Berlin. It wasn't to be the same route as the last raid, she told Olive, pointedly. A new route might oblige a longer time spent over land, running the gauntlet of flak and fighters. Under such conditions, the survival of the stream would be left more than ever to luck, and – where Love was concerned – to Lofty's assortment of deities, his polyglot Gods.

The Lancasters of 629 went off into the early dark, Love taxiing last, the Merlins giving out their bone-shaking roar. Flying Control was to look for them returning after midnight. But it was not much after six when Olive was hailed by Jig – its heating had gone unservicable. She cleared them to land, and no sooner had the crew's feet hit the hardstanding than the wing commander was upon them. He was furious. Maximum effort was no respecter of a crew's comfort. And – the wing commander told the pilot – if the squadron could do without armoured panelling (most of which had been taken out of its Lancasters by order of Bomber Harris) then Jig could bloody well do without its hot-air blowers.

It was just after midnight when the rest of the force started in. Three came in quick succession, and then another two. Although Olive's watch had ended she resolved to wait for the remainder. Half an hour later there was still no Love, and no Ink. Betty sat at her station and gnawed the end of her pencil. She was trying not to look at her housemate.

Then came the call, 'Ping-Pong Ink from Tussor, how do you read me, over?'

'Tussor Yokel from Ping-Pong Ink, loud and clear,' Betty replied. '2000 feet, if you please.' Now only Love was outstanding. The Flying Control Officer gave them until 2 a.m., because that was all the air-time the Lancaster had fuel for.

'Let's have a game of Ludo,' the Flying Control Officer said, with greater cheeriness than was needed. He unfolded the board on his desk and plumped down the counters with fat, nicotine-stained fingers. The WAAFs squabbled about the colour they wanted, and Olive eventually let Betty have the red. Half an hour later, despite having two of her counters in peril on a board crowded by rivals, Betty got up to make them a brew. Olive scalded her lips on the tea, and then burned the wound anew with the heat coming down the tube of her cigarette.

She wondered, in the one lucid moment she was to have that hour, whether it had been worth it – saving Duncan.

Olive had just got her last counter home when the Flying Control Officer of Middleton St George called. He told them Love had missed the entry point on the return leg and the navigator's south-easterly correction had got them off the North Sea and back over England just in the nick of time. While the staff on watch in the North Killingholme tower played Ludo, Love's crew were enjoying North Yorkshire hospitality – eating ham and eggs and being ribbed by their peers for having lost the British Isles. The Flying Control Officer at Middleton St George said they could be expected back by late morning.

So she went home, the bike wobbling and jouncing over the track, tears dripping off the end of her chin, and nose. She had discovered that there was a cost to relief – the mind grasping at the thrown line, but the body still floundering in panic. Even when she woke at nine the next morning it was to the sense that Lofty and Evelyn had bought it, and it was not until she'd ridden back to the field, and seen Love sitting on the tarmac with the petrol bowser beside it, that was she was able to relax.

After their second trip to Berlin the Station's aircraft did five minor operations, then dud weather took the squadrons off the battle order. On the 1st of December an isolated flurry of snow fell on the aerodrome, and people gathered in the NAAFI and the mess to talk about the possibility of another bad season. A colder than usual winter meant the Lancasters would haul themselves into the air, and to the target, only to return with the leading edge of their wings sheathed in ice. But the hours of winter dark had to be capitalised on at all cost. If the only encumbrance was cold – and not cumulus nimbus or fog or some other meteorological obstacle – then it would have to be coped with.

When the snow flurries stopped, so did the speculative talk.

At their cottage in the village, the four WAAFs listened to Cathy's record collection. Betty showed a liking for the noisiest of the Beethoven symphonies, and played these loudly until Cathy managed to get her interested in Mahler. Olive liked the ragtime tunes best, and on the days when no one else was in the house she would push the furniture to the skirting boards and dance. Not once did she invite Evelyn to join her.

The gunners hadn't been long on Station, and had not yet

accrued leave. Since Olive's schedule did not mesh with theirs, she did not often see them – if she did it was only for tea and a wad at the NAAFI. The one afternoon they all found themselves free, Lofty suggested a bicycle ride and they set off, travelling line astern, awkwardly bundled in their woollens; pedalling into a headwind that made the task too strenuous for talk. Olive bicycled just behind Evelyn, and every so often she'd see her pale profile – her cheeks stung red by the wind.

Just before the Group stand-down for the full-moon period, Love flew to Leipzig. Evelyn experienced her first heavy flak on the return journey, near Frankfurt. A Lancaster below them had been hit, and she'd tracked it through its flaming descent while the rear turret filled – spectrally – with the smell of cordite and cinders. The flak was a silent battering, and Love's crew felt it most in the slipstream of aircraft flown by inexperienced pilots – men who'd imagined flak could be evaded and whose Lancs jigged and jostled their way through the bomber stream, sometimes directly into a burst of flak.

Olive heard about this operation on one of the rare days their free time converged. The two of them had taken advantage of a clear day to make the long ride to Goxhill Haven. Not confident that the winter sun had warmth to it they had swaddled themselves with every woollen to hand – those gloves and scarves and vests knitted by Mrs Macintyre with such industry at the start of Duncan's war. Evelyn's jumper was darned by wool that didn't match the colour of the original – her brother's work.

'At least there's no wind,' Evelyn said, as she slipped through the stile. She'd not been in Lincolnshire long enough to know how unusual still air was.

A dog from the farmhouse next to the haven wandered out of its gate, and stood looking at the two strangers before strolling over to sniff the front tyre of Olive's bike. Then it slipped through the stile after Evelyn, tail thumping.

'Hop it!' Evelyn shouted, and the dog hunched its shoulders, and spread its front legs in supplication. Evelyn had spent too much time getting the ginger fur off Duncan's woollens to stand the acquisition of any more animal hair, so said, 'Off, you brute,' and toed it with one heavy boot. The dog retreated, whining its reproach.

The rear gunner and WAAF walked towards Immingham beside the slick, open mouth of the Humber; past the grey concrete teeth of the anti-invasion obstacles exposed by the tide. Wading birds stood on their reflections, curiously quiet. The only noise was the distant running up of an engine.

Evelyn cocked her head. 'Hurricane,' she said, and after they'd been walking for another minute they saw the fighters go up. Evelyn turned her face to the sky to watch them go.

'You must miss it,' Olive said.

'Not for the moment.'

The reeds down by the water were standing straight in the air, their feathery tops shining a bluish-silver in the sunlight. Evelyn peered down the grassy bank. 'This will be nice in summer, when it's warm and the ground is dry. You could lie here and watch the American fighters come in.'

Someone could, Olive thought, but not you. Not me.

Evelyn was looking speculatively at the ground.

'Don't you dare!' Olive said, 'You'll ruin your coat.'

'You can't ruin a greatcoat that easily.' Evelyn lowered herself onto the thick grass of the bank, stretching out so that her head was at the rise. 'Here,' she said, unbuttoning her coat and folding out one side of it so that the lapel faced the ground. 'Try it.'

Olive didn't think there was room enough in that coat for two but lay down beside her, the cold of the ground and the warmth of Evelyn's body equally shocking.

'Just for a second,' Olive said, 'or the chilblains will get us.'

'I have never known what a chilblain is. They itch, apparently. But I've discovered that itching is the property of a great many things.'

Olive rolled onto her shoulder so she could see Evelyn's face. She traced one finger over the marks of the rash around her mouth, and stopped with a fingertip resting in the declivity of her dimple. 'It looks like shaving rash, but you're a beardless wonder,' she said, and Evelyn's dimple deepened with a smile.

'I shave. Not every morning. Just so long as someone every so often sees me with the towel and the razor, or emptying the suds.' Evelyn shut her eyes, and Olive could see her eyelashes trembling. 'If I can bomb Berlin and Leipzig, shaving shouldn't be a challenge.'

She was quiet for a moment, then – her eyes still closed – she began to tell Olive about Leipzig. The cold, the silent bursts of flak, and Lofty's advice to Pendleton to leave the stream. Doc's reluctance to do so had disappeared as they'd flown inside the light of another aircraft burning. Then, on the crew bus to interrogation, Lofty had joked in too high a voice that he enjoyed visiting an old friend as much as the next man but intended to send his apologies the next time they went anywhere near Leipzig, or Hanover.

'Lofty feels Tommy's crew is out there somewhere – ' Evelyn went on, ' – in the air.'

'Poor Lofty.' Sitting up, Olive put her hands to her lips and blew on them before adding, 'It really is quite cold. And wet.' She stood. There was a damp impression in the fabric where her hip had pressed into the bank, indeed, the whole coat was muddy and sodden in patches. It hung more heavily than usual when Evelyn put it on.

'You look like you've had to bale out and walk home,' Olive said.

'Remind me next time that beds are for lying in.'

They walked on a little further, but when Olive's teeth started to chatter Evelyn steered her back along the banks of the haven to the bikes. She promised exercise would keep them warm until they could get to the Black Bull at East Halton, where they'd be able to fortify themselves for the last leg home. It was that prospect of a nip of spirits – on top of the famishing she'd let herself in for at Skitterbeck – that got Olive into the serviceman's pub with Evelyn.

At the entrance to the pub, Olive reached out to clutch at the muddy sleeve of Evelyn's coat. 'What if I drop my guard and say something stupid?' She was afraid the wrong pronoun would slip out.

'I'll order,' Evelyn said, and opened the door for her friend.

The pub was crowded, as usual, and a noisy lot of sergeants were forcing one of their friends to drink from the back of his beer glass. The newcomers gave them a wide berth to take the only empty stools at the bar. They'd barely had time to bend their elbows when a sergeant pilot clapped Evelyn on the shoulder and she lost a quarter of her pint to the floor.

'Bet's off then. You do drink,' said the sergeant-pilot happily, then, to someone over his shoulder, 'I told you Duncan wasn't the teetotalling type!' He slipped an arm around the gunner's shoulders. 'Don't be snotty, Duncan, bring your girl to join us.' Offering his hand to Olive, he said, 'Pendleton, at your service.'

Pendleton was an amiable-looking young man with a high forehead and hair receding at the temples. His nose was crooked, and flattened at its bridge, and Olive thought that might account for his adenoidal voice. Evelyn's drawl sounded deep by comparison.

'Since you're at our service you can make up for this lot down my front,' Evelyn said. Olive had to admire the ease with which she fell to their banter.

'Pardon me, ma'am,' said Pendleton to Olive, 'the gunner's thirsty.' Love's pilot bought the drinks and, followed by a sergeant with carroty hair and freckles, led the new arrivals back to the table they'd left in Lofty's care.

'You should have sung out when you saw us,' Evelyn told him.

'Sung out? In this?' He waved about at the close-packed tables; the chain of bodies at the bar. 'You must be joking. But I managed to scrounge a couple of chairs for you.' He banged his palm on the seat of one next to him, and Olive sat on the edge of it. She did not intend that Evelyn stay. Lofty was saying how democratic their assembly was – 'we let anyone in. Even pilots.' He grinned at Pendleton. 'This one – ' he nudged the redhead, 'is only biding his time until he can pry that American off the piano stool. Then he's going to lead the pub in a singalong. Aren't you, Blue?'

The wireless operator shrugged, and took a sip of his beer.

'We're only here for one drink,' Olive said, giving a warning look at Evelyn.

'No such thing as one drink. They multiply on the sly.'

Evelyn picked up her glass and held it to her chest. 'Not if they use protection.'

'Ha!' Lofty toasted Evelyn, and, with nose wrinkled in distaste, said, 'You look like someone's rolled you down the pitch after play's been called for rain.' He plucked at a sleeve of the gunner's greatcoat. 'I could grow mushrooms in that.'

'Yes,' Olive announced, standing, 'and that's why we have to go home.'

'They don't want *us*,' Pendleton told Lofty. 'They've got each other.'

'And I have you, skipper,' Lofty said, reaching over to plant a kiss on the other man's forehead.

Evelyn and Olive were lucky enough to get a lift back to the Station, and before they went to eat at their respective messes,

Evelyn asked Olive if she could come around to the cottage that evening. She had nowhere else to go, and thought it would look odd hanging around the Station on a leave.

'Go on then,' Olive said, 'so long as you understand the rules.'

But Olive herself was struggling with the rules: those of her own invention, and those of the RAF. Fraternisation might be discouraged, but it went on. It was sensible to keep Evelyn out of the way of Cathy, not because she was a superior officer but because her perspicacity might prove awkward. Olive's instinct was to keep Evelyn away from women in general.

But the rules of Olive and Evelyn's association were idiosyncratic and had no broad principles to follow – they seemed to be more a matter of no dancing, no sharing of the domestic chores, and no conspiratorial whispering. Nothing so clear as King's Regulations.

When the rear gunner arrived, Olive was fetched from her bath by Betty, who was in such a hurry to get off on a date with her American that she gave the man on her doorstep a quick look up and down, then flicked Olive a thumbs-up sign from her perch on the back of the American's motorcycle.

'Cheerio. Have fun. Don't do anything I wouldn't do,' she called.

They had the house to themselves. Cathy and Violet were on a watch. They listened to ragtime records, and laughed at Colonel Chinstrap on the BBC while they ate their bowls of syllabub. It grew late and Olive let the fire go out but still she and Evelyn stayed in the cooling lounge, staring into the glowing bed of coals. Evelyn was sitting sideways in her easy chair, her long legs draped over its arm. Sometime in the last half-hour she'd returned to her habit of worrying a lock of her hair. But there was not one long enough to do, and every time she'd put a hand up to her forehead, she'd realise, and look irritated.

'Olive,' she said. 'It's started to snow.' It had, not long since, and the outside of the window glass was latticed with ice. 'I'd rather not go back to the aerodrome in that. Sober,' she added, just as 'God Save the King' came on the radio. 'Can I stay?'

Olive – conscious of the darkness, and of the empty house, and of the passing hours of Evelyn's leave – said, 'Violet will be home from her watch soon.'

So Evelyn stood, and put on her coat. Olive followed her to the door, and switching the hall lights off, flipped back the blackout curtain.

Evelyn stepped out onto the doorstep, snow settling on the shoulders of her coat and on its upturned collar. She stopped to light a cigarette, and Olive heard the fizz and pop of the match as she held it to the weather.

She turned around, brushing loose tobacco from her bottom lip with a thoughtful, rather than a fastidious, gesture. 'I'd rather not go,' she said. The hand holding the cigarette was shaking and she steadied it by leaning on the doorframe.

Olive, she said.

Olive was holding open the door. After a moment she asked, 'How do you think it would look, you staying?'

Evelyn flicked her cigarette into the snow, and said, 'It would look just the way you'd like it to. It would look normal.'

Chapter Twenty-Two

The Caterpillar Club

The crews of 629 got Berlin for an early Christmas present. The day after there was a maximum effort at inebriation. Then it was fireworks over Berlin, and three crews flying from North Killingholme lived just long enough to toast the New Year.

When the Group stand-down for the full moon came some crews disappeared on leave while the servicemen and women not on operational duty had a quiet week seeing the aircraft in from daylight exercises, and haunting the local pubs. Evelyn and Lofty kicked around the aerodrome, and Lofty began his Dorian Gray Project – hauling an easel and canvas out to the edge of the hardstanding to paint L-Love and her crew. The finished work he stacked under a tarpaulin against the wall of the crew hut, strictly forbidding anyone from looking at it. During his sleepless nights, he toyed briefly with meditation – the sort of thing that Hindu swamis did; and Tibetan monks in their mountain monasteries, plumbing the fleshy depths of their spiritual world.

'I shall pray us into clean air,' he told Olive one day when she met him in the NAAFI. She saw he wasn't joking.

Even before the stand-down, Olive had started joining the lines of ground crew, WAAF and admin staff who'd gather at the edge of the tarmac to see the planes off. Some would wave with such vigour anyone would have thought they were farewelling the king, while others stood quietly as the bombers roared past. There were always three or four people left staring into an empty sky long after the rest of the Station's complement had gone sensibly indoors. Olive had become one of these people – standing too long in the cold for much the same reason she'd stayed on the cliff above the sea at Hamble after reading the letter in which Marjorie had broken it off with Evelyn.

Guilt at what she was doing had rooted her to the spot.

The week it was first rumoured that Olive and the gunner were an item, people treated her with great gentleness, as if she was an invalid recovering from an illness likely to relapse; someone who could not to be trusted to recognise the symptoms of her own infirmity. She'd been handled with such solicitude only once before: the hour after she'd got the telegram about William being missing. Knowing that only made the irony deeper – she had come to be surrounded by people who could no longer distinguish romance from loss.

This was not a failing Evelyn shared. She did not think Olive foolish. She had her victory, and the company she craved. Evelyn had Olive, and all her losses were behind her.

It was during the stand-down that Duncan was due in Liverpool to board ship. It was a nervous few days for the conspirators, and they spent as much time as they could together, too anxious to bear the wait alone. If Duncan's papers were questioned, if he was exposed, they could expect to be tumbled themselves soon after. During this time Olive made Evelyn spend her nights in the crew hut. The idea of their being found together frightened her too much.

But the Air Force Police did not come to haul them away, and no one was called into the wing commander's office to account for the sudden change of sex of Evelyn Macintyre of the ATA. When it seemed as if Duncan had got away safely on the first leg of his voyage, Lofty's insomnia lifted, and the men who'd shared their hut started to complain about both gunners' snoring. Evelyn used this as an excuse to return to the cottage.

When she was there, Olive tried to keep her away from her housemates. Luckily for Olive, the household share of scandal soon shifted to Betty, who was about to be discharged. She'd missed her period, and although her housemates had tried to jolly her along by telling horror stories about the effects of a wartime diet and stress on their menstrual cycles, she was inconsolable. She said she'd known when it happened, not from the broken rubber but by the 'funny feeling' she'd got during intercourse. Hearing this, Violet and Olive had glanced at each other but said nothing.

The girls counselled Betty to wait. If her periods came she'd look pretty silly marching before the section officer to put herself up for a Paragraph Eleven. Then, when it became obvious to all four of them that Betty had waited too long, they changed the tenor of their pep talks in favour of Paragraph Eleven. Wasn't it one of the few ways a girl could get out of the service? Then she could put her feet up. This optimistic talk fell flat, so Cathy dropped hints about folk remedies she'd heard mentioned, and the possibility of an obliging doctor. And finally – when Betty told her American, and he proposed – Violet and Cathy and Olive enthused about what fun Chicago would be, with its gin palaces and gangsters.

'They don't have those anymore,' Betty said and, dry-eyed, put the second movement of the *Eroica* on so loudly the gramophone funnel danced.

Betty's pregnancy was their personal disaster for January, but Berlin was the Station's in general once the stand-down ended. The Lancasters bombed cloud, or the burning tails of sky-marker flares everyone hoped hung above the target. What was happening to Berlin itself, nobody could say. As with most operations, the crews took themselves to the target and bombed – flying level to let the camera mounted in the belly do its work – then refrained from asking questions that the photos of their bombing pattern couldn't easily answer. It was easier to think the target was getting a pasting. It had to be – just by the sheer tonnage of bombs chucked its way. Arthur Harris had promised Berlin as the key to German morale: knock it out, the 'Butcher' said, and the war would be over. So, it was Berlin for the squadrons of Bomber Command, all through January and on into February.

By then it was clear that the losses were mounting. 629 Squadron had lost I-Ink and B-Beer, and N-Nuts had gone in, trailed to the ground by the puffball white shapes of four parachutes. Also alarming to Olive were the rumours of old friends or boyfriends who'd failed to return to their Lincolnshire and Yorkshire stations. Not that anyone talked about this openly on the Station. Briefings went on as they always had – empty ritual for everyone but the navigators. Crews buttoned their lips and listened, even as the meteorological officer promised weather conditions they knew they'd never see.

If Evelyn was rattled, she didn't let on, and Lofty told Olive – too often for it to give her any comfort – that the rear gunner knew her stuff. If he was to be believed, the crew of LQ-Love worked like a Swiss watch, and Evelyn hadn't done anything flighty since hosing cloud on their first tip to Berlin. 'Nothing to be ashamed of there,' Lofty told her when they were having tea at the NAAFI. As for Evelyn, she restricted her complaints to the worsening rash on her face. On the advice of the medical officer (whom she'd nerved herself to see) she washed the inside of the mask with a cloth soaked in distilled water, and when that hadn't worked, she'd made herself a silk balaclava to wear on every operation.

Having heard nothing to the contrary, Olive and the gunners presumed Duncan was nearing Australia – Evelyn would only have to sit things out for another month or so. Besides the wait for Love when it was on the battle order, the worst of Olive's problems was the fact that, for obvious reasons, neither Duncan nor Evelyn had been able to send a letter home. She had already received word from a concerned Mrs Macintyre. She'd replied that she'd seen Evelyn safely off; and that Duncan was fine, and would write as soon as he could – one of the lesser lies she'd been forced to spout that winter. Olive herself missed Duncan's letters. He'd written to her faithfully since she'd left Australia and his silence now came as a shock, even though she knew its cause. The problem of unsent letters was surmountable: people might wonder, and lose patience, but the situation would sort itself out eventually. The real problem for Olive and Evelyn and Lofty that February was one they could not have foreseen.

A letter had come to Love's rear gunner at the crew hut – a wad of pages in a comfort fund envelope addressed to Duncan Macintyre. The return address was for a hotel in London that everyone in the service knew, but no name appeared above the sender's address. Evelyn put the letter in her tunic pocket and carried it to the house on Church Lane that evening.

'How odd,' she said, holding the envelope up to Olive's light. They were sitting on the bed with Cathy's bar heater popping and creaking into life on the floor beside them. 'Should we open it?'

'Of course we should,' Olive answered, and took the thing out of her hand. 'Duncan will want to know what it said. When we write.' They had lately begun to use the word *when* rather a lot in reference to Duncan. Their favourite of these was: 'When Duncan's safely home...' So, in Duncan's no-nonsense way, Olive ripped a corner off the blue envelope and wriggled her finger along the crease to unseal the flap. But when she slipped out the pages and read

Dear Duncan, This must be a shock

she had to pass the letter to Evelyn.

'It's from Crowe,' Evelyn said, after a quick scan of the first page, and then – as if it mattered – added, 'He's been promoted to Flight Lieutenant.' Olive expected her to read the whole thing out loud but she summarised, as if reading one of the newspapers Olive had been too lazy to follow at Hamble. Then it had been 'Troop train derailed in Suffolk', or 'Tea ration's down again' – Evelyn making sure her friend did not stay ignorant, but sparing her the complication of the details.

Tommy had been hit over the target. A piece of flak had come up through the deck, cut straight through the navigator's table and painted the back of the blackout curtain with his brains.

'That,' Evelyn said, embroidering her synopsis, 'is a direct quote.'

Crowe had re-balanced the fuel load. T-Tommy kept on with one engine feathered but they hadn't had the power to clear her tail when a German fighter found them. Solomon had already baled out so Crowe chivvied the flight engineer out the hatch before leaving the controls to the automatic pilot. He had come down near Aachen with no injury but the sprained wrist he'd got in the scramble to the bomb aimer's emergency exit.

'It seems everyone else bought it,' Evelyn said, and sighed. She was thinking about the gunners Crowe had found so that Lofty and Duncan could take their leave.

Crowe had come down in a forest with no idea what had happened to the other members of his crew, although he'd heard a pistol fired some way off when he was burying his parachute. On his return to England he learned that the bomb aimer and flight engineer had both been taken captive – the Red Cross had passed on their names. Duncan, he wrote, was not to worry about them. In her telling, Evelyn frowned at something on the page and declared, 'Crowe's very pleased with himself here. The forward planning of his escape provisions. The crew had always given him a ribbing about him wasting effort on a contingency, and now he's been proved right. He wants Duncan to follow his example and prepare for the worst.' She laughed in a way that Olive didn't like and added, 'What preparations could *I* possibly make for baling out over Germany?' If Evelyn baled out, and was caught, she would almost certainly be shot as a spy. Not for her the prison camp, and the duty of escape.

Crowe had ripped the tops off his flying-boots and stripped down to the civilian clothes he customarily wore under his flying suit. He had taken off the button of his fly that was to serve as his compass. He'd sorted through his escape kit to make sure nothing had a manufacturer's name – a tube of toothpaste could get a man killed.

Then he'd walked into Holland.

There he had approached a Lutheran Priest as the man was unlocking his church. He'd touched the sleeve of his cassock, and declared himself to be RAF. *Amerikan Engelsch* he'd said, standing there in his stinking clothes, his injured hand curled like a leper's.

After more than a month in the cellar of the church, Crowe was passed along the escape route, and eventually found his way back to England, in the hold of a Dutch fishing boat.

Evelyn's telling of the escaping pilot's narrative complete, she handed her friend the letter. Olive read:

> I'll bet that Lofty sees the joke in my being saved by the Lutherans – I might be Elect, but the gentlemen at HQ who debriefed me were pretty sure I made it through by skillful use of escape craft. So they've got me doing the rounds of operational stations and training units lecturing on evasion. I mean to make it your way as soon as I can and look forward to seeing you very much.

This last Crowe had underscored.

The American concluded his letter with an apology, although Olive couldn't see why. It wasn't his fault that Tommy went in, and the American's letter showed he had tried his best to get the Lancaster out of danger – an aircraft so sluggish, and a stick so heavy, that the flight engineer had to tug on his shoulders to help him pull up the throttle, and get the Lancaster out of its drunken corkscrew. Olive thought that Crowe was apologising not for losing T-Tommy, but for having abandoned Duncan.

Olive put down the letter and went to where the bottom of the stairs protruded from the ceiling, the alcove that captured, and held, the warmth from the heater. She took off her uniform and hung it on the line she'd strung there, then – in nothing but her blackouts – got into bed beside Evelyn. To get comfortable in her single bed, they both had to lie on their sides. Spooning was the best way to do this but Olive wanted to be able to see Evelyn's face, so she lay with her back to the cold at the blanket's edge. She put her fists between her knees to warm them, while Evelyn rested one palm, proprietarily, over Olive's left breast, the other cupping the nape of her neck.

Evelyn's eyes were shadowed, and dark, and grave – and not because she was preoccupied with the prospect of Crowe's return.

'We must think,' Olive said, and Evelyn looked anxious for a second. Fearing disavowal, she saw evidence for it everywhere. But when Olive added, 'You'll have to write and tell him not to come,' it was clear she was just preoccupied.

'I'm having enough trouble keeping up the gunnery log without having to write a whole letter.'

'Writing a letter can't be as painful as Crowe appearing in the mess one morning while you're having your egg and ham.'

Evelyn had to admit that was true.

All along they had said *just for a few months*, and their luck had held. Until now: until Crowe.

'You could write to say you don't want to see him,' Olive said. 'That it's best, considering.' She could feel Evelyn's dissent before she muttered a 'no' – her breast cooling as Evelyn took her hand from it.

'I won't do that. It's a disservice to them both. Like sending a telegram to say someone's dead when they're perfectly fine.'

Olive put the squared edge of her curled hands against Evelyn's stomach, one knuckle covering her belly button. She considered their situation. Evelyn's attention was taken up by the role – the ruse – she'd committed herself to. Any further difficulties would be left for her, or Lofty, to solve.

Olive and the gunners were in the NAAFI when Lofty came up with a solution, despite – as he put it – their being 'in the cactus'. He'd been deep in thought, demolishing a rock-hard bun by hitting it with the bottom of his saucer. The girl behind the counter was giving him looks but Lofty kept right on with this battering as he set out his plan.

'Say you'll see him during our next 72. And if we've not heard from Duncan by then just let Crowe know there's a flap on and that all passes are cancelled. What with the flicks to Berlin he's unlikely to think anything of it, particularly now that he's so far up in the gods he can't see what's on stage.'

The girl from the Women's Voluntary Service came out from behind the counter, swinging her tea towel menacingly. 'There's a war on, you know,' she said. 'Scarcity. Don't suppose you've heard of it?'

Lofty looked down at the pebbly mess on his saucer, and coloured. 'That wasn't rock cake – it was shell casing.'

She made no move to take his plate, but did wave her tea towel over it. 'Why don't you drop it on Berlin then? Next time you're there.'

'I do believe I will,' he yelled at her. 'And while I'm at it I'll tell the gunnery leader it was your idea to pepper the German people with baking goods!'

Late in February Lofty had an argument with the crew about the painting for Love's nose. He thought she should be 'Fool for Love', but couldn't get the others to agree on the image to go with such a name. He did manage to convince Pendleton not to paint a row of bomb icons beneath the kite's name. The Germans were never pleased at evidence of a crew's destructiveness, and if Love survived a crashlanding, that row of bombs would be a sign around the neck of every member of her crew – a sign saying: 'I burned the citizens of Hamburg'. In the end a leading aircrafthand got up his ladder and painted a red queen of hearts over the words 'Lucky in Love' while the crew stood below, shouting instructions. The paint dried in time for them to show off the new decoration for their operation to Stuttgart.

Meanwhile, the Station optimists looked out for a spring still technically some way off. A few straggly jonquils appeared at the border of the vegetable garden the WAAFs in the cottage had put in just before Betty had left them, with the Beethoven records tucked under her arm.

It was about the time the jonquils appeared that Cathy went to London on a 48, and Evelyn and Olive had the cottage to themselves. They spent all the time they could together there, although Olive had her watches to work, and Evelyn put in regular appearances in the crew hut to make sure there was no talk of gunners fraternising with WAAFs.

Lofty was painting once more – this time watercolours of local flora. One of these he gave to the vicar of St Deny's to auction. It sold for a pound, and Lofty could say he'd helped fund the cleaning of the church's northernmost eave of its pigeon droppings. Then the mid-gunner was interviewed for his warrant; Lofty impressing upon the Wing and Group commanders his warm support of the egalitarianism of Bomber Command. He told Evelyn afterward that he didn't care if they gave him a half-ring for his sleeve – if they didn't, he could hardly be worse off.

The days between LQ-Love's first and second trip to Stuttgart saw the last of their good luck. The day Lofty got his warrant, and celebrations in the sergeants mess, Cathy came back from her leave from London to tell Olive about the man she'd met.

Olive was happy for her friend for the five minutes it took her to make toast, to spread it with margarine and to pass the plate over to her. Then Cathy told her the man's name and Olive dangled the edge of the tea towel in the gas flame in her fright.

Catherine Derrick was no fool. She'd seen the look on Olive's face, and wanted an explanation.

'You think he's not suitable,' she said, her mouth barely opening to let the words out. 'Because he's American?'

'I don't think you're as silly as Betty if that's what you mean.'

'What *do* you mean?' she asked, and Olive saw that she was on the verge of tears.

'I'm not fit to advise people on their love-lives,' Olive said more gently, taking control of her own sense of shock, 'and you shouldn't give two hoots what I think. It's enough that you like him.'

'You knew the name when I said it,' Catherine replied, having regained her aplomb. 'Go ahead and tell me what you know. I don't want to be one of those women who flings herself about over a man her best friend thinks is a heel.'

'What I understand is that he's not terribly fond – ' Olive said, keeping hold of Cathy's gaze, ' – of women.'

She watched this settle, as a mine does in wet sand. 'Oh,' her friend said, empty-faced, then: 'Who told you that?'

'Lofty,' Olive lied. She had no intention of bringing Duncan into it. 'Curtis Crowe was his last skipper – their kite went in over Aachen.'

'If you'd said anyone else I might have had a hope of laughing it off as gossip. Yank-bashing,' said Cathy, picking at the corner of a slice of toast. 'But even an odd bird like Hilliers couldn't get the character of his own pilot wrong.'

'I don't know that it's a matter of *character*,' Olive said, but her friend was no longer listening. After Cathy went to her room to unpack, she cleared the kitchen, clanging dishes and banging cupboard doors. She was angry that she'd never met the man so pivotal in the lives of people near her. She should at least have been able to picture him – from the photographs Duncan had sent from Lichfield, from the story of his singing during the run-up to the target, or walking through the forest of frozen, skeletal birch trees in Holland. Crowe the Evader. But Crowe seemed like an abstraction, an idea. Perhaps he was admirable – in the way that icebergs were, or the Air Vice Marshal. But not someone with whom a person could stand close acquaintance.

For the next few days Cathy was quiet about Crowe, and Olive hoped she'd given up on him. But what her friend had done was to write and confront Crowe with an accusation against his character, something she'd 'heard' – she did not offer the precise source of the slur. She promised herself that if he wrote back to deny the rumour, and if his excuses sounded in the least like a flannelling – she'd drop him. But if he replied candidly she'd keep him as a friend. She was surprised when Crowe replied with a short letter to say the accusation was true in its more serious implication, but false on its face. He did like women, and he particularly liked her, and if she could master her qualms about his sexual history (and he did not expect her too) then he'd be honored to woo her.

And Catherine Derrick – priest only to her own conscience – replied that she would save her next leave for him, and if he was to come to a dance, or to take her to the Station pictures, then he would be welcome. Lincolnshire was easy striking distance for a man with a petrol ration for the motorcycle taking him on his lecture circuit. At the end of her letter, she'd added: *If you come, you can catch up with Tommy's gunners.*

So Curtis Crowe was invited to North Killingholme. In her hopefulness, and her innocence, Catherine Derrick would imagine he'd come in answer to her letter. But Olive knew it would be Duncan he'd come for.

After Cathy told Olive that she'd asked Curtis Crowe to visit her, Olive could not shake a sense of foreboding. Evelyn would have to shed her role as Duncan earlier than had been planned, and present herself to the Air Transport Auxiliary at White Waltham, saying she'd changed her mind about going home. The game was up. Olive spent her whole watch in the Flying Control Office getting used to that idea, and by the time she left the tower imagined herself reconciled to it. Evelyn would be safe, and only Duncan's *name* would be in trouble. A name couldn't suffer, could it? A name was not something you could weep and wail and gnash your teeth over, and – she told herself, trying not to think too hard about the efficiency of the war office – the RAAF couldn't do much without a body to fit the name of a defaulter.

But Olive didn't get the opportunity to say any of this to Evelyn and Lofty until a day later. Love had been on the battle order for Stuttgart. The gunners were in a good mood when she met them outside the mess – Lofty was playing with the wingco's new dog as Evelyn watched them berserk about between the buildings of admin, getting in the way of the clerks and technical officers making their way from desk to dinner.

When Olive finally caught the mid-gunner's eye, she yelled, 'Come for a walk?' and he loped over to join them.

'Thirteen down,' Evelyn told her as they headed for the gates, and Olive saw the source of their mood. Twelve ops was the magic number, kill or cure: if a crew could make thirteen ops they could make thirty, or so the popular wisdom went.

'Sh – , *he's* had the rite of passage,' Lofty said, and coloured so that the few freckles left over from summer stood out vividly. 'Old age and an easy death are the worst we've got to look forward to now.'

She explained that might not be the case if Cathy managed to entice Curtis Crowe to North Killingholme. Without her needing to press the issue, Lofty agreed it was wisest that Evelyn pack it in. Soon.

But Evelyn was recalcitrant. She didn't want to quit, not when Duncan might still be in transit.

Bloody slow transit, Lofty said, and she ignored him.

In any case, Evelyn went on, wouldn't Cathy get more precise notice of Crowe's arrival? Any visit had to be timed to watch rotations, to days off, or leave, and if Olive kept her ear to the ground she'd know almost as soon as Cathy did when Crowe was due to arrive. And then she could give warning.

'It's not the disaster you imagine,' Evelyn said, lighting a cigarette for Lofty.

So they let Evelyn have her way. And since Olive didn't really want her to leave in the first place, this was – from her – no difficult concession.

Chapter Twenty-Three

Rivals

Over the following days Olive grilled Cathy on the subject of Crowe. She thought her interest only fair given how nosy Cathy had been about her affairs.

The couple were writing to each other every second day. Crowe wrote to Duncan sporadically, but the fact that he wrote at all demonstrated that Cathy wasn't the only person on his mind. He was perfectly candid; writing that he'd been seeing a girl but Duncan oughtn't mind – as ever, he'd keep such matters separate. And since Duncan seemed to be dragging the chain about *their* meeting, Crowe couldn't help but wonder what was on the gunner's mind. *Are you alright?* he'd ask, or, with a sharper edge, *Tell me you're alright!*

Evelyn agonised over her end of this correspondence, wanting to write something true to what her brother *might* have felt. But her version of her brother's feeling left out his tiredness, and all of his fear. She had long since put the image of the young man weeping in the showers out of her head. *Be patient,* she told Crowe in her best version of her brother's handwriting. *It's just the shock of having someone back I thought was lost.*

That letter Evelyn posted in Lincoln, while Lofty stood, hands in his pockets, peering up at the cathedral. Olive was at the other end of the stone bridge looking into the waters of the Witham, her elbows on the wet stone railing. Students in their long coats and mufflers were streaming down the hill towards them. Lectures were over for the day so they were off to the pubs they'd fought to keep their own in a town filled with thirsty servicemen.

Lofty had his heart set on the Saracen's Head, but Evelyn wouldn't hear of them going to 'that pit' – even the assurance of anonymity was not enough to tempt her. So the three of them followed the students along the walkway by the river and claimed a table in a pub that looked as old as the cathedral. It had a great, smoke-blackened fireplace deep and wide enough that the crew of a Lancaster might have stretched out side by side on the stones of the grate. The only other service people in the place were a pair of lost-looking Wrens hemmed in at the corner of the bar.

Olive and the gunners met each other pint for pint, Lofty slowing to his companions' more delicate pace. At some point he started a philosophical discussion with some students, shaking his finger in the face of a young man who'd announced that a truly socialist state was impossible. Olive was almost drawn into their argument, but Evelyn put an arm around her, and kissed the side of the face she'd had turned at Lofty. Then Olive saw one of the Wrens look their way and give a tiny smile of sympathy and approbation.

Olive understood, in that look, the license she'd been given. She had loved Evelyn Macintyre since she was twelve years old, when Evelyn had taken her up on the Macintyres' best black mare, and ridden with her to school. But the time she could love Evelyn easily was rapidly running out.

'Good grief, what's up with her?' Lofty asked Evelyn, forgetting his argument. Olive had stood up and was elbowing her way through the crowd of drinkers to the door. 'Anybody would think she'd just got a telegram.'

Frowning, he glanced at her empty pint.

Evelyn pushed herself out of her chair. 'I think I'd better go after her,' she said. Lofty followed after stopping to drain what was left of their drinks.

Olive was leaning over the wall beside the river, with her back to them. Somehow her hat had fallen into the street. When they came to stand at either side of her she said weakly, 'I'm alright. You needn't have come out.'

Thinking she must be drunk, Lofty picked up her cap and then he and Evelyn each took an arm and walked her up and down the towpath, up and down in front of the blacked out windows of the pubs, and houses, and the fat black mouth of the sheds that, in better years, had sheltered the markets. Olive found that her knees bent too much as she walked – her body seemed to want to lie down, just to lie down and be done with it, but she was being held up at either side by her friends. A few people passed them on the path, but in the dim radiance of the glimmer lights there was not much to see that hadn't been seen before – just another WAAF the worse for wear from drink.

But there was one person who took a keen interest in the gunners walking a young woman between them. This good Samaritan was himself RAF, for he wore a flying jacket and dark, neatly creased trousers. The stranger sat astride an idling motorcycle, at the other end of the short stone bridge that spanned the Witham. He lifted one white hand in the darkness, and waved.

'Lookout, here comes a nosy parker,' Lofty said, as the motorcyclist nudged the front wheel of the bike onto the cobbled bridge and puttered their way. But before he could tell the man to mind his own business the motorcyclist had passed them, his machine backfiring as it geared up. After that, the only interference Olive and the gunners encountered was a young woman who'd loomed out of the dark like a pike from a fishing hole to ask whether they needed a better balance of ladies.

'Piss off, you tart,' Evelyn said.

'Not good enough for you, eh?' the girl yelled and, swearing loudly, went down the towpath, back the way she'd come.

By the time they were sitting on the bus on their way back to the Station, Olive had recovered, and Lofty was telling her how much he admired her qualities as a cheap drunk. But Olive would not bite. Evelyn sat quietly beside her friend, every so often squeezing her hand, but Olive's anxiety only deepened at the thought that Evelyn knew it was not drink that had undone her. While aircrew and WAAF of the station sung bawdy songs, and chattered about them, Olive rested her forehead on the glass, staring out of a window blacked-out years before with broad blue stripes, like the undercoat to an expressionist canvas.

The crews went to Frankfurt again, then to a particularly hairy raid on Berlin. Lofty and Evelyn were halfway through their tour when Evelyn confided to Olive her hope that she'd make twenty-five before she had to pack it in. Twenty-five was the limit for the American crew of the Liberators that flew the daylight raids. Olive thought twenty-five was enough for anyone, but for Evelyn it was a point of honour. Duncan's safety was one thing – service another. She'd shown a woman could do it, even if she'd only shown it to two people.

No aircraft from North Killingholme flew the minor raid to Aulnoye, and that meant whoever was not on duty could sign-out from the Station or stay to wangle a telephone line, if such a line was free and the reason for wanting it convincing.

Olive was denied such leisure. She had watch, and spent the hours of 8 a.m. to 4 p.m. listening to the air above the Station for aircraft lost, diverted, or marking their proper course with a call. She was therefore busy, and had no idea what was – by then – happening to Evelyn.

Doc, the Skipper of LQ-Love, had gone to the mess looking for his rear gunner. The squadron leader was asking for him. This request had forced Love's gunner into a flat spin. Evelyn had run to the crew hut, where she'd buffed her shoes and buttons and checked that her cap was not at an insolent angle. That she'd been called before the squadron leader meant it was an operational matter. She hoped it was about the warrant – Duncan's refusal to progress in rank would have baffled the officers at Group.

The two men in the small office with its windows overlooking the runway were laughing when she arrived, that full-bodied laughter the crews learned early in their wartime indenture, and – if they'd lived long enough to get rings on their sleeves – took with them into command positions. Evelyn composed herself before knocking on the door, and entered the room with her face unreadable as a cat's. She marched smartly up to the desk and saluted, then stood to attention staring over the head of the squadron leader.

The squadron leader took the measure of the man before him. Macintyre stood with his shoulders hunched – quite some achievement for a man standing at attention, but less so for a rear gunner. Gunners were generally small of stature to start with, but all became – by degrees – even more crimped and compacted by their time in the turret, a confined place that nevertheless offered a grand view of air dark and crowded – of aircraft aflame, of flowering flak and German cities burning. Such sights contracted the spirit to match the frame. Still, Macintyre was a lively-looking specimen, what with those widely spaced, intelligent bluish grey eyes. But there was something weak about the man's mouth – it was too sumptuous, like the mouths of some of the squadron leader's fellow students at Oxford, young men who'd only lasted a semester, and had drunk too much.

'You wanted to see me, Sir.'

'I did, Flight Sergeant. My curiosity got the better of me.'

The squadron leader knotted his hands together as a pastor might before leaning in to lecture his parishioners. 'I hear you refused to be interviewed about your warrant.' At that, the man before him relaxed. 'You're sixteen operations in, with another forty under your belt from Elsham. A commission could follow a warrant for a chap with a record like that.'

Evelyn met the squadron leader's eyes for a moment. He seemed amused, if slightly bored – not the expression of a man who suspected one of his complement was an impostor.

'I don't mind, Sir.' Evelyn answered, mastering her nerves. 'I'm happy at my work as I am.'

'Louder, Flight Sergeant. Let's hope that's not how you talk on the intercom.'

Evelyn cleared her throat, and fairly bawled: 'I'm happy at my work.'

'So happy and so busy you've got no time to see the man who put you up for a half-ring?'

Evelyn said nothing to that, but the back of her neck started to burn.

Noting the gunner's silence, the squadron leader prompted: 'We've not been depriving you of leave, have we?'

'No Sir.'

'So you *have* had leave?'

'Yes Sir,' Evelyn said, in the quiet voice she'd started with.

'And you spent it on Station?'

'Yes Sir.'

'Now why would you do that?' The squadron leader raised

his eyebrows, and as he did Evelyn saw that he was probably no older than Duncan.

She only had a second to think, so – imagining what Lofty might say – said, 'Because we're skint.'

'*We* being who?'

'Flight Sergeant Hilliers and myself.'

'Your skulking around North Killingholme couldn't be anything to do with a romantic attachment to a WAAF in signals then?'

That was not what she'd expected. Evelyn blinked. 'Not at all, Sir.'

Then someone behind her said, in one of those American accents familiar to her from the ATA and, more recently, the drinkers packing the bar at the Cross Keys, 'That's got a ring of truth to it. The Duncan I remember would never get himself mixed up with a WAAF.'

'Is that right?' the squadron leader said to the American standing behind her. Then, to the gunner, 'See how your old skipper stands up for your reputation?'

Curtis Crowe strolled over to the window, and stood looking out of it. In a musing voice, he said, 'Whether this is the Duncan I know is another question altogether.'

Evelyn stole a look at the American she'd been writing to for the past month. His tie was knotted loosely around his thick neck, and he held his cap in his hand. His hair was dark, except at the temples, and at his neat parting a cowlick shone. His eyes were a warm brown, and deeply lined at their edges. *Of course*, thought Evelyn – as if the fact was important – *he's years older than any of us*. Crowe raised his lips in a smile, exposing his teeth (as Americans often did), and she looked down at the floor, at the shining tips of her regulation issue shoes. Then she brought herself to a more rigid attention, wavering in place as if she'd been held on parade for hours.

Crowe was saying that the Duncan he'd known wouldn't have passed up a chance at a warrant. 'Not if it meant an increase in pay, and more money saved towards the veterinary practice.' He picked up a mounted skeleton of a bird the squadron leader kept sitting on the corner of his desk and, turning the thing to the light, said, 'And what about that sister of his. She was paid at a pretty good rate by the ATA. Outdoing her must have had its attractions.'

Crowe had not yet looked directly at Evelyn, and now, peering at the bones of the bird's wings he said, 'How the hell do these things fly?' Sighing, he put the skeleton down. 'The fact is, people change.' Finally he looked at her with such intensity Evelyn was afraid the squadron leader would notice. 'So how is your sister?' Crowe asked.

Evelyn's face felt wooden. 'She's gone home to help our father out on the farm. She should be there by now.'

'That must be a relief for all concerned.'

Evelyn nodded, and felt the muscles in her back slowly begin to unclench.

The squadron leader had meanwhile picked up the first of a stack of intelligence reports. These seemed more interesting to him than the gunner and the American Flight Lieutenant standing in front of his desk.

Evelyn stared at Curtis Crowe. Here was the man who'd been flying for the RAF since late 1940, when he'd started in Fighter Command; the man with a DFC; with thank-you letters from Winston Churchill and from Queen Mary; a man whose idle requests were listened to, and whose anger was respected; the man who – the night Duncan insisted they check on Ida's house and they'd got caught in an air raid – had let her brother sleep in his arms in a crowded street shelter in West Ham.

The man who had engineered a leave for Duncan and Lofty, and had therefore saved them.

After a glance at the squadron leader – he was oblivious, still shuffling papers – Evelyn found her resolve. She walked up to her brother's lover and put out her hand to him. Although Crowe was slow to raise his hand to take hers, his grip when he did so was strong, and his hand warm.

'I can't say how glad I am that you came through,' she said. 'Lofty and I owe you a debt. I'm going to make sure they understand that at home, and that they know you're safe and well. But letters take so long to get to the other side of the world; if you don't hear anything that's all the silence means – that it takes time.'

'You don't need to thank me. I've always wanted to take care of my crew. To do what's best.' Crowe's moustache twitched upward in a smile. 'Can't change those habits now.'

At that the squadron leader looked up, and Evelyn knew that it was time for her retreat.

'May I be dismissed?' she asked, and the squadron leader flung up a lazy salute.

'Go on then, Flight Sergeant. Consider yourself billed. And I don't want anything getting back to me about your poor choice of a target for tonight. If you must get serious with a girl, make sure she's not in the Station complement.'

As soon as Evelyn was out of the admin building she ran into the blast shelter and vomited all over the shoes she'd buffed a half-hour before. Once the retching brought up nothing but bile she sprinkled sand from the bucket by the door over the little steaming pool of her vomit, and used a handkerchief to clean her footwear.

Then, feeling like some conjurer's helper sawn in half for an audience, she walked back to the crew hut. Lofty was lying on his bed reading. Luckily there was no one else there because when she told him what had happened he threw his copy of the *Tibetan Book of the Dead* at the shelves on the opposite wall, and it knocked over Blue's beer stein from Magdeburg, the one he'd got in exchange for three months of his chocolate ration. The stein broke in two and rolled under a bunk, but Lofty ignored what he'd done. Evelyn followed him to the door only to see the mid-gunner set off at a run between the huts, towards the gate.

Lofty waited there a half-hour, then an hour, and despite the pathetic lack of props to his story, told the sentry he was composing a sketch of the scene. When finally he saw Crowe walking the perimeter towards him he went out to meet him.

Lofty stopped in front of his skipper. 'One moment, there's

me thinking I'll not lay eyes on you again,' he said, in wonder at himself, 'then the next moment, I'm thinking any time would be too soon.'

Crowe took his cap off, and sighed. He looked like a fighter waiting for his opponent to throw the first punch.

But Lofty only put out his hands to take the one Crowe still had free. This he did with the vigour of a child trying to bring down ripened fruit by shaking the branch.

Later that day he came to tell Olive about the encounter with Crowe, and to say that Evelyn thought it best they stay away from each other for a while. There was too great a chance Crowe would turn up at Woodside cottage. Even if he were ready to keep their secret, a social engagement with him would be far too ticklish. Evelyn was worried, too, that confirmation of the rumour about Love's gunner and a WAAF in signals would fetch up at the squadron leader's door. If the squadron leader found out, so would Olive's squadron officer, and she would be sent off Station.

Lacking Evelyn's side of the story of her meeting with Crowe, Olive was left to shape the encounter whichever way her imagination took her. She saw Clark Gable in the natty best blues Crowe would have been issued after his return from Europe; Clark Gable shaking the squadron leader's hand. These images had all the fantastical qualities of her hope that they'd got away with it – as if the rest of Evelyn's indenture as a gunner, and the fifteen operations left to do were mere technicalities. They had done it.

That feeling lasted for a day, and then she started missing Evelyn. LQ-Love was on the battle order for Essen, and she thought it wouldn't hurt if she stood by the runway to watch them leave. But she was not the last person out in the cold waving the planes off since she had to get back to the Marconi, her notebook, and the shove ha'penny board.

While the cities of the Ruhr were closer than Berlin, or Leipzig, the night's operation was a bumpy one. Happy Valley had more permanent flak batteries than any other part of Europe. It had its own special feature in the mobile batteries, those flotillas of trucks with guns, bolted onto their backs, that lobbed thirty-pound shells. Navigators dreaded these because it was impossible to plot a leg to avoid them: like fighters, they were simply there, or not – and if they were there, then the crew would know about it. So when all of North Killingholme's aircraft returned, the relief was general. Things were particularly cheery in the Watch Office when Olive hung the strap of her gas mask over her shoulder and got ready to give up her seat to the WAAF come to relieve her.

It was unusual for her to come off a watch just as the crews were finishing their interrogation, but as she bicycled from the tower she saw men drifting out of their debriefing at the Nissen hut, their faces lit red by the embers of cigarette ends.

The wireless operator of D-Dog, a Geordie with whom Olive had danced a number of times, stopped to whistle at her while his friends stood stamping their feet on hardstanding bright with frost.

'Parky innit?' Dog's mid-upper gunner said as Olive came to stand beside them.

'It would freeze the nuts off a brass monkey if it weren't already nutless,' agreed Dog's bomb aimer and Olive patted him on his sleeve and said no one would know what was what under the lot of clobber he was wearing.

''earts of bleeding steel, that's what,' the gunner said. Olive noticed that his teeth were chattering and that he'd every so often clench down his jaw in a grimace. Either he was feeling his benzedrine, or his nerve had gone. She looked away from him at the door to the hut.

'Love's just winding up. They had a spot of bother finding the target,' Dog's pilot said equably. They'd all had a spot of bother finding the target at one time or another. But however common that problem was, it had to be explained to the WAAF intelligence officer's satisfaction, and that took time.

Dog's crew drifted off to their supper; to the stout and singing that would unwind them sufficiently to sleep. Essen was not so far that any but the unwary sprog would take a wakey-wakey tablet, so by 0200 or 0300 the mess would be quiet; the crews snoring in their bunks.

Olive peered at the pale splotches of radium on the dial of her watch. The watch given to her by an aspiring suitor at Spaulding Moor. The suitor was long since dead, but his watch still ticked – the secondhand sweeping over the radium in its regular circuit. 0035. Olive's stomach didn't like the hour of night, and it told her so in no uncertain terms.

Then the last crew came out, more subdued than the ones before them. They had spent their bluff on the WAAF at the interrogation table.

'Jeez I'm knackered,' Blue said, stretching up to touch the dewy curve of the hut's roof. 'You lot can have my dinner, I'm off to get some straight and level in.' And he walked away, chaffing his gloved hands against the cold.

Sleepy was wide-awake, with no appetite. 'What I need is a beer and a chat,' he said and went off to the sergeants mess with the bounce of bennies in his step.

That left Bashful, Happy, Doc and the gunners, and Olive walked them to the door of their mess, Lofty and Evelyn strolling slowly enough that anyone would have thought it a summer day. The gunners dwarfed Olive, Lofty nearly as wide as he was tall in the padding of his flying suit, the rear gunner more bearlike still. Olive felt like the oysters walked down the beach by the Walrus and the Carpenter.

'How was it?' she asked, and Lofty shrugged.

'It was a milk run. Sadly, we left our delivery on the wrong back step.'

Evelyn laughed at that, smoke from her cigarette indistinguishable from the vapour of her breath. 'We did rather.'

'Never mind,' Olive said, because she didn't.

'*We* don't,' said Lofty. 'It's Sleepy and Doc in the old excreta, not us. Sleepy got a case of premature ejaculation. He feels a bit burned about it.' Lofty threw his own cigarette into the dark and waved at the sky. 'But as you can see the sky is not falling, and we have not been struck by bolts of lightning hurled by Butcher Harris, so we don't give a tinker's.'

They had come to the door of the mess through which the rest of Love had disappeared.

'I can't go in there,' Olive said, nodding at the crew mess. Then, to Evelyn, 'I'll wait for you.'

The rear gunner's face was pale, and Olive wanted to kiss those sharp cheekbones; the rise of her brow.

'You'd better not,' Evelyn said, and gave her one of her austere looks, but Olive was there when Love's crew came back out. She'd had to hang back in the shadows to avoid the squadron leader – he'd flown as a supernumerary with the sprog crew of P-Peter, and Olive didn't want to cross his path.

She convinced Evelyn to walk a couple of circuits of the perimeter track with her, as if the hour was no impediment. But there was no romance in it – just cold, and a creeping sense of discomfort that was not physical in its origin. Behind the Avro Hangar they kissed, and when Evelyn made to step back Olive clung to her neck.

'Don't say anything,' she warned, feeling the muscles in Evelyn's neck tense, but it was only a yawn that had stretched them.

Evelyn detached herself. 'I'll take you to the gate,' she said, and they walked the last of the way in silence.

After the operation to Essen there were a few quiet nights, the boon of bad weather. Olive had begun to feel that Evelyn was avoiding her, and her mood became increasingly leaden. The afternoon Evelyn spent in her bed should have broken Olive's mood, but instead her anxiety deepened – convinced, as she was, that Evelyn's gift of her company had been a concession.

LQ-Love was on the Battle Order for Brunswick but the operation was scrubbed while the crews sat in their Lancasters waiting for their take-off order. Since Olive had gone to wave them off she walked to dispersal to meet them. Evelyn was at the grassy edge of the hardstanding up-ending the contents of her thermos onto the weedy grass. Tendrils of steam rose from the ground before the toes of her boots.

'Sign out and come to the cottage,' Olive said, catching the gunner's thickly padded arm. But Evelyn shook her head, the mask wobbling beneath her chin.

'I'd better not.'

Olive blinked, then squeezed her eyes shut. 'What point can there be,' she said, slowly, 'what possible point, if we are not to see each other?' After a second she felt Evelyn take her hand.

'Meet me in the air-raid shelter in half an hour,' Evelyn said, and then Olive heard the sound of her boots on the hard-standing.

Evelyn came to meet Olive in her best blues, but wearing a bulky woollen jumper under her tunic. Coiled about her neck like an enormous scarf was one of the service blankets from her bunk, and she laid this on the concrete floor of the shelter and stretched out on it, looking up at Olive, her eyelids lowered. Olive folded herself down upon her friend, lying at a diagonal, with her chest against Evelyn's, and her legs on the blanket. She pressed her forehead against Evelyn's warm cheek, feeling the fragile fall and rise of the pulse in her neck where her lips lightly rested.

Evelyn pulled herself up against the wall, carrying the slighter woman with her. Fishing in the pocket of her greatcoat she found Duncan's Ronson, and waved its flame over the ends of two cigarettes. She put both in her mouth and drew until their ends were brightly burning, then she passed one over to Olive.

'It's not about you, if that's what you're thinking,' Evelyn finally said, her voice a puff of pale vapour in the dark. 'Nor am I giving you the push.' Blowing smoke past Olive's cheek, she smiled her lopsided smile. 'One day when this is all over, I'll fly you to Nice. Or Marseilles. Or San Remo. We'll take a villa. No one pays attention to the English in the South of France – there's so many of them there – hiding from their relatives or their spouses; from English manners, and the cold.' Evelyn wrapped her arms around Olive and spoke into her hair. Her breath was warm. 'I'll be able to take you on my arm to the Casino at Cannes, and no one will whisper.'

Olive wanted to sink through the concrete floor of the shelter into the soil beneath. What Evelyn was describing she could not imagine, and her mind could offer no future in its place.

'You must promise not to leave me,' Olive said, knowing, as she did, that this was a pledge she herself could never give.

'Alright,' Evelyn said, 'I promise.'

Chapter Twenty-Four

The morality of altitude

Olive slept in that morning in late March. There was to be no flying and since she was not on shift until midnight, she had the day to herself. Cathy brought her breakfast at eleven: two bits of toast and marg, a peeled carrot, and a cup of tea. Cathy suggested they go out for a ride. The weather was clear and bright – just what a spring day should be.

'Oh go on, give me a minute,' Olive said, pushing the crusts to the side of the plate.

The two WAAFs set off towards East Halton, at times riding abreast; at others weaving about to take up the whole of the road. It was a good outing, and at its end Cathy insisted they stop for a beer at the Cross Keys. She wanted to talk without having to shout over her shoulder.

The pub was dark and smoky, and there were very few men in blue about. The lounge was full of the Americans from Goxhill and one of these was Betty's husband. Once he'd got over his embarrassment at seeing them he came over to tell her news. She was boarding in Lincoln. Despite rationing, and thanks to the baby, Betty had gained ten pounds. He wondered whether she was incubating a Liberator in there.

Olive was taken by surprise when Cathy told the American that she had news to pass on to Betty – she'd got herself into a romance with a Yank airman and it was serious.

Olive seemed to lose interest in her pint. She asked, 'What do you mean, *serious*?'

Cathy – who never presumed to know anyone's mind – replied, 'I'm serious about him.'

There was an awkward silence for a minute or two, then Olive looked at the people drinking at the tables around them and said, 'Where's our lot?'

'If they're not here its because they're driving the bus tonight,' said Betty's husband, and it dawned on the WAAFs that he was right.

Their ride south was subdued. At the crossroad to the village they leaned on their bikes, Olive with a foot down in the weeds by the ditch, to look through the gaps in the hedgerow by the aerodrome. Sure enough, the Lancasters were out on the tarmac with ground crew busy about them. Tractors towing armaments crisscrossed the hardstanding, as did the petrol bowsers.

'That doesn't look like prep for a minor raid,' Cathy said, and then sat straighter on her saddle and rode home to get her kit.

Although Olive herself wasn't due on watch for eight hours, she followed Cathy to the aerodrome. The Flying Control Officer told them it was to be a maximum effort, a light bomb load and ladles of gravy.

'We're not quite sure where all that fuel will take them, at this point. Group could call at any minute.'

Olive knew what all three of them were thinking: Berlin – a dicey enough do without a full moon to light it.

Cathy went to inspect the communications log for the earlier watch. Olive was edged out of the tower. She'd hear the target soon enough wherever she was on Station, as nothing travelled faster than rumour, and no rumour travelled faster than at the NAAFI.

Talk at the tables there was moody and tense. One off-duty aircrafthand, a mechanic by the look of the black rings under his nails, kept saying 'But it's a full moon!' as if the rest of the people there didn't know. Most of the aircrew seemed to think that amount of fuss for an operation sure to be scrubbed was wasted effort. And if the thing did go ahead, there'd be worse wastage. So why bother at all?

'Anybody would think we weren't due a rest,' growsed one sergeant of the RCAF.

'You might get a longer rest than you bargain for if you go saying things like that,' added a young man wearing the sparks brevet of a wireless operator.

'If I was the wing commander, I'd tell them where to stick it,' said another.

Blue, Love's wireless operator, was in one of these growsing groups, standing with his foot on the seat of a chair. Lofty was not with them, and neither was Evelyn, but Doc was blowing smoke rings at the ceiling nearby, and egging on his W/Op.

'Go on, you tell 'em, Ali Oop,' he said.

'What's all this chin-food about? I'd rather go anywhere than sit on the tarmac like a bloody idiot. There's no future in it. If they keep scrubbing ops, I won't see Perth until 1954.'

'You can't see Perth now, it's so small,' another man in the pale blue uniform of the RAAF teased. Olive knew him slightly. He'd had a greengrocer's shop in Surry Hills and had given her advice on what to put in their vegetable patch.

While the Australians bickered, Olive asked Doc where Lofty and Duncan were and he looked at her as if through the wrong end of a telescope.

'At the firing range.'

At the range there were only a few sprogs manhandling a Vickers gun. For a while Olive watched them working off their nerves by shouting abuse at each other and at the gun, then she went home.

When she returned to the field some hours later the furious activity had settled, and there were fewer aircrew about – the navigators were in their briefing. In the Flying Control Office Cathy was filling in the list of aircraft on the battle order. It was a long list. The only plane not on it was King – it was still showing far too much daylight to fly anywhere. It would be the only aircraft left sitting on the tarmac when the balloon went up.

Brushing chalk from her fingers, Cathy came over to Olive, and although her junior could quite well read the target herself, said, 'Nuremberg.' Olive saw flags draped over neoclassical buildings, marching figures, and a little dot on the map near Berlin – a long way away, and just another target. She was too tired to think more about it.

'I'm going to go get my dinner,' she said. She and Cathy and Violet were always doing that – eating on Station spared their ration books.

'Lucky you, I'm famished.'

Olive promised she'd cadge something for her.

She ate at a table with six other WAAFs, two of them girls who ran the bomb tractors. They'd had a relatively quiet day – the petrol bowsers were on the go, but they weren't. Maximum effort to a distant target meant you had to send a *lot* of planes because each one had its weight accounted for by the fuel it was carrying. Bombs destroyed cities, but the aircraft off to Nuremberg couldn't afford to carry many. It was like sending a mob of three-year-olds to do a stoning: you could only kill the victim through weight of numbers.

'I did a job for your boyfriend today,' said a WAAF armourer Olive had seen but never talked to. At first Olive thought she was talking to someone else, but then the girl said, 'I took two sections of perspex out of the turret to give the guns a better radius of movement. It's dead fashionable at the moment.' She was ferrying mushy peas to her mouth but when she saw Olive's face she put down her fork and gave her hand a good squeeze. 'He'll be alright, love.'

Olive thought it was unlikely she'd get to see Evelyn and

Lofty – they'd leave their briefing for the crew room to suit up, and then would be taken by crew bus to dispersal. There wasn't much Olive could do, so she played Ludo in the WAAF mess, and wrote a letter to her father. When she heard the massed rumble of the Merlins she knew that the last checks were being made, and the crews would be on the field. Though she was breaking regulations, she made her way to the edge of dispersal, until she was near enough to see the Lancs emptying their crews, groups of men in their fat flight suits and Donald Duck yellow Mae Wests standing under the wings of their planes, talking to ground crew. It was not a scrub, then, but a delay. Olive hitched a lift with the mobile canteen as it puttered its way about the perimeter. When finally it came to Love, Olive asked the WAAF serving to pour her a cup of tea. This she carried over to the crew.

'One sip can't hurt,' she said, and handed the cup to the first outstretched hand. It was Lofty's.

'If I spend my trip at the Elsan I'll know who to blame,' he said, blowing on the tea. Olive could see every detail of his flight suit, and his face, and even the shadows of the tendons in the hand that clutched the cup.

Lofty looked up into the clear moonlit sky and, taking a sip, he said, 'Oh Father, if it be possible, let this cup pass from me.' At which point the flight engineer, who'd been next in line to drink, folded his arms back over his chest.

'Oh go on,' said the man with a leather patch on his flying suit that said Flt/Sgt Macintyre. 'Give me a sip.'

Lofty passed the cup to Evelyn, and from her it went to Happy, the navigator, who for once was not. 'How would you like to fly at 16,000 feet in this? All the way to the Rhine?' he asked, and took a good swig of the tea.

Olive thought about that for a second, and then Evelyn said, 'If it was Olive she'd have to fly lower than that. I don't think she knows where the Rhine is.' And they all laughed their heads off.

'This tea's cold,' said Blue, and then, to Sleepy, 'You hogged it.'

Sleepy jigged about, his harness jangling, and Olive wondered if he'd already taken his benzedrine tablet. 'That'll be through us in a second and we'll have to re-christen the tyre.' He nodded at Olive. 'If there's no objection from the ladies.'

But even if their bladders had been full, the men of the crew of Love were too nervous to relieve them. It dawned on Olive that she was making their wait worse, for they had to put on an act for her, and for each other, as long as she was there.

'I'd better go,' she said, and kissed Lofty's cold cheek. He held both her hands a minute, and looked into her face like a dog worried about its master. Then, much to her surprise, he brought her right palm up to his mouth and kissed it.

'There's my girl,' he said, in just the same way he had when he was lying on the sitting room floor at Robin Hoods Bay.

'Snow White kisses *all* the dwarves goodbye,' Pendleton said. So Olive did, leaving the rear gunner to last.

Later Olive would try to conjure Evelyn at that moment: how her face was paler than any of the crew's; that her lips tasted sweet from the glucose tablet she'd just eaten; that she trod on her toe by mistake when they kissed. Later, she would think about those things so much that everything else would drop away – and what dropped farthest and fastest was how she herself had felt. It was impossible to have a full memory of that moment, just as it was impossible to watch a total eclipse and, in the instant of totality, see the shadow of the moon rushing at you, the disappearing sun; the colour of light at the horizon. Something will always be missed, and there will never come a chance to see any of it again.

Olive would remember that Evelyn put her lips in her hair for a second before pushing her back towards the NAAFI wagon, the driver of which had kindly waited.

'I'll see you later,' she called.

Later, Olive was on watch. The men and women serving around her in the Flying Control Office were subdued, understanding what it meant that the crews had been asked to fly at a low ceiling under a moon so bright it was like daylight. Olive did her job, and waited. The estimated time over the target for the lead aircraft was 0100, and it would take the crews another three hours or so to negotiate their return. The only aircraft they could expect to see before 0400 were the ones that turned back on the outward leg, as two of North Killingholme's did. It was through the crews of those early returns that they heard about the vapour trails from the bombers' engines webbing the skies over Denmark and Germany, contrails so crisp-edged that the gunner who'd logged them thought they looked solid enough to walk on.

Olive won at shove ha'penny, and as his penance for losing, the Flying Control Officer took charge of the tea for the rest of the night. Then Olive knitted, a ball of air-force blue wool pinioned beneath her soldering iron. 0400 came and went without a peep from the radio-telephone, at which point they knew that the broadcast winds had been wrong. Something had detained the stream. It was 0500 when the first call came in, and the next was not until twenty minutes later. After that, the aircraft meandered home – few enough, and none of them Love. Olive recorded the instructions in her best hand, as if squared letters on the page of the log could keep disaster in check, but when she heard Lofty's voice – flattened and shrunken though it was – calling for crash tender and blood bus, the lines of her printing kinked and broke and staggered over the page.

'We're going to pass over the fields to the north and those of us who can are baling out. Then Macintyre wants permission to come around and try the north-eastern approach for an emergency landing.'

'Please confirm your approach altitude,' Olive said, crisply.

'That I can't say, sorry.' Then, Lofty said something Olive could not at that moment comprehend, although later – when she was sleepwalking her way through the churchyard on her way home to the cottage – she'd recognise it: he'd quoted the two-line inscription from a stone near the chapel door: *Ye mortals be ready at my call/ and think how sudden is our fall.*

Olive answered Love's mid-gunner the only way she could, although the Flying Control Officer was trying to tell her that they could not guarantee Love air-room to manoeuvre – aircraft were coming in all over the south-east and some of them had inoperative wireless, prime conditions for a collision in the air or on the deck. To give this emphasis, the Flying Control Officer was pointing at the ceiling like a biblical prophet at a cloud of locusts. LQ-Love would be safer setting down in a satellite field.

'Love from Tussor Yokel,' Olive said, hoping its pilot could hear her. 'Fire tenders standing by.'

Finally she heard Lofty say, 'Watch out for Evelyn,' then 'I'm off to open my brolly now,' and Olive got an earful of static.

'Can you take over for a sec?' she asked the WAAF signals officer and before her superior could answer Olive had pulled off her earphones and was running to the door.

The Flying Control Officer followed her out and both of them watched Love do its agonisingly wide turn and make for the runway.

'At least the landing gear is deployed,' the Flying Control Officer said, for they could see the wheels, and that the bomb bay doors were closed. 'And there can't be much fuel left to burn.'

The port wing was down, and when it levelled out the tail seemed low.

But Love's approach demonstrated a superb bit of flying: the pilot did a perfect three-point landing – then both front tyres exploded, the stripped hubs gouging the runway; the feathered props shearing off to fly in gleaming shards behind the wings, while the two air-screws still turning simply evaporated. The bomb aimer's position, already holed and gaping, folded inward, as if the Lancaster was trying to swallow itself.

Olive saw all this in the green light of a distress flare, and then the starboard wing snapped off from the spar and the air around the fuselage began to burn, the flames wrapping red hands about the body of the Lancaster where its fuel burned, and darting orange fingers into the holes of the fuselage to find the Glycol tank. For a second, too, there was a deeper crimson glow behind the starred mess of perspex in the cockpit, a reflection of the fires breaking out abaft as the tracers exploded in their magazines.

Olive could not feel the heat of the explosion where she stood. At her feet dawn frost still glazed the grass, the light from the flames reflected on its pale blades.

So she discovered there is *always* something left to burn.

She could not go any nearer to the crash than the bottom step of the control tower, although a WAAF from the signals room ran by and, taking Olive's bike instead of her own by mistake, pedalled off towards the fire. Olive numbly supposed that the girl knew someone in the crew, as she did. After a little while the WAAF who'd taken Olive's bike came back, riding out of the dawn with her cape flapping behind her.

She had been seeing one of Love's crew, but when she told Olive his name it didn't mean anything to her. Olive had only known them by their nicknames.

'Blue,' added the Signals WAAF, and looked at Olive as if she'd killed him herself. 'The flight engineer and mid-gunner parachuted, and they've got the pilot out but he's in a state. They'd bundled him into the ambulance and gone but you could still smell – ' She was wide-eyed, raving – even so, Olive could not forgive it and ran up the stairs so she didn't have to see her stupid face.

She sat back down before the wireless, and slipped her headset on. There were still aircraft aloft. She listened to those voices in the air for a few seconds, and then the WAAF officer in charge tapped her on the shoulder and said she'd take over. The WAAF officer was kind enough about it but clearly thought Olive had brought it on herself.

Outside, the chance lights had been turned off, and as she walked across the aerodrome tiny drops of water blew out of a cloudless sky – spray from the fire tender's hoses. They were cooling the wreck of LQ-Love so they could drag it off the runway.

Chapter Twenty-Five

Maximum Effort

The hospital at South Rauceby had one of the best burns units in the country, and the men who were patients there sat under shaded cupolas in the walled garden playing cards, and chess, making their moves with hands mummified by bandages or with skin shiny and red as Murano glass.

None of these men could bear the sun directly, and some spent their brief indenture at Rauceby under tents of cotton, or suspended by straps above their beds so that the torture of their own weight on the wounds would not be too great. The wards were full of blind men with saline compresses over their eyes. Some had second-degree burns in their throats, and others were waiting to see the plastic surgeon, McIndoe, to see what could be done about their melted lips.

Olive would always be glad that Lofty did not see South Rauceby. He'd been escorted out of the wing commander's office the morning after the Nuremberg raid, four hours after Olive had found him walking a wounded little circle outside the interrogation hut. He was limping, and dirty, and had been crying, and the two of them sat in the blast shelter in the blue light of the dawn while he stuttered out his story.

Love had been hit by flak on the return leg, over Metz, a great shuddering blast near the nose of the Lancaster that had killed the bomb aimer outright, and had mortally wounded Pendleton, the pilot. Blue caught shrapnel in his shoulder and Happy, the navigator, had a stomach wound and when Lofty came down from the turret he'd taken both men back to lie on the floor above the bomb bays. Up the front of the plane he'd found Bashful, the flight engineer, with his hands below Pendleton's on the control column. Its shaft was cracked and Bashful was clutching it as tightly as a strangler would the throat of his victim. Glancing at the instrument panel, Lofty saw that something still showed on the clock, although the judder in the remaining engines did not feel promising. And Pendleton was dying, the wind through the smashed perspex blowing his blood in dark streamers from the back of his seat.

''int it,' he seemed to be saying, and it was a moment before Lofty realised he wasn't talking about their bad luck.

Spinning one hand about the other he yelled, 'Bash, he thinks we should splint it!' Lofty saw the flight engineer's eyes widen – he couldn't let go of the column, holding it was all he could do to keep the aircraft from plummeting. At that, Lofty scrambled his way back through the Lancaster.

He shook the navigator gently by the shoulder and, putting his mouth as near to the man's ear as he could, yelled, 'Are we on course for Dieppe?' Dieppe was the official exit point at the coast, but Lofty remembered Pendleton, not twenty minutes before, asking the navigator to make the shortest course for home he could, allowing for the head wind. The pilot had gone shy of the stream. On the way over they'd seen too many aircraft downed to think there was any safety in it, so many aircraft that the gunners stopped counting the light of their corpse-candles after Liege, where the fighters found the bomber stream.

'Maps, maps,' mumbled Happy, like a man dying of thirst who begs for water. So Lofty went behind the tattered blackout curtain to the navigator's desk to peel the map from where it had been plastered by blast to the headroom buffer. He couldn't find the compass, but did retrieve a pencil stub. By the time he returned to give the navigator the map, Blue had fallen over sideways. Lofty laid him out.

It was only then that he thought of Evelyn. There was no point plugging in his intercom, he knew that had gone in the blast. Without it Evelyn might very well imagine that loss of contact was the most that had gone wrong with Love.

Or she might be dead.

Lofty squeezed Happy's shoulder until the navigator turned his grey face up from the map; he pointed towards the tail of the Lanc.

'Just going to check Macintyre,' he yelled, moving his lips as wildly as a ventriloquist's dummy to give the navigator the gist despite the roar of Love's last labouring engines. Spurred by the thought of those engines Lofty slid over the tail spar, banging the Elsan's lid with the toes of his boots. He could see the back of Evelyn's helmet through the perspex of the window in the turret door, and as he looked a pale slice of profile came into view, the fat collar of goggles around her neck. The gunner was still dutifully scanning the air beneath the Lancaster for fighters.

Lofty saw no point in banging on the glass, so he slid the turret doors open and pummelled the back of Evelyn's flying suit, hoping not to startle her so much she'd put her face into the edge of the reflector sight. But she turned calmly and when Lofty tapped his helmet where the intercom earpiece was and shook his head she nodded.

Getting her to leave the turret took persistence, and some wild gesturing, but eventually the tail gunner slid clumsily over the spar after him, pulling her parachute from the rack as she went. The next difficulty Lofty encountered was getting himself heard: the farther up the plane they went, the noisier it got, so he took the navigator's pencil and, flipping the map, wrote: 'Pilot, W/Op and B.A. dead, stick near u/s – don't know what else. Bashful in pulpit. Can you fly Love?' Happy had scrawled his best guess of their position on the map and Lofty put this under Evelyn's nose, the map pulling at his glove in the wind from the holed fuselage. From his seat on the floor, Happy watched the dumb-show, too weak from loss of blood to be puzzled by the fact that the gunners were in conference about flying the Lancaster.

Evelyn took the pencil from Lofty, carefully, her thrice gloved hands indelicate tools, and wrote: 'Ailerons ok? Rudder? Hydraulics?' and when Lofty did a vaudeville shrug she scowled at him and made her way up to the cockpit to see for herself.

Bashful was so tired from holding the aircraft level that he only blinked at the gunner pulling at Pendleton's corpse to clear the pilot's seat and then, when a pair of hands were in place over his, he let go and went aft. He came back with a hammer and wire to splint the control column and, once that was done, Lofty went back to help the flight engineer go over the wireless set. He felt like he was sleeping with his eyes open then, because he later could not say what it was that Bashful did to get the intercom working, but it suddenly *did* work. And so – the flight engineer told them – would the wireless, once they were in range.

The navigator was shaking the map at Lofty, and when he bent to look he saw *nearer Ostend than Dieppe* written in large uneven letters. Having used his remaining strength to haul himself upright in the astrodome and take a star-sighting, he'd annotated the map and – putting his head down on the pillow of his parachute – died. Lofty found him just as he heard Evelyn say Happy was spot on. The Westerschelde had become visible to their north.

After that there was not much talking. The three surviving crew members stayed in the cockpit watching the wall of search-lights ahead. None of them could have imagined they'd make it: not at their altitude, not without the engine power needed to evade attacking fighters.

But Love's pilot had one trick left up her sleeve, and it saved them for their passage home. The stream, such as it was, had spread for forty miles. Aircraft were leaving the enemy coast all along the length of the searchlight belts – one of these a Halifax more damaged than Love, and when the bright fingers of the lights plucked the Halifax out, Evelyn took the advantage of its shadow and rode the blind spot of air above it until they were out over the North Sea, and safe.

She brought the Lancaster down to 3000 feet, low enough that they'd be able to see the silver line of the breakers on the coast south of Felixstowe, and then it was hedgehopping across Suffolk and Norfolk – Love's pilot glad, finally, of the full moon's light on those landmarks so familiar to her.

'We should set down,' Bashful said, once they'd crossed the Ouse and were within striking distance of the aerodrome at Sutton Bridge.

'No,' said Evelyn. 'We can make Killingholme.'

'She was used to getting the planes to their destination. And there was nothing wrong with the weather,' Lofty told Olive the morning after the raid. She had taken him into the blast shelter, where they could talk properly. He was crying. The tears had streaked his oil-grimed cheeks, and Olive saw the tracks come to shining, iridescent life whenever he turned his face to the sunlit doorway.

'She thought if Love could get that far, she could get home and since it was such an expensive bit of machinery we should try to bring it in. All those chits and schedules in the ferrying service must have gone to her head. She was dead set on delivering that

Lancaster, so long as it didn't cost Bash and me anything. She said she'd get us near enough the field to bale out – so near our dear old beds we could walk to them.' Lofty paused to take a deep breath, and when he spoke again his voice had dropped so low that Olive had put her face beside his in order to hear him. 'That was Evelyn's idea of maximum effort. She did St Denys one better – the head carrying the body from its place of execution. Not that it made any difference in the end.'

Olive lit Lofty a cigarette and both sat staring at the weedy outlines of the bricks beneath their feet. The hand to which she'd passed the cigarette was black with oil, the index and middle fingers patched yellow with nicotine at the second joint.

'I had better go and clean up,' Lofty said, and stood, holding the wall for support. 'Someone might want to see me.'

Olive stood by the curving, grassed wall of the blast shelter and watched Lofty walk back towards the crew hut. He walked like a man drunk, or concussed. After he'd gone she stood watching the empty path between the Nissan huts along which he'd passed – as if expecting someone else to appear there, to wave her on, or to come to meet her.

But no one came.

Later that day she tried to find out what had gone on the intelligence report, but the WAAF intelligence officer brushed her off.

'Sorry. Can't say,' the IO said.

But D-Dog's gunner could. Debriefed, the flight engineer of

Love had been heard wondering how well the RAF trained its gunners that they could fly a Lancaster, and land it, when push came to shove.

'If push came to shove in Dog we'd all go for a bleeding Burton,' said Dog's gunner. 'I don't know how 'e did it, but if they patch 'im up I'll be first in line for lessons.'

Chapter Twenty-Six

No Killingholme hero

The hospital at South Rauceby may have had one of the best burns units in the country, but the doctors on staff there were unprepared for the sight of F/S D. J. Macintyre, Aus. 415732, air gunner.

The nurses had snipped through the straps of a bloodied Mae West, and then sent for stronger shears to deal with the mesh of filaments running through the fabric of the electric insulation suit. There were places where cloth and leather had fused with the gunner's skin, and it was a delicate and exacting procedure to separate the body from its armour of uniform. But finally the last of the charred kapok was pulled away, and all that remained to deal with were the silk leggings and vest, those most intimate of second skins. As one of the nurses carried out the harnessing to add it to the bloodied, knotted pile outside the doors of the operating theatre, the other dealt with the remaining cover: noticing, as she ran the shears up the side seam of each leg, that the underclothes had been hand-stitched from parachute silk. Then, she and the doctor had both stood back from the table, had stood and stared at the person lying there before them.

So amazing was the naked body of the patient from North Killingholme that a call had been immediately put through to the wing commander of 629 Squadron. No less amazed, the wing commander had summoned the survivors of LQ-Love to his office.

They'd not yet got around to calling Olive, although she knew they would. But Olive was not there to be called. She was on the London and Northeastern Railway, changing at Brocklesby for Lincoln, changing at Lincoln for Sleaford for the bus with the blue-tinted windows that would take her to Rauceby. No wartime dash could be made quickly, and she had a watch at four, but Olive took her chances: she might never get to Rauceby again.

South Rauceby had been a little District hospital, and then, once the war began, a clearing station for 1 and 5 Group. Since then it had grown on a steady diet of burned and broken men from the fighter and bomber stations of Lincolnshire. Like many wartime affairs, Rauceby had outgrown its allotment, and now Blister huts sat around the original hospital building, close up against its walls. It was to one of these temporary-looking affairs that Olive was directed.

The burns ward was a long, low hut with its sides partitioned along a central corridor. In the room nearest the entrance Olive saw a bath loomed over by an assembly of pipes. At either side of the corridor beyond were the patients, five beds to a room. The beds were divided by low cupboards, and had men lying or sitting in them. At the end of the hall she came to an open door that gave on to the nurses station. Two women were there, in blue uniforms stiffly starched. Above them hung a sign saying: *QUIET.*

When Olive asked after the gunner brought in from North Killingholme the more senior nurse looked at her with interest, and then led her out the back door of the hut to the shaded garden. There was no one else about.

'The patient is in a stupor from the morphine, and won't know you're there. It's too soon after the accident for you to expect much.' When Olive didn't say anything the nurse went on, 'There are substantial burns to the head, arms, and legs, and the patient will be blind for a month, if – ' here she paused, looking for the pronoun, ' – *the patient* lives that long. Even then their eyesight will only improve if the surgeons can graft new eyelids. In short, your *gunner* – ' the stress on the word was unmistakable, ' – is a very sick girl.'

'Would you let me see her?' Olive asked. 'I won't be a bother.'

The sister sighed, and looked her up and down. 'I'll have to tell the doctor you're here, and he'll probably tell your squadron officer, who'll tell your wing commander, who'll tell the Group captain.' The nurse drew a chair up to one of the tables and waved the WAAF into it. 'You'll have to wait – there's only one visitor at a time allowed for a patient in the private room. I'll fetch you when the flight lieutenant's gone.'

Olive did not want to run into any of the officers of the squadron and so was willing to wait. It was only when she'd lit her second cigarette and was running through the names and faces of the senior officers of 629 that she began to suspect it was not one of that complement, but Curtis Crowe. By then the nurse had come back. Startling her, Olive ran around the back of the building, hoping to catch sight of the American on his way to the gate, but all she could see was a young man in dressing-gown and slippers pushing a man in a wheelchair around the flowerbeds.

When Olive returned to the hallway the nurse asked, 'Are you ready now?' with an irritated little bow. 'You'd better steel yourself. This will be a shock, and you're *not* to show it in your voice if the patient wakes.'

The shades were down in the room, but someone had opened a window. Even so, the smell that permeated the hut was strongest there. Roasted meat on the turn. Olive baulked at the doorway, and the nurse took her by the arm and led her to the only chair in the room, then left.

The gunner was swaddled in bandages broken only at her raw and swollen mouth. Olive thought it could have been any body lying there, with its fat muslin arms cantilevered out from the bed. Then came a whimper and Olive knew it was Evelyn from the timbre and shape of the cry, though it was a sound she'd never heard her make before.

'I'm here. It's Olive,' she said, but the figure in the bed had lapsed back into silence. Olive carefully rolled back the sheet until she could see the place where the dressing ended, at the décolletage. She touched the dark mole that sat squarely above the place where Evelyn's collarbones met, and lightly patted the unblemished skin above her breasts.

'That's my darling,' she said. 'My dear.'

Olive was back at the Station in time for her watch. It passed without event, but at eight the following morning when she arrived at flying control she was told to report to the WAAF squadron officer, and another girl took her seat at the radio-telephone.

The most senior WAAF officer on the Station had an office in the admin building. It was a small office, and that morning seemed smaller than ever, with the wing commander and the squadron leader flanking her desk. Olive knew the wing commander had been in the Royal Flying Corps, then the RAF, and had flown a tour on Hampdens, and another in Wellingtons – he was all the more terrifying a figure for having survived so long, at such poor odds.

All three officers were staring at Olive.

'Corporal Olive Jamieson,' the Queen Bee said, but not to the WAAF in question. She'd passed her subordinate over to the wing commander, and was following formality.

The wing commander looked Olive up and down and said, 'We won't keep you long, Corporal, as no doubt you've got a train to catch. We just wanted to have a good look at the WAAF who let a crew go up with someone who'd never been trained as a gunner, and who wasn't in the RAF. We were wondering what type of girl you'd be. Squadron Leader Hoyle thought you must be thick – a bit shy in the old brain department – but the squadron officer tells us you were a competent R/T operator with a good service record. That piqued our curiosity even more.' He paused then, and looked for a response from the WAAF before him.

But she had nothing to say.

The wing commander's moustache twitched and he said, 'Squadron Leader Hoyle once met your bogus gunner to talk about "his" being embroiled in an on-Station romance. What that bit of information does to the impression of the whole business I don't like to say. A poor show under the best of circumstances, but in a case like this much worse. Distastefully so.' Glancing at the squadron officer, the wing commander coughed uncomfortably and said, 'But enough said. We're not writers for the gutter press, so that part of it is your business. The rest, alas, is not.'

Olive looked at the floor, feeling faint.

'You will only hear this once – here, in this office. And I think you'd better look at me while I say it.' The wing commander glanced at the senior officers beside him and then, in a quiet voice, said, 'I've heard no complaints about the quality of Love's air gunnery and your friend certainly did a marvellous piece of flying to get that Lancaster down. Had the kite's tyres not blown and the thing gone up in flames I'd have told her that before handing her over to the police. Now no one beyond the four people in this room will ever hear that commendation. And neither should they. Imagine what Lord Haw-Haw would make of the information that we had a woman in our bomber crews. Not to mention the questions in the House. Unconscionable. The furore at Australia House is quite enough for me to be going on with. I'm cautioning you never to speak of this again. Once I have placated the Group leader, the subject will be dropped. And even if your friend acted heroically at the end, the fact that she was in a position to do so stinks to high heaven – as does your part in putting her there. She was no Killingholme hero, and neither are you. You're not fit to serve.'

'I'd say not,' the Queen Bee added.

The wing commander steepled his fingers and leaned his chin on them. 'An unfortunate turn of events has made my job, and that of the Ghoul Squad and the Office of Military Records, much easier – although I doubt it will help your conscience any, Corporal Jamieson.'

The wing commander slid a stapled sheaf of papers across the desk to Olive. As she was standing a foot or so out from its edge, and did not reach for the file at his prompting, the squadron leader picked the papers up and put them into her hand.

Olive saw that she was holding a roneo sheet much like the pages of the battle order tacked up before operations. But this list was longer: column upon column of surnames, followed by forename, rank and serial number. The list's title was not a target, but a name with sibilant honorific: SS *Khedive Ismail*.

It was a casualty list. And on that list a name and registration number had been circled:

<u>Evelyn Ames Macintyre, 3ICJ-743-6, Air Transport Auxiliary.</u>

The wing commander explained that the *Khedive Ismail* had sunk six weeks before, and that the Air Transport Auxiliary had been duly informed of the death of one of their rank. He'd had a telephone conversation with their Director of Operations, who'd been kind enough to send over the casualty list. An account of the sinking he'd gleaned from the *Times* – one of those newspapers Olive never read. The SS *Khedive Ismail* was an Egyptian transport requisitioned for troop carrying. She'd sailed crowded with men from the Western Desert; with nurses changing their theatre of duty; with Wrens in dusty uniform and female drivers of the Transport Corps – and a thin young man in the uniform of the Air Transport Auxiliary. On the 12th of February, off the coast of Ceylon, the ship was torpedoed and had sunk in less than two minutes. Some of those who'd survived the sinking were killed when the area was depth-charged by the Royal Navy in their attempt to force the Japanese sub to the surface. There was havoc in the water, and none of the survivors could say what had happened to those around them not left alive to account for themselves.

But, even before hearing this, Olive understood everything she needed to.

The list she was holding told her they'd done it all for nothing, after all.

Chapter Twenty-Seven

Burns

She was discharged a week later. Not long after the paperwork was filed, she received notice from the Ministry of Labour that she was to be re-drafted as a worker in a factory making utility furniture at High Wycombe. She'd thought a place on the belts of a munitions factory would have been worse punishment, but that was before she discovered the factory was located under the flight path of the ferry pilots from White Waltham. Each day she would hear the droning of their aircraft, even over the sound of the lathes.

Of the end of her stay at North Killingholme – the days it took to process the discharge – she was to remember very little. The only people capable then of pricking the skin of her grief were Catherine Derrick, and Curtis Crowe, whom Olive finally met.

Crowe had been Evelyn's last visitor. He'd convinced the nurse to let him stay through the quiet hour before dinner, while Olive had been hustled out the minute the hand of the clock clicked around to four so that the nurse could see to the bandages. At seven the nurse came to do the next change of the patient's dressings and fussed about with the flowers Crowe had left before noticing that the patient, normally silent in her swaddling of bandages, had sunken into a stillness of a higher order. She'd gone to fetch the doctor.

The service for Love's troublesome gunner was held in the hospital chapel, and it was there – two days after Olive had heard she was to be discharged – that she met Curtis Crowe. He came in with Cathy, shaking rain from his umbrella and walking gingerly over the already wet linoleum of the annex to the chapel. In person, he looked nothing like Clark Gable, and as he stood holding Cathy's dripping coat, Olive saw him raise the toe of his right shoe from the floor and tap it agitatedly, as men do at the podium when they're nervous of public speaking, or on a platform when the train is late. Crowe no longer wore a moustache, and the set of his face was not what it had been in photographs.

He took off his gloves before shaking her hand. 'I'm sorry that we meet under such lousy circumstances,' he said, then, glancing at Cathy, 'Duncan was always talking about you. And I'm sure his sister would have too, if she'd had the opportunity. Both had a great capacity for loyalty, it would seem.'

'But you never met Evelyn,' Olive said, in such a way it might have seemed an accusation.

'I had the pleasure.' He could say no more, as Cathy was looking at him with interest, and she was no fool. Then he asked, 'Has Lofty managed to get word to you?'

Olive shook her head.

At the pulpit the chaplain opened his Book of Common Prayer with a dry rustle of pages, and the mourners sat and listened to his service. Although Olive knew whose body was being commended to the crematorium, she spent whole minutes thinking it *was* Duncan's funeral. Certainly Cathy thought that. As to Curtis Crowe, he kept his dark brown eyes fixed firmly on his knuckles, and his grief was glacial.

Then there was an awkward few moments on the stairs outside the old hospital building. The army chaplain shook their hands as if it was an ordinary Sunday service.

'It's a terrible shame,' he said, and seemed to mean it.

They stood in a little huddle after the chaplain had gone, cold wind tugging at the hems of their coats. Crowe passed his packet of Lucky Strikes around.

'When will we see you back at the cottage?' Cathy asked Olive. She knew Olive's kit was packed, and sitting on her bed. There was nothing left to do but say goodbye. As she spoke she put her hand out beside her and Crowe caught it; chafing it between his bigger, gloved, hands.

Olive remembered how Evelyn had liked to do that for her.

'I'll be back soon,' she said. 'I just want to have a word with the doctor.' The chapel was adjacent to the burns ward, and Olive hoped to find him on his rounds.

'We're just going to go for a drink, if we can find one. Join us later if you like,' Cathy said, and then Crowe took her off on his motorcycle.

The doctor was checking the state of the men's sight. Those just a few months out from their accident had not yet been able to close their eyes, their eyelids having been burned off or fused onto the promontory arch of the brow. Now they turned their eerie, wide-eyed stares on Olive, not used to seeing women out of uniform. She smiled and chatted to one or two of these men, all the while hoping the doctor would finish what he was doing so she could talk to him. After he'd been to the last bed, Olive was ushered into the hallway and asked what she wanted. She explained that she'd been a friend of the girl in the private room, and wanted to know how she'd died.

Brushing at a smudge of gentian violet on his coat, the Doctor said, 'The patient simply stopped breathing.' The stain had spread to his fingers and he wiped these on the wall before looking at Olive. 'These things happen.'

She nodded. Of course they did.

'Perhaps a tracheotomy became necessary and there was no one there to give it. Swelling in the throat, you know. It sometimes can be a problem. So can shock, secondary infection and septicemia. Occasionally those with disfiguring or profoundly debilitating wounds just give up hope – in which case we'd be hard put to give an immediate cause of death. Perhaps she lacked heart at the end. It wouldn't surprise me. She was just a girl.'

'I see,' Olive said, to head off what was coming – some platitude about it being for the best.

The last time she saw Evelyn awake was when the tea trolley went rattling down the corridor to the other, fitter, patients. She'd started into consciousness, tugging at her straps – her first time far enough above the cloud of morphine to assess her situation.

The nurse came and stood at the bedside making soothing noises, and then turned to Olive. 'She wants to relieve herself. Why don't you just help her on to this,' she said, handing her the bedpan, 'and I'll come back to check on you in a minute.'

But when Olive tried to slip the pan under Evelyn's buttocks she cried out – the wounded cry a dog makes when beaten by its owner.

Olive ran for help.

The nurse walked her briskly back down the corridor. 'They need to feel a confident hand. If you're scared, they're scared,' she scolded, and left the WAAF standing in the hallway while she did what was needed.

When Olive got back to Evelyn's bedside, she was once again insensible, and at four the sister came to chivvy her off the ward.

'I see,' Olive repeated as the doctor turned to go. Then she said, 'It might be for the best,' and went to catch the bus to Sleaford.

Epilogue

1956

It was not long after the Royal Visit to Australia and New Zealand that Olive and Norm flew across the Tasman to Wellington. He had a week of advisory meetings with their Ministry of Works and Electricity on a hydro-electric plant for the central North Island. Norm found it hilarious that the minister running the show was named Watt, but his amusement thinned after a day of meetings at Old Government House. While her husband worked, Olive walked the steep streets of Wellington – a city cleaned by the winds that scoured it.

Norm had no time at all to be a tourist. He'd agreed that his wife should do what she liked with the trip; so Olive had arranged to visit Lofty.

Oddly enough, Norm was the one who'd found Lofty. A year before he'd come home from his office with a letter from the Treasurer of the Australian and New Zealand Association of Civil Engineers that accused his fellow committee members of understanding as much about accounting 'as dogs know about toothpaste'.

'Didn't you know a Lawrence Hilliers during the war? See – ' Norm had said, waving the letter under Olive's nose, ' – he signs himself "Lofty" Hilliers.'

Lofty had returned to engineering after the war until an association with the asbestos mines in Upper Takaka put him off. He'd since moved through an assortment of projects around Nelson and Golden Bay, the district inside the curving spit of land at the western tip of New Zealand's South Island. The Golden Bay Cement Company was where he'd settled.

He came to fetch Olive from the tiny airport at Nelson, walking out from under the shade of the terminal wearing the same dark glasses he'd worn as a gunner.

'Olive Jamieson,' he said, reaching out to take one of the two bags she was carrying. 'Where have you been all this time? Maisie's been going mad without you.'

'Maisie was mad to start with.'

'Funny that,' Lofty said.

They stood looking at one another, and while Olive thought Lofty had aged all he could think was how beautiful her uneven face still seemed, and how appropriate it was that they should meet on tarmac, to the sound of a dwindling engine.

They drove through Nelson's suburbs, and on to Motueka.

'Look at that beautiful bloody stuff,' Lofty said, waving out the open car window. Acres of hops and tobacco filled the farmland at either side of the road – the whole valley a rich hinterland for his addictions.

In a place called Riwaka Lofty stopped to gas up the car and to check the water level in the radiator before heading up 'the Hill'. He seemed proud that the locals only called it a hill because it was the shortest peak in the mountain range. 'We Kiwis are a self-deprecating bunch. Even our mountains are modest.'

'All except for you that is,' Olive said, and bludged another cigarette.

They drove the great snaking bends of the road over the Takaka Hill in dusk light, the car filling with the scent of the bush that hemmed the road.

'Beech,' Lofty said, and Olive looked sidelong at him.

'Beech smeech.'

It was dark by the time they reached the house he'd rented from the cement company. This stood on a narrow promontory of land between a tidal flat (Olive looked dutifully off into the dark in the direction he'd pointed) and the sea.

That night they had a supper of cold meat and salad, and Lofty brought out a bottle of whisky before showing Olive photographs of his wife and eight-year-old daughter in Christchurch. In one of these Olive saw a pretty young woman and a pouting child perched on bicycles, a dusty bank of blackberries behind them; in another the child and her parents sitting on a picnic rug surrounded by neatly manicured lawn, punts on the river behind them.

'It looks like England,' she said.

'Doesn't it just? Imagine me living there.' Lofty shook his head and put away the photos.

The spare bed she was to sleep in belonged to Lofty's daughter.

She and her mother were coming up for the school holidays, and Lofty intended to row the dinghy out to the islands to give them a glimpse of the hermit.

The next morning he drove his guest to the beach beyond the inlet, its one or two houses sitting in bush and farmland; facing yin-yang shaped islands at the easternmost edge of the bay.

'The hermit lives on that one,' Lofty said, pointing to the island nearest. Olive could just make out the roof of a shack. 'Been there since the First World War, poor bugger.'

'We have an old soldier like that living in a cliff in the Blue Mountains.'

'I don't know how they can bear it,' Lofty said, and balancing the brim of his hat, got back into the car.

He took Olive to Tarakohe to show her the Cement Works, and then they went a long, and dusty, fifty miles further along the road to Collingwood, a seaside town at the base of the mountains dividing Golden Bay from the West Coast. They passed a church and fire station, and then Lofty followed the road to the sea so they could eat their picnic lunch on the crumbling pier. In the time it took him to wolf two ham sandwiches he'd explained the key points of the town's history. Collingwood had once been slated to be the capital city of New Zealand. Then the silt came, and the deep waters of its harbour turned to tidal flats. And not long after, a fire burned most of the town down to its foundations.

'I can't see it coming back from that,' Lofty said, looking critically at the rind he'd pulled from the crust edge of his sandwich.

'Do you ever wonder what they look like,' Olive asked, 'the old aerodromes?'

Lofty and Olive both looked around then at the flaking paint on the seaward-facing wood of the houses on the hill, at the gaps in the planking of the pier. Neither ventured their thoughts.

Finally Olive asked why his wife wasn't with him.

'Oh, she can't stand me in a day-to-day sort of a way. Loves me from afar, she does.' Brushing the crumbs off his hands onto the legs of his trousers, he said, 'The marriage isn't your average thing, but we're going to stick with it. That's more than some can say. I'm not sorry. One true love in a lifetime is enough for me.' At this, Lofty flicked the ash off his cigarette with vigour, and she wondered whether he wanted her to guess whom he meant.

'I wouldn't stop counting yet,' she said, carefully.

'I haven't stopped counting – just paused on the beat, so to speak,' Lofty answered, and glanced at her for a second, his eyes bright. 'One and one and one,' he said, and tipped a tobacco-stained index finger at her. Then he slipped on his dark glasses and looked out to the white line at the ocean's rim – the low dunes of Farewell Spit. 'Thought I'd run into you sooner or later. But now that I think about it, you weren't exactly after me like a terrier down a rabbit-hole.'

'I'd rather think of myself as a pig after truffles,' Olive said, and unselfconsciously covered his hand with her own. 'There's years and years of preparation in truffle farming. Wouldn't you rather be a truffle?'

'I wouldn't. Never get a moment's peace as a truffle. First it would be snouts and then it would be some prat shaving bits off you to go in an omelette. Believe me, rabbits have the better deal.'

'Not during the war they didn't,' Olive said, thinking about the land-girls and their shotguns, the hungry evacuees learning how to poach.

'I've heard there were better deals going to some in that war, but I've yet to see the proof of it.' Lofty swung his legs, his well-shined shoes disappearing under the edge of the pier on the inside of every arc. Down in the water shining minnows fled from his shadow. 'When I was a binder at Staxton Wold I used to sing to make the time pass,' he said. 'That's where they sent me after they took my rank, after I got out of the detention centre.' He smiled a tight little smile. 'They couldn't convene a court martial, not if they wanted to keep the details of the case quiet. So it was the binders for me.'

A binder was a man on a bicycle. The bicycle was riveted to a spoke that drove the cogs that turned the radar's aerial. The binder rode in little circles in the darkness of the concrete bunker under the Ground Control Intercept Station, day in day out.

'Does three blind mice ring a bell?' Lofty tipped back his head and his Adam's apple wobbled as he sang:

Three blind mice
Three blind mice
See how they run
See how they run

They all ran after the butcher's wife
Who cut off their tails with a carving knife
You never have seen such a thing in your life
As three blind mice

'Always got the lyrics wrong, I did.' He took a sip of the tea he'd poured from the thermos minutes before. 'At Staxton Wold they thought I must be LMF. Why else would a man who'd been aircrew end up in a place like that? So there's me singing in the dark like a Welshman in the mines, waiting for the ceiling to fall in.' Lofty paused. 'Are you going to have that?' he asked, pointing at the only remaining sandwich.

'Go ahead,' Olive told him, and he peeled the top layer off the bread, looked inside at the limp lettuce and the clots of egg, and nodded, as if he'd thought the filling might have scarpered.

'I'm sorry, Lofty. I should have found you sooner.'

'Isn't this sooner?'

He stood then and they gathered the picnic things and walked back towards the car. Inland, there were banks of dark cloud rolling off the mountains. Where the pier met the rock it was bedded in, Lofty stopped and put a hand on the fat rusting cable that anchored the jetty's uprights. 'The worst bit was not knowing what had happened. I wrote to you and nothing came of it, and then I wrote Bashful and got a letter back saying he'd bought it in the raid on Gelsenkirchen. So finally I wrote the War Office and they told me that Duncan Macintyre had been cremated at Rauceby. I didn't find out about my Duncan until a few months after that.' Lofty wetted his lips with his tongue, and looked away. 'I wrote to his parents. I'd thought their answer would tell me if he was safe; that they'd use some kind of code that I'd miraculously crack. But what I got was a very nice letter telling me Duncan and his sister were both dead, and how sorry they were I'd not heard.'

'The discharge meant your letters didn't find me,' Olive said, deciding not to mention the one that she'd found waiting for her at Ida's, and had thrown away unread.

He nodded, but she knew he was shrewder than that.

They walked on to the car, and Olive pulled the battered leather schoolbag from the backseat.

'I brought something to show you,' she said, prying the clasp open. The paper inside the case fluttered and twitched in the breeze.

'What's that then?' Lofty asked, as she plucked the first letter from the pile – one of Duncan's to Evelyn. She handed it to him.

'I've got them all. The pile Duncan left with Evelyn, and Evelyn's own,' she said. 'I salvaged them before the Committee of Adjustment could go through her things. There's mine, and all of yours.'

'You surprise me,' Lofty said, as if to the letter itself. 'I didn't think you were the type to hold onto things.'

Olive looked at the sandy ground. *That's right*, she thought, *I am just a pair of empty hands.*

But all she said was, 'I've always liked a good letter.'

Lofty shrugged, and hefted the case. 'We'll never get through this little lot in a day.' Then, flattening the creases on the page, he said, 'Who'd have thought mice could write?'

The wind was strengthening, and cloud had spread to block out the tops of the hills. The mountains. Both still could put a height to the base of that cloud if they had a mind to – the ability to measure clear air a hard-dying habit.

'I'll leave them with you for a while, if you like,' Olive said, taking back the letter. 'But we can make a start on them now. See how many we can get through.'

And they walked back out onto the crumbling pier.

Acknowledgements

Some readers may already know that there was no 629 Squadron active operationally during the Second World War. The number 629 was being held in readiness for a new squadron, but the war ended before its use was required.

Any historical novel requires substantial research, and this is no exception. I would like to thank the Australia Council for the Arts for making that research possible. I would also like to thank the staff of the Documents section of the Imperial War Museum, Lambeth, and of the War Memorial Canberra, and the Aviation Heritage Centre, Maidenhead, for making available to me the diaries, logs, letters and published ephemera without which it would have been impossible to imagine wartime life on the home front and in the operational stations of Lincolnshire. Of the material in these collections, the following proved most useful: Typescript by Miss R. Britten, IWM ref no. 94/27/1 (a report about a WAAF intelligence officer's supernumerary flight on an operation, and her feelings on their subsequent forced landing); Miss N. Fry ms IWM ref 93/22/1 (on WAAF R/T training and wartime life); J. Ralph ms. Diary IWM ref 96/4/1 (ditto); Mrs E. M. Wilford, ms, IWM ref 88/2/1 (ditto); 'Diary about life in Grimsby during the Second World War', IWM ref. Misc 45 item 762; Papers of Warrant Officer Cecil Cawley (Aust War Memorial ref PR 3165); Papers of F. Dale, Air Gunner (Aust War Memorial ref PR90/135); and from the transcripts of interview for the Keith Murdoch Archive at the AWM, the recollections of: Peter O'Connor, navigator, RAAF (ref S00521); Frank Dixon, pilot, 467 Squadron; Arthur Hoyle, navigator.

Published sources were likewise invaluable. Eric Partridge's *Dictionary of Force's Slang* showed me that I'd been raised speaking RAF slang, and that a single word can say more than pages of written history. For all that, I couldn't have done without Angus Calder's social history, *The People's War: Britain 1939–1945* and would likewise have been brought up all standing without Martin Middlebrook's operational reference work, *The Bomber Command War Diaries* and his military history, *The Nuremberg Raid.* I learned much of the work and life of women in the Air Transport Auxiliary from Lettice Curtis's memoir, *The Forgotten Pilots.* I couldn't have done without Mary Lee Settle's literary memoir of her time in the WAAFs, *All the Brave Promises*, and Sylvia Pickering's *Tales of a Bomber Command WAAF* and Pip Beck's *A WAAF in Bomber Command* told me a great deal about who did what and ate what, where. David Scholes, *Air War Diary: An Australian in Bomber Command* gave me a good sense for what aircrew did with their leave, and their nights free from ops. Fiction of the era was similarly useful – notably Paul Gallico's *The Lonely* and Nevil Shute's

Pastoral and *Requiem for a Wren* (this latter I'd not re-read until after I'd finished writing this book). Likewise, I have not seen a copy of Han Suyin's *Winter Love* since reading it in 1981, but remember well its evocation of the dreariness, and the compunction, of wartime life – the dreariness and compunction relieved by love, and underlined by its inevitable loss.

Thanks are due to Alan John, bomb aimer, 75 Squadron RAF, for his generousity in talking about his crew, and his time in Bomber Command. And to the family of Pilot Officer, Brian McDonough, 236 Squadron, Fighter Command, much more is owed. P/O McDonough was one of the 'few of the few', an Australian killed during the Battle of Britain. But he was also one of another 'few' not honoured by histories of the war.

The photograph on the cover has been reprinted from *The W.A.A.F. in Action* (London, Adam & Charles Black, 1944). Every effort has been made to contact the copyright holder, unsuccessfully: I would be pleased to rectify this omission in future editions.

I am grateful for the support of the Writing and Society Research Group at the University of Western Sydney, and to the staff of the School of Humanities and Languages and the College of Arts for their appreciation of the research practices involved in the writing of historical fiction. And, for their sound advice, a warm thanks to my first readers: Jane Goodall, Jill Dimond and Elizabeth Knox.

This project has been assisted by the Commonwealth Government through the Australia Council, its arts funding and advisory body.